INSTINCTS
& IMPOSTORS

INSTINCTS AND IMPOSTORS (Amplifier 5)
and RECON MISSION: BEE (Amplifier 5.5)
Copyright © 2022 Meghan Ciana Doidge
Published by Old Man in the CrossWalk Productions 2022
Salt Spring Island, BC, Canada
www.oldmaninthecrosswalk.com

Library and Archives Canada
Doidge, Meghan Ciana, 1973 —
Instincts and Impostors/Recon Mission: Bee/
Meghan Ciana Doidge —
PAPERBACK EDITION

Cover design by Gene Mollica Studios
Models: Devon Ericksen & Jonathan Cannaux
Oracle Cards designed by Elizabeth Mackey Graphic Design

ISBN 978-1-989571-51-4

THE AMPLIFIER SERIES: BOOK 5

INSTINCTS & IMPOSTORS

MEGHAN CIANA DOIDGE

Published by Old Man in the CrossWalk Productions
Salt Spring Island, BC, Canada

www.madebymeghan.ca

Instincts and Impostors is the fifth book in the Amplifier series, which is set in the same universe as the Dowser, Oracle, Reconstructionist, Archivist, and Misfits of the Adept Universe series. While it is not necessary to read all three series, **in order to avoid spoilers** the ideal reading order of the Adept Universe is as follows:

More books in the Amplifier, Archivist, and Misfits series to follow. This reading list doesn't include the shorter stories interspersed throughout all of the main series, but more information can be found at: www.madebymeghan.ca/novels

For Michael
Who always encourages me to take
my instincts seriously.

Author's Note

Instincts and Impostors is the fifth book in the Amplifier series, which is set in the same universe as the Dowser, Oracle, and Reconstructionist series.

Sage

WISDOM

I'D LED A DEADLY SQUAD OF GENETICALLY EN-
hanced, uber-powerful magic wielders through
life-threatening missions multiple times in the first
twenty-one years of my life.

When marked for death, I'd led the escape from
those who'd bred us, controlled us. Utterly annihi-
lating the Collective's compound, and destroying
everything that had gone into creating us—the Five.

I found Christopher and Paisley a home, a safe
haven. Then, despite being bred and raised to be a
sociopath, I learned to love. And even some of the
nuances of the act of loving.

To protect the life I'd built, I'd faced off against
black witches. Survived demons. Held powerful dark
sorcerers at bay. I had thwarted an immortal entity.

And despite all that, I was nervous.

About attending a coven retreat. About revealing any part of myself to witches of the light.

Witches who could hurt me without a lick of
magic or a single sharp blade. Just by denying Opal
the future she wanted.

Because of me. And everything I could no longer hide. Or hide from.

ONE

KEEPING SLIGHTLY BACK FROM THE BEDROOM WIN-
dow that overlooked the backyard and the gardens so
the sorcerer and the dream walker wouldn't catch me
spying on them, I watched as Aiden bent his head,
all his concentration fixed on listening to Opal. He
was so much taller and deadlier than the little witch.
Yet everything about the gesture indicated that
every facet of the sorcerer was currently focused on
our…daughter. Our soon-to-be daughter. Because
that was the choice she'd made.

I just had to get through the next three days.

The coven witches didn't care that Aiden and I
weren't officially married yet—that wasn't what was
holding up the release of the adoption papers. But
they did want to meet Opal, as part of inducting her
into the coven.

And that was Opal's choice as well. She'd gotten
friendly with a second-year witch, Juniper, during
their last few weeks at the Academy. Though Juniper

was a year ahead of Opal, she had sought out the young witch after the invitations had been issued for the coven retreat.

Juniper was also being inducted into the Godfrey coven, and Opal had decided to join her.

The little witch had informed us of that decision with her typical bright confidence. And even when I tried to confirm that she wasn't choosing that path only for fear of losing me, of losing Aiden and Paisley and Christopher, she'd stubbornly jutted out her chin and reiterated her decision.

Outside, Opal was holding out her hand, palm down, as Aiden took a step back. A light-blue shimmer of magic appeared under the dream walker's hand, and she started moving along the edge of the garden fence. Slow steps. Her head was bowed. From what I could see of her expression, her body language, she was serious and focused.

She was looking for a grounding stone, which she needed for the induction ceremony. The coven had supplied a list of necessary items as soon as Opal had asked to take part. So I'd spent the last week collecting everything she needed, including a tailored cloak in the coven's specified color, royal blue, that had to be ordered from a witch who specialized in such things.

Aiden glanced up at the window, catching me spying. He flashed me a grin. I smiled back. Thankfully, the expression wasn't forced even though I was nervous.

Yes, nervous.

I had led a squad of genetically enhanced Adepts through life-threatening missions multiple times in the first twenty-one years of my life. I'd run from those who'd bred us, who had controlled us. In the process, we'd annihilated the secret compound in Peru where we'd been raised—along with all the research that had gone into creating the Five. Then, for eight years after that, I'd kept myself, Christopher, and Paisley one step ahead of those who would have enslaved us for our magic. I'd built a home. I'd learned that I was actually capable of love. I'd managed to not outright murder my soon-to-be father-in-law—one of the Collective who'd made me—and had actually saved his life from an immortal entity calling itself 'the mother of the dawn.' The Hallowed.

And I was nervous. About meeting witches of the light.

The kind of witches who held their annual coven gathering at a five-star resort on the beach, and who gathered flowers and made healing tinctures and all that other sunshine-and-charm sort of magic.

Those witches made me nervous.

Because I held way too much power. And, if I was being completely honest with myself, I had a habit of beheading first and asking questions later.

Actually, I rarely bothered with the questions.

Except for Opal.

For Opal, I would do anything.

"I'm heading out," Samantha said from the doorway behind me. "I'll keep you posted."

I turned. The dark-skinned, dark-haired tele-kinetic was wearing black cotton pants and a tight black T-shirt instead of her usual leather. Due to the warm weather. She had a small duffel bag slung over one shoulder, her laptop and other tech gear in a hard case. Also all black. She was on her way to join up with Daniel, aka Fish, somewhere in Europe. She had delayed the trip—more than once—because she'd wanted to see Opal before she went.

"Well," she sneered, "I'll keep Christopher informed."

I nodded, crossing back to the bed, where I had two suitcases lying open, one for me and one for Opal. They were packed for the coven retreat. For the third time. Opal had arrived home last night with Aiden's youngest sister, Ocean, and had needed all her laundry done. And I was bringing way too much.

Samantha huffed. Then she dumped her bag on the floor, crossed to me, and slung her now-free arm around my neck. Taller than me, she pressed her face to the side of my head and held me for a moment. Power shifted between us, mostly simmering around the blood tattoo on my T4 vertebra. A tattoo that tied the telekinetic to me—for life, as far as we'd been able to figure out. "You could at least hug me back," Samantha muttered into my hair.

I wrapped my hand around her forearm, skin to skin, and my other arm around her waist.

She rocked me slightly. And I allowed the contact, though more magic flared between us. Even when I wasn't actively amplifying Samantha, I was still feeding power to her. That passive transfer had always happened to some extent, for anyone who spent any regular time around me. But it had gotten much more difficult to suppress since the Hallowed had triggered my latent empathy. Somehow weaponizing it.

As if I needed more weapons at my disposal.

"If we find Bee," Samantha asked softly, almost tentatively, "we can bring her back, right?"

"We've talked about it. Extensively," I huffed, slightly pissed that she was bringing up the topic. Again.

There were many, many reasons that the Five couldn't, shouldn't reunite. And the biggest one, not including Christopher, was out in the yard right now looking for a grounding stone that 'spoke' to her. Her tie to her home.

I would never do anything that might compromise the security of Opal's home.

"There's that other property," Samantha murmured. "It's a blank slate. Now that you're done with it."

She meant the Grant property, claimed in the aftermath of Opal, Jenni, and me being kidnapped by Ruwa, Aiden's ex, and the collapsing pocket of the demon dimension. "It's in Opal's name."

"We'll lease it."

I sighed. "You don't know that this new lead will even pan out," I grumbled.

Samantha released me, grinning. Like she'd won this round of the debate. "It will. Knox is getting glimmers."

"Christopher is constantly getting glimmers."

Samantha scooped up her abandoned bag and stepped out into the hall. "Got to say my goodbyes."

She was jogging down the stairs before I could say anything else. Not that I actually had anything else to say. Samantha had been living at the farm full-time for the last few weeks, ever since she'd hauled Christopher to Europe, following another lead on the whereabouts of Amanda, aka Bee. The telepath who made the other four of us the Five. But that lead had gone cold, assuming it had ever been warm to begin with.

I knew that if Bee didn't want to be found, it was best to leave her alone. Any telepath of power couldn't be compromised or taken against her will—not for long, not for the eighteen months she'd supposedly been missing. And as far as I knew, Bee was the most powerful telepath in the world.

So she wasn't responding to emails? I didn't respond to emails either.

By choice.

I zipped up my suitcase, refusing to repack it a fourth time. Lani would arrive in a few minutes. The part-time intuitive/full-time mechanic was taking the drive up to Tofino on the west coast of Vancouver Island with us, but hadn't agreed to do more than simply meet with the Godfrey witches. Or as she'd put it, surf, eat fresh crab, and baby herself.

Ocean was joining us as well. Aiden's sister had applied for an internship with one of the Godfrey witches over the summer. Then she'd head back to the Academy for the first year of her specialization in potions.

Christopher and Aiden were rather put out not to be included, but coven gatherings were witches-only events. Except for me. Because I was Opal's guardian, the witches couldn't stop me from coming, though I had no plans to participate in any of the weekend's sessions or lectures.

As I was closing Opal's suitcase, Paisley lumbered into the bedroom, currently in her extra-large blue-nosed pit bull form. Shoulders rolling and ears flattened on her head, she made a point of not acknowledging me as two tentacles flicked out from her neck and wrapped around the handles of the suitcases.

"Thank you," I said, running my fingers over her head.

She dodged my touch, abruptly turning back the way she'd come with the suitcases suspended off the ground.

Speaking of those who were pissed about having to stay at the farm instead of meeting the witches.

I didn't miss the irony.

Everyone in our household wanted to go, except me.

Shaking my head at the demon dog, I grabbed Opal's new backpack from her bedroom—a bright-orange, boxy-shaped, vegan-leather bag that was an end-of-year gift from Aiden. Then I headed downstairs myself, trusting Paisley to put the suitcases in the trunk of the Mustang rather than absconding with them. The backpack was one of multiple gifts my dark sorcerer had bestowed upon the little witch the moment after she returned home with a bright smile, and a suitcase stuffed full of dirty clothes.

"GOT IT!" OPAL CRIED AS SHE CLAMBERED INTO THE kitchen through the partially open French-paned doors that led to the back patio. "Well...I found three possibilities." She was holding three rocks, each ranging in color from light to dark gray. Each was flat with smooth, rounded edges and about the size of her palm.

Aiden was on the dream walker's heels. His hair was currently long enough to fall over his brow and slightly curl at the nape. A few weeks of not shaving, and his scruff was verging on a beard. And I certainly didn't mind the new sensations his less-than-perfect grooming brought to our lovemaking. Not one bit.

The sorcerer flashed me a knowing grin. On the other end of the kitchen island, I finished tucking nut mix and ginger snaps into Opal's backpack and valiantly tried not to respond to the spark of heat in his own gaze. He couldn't read my mind, of course. But apparently my magic beckoned whenever I was thinking of him in a certain way.

So...pretty much whenever I laid eyes on him.

"See?" Opal said, skirting the kitchen island and holding out the stones.

I had to tear my gaze away from her wide grin and bright blue-eyed gaze to take in the rocks she'd collected. I was so happy to have her home that I had to keep stopping myself from running my fingers through her bouncy gold-and-silver-tipped dark curls.

"Is that quartz?" I asked, noting a jagged white vein slashed through what looked like granite on one of the stones.

"Yep," Opal said, still grinning madly. "That one might be the best. It hums a little bit more. That's good, right?"

I gave in, touching her shoulder lightly while trying to keep my magic to myself. Opal deserved to grow into her witch magic as naturally as possible. She was already the only first-year student at the Academy with a specialty—dream walking. She didn't need to be further set apart from her classmates.

No. She was in second year now.

Only five more years until I could have her home full-time. Assuming she didn't specialize even further, as Ocean had chosen to do.

"Yes," I said, realizing that I hadn't answered Opal. "Perfect."

She bounced slightly under my hand, then took off into the house. "I'm going to show Ocean. And Paisley."

Aiden crossed around the island and swept me into a hard kiss. I allowed myself to soften against him, settling my hand on the back of his neck and just enjoying the warmth of his touch.

"I'm being a baby," I murmured against his lips.

"I'm the one who has to be without the both of you for three days. I still had one more gift for our little witch."

I laughed quietly. "More gifts, Aiden?"

He just grinned unrepentantly. "I'll keep an eye on the place."

"Did Samantha say goodbye?"

"Yeah. She made a last attempt to persuade Christopher to go with her. He opted to continue adding compost to the tomato beds."

Being clairvoyant, Christopher didn't do well off the property. Though he was blood tied to Samantha as much as he was to me, he was more grounded in an environment that he could control. Away from the influence of too many people, too many lives to navigate possible futures for in his head.

"Has he…Samantha said he'd been getting glimpses of something?"

Aiden brushed his fingers gently across my cheekbone, then over my ear, catching and smoothing his fingers down a long length of my hair. "You know he'd tell you."

I huffed. I did know. I just wasn't feeling wholly rational at the moment. Apparently, Christopher wasn't the only one who needed the grounding of a chosen environment, a chosen family.

"Keep him and Paisley in line," I muttered.

"Come home quickly. I'm not sure either of them will listen to me…at all. So, if your orders wear off—"

I grimaced. "I'm not their commander."

Aiden snorted. But whatever he was going to say was overridden by two sets of footfalls—young teenager and demon dog—pounding down the stairs, followed by the sound of the front door being wrenched open.

"Lani is here!" Opal crowed from the front of the house.

Aiden kissed me gently. Then, threading his fingers through mine, he grabbed Opal's backpack from the counter and tugged me with him out of the kitchen.

And yeah, I was dragging my feet. As childish as that was.

Except I'd never had a chance to be childish. Not even when I'd actually been young enough for that to be suitable behavior.

That thought was all it took for me to pick up my pace.

Because Opal deserved the childhood I'd never had. She needed a family, yes. But also an education and a sense of being. Of place.

And for a witch, that place was a coven.

The Godfrey coven was the most powerful in the world, according to both my lawyer and my lover. So it would do just fine for my Opal.

AFTER NOT EVEN FOUR HOURS APART, I ALREADY missed my deadly sorcerer. As if the invisible, involuntary bonds of magic that tied us were stretching thinner and thinner the more road my 1967 Mustang convertible chewed up between Lake Cowichan and Tofino.

Of course, my current mood might also have been tied to the fact that I apparently never did anything in half measures—and I was about to spend three days among a coven of witches who'd never laid eyes on me.

Specifically, and even more worrisome, they had never beheld me with their finely tuned senses for power.

Witches were judgemental. So was I, obviously and always. But I needed the next three days to go smoothly, because I wanted to adopt Opal. And the witches could potentially stand in my way. In our way.

Normally, I just drained or decapitated people who stopped me from achieving my goals. But in this situation, that would have the exact opposite effect than I intended. Hence, the extra emotional ache with each kilometer I was putting between me and my sorcerer, my Aiden. He was the smooth, cultured, and charming half of our partnership.

And I?

I was pretty much only a blunt instrument.

I wasn't anyone's idea of a mother.

Except for Opal.

Thankfully, the little witch's opinion was the only one that mattered.

The traffic had thinned slightly after we left the main highway and started cutting across the island toward the coast. But it was still steady enough that, even while winding through the mountainous pass, we were never the only vehicle headed west.

I eased off the gas as we neared a junction, already knowing we needed to make a right turn but still taking the time to read the signs.

Thirty-three kilometers to Tofino.

Opal and Ocean were chattering away in the back seat of the Mustang, as they had been ever since we'd left Lake Cowichan. Though apparently the drive through Cathedral Grove could reduce even teen witches to exclamations of amazement at the size of Vancouver Island's old-growth evergreen trees.

Lani, in the front passenger seat beside me, was as sprawled as much as her seatbelt would allow, arm resting along the top of the door, window rolled down. Her short dark-brown hair danced in the wind, her tanned face tilted upward to the sun. The intuitive had been quiet for most of the drive, but was seemingly content.

Thirty-three kilometers until I met Pearl Godfrey, the head of the witches Convocation. And the rest of the coven. Until the women who might have the final say in allowing me to adopt Opal met me.

Me.

And everything I couldn't easily hide since my encounter with the Hallowed—the ancient entity that Cerise Myers had fully unleashed on Kader Azar after he'd outright accused her of slowly trying to kill him. Aiden's mother and father.

I would have walked away from all that family drama. I could have done so easily. Except that Cerise had used Aiden's blood to anchor the entity through him, in order to reach Kader. So my dark sorcerer could have been consumed by his own mother's vengeance. Instead, the Hallowed—the mother of the dawn, as the entity referred to itself—had decided that I was its perfect vessel. And in the brief moments it possessed me, it heightened my abilities, specifically weaponizing my latent empathy. I also no longer needed skin-to-skin contact to amplify or drain others, or to read or manipulate their emotions.

No matter how much I struggled to dampen my power.

I kept my grip on the steering wheel light, making the sweeping right turn without hesitation. Ignoring the ball of trepidation currently lodged somewhere in the vicinity of my heart.

Lani gestured to the left, calling back to the teen witches in the back seat over her shoulder. "You'll start to see glimpses of the ocean now. Though the trees have really grown in since I was here five years ago."

Cedar and fir trees edged both sides of the two-lane highway, seemingly stretching out endlessly—as had been the case for most of the drive, in between the small towns and tourist spots we'd passed through. Though the road had wound through the mountains for the bulk of the drive, its curves sharply dropping off steep cliffs bordering large lakes, it ran straight before us now for as far as I could see.

The June day was beautiful, sunny but not too warm. Endless blue sky stretched over us, dotted with a few wispy white clouds.

Opal gripped the back edge of my seat, pressing against her seat belt as she shouted over the wind, "Can we stop, Emma? At the beach?"

"Check-in is 4:00 P.M.," I said, raising my own voice. "And the hotel is on the edge of a gorgeous beach." I had studied the resort property and the two small towns that bordered it with the same thoroughness I applied to any mission. Including getting freshly updated satellite images from contacts of Samantha's, and detailed weather reports.

I had three emergency escape routes meticulously mapped out—by road, sea, and air. Not as many as I would have liked, but there was only one road in and out of the tiny town of Tofino. I was surprised that the Godfrey coven chose an area for their yearly gathering in which they could be so easily contained. But coven witches had their own way of doing things. And that usually came with a large dose of superiority and arrogance.

Yes, I was aware that I was being exceedingly judgemental. Again. That was why I needed Aiden to smooth all my blunt edges.

"Oh, look!" Ocean cried, drawing Opal's attention to a glimpse of blue sky meeting gray sand, and the crashing, frothy-white surf through the evergreens edging the road on our far left.

Lani smirked at me. "You know the check-in time is just a suggestion."

I grimaced. "The first activity is a meet-and-greet."

"I know. You made me memorize the schedule for the next three days, the layout of the hotel, and individual bios for each of the witches."

She paused as if expecting me to respond. But since I'd already supplied her with everything she needed to successfully navigate her first meeting with the Godfrey witches, I felt no need to elaborate. Though the cheat sheet detailing all the Godfrey coven witches had been Aiden's meticulous work. I would have just lumped them all into the same category—possible enemy combatant, low risk.

Low risk for me, anyway. Because there were few Adepts who could stand against me.

A fact that was more disconcerting than empowering these days.

I had more to lose now than just my life.

Lani chuckled quietly. "The meet-and-greet is over tea. That should make you happy."

Not even ginger snaps would make afternoon tea a pleasant experience with strangers who had far too much potential control over my life.

Lani brushed her fingers over the back of my hand, barely touching me. Her witch magic, typically manifesting as a heightened sense of intuition, tingled across my skin, along with a brief sense of her easy resolve and contentment. Though my once latent empathy didn't actually need skin-to-skin contact to trigger. Not anymore.

Lani might have been only a part-time intuitive, but she was a full-time friend. She had likely meant the touch to be comforting, but I accepted the magic that backed it much more easily than I could accept being taken care of.

If nothing was tweaking Lani's senses, then everything was going to be okay.

At least for the next hour or so. That was as far out as we'd been able to test her intuition, since setting up such tests was rather difficult. Aiden and Christopher had taken to pranking Lani to trigger her power, and I didn't really approve of that methodology. Especially when those tricks involved me.

Another exclamation erupted from the back seat of the convertible, drawing our attention to the left again. For the briefest of moments, another view of a gray-sand beach broke through the trees. If not for the roar of the wind already buffeting my ears, the sound of the pounding surf would no doubt have been impressive.

"Surfers!" Opal exclaimed, picking out black dots among waves that had to be at least four meters high. Even in June, my research informed me, the water was cold enough that surfers wore wet suits if they were in the ocean for any extended period of time.

"But no sharks, right?" Ocean howled over the wind.

"You know there are!" Opal huffed, exasperated. "We looked it up!"

"But not near shore," Ocean muttered, reassuring herself. "Not man-eaters."

"Don't worry," Opal crowed gleefully. "The orcas will eat you before the sharks."

I glanced at Ocean in the rearview mirror. The eighteen-year-old potions specialist in training looked utterly aghast. "But not near shore, right?" she repeated, brushing strands of the dark-brown, blond-tipped hair that had worked free from her loose bun away from her light-blue eyes.

Lani laughed. "You don't have to surf, Ocean."

The Myers witch huffed, crossing her arms. "You don't know witches. If I show any weakness, they'll freeze me out."

Lani smirked in my direction.

Though Ocean wasn't wrong.

Coven witches had expectations. Those expectations wouldn't impact the intuitive because Lani didn't want anything from the coven. Ocean, however, was seeking guest status and an apprenticeship.

Signage started appearing on either side of the road. I shifted my attention, noting the sparsely spaced side roads, the park trails, and the turnoffs to other resorts as they passed, orientating myself.

The sign for the Wickaninnish Inn appeared up ahead on the left. I slowed, once again ignoring the trepidation that had taken up permanent residence in my chest.

I wasn't scared of witches. Not even a full coven. I could drain them all without laying a single finger on any of them. Depending on the strength of their shields, both physical and mental, I might even be able to beguile them, bend them to my will, from a distance. Though I hadn't been comfortable testing that new ability.

I hadn't received a single hint from my Adept lawyer, Ember Pine, that there were going to be any issues with the adoption. So it was definitely possible that I was getting caught up in my own insecurities.

I turned up the drive, dropping my speed further. Tall trees closed around us as I followed the signs to the resort's lower parking lot. The rooms set aside for the coven were in a secondary building. And even though I'd never stayed in the luxury hotel before, I knew how many steps there were from the lot to the entrance and then to the reception desk. I'd memorized the locations and menus of the cafe and the restaurants. I even knew the artists—a sculptor and a metalsmith—who were currently being featured in the lobby.

I wouldn't stumble.

I would help Opal, Ocean, and Lani meet the coven. I'd keep my own interactions with the witches to a minimum. Then we'd go home, and sign the adoption papers soon after.

Three days. Two nights.

I could do this.

I would do it.

GRANITE DANCING BEARS ON WOOD-SLAB PEDESTALS marked the entrance to the inn. The heavy wood-framed glass door swung shut behind us as Opal and Ocean raced through the open room, down a few steps, and through a plush seating area, weaving around more stone and wood-hewn indigenous artwork. Wooden stairs, railings, and casings dominated the main areas of the inn. Charcoal-gray stone tile stretched throughout. The building was perched along the edge of a cliff, with the treed shoreline stretching out for kilometers beyond it.

The teen witches practically plastered themselves against the expansive windows overlooking the sandy beach and the crashing surf below. Lani eyed them with amusement, sticking by me as I crossed toward the reception desk, where an employee was situated at a computer screen. We'd left our bags in the Mustang.

The front desk clerk looked up as we approached, smiling politely. Her skin was naturally tan, and she wore her light-brown hair tidily pulled back at the nape of her neck. Her navy jacket and skirt were paired with a white collared shirt, but no name tag. I quickly surmised, given our luxurious surroundings, that a name tag would have been considered too…ordinary?

"Emma Johnson?" She had a European accent that I had no hope of identifying, even as she somehow identified me on sight. "And Lani Zachary?"

"Yes," Lani said, smiling—and not at all thrown that the woman apparently knew who we were.

"Your party is expecting you." The clerk's fingers flew across her keyboard. "Ms. Johnson, I have you in the Frank Island Suite as requested. But we didn't know if you were bringing one or two pets?"

Pets? I cast Opal a sidelong look. The two witches had abandoned the stunning view to peer into a glass case that appeared to hold jewelry. For sale by local artisans in keeping with the rest of the art, I presumed.

"One," I said, sighing internally. Apparently, the young witch thought Paisley might be joining us, even though I'd asked the demon dog to stay on the property with Christopher and Aiden. "Thank you."

"Our pleasure." The clerk folded two key cards into a small envelope. "There is a dog wash station just outside your room. For the sand. And a bed, bowls, and treats waiting in your suite." She slid the envelope across the high counter toward me.

The head of a seal—cast out of metal and ridiculously lifelike—was set on the wooden counter. Staring at me. I took the key card envelope and tried to not stare back at what I assumed was supposed to be art. Entranced even as it repelled me, I quashed the urge to stroke the decapitated head.

Christopher would have been all over the symbolism, since he continually saw me going around beheading people. But rather deliberately, I hadn't packed my blades for the trip. Technically, they were only a thought away thanks to the recall spells Aiden had embedded into the gemstones in their hilts, then had spent hours teaching me to trigger earlier in the year. Though we hadn't tested that magic at this distance.

Lani bumped me with her shoulder.

"The Wi-Fi password is on the back," the front desk clerk said with a patient smile, as if she'd been waiting for me to look over at her. "I have you staying for two nights."

"Yes."

"We are at your disposal."

"Thank you." My tone was stiff, but recognizing that I was uncomfortable with the interaction didn't ease it at all.

The clerk then turned her attention to Lani. "Ms. Zachary, I have you and your guest in the neighboring suite, but I do have a room available on the second floor, if you prefer."

"Ground floor is fine," Lani said. Ocean was rooming with her, Opal with me.

"Lovely." The clerk moved through the process of getting Lani's key cards tucked into another envelope.

A dark-skinned, barrel-chested man wearing a fuchsia dress shirt stepped out of the back room. "Welcome to the Wickaninnish." Again, I didn't recognize his accent. South African, perhaps? "The rest of your group has gathered for tea in the upstairs library, if you wish to join them directly. May I park your vehicle? And bring your bags to your suite?"

My stomach soured. If there were other witches in the building already, I couldn't feel them. "We're already parked."

Lani plucked my car keys out of my hand. "The pretty Clearwater Aqua Mustang. Feel free to drop all the bags in either room. We'll sort them out from there."

"Very well." He smiled broadly. "Please let me know if there is anything else you need. The stairs are to our right." He gestured, though the stairs couldn't be seen from the reception desk. "One flight up will take you to the library. But your suites are at the end of the main ground-floor hallway."

The clerk slid an envelope with Lani's key cards across the counter. "Can I make any restaurant or tour reservations for you? There are maps of the area and other information in your rooms, but they're available at both main desks as well."

"We're fine for now," Lani said. "Thank you." She touched my elbow lightly, and I turned away at her prompting.

I settled my gaze on Opal. The young witch was now inspecting a seal statue set beside a brown leather couch. The statue appeared to have been cast by the same artist who'd created the disembodied head perched on the counter behind me. Ocean was back at the window, her gaze awed.

"What exactly is bothering you?" Lani asked in a low murmur. "Do you think the Godfrey witches might try to…harm us in some way?"

I shook my head. "No. That would look bad for them. Especially with us escorting prospective members."

"So...bad PR makes for good witches?"

I frowned, not understanding the reference.

Lani shook her head slightly, then followed my gaze to Opal. The young witch floated over to a granite bear statue, petting it. "Is it the socializing? You...aren't particularly...social..."

I nodded. That was a good enough excuse for what Lani obviously thought was some odd behavior. I'd also never checked into a luxury hotel before. And I'd never loved a child, a person, so much that the very idea of not being able to have them in my life was suffocating me from the inside out.

Opal looked up, catching my eye and smiling broadly enough to flash her crooked eyeteeth. Despite her tumultuous background, the little witch was far more adaptable than I was. I held up the tiny envelope with the key cards, and she skipped toward me. Her gold-and-silver-streaked dark-brown curls bounced around her head.

She had grown so much since I'd first laid eyes on her almost two years ago in San Francisco. When she'd been kidnapped and almost drained of blood and magic to fuel a spell meant to hold me.

It hadn't.

I took one of the key cards, tucking it into the pocket of my sundress with my credit card and the fold of twenty-dollar bills I'd remembered to grab from the ATM at the last minute. Then I offered the envelope with the room number and Wi-Fi password to Opal. Still grinning, she tucked it in the inner pocket of her bright-orange backpack. I caught a glimpse of her iPad and a few spellbooks before she zipped it back up.

"So…the beach?" the young witch asked.

Ocean had wandered over, taking a key card from Lani. "Tea first," she grumbled, feigning disgruntlement. "We don't want to be late making our first impression."

"Yes," I said, indulging my nerves by settling my hand briefly on Opal's shoulder. "Tea. Then we'll walk the beach."

"Juniper and her aunt, Olive, arrived about an hour ago. Juniper texted." Opal bounced shallowly in place, not remotely concerned about meeting the witches who controlled her future. "Ocean wants to intern with Olive. She specializes in herbology."

"I remember," I said, recalling all the details about Olive from Aiden's cheat sheet.

"Upstairs, right?" Ocean asked, tugging her dark-brown hair out of its messy bun and flipping its practically white tips over her shoulders. With a whisper of magic, it fell into a straight, silky sheath.

"Yes." I quashed the urge to run my fingers through my own sure-to-be tangled hair.

Ocean stepped away, drawing Opal with her. My hand fell to my side. Ocean had been born and raised a Myers coven witch. The Godfreys might have been primarily located in Canada, rather than France, but Aiden's sister would have no issue fitting in.

Lani squeezed my hand lightly, releasing my fingers as quickly as she'd touched me. Then she followed the younger witches around the corner to the main stairs.

For what might possibly have been the first time in my life, I trailed behind. I rectified that lag the moment after I recognized it, lengthening my stride and catching up with Opal halfway up the wide wooden stairs. As we hit the first landing, I caught our reflections in a large mirror set in a wood frame that appeared to have been cut from a huge tree, then sanded just enough to smooth the grain but not change its natural shape.

Opal was grinning, her bright-blue eyes gleeful. All long limbed in shorts and a T-shirt printed with the Academy's coat of arms, with her backpack hanging off one shoulder. She still barely came up to my own shoulder, and her light-brown skin was a sharp contrast to my practically translucent complexion.

I deliberately softened my expression, taking Opal's hand. She was mine to hold, to protect. And the damn witches were going to know it the moment they saw us together.

A cool rationale settled over me, similar to the outset of any mission that required my undivided attention. We traversed the landing, then climbed the second flight of stairs with Ocean and Lani chatting quietly behind us.

The first hints of witch magic tickled my senses.

OVER A DOZEN WITCHES—MOST OF THEM DECADES older than Opal, judging by appearance—were arrayed in a lofted room that was open to the hotel lobby below, sharing the same span of windows overlooking the beach. The view beyond the wooden railing was just as impressive as it had been one floor below.

Though it contained a few well-stocked bookshelves, the library seemed to be geared more toward lounging. Cozy leather couches and high-backed fabric chairs proliferated the space. Photography and travel books were piled artfully on the coffee and side tables. A tea service and tiered trays of baked goods were set on a long table to the far right.

A silver-haired witch, standing against the far railing in the very center of the room, turned as we stepped onto the landing at the top of the stairs, setting her teacup in a saucer. But it was the strawberry-blond witch standing closer to us, seemingly in her early forties, who smiled at us broadly as if utterly delighted. Then she swiftly closed the space between us, with both of her hands held out to Opal. She was dressed in a short-sleeved blue silk wrap dress with open-toed heeled shoes. Her smile was utterly genuine and epically charming.

Scarlett Godfrey.

Not that I'd ever met or seen a picture of the vibrant witch. But Aiden's description of the scion of the Godfrey coven was exceedingly accurate. Daughter to Pearl, Scarlett also occupied a seat on the witches Convocation. And based on the unmistakable shared genetic traits—both women had striking facial features, a petite stature, and indigo-blue eyes—her mother, Pearl, was the silver-haired coven leader steadily watching us from across the room.

"Opal, yes?" Scarlett asked, still smiling broadly. "I'm Scarlett. We're so pleased you could join us."

Opal curtsied playfully instead of taking the strawberry-blond witch's hands. To the utter delight of Scarlett, whose laughter was just as delightful while ringing through my ears.

Charm. Charisma. Beauty.

Godfrey witch traits. Again, according to the dossier that Aiden had put together.

A pretty mask for a witch powerful enough to almost completely dampen her power signature even while only a couple of steps away from me. Though given the generally muted tenor from the gathering, it was obvious that some powerful charms were being utilized by all the witches. Or perhaps the entire library had been warded for the duration of the afternoon tea.

"Opal! Ocean!" a wavy-haired blond in her teens called from the other side of the room. She appeared to have commandeered a tray of cookies.

Opal waved.

Scarlett glanced over her shoulder. Then, still grinning, she gestured toward Opal. "Go, go."

Opal glanced at me, and I nodded. She took off toward the teen, who I assumed was her second-year friend from the Academy, Juniper.

We had drawn the attention of all the other witches now, but they maintained their quiet conversations in between moments of glancing our way. All the witches identified as female in the Godfrey coven, according to Aiden's notes. Males wielding witch magic were slightly more rare but not that unusual—so the fact that the Godfrey coven appeared to not have a single male in it was highly unusual. A mystery that even Ember Pine couldn't illuminate.

Ocean offered Scarlett a nod. "Ocean Myers."

"Scarlett Godfrey." The older witch tilted her head thoughtfully. "I understand you want to talk with Olive." She nodded toward a tall, slim witch adorned in shades of orange. "About a summer internship in herbology?"

"Yes." Ocean grinned enthusiastically. "I know the Godfrey coven doesn't have a potion master per se…but maybe you will consider an application from me?"

I blinked at Ocean.

So did Scarlett. "You…wish to relocate?"

Ocean squared her shoulders, perhaps thwarting an impulse to shrug. "I have at least another year of specialization I can do at the Academy, but I can sell my creams and other products from anywhere in the world. So…yeah."

Scarlett's gaze sharpened. Not that I thought there was much the witch didn't already see from under the guise of her heady charm. "We would never turn down a member of your talent, Ocean. But leaving your coven…"

31

Ocean shrugged. "No biggie. The Myers coven has several potion masters."

Scarlett nodded, but didn't seem at all convinced.

Feeling betrayed by her mother, Cerise, as we all were, Ocean hadn't wanted to return to the Myers coven. She had actually transferred for the last few weeks of the term to the Academy's American campus from the UK, but I hadn't been aware that she wanted to stay with us beyond the summer.

Ocean glanced at me, smiling tentatively.

I smiled back, the expression tight on my face even though I was trying to be supportive. "Aiden, Opal, and I would be pleased to…sponsor you." I had to reach for that term, but I was fairly certain it applied equally to the coven and Canadian immigration.

Ocean wrapped her arm around mine for a moment, squeezing. The gesture drew Scarlett's attention. Then the young witch swiftly crossed toward Olive, already smiling widely and politely.

Adepts didn't touch unknown magic users terribly often. And most Adepts kept an even wider berth from me—even more so once they got to know me.

Scarlett met my gaze. "Emma. Thank you for bringing Opal."

"Thank you for inviting us." I angled my shoulder toward Lani, who'd stayed a step back. "My friend, Lani Zachery."

I might have hit the word 'friend' rather hard, given the knowing smirk that Scarlett quashed as she nodded toward Lani.

"Nice to meet you," the intuitive said, keeping her hands stuffed in the pockets of her shorts.

Scarlett's gaze flicked over Lani's shoulder, and she couldn't quite stop herself from narrowing her eyes as another witch stepped into the library. The newcomer appeared to be in her mid-to-late forties, with light-brown hair cut bluntly at chin length. Her blue eyes were the lightest I'd ever seen on a witch, and her skin was pale.

However, I assumed it was the raven perched on her shoulder that had raised Scarlett's well-disguised ire. Though it seemed doubtful that anyone without the sight for magic could see the imposing hooked-beak corvid that was likely also the newcomer's familiar.

I'd never actually seen a familiar in person. Not all witches had the inclination or capacity to attract a willing and compatible familiar in the first place, and those who did carefully guarded the animals with which they'd bonded.

"Mercury," Scarlett purred, suddenly sounding the opposite of delightfully sunny. "How nice of you to join us."

"How annoying of you to summon me." Mercury's accent was British through and through, pointed and clipped.

The raven took in the entire room with a sharp-eyed gaze. Then that gaze settled on me, not shifting even as the witch all but shouldered past us to cross to Pearl.

A sandy-haired witch in her late thirties, who was knitting while she walked, moved to accompany the newcomer, Mercury. Though she appeared to be transfixed by the raven more than the witch.

"Kelly Godfrey," Scarlett murmured quietly. "A second cousin on my father's side."

"From Salt Spring Island?" I asked, though I already knew the answer. "She raises alpaca and cashmere goats?"

Scarlett nodded, still watching the trio by the railing—her mother Pearl, Mercury with her raven, and Kelly who was trying to get the bird's attention. But the raven's head remained twisted back, its gaze still on me.

"That's weird, right?" Lani asked in a low murmur, likely thinking she was speaking only to me. "Walking around with a huge bird on your shoulder? Even for a witch? Aiden didn't mention it on his cheat sheet. And neither did Ember."

Aiden's dossier on the Godfreys had mined much of its information from the witch lawyer, and I knew that Lani had been chatting back and forth with Ember via email since they'd met briefly earlier in the year. I thought that the slowly building friendship between lawyer and mechanic might have been one of the reasons Lani had decided to come with us to the coven retreat.

Scarlett, her lips twisted into an amused smile, answered Lani before I could. "Yes, it's weird. Mercury is a visiting member from the Dunkirk coven, from London. An animal mage. She's been partially based in the Vancouver area for the last five years, in between traveling and private contract work. Ember Pine is very thorough, but I doubt she's met Mercury. Or our youngest member, Burgundy." She nodded toward a curvy witch in her twenties, wearing a cotton crinkle skirt and a yellow T-shirt with a pink-printed Cake in a Cup logo. For a bakery, I presumed, given the picture of what appeared to be a cupcake in a mug. She was in the process of shaking Ocean's hand, rather enthusiastically.

Scarlett laughed softly. "Correction. Burgundy has been our youngest witch for a couple of years. She was very much looking forward to meeting Ocean, Juniper, and Opal."

"Fresh blood," I said before I could edit myself. "To expand the power of the coven."

"The Godfrey coven welcomes new members," Scarlett said neutrally. "But I believe you will quickly find that we have no need to…expand, as you put it."

Ember had said as much when we'd first discussed Opal's guardianship. The lawyer had explained that the Godfrey coven already had numerous nonwitch members, including necromancers and sorcerers, as well as an amplifier and some sort of seer.

But my inherent and all-encompassing distrust of organized bodies of magic users ran rather deep.

"Burgundy is studying healing," Scarlett continued easily, as if I hadn't just rudely accused her coven of being power collectors. "She will have a lot in common with Ocean." She glanced at me, then at Lani.

"Come. You might as well get meeting my mother over with." Her self-deprecating smile didn't quite warm her eyes, nor did it linger as she crossed toward the silver-haired witch.

I touched Lani lightly on the arm as she started to follow, whispering to her, "You can see the raven clearly?"

Lani glanced toward the corvid in question, tracking Mercury Dunkirk as she crossed toward the long table to get some tea. Kelly Godfrey was trailing behind her, still knitting. "Shouldn't I be able to?"

"It's magically cloaked."

Lani met my gaze, grimacing. "So…I can see magic now?"

Aiden had added Lani's blood to the boundary protections around the property after I'd amplified the intuitive enough to pull forward her latent witch talent for finding and fixing lost things. But even though Aiden had offered to work with her, the mechanic hadn't been terribly inclined to train that innate talent.

I eyed the raven a little longer, then glanced around the room in search of anything else that might have been magically cloaked. Nothing stood out, though, so I couldn't test Lani's sight further. "I'm not sure," I finally murmured. "Maybe there's something wrong with the raven, and your senses are picking up on that."

"Like the fact that it's just creepily sitting there on a person's shoulder?" Lani huffed. "It should be out in the wind, fishing in the surf."

I eyed the intuitive.

She grimaced at me. "A few months ago, I would have been exceedingly pleased to have you look at me like that, Emma."

"But…?" I smirked.

"I'm not a puzzle."

I grinned at her. "I would have thought you'd like to be intriguing."

"Do you?" she snapped.

She had me there. I hated drawing attention. Though in my case, that was because I often had to resort to incapacitating people who became enamored with my magic and the idea of using me.

"The raven feels wrong to you. For whatever reason," I said, as if the nuances of how Lani's magic worked weren't at all intriguing. "So you can see it."

Lani grunted noncommittally. "Mercury is something pretty to look at, though. Miles and miles of creamy skin. And those white-blue wolf eyes." She flashed me a grin. "I might grab some tea first."

I shook my head at her, but she sauntered off toward the treats with her hands still stuffed in her back pockets. She was far more confident among unknown magic users than I was, even though I was the biggest predator in the room. In the entire area, perhaps.

The silver-haired witch was watching me. Pearl Godfrey. Her indigo gaze was piercing, a much darker blue than even Aiden's eyes. But somehow still neutral. I couldn't feel even a hint of power from her. Yet.

It was possible I was wrong about being the biggest, baddest Adept in the library.

That didn't make me feel any more settled, though.

I glanced over at Opal. She was clustered with a small group of younger witches—Ocean, Juniper, and the healer Burgundy—nibbling on a chocolate chip cookie and listening intently to everything the older three were discussing.

Chocolate chip had been her mother's favorite cookies.

The little witch met my gaze, grinning widely. Happiness practically thrummed under her skin, gleaming from her eyes.

She belonged among witches. And she deserved to belong to the most powerful coven I could find for her.

I smiled back at her. Then I turned that smile on Pearl Godfrey, reaching out as I crossed the room to shake her hand.

For Opal, I would do my best.

I couldn't match the Godfrey charm. And apparently they had no need for an amplifier, so I couldn't use that either. But just based on the ages of the witches arrayed across the room, and Scarlett's reaction to the idea of Ocean leaving the Myers coven, I already understood that the Godfrey coven would want Opal—maybe even desperately—for her youth and her abilities.

And we were a package deal.

I just had to make certain the witches understood that fact. Without inadvertently putting on a massive power display that might have them running away as quickly as they could instead.

Hence leaving my blades at home.

And my deadly sorcerer.

Pearl Godfrey met my gaze. Closer up, I could see that her indigo eyes were the exact same remarkable shade as her daughter's. But she carried none of the easy charm that spilled from the strawberry-blond witch. The coven leader slid her hand into mine without hesitation, and only then did I pick up a simmer of all the power she kept neatly contained. A vibrant, almost electric hum streaked through my fingers and shivered up my arm. But not a hint of emotion even tickled my empathic senses.

The only other Adept I'd ever touched who could so effectively hide their power, and emotions, from me was Kader Azar.

Pearl smiled, the expression perfunctory. "We're pleased you could bring Opal, Emma."

"Of course," I said, suddenly not at all certain of myself. "It was what Opal wanted."

Pearl narrowed her eyes at me for a moment. But then she simply nodded, squeezed my hand briefly, and released me. "Tea?"

"Ah…yes?" I wasn't certain why that had come out as a question, regretting the display of weakness instantly.

But Pearl stepped away without another word, without another glance at me, instantly dropping into a conversation with another witch as they headed toward the tea service.

Well, that had been…anticlimactic.

And now I didn't know what to do with myself.

Again.

Seriously, even if it left my soul aching, beheading my enemies was far easier than any of this.

TWO

A DARK-HAIRED, DEEPLY TANNED SORCERER CLAD IN nothing but blue jeans was sprawled on the bed in my suite, propped up on pillows just high enough to watch the surf pounding the gray-sand beach out of the windows.

I had no idea how Aiden had gotten to Tofino—or into the room for that matter. But I had just spent the previous hour trying to not act like a sociopath while sipping tea and surrounded by strangers, then had gratefully escaped when Opal and Juniper headed to the beach. So in that moment, I really didn't care how the sorcerer came to be in my bed.

Smirking, I stepped through from the living room area and past the luxurious bathroom that opened up on my right, replete with soaker tub and walk-in shower. I rounded the bed, intending to give the sorcerer the tongue-lashing he deserved for disturbing the sanctity of an invitation-only coven gathering.

Except…he was napping. Sprawled in the sun spilling partly over the bed, like a contented cat.

And I just stopped.

Stopped and stared at him with my heart aching. Just a little. Over the sheer beauty of him.

Aiden.

Mine.

He cracked one blazing-blue eye open, smirking at me, then running his hand down his chest and stretching to show off all his hard-earned muscle.

I was shimmying out of my underwear even as I climbed over him on the bed.

Surprise flickered across his face, but then my mouth was crashing over his as I tugged awkwardly on his buttoned jeans, trying to get them off without actually breaking contact with him.

He grabbed my low ponytail with one hand, tilting my head to ravish my mouth, while lifting his hips and shoving down his jeans and underwear with the other hand. I wrapped my fingers around his girth as it sprang free of his boxers, stroking a few times—fast and probably a touch too hard. But he didn't complain as I settled over him, taking him inside me while he was still kicking his jeans and boxers free of his ankles.

He groaned. The noise shot through me like liquid fire. I lay low over his chest, the angle where our bodies connected likely too shallow for him but perfect for me to take my own pleasure. Rubbing, rubbing as I kissed my sorcerer, my Aiden, and tried to ignore what was very much an overreaction to us being parted for less than half a day.

Magic poured from me, from him, tangling around us in a web of invisible power.

I was panting now, bolts of pleasure streaking through me with every groan and gasp I wrung from Aiden.

I came.

Hard. And fast.

I lost control of my own limbs for just long enough for Aiden to gain that control. He flipped over with me, pressing my knees wide to the sides as he rose above me. Hands pinned to my thighs, he drove deep, keeping up the vigorous rhythm. I had to muffle my own cries from the sheer intensity of the pleasure he wrung from my now extremely sensitized flesh.

Our empathic connection, intensified by our skin-to-skin contact, flooded with the potent pleasure Aiden was also riding—a wave that crested, then exploded just as the waves thundered against the beach outside.

Still braced above me, Aiden jerked, then stilled, buried deep inside me. He groaned harshly.

Surfing his emotions, I orgasmed a second time.

My sorcerer blinked down at me, shaking his head. Then he laughed huskily. "Hello to you too."

I wrapped my legs around him, tugging him closer for a sweet, gentle kiss. The kiss I probably should have welcomed him with.

He laughed again, breathlessly happy. Then he slid off me.

I groaned playfully, in disappointment.

But he just grinned at me, padding to the bathroom and wetting a washcloth. He rejoined me, washing my thighs and between my legs. His gaze was locked to mine, burning with fierce possession now. He liked the submission, liked that I allowed him to tend to me.

He kissed my belly—my dress was still shoved up under my breasts—his lips tracing the lines of the faded scars slashed across my abdomen. Scars from the fight against Silver Pine's greater demon.

"Again?" he asked huskily, speaking against my skin.

I threaded my fingers through his thick hair, turning my attention out the window. The tide was low. The rocky outcroppings nearer to shore and the few evergreens between the beach and our suite didn't offer any visual protection. Anyone could have walked past our windows and seen us, though I couldn't really bring myself to care.

"Opal's on the beach," I whispered finally. "I said I'd join her after I made certain the luggage made it to the room."

Aiden huffed, playfully peeved. But then he wandered back into the bathroom to rinse the washcloth and quickly bathe himself. I rolled over onto my stomach, rejecting the breathtaking view outside for the stimulating view inside. Aiden's backside was glorious.

Catching me watching him in the mirror, he flashed me a grin.

Magic shifted, giving us barely a moment of warning before a large, blue-nosed pit bull trundled into the bedroom area—carrying the hotel dog bed that had been set next to the closet in the front hall of the suite.

Paisley.

The demon dog was supposed to be guarding Christopher at the property.

I sighed.

She shouldered past Aiden in the doorway of the bathroom without acknowledging either of us, stepping out of my line of sight.

Aiden quashed a grin, then raised an eyebrow at whatever the demon dog was doing. "The tub? Did you want me to light the candle for you?"

Paisley grumbled offishly.

Aiden looked at me, grinning and shaking his head playfully. "Apparently, Paisley can get a lock on you even over two hundred and seventy-five kilometers away."

"Neither of you are supposed to be here," I said, though without much heat. After two orgasms, it was rather difficult to get riled up. Or perhaps I just didn't want the warm glow to ebb too quickly. I felt like myself for the first time since we'd left the house, since I'd spent too much time packing for the trip.

"Christopher is going to be pissed that we've both abandoned him."

"Did you teleport?" I kept my tone as light as possible, but the question was loaded. I knew that no matter how much it worried me, I couldn't dictate what Aiden did or how he did it. Just as he couldn't stop me from doing what I thought was the strategic choice either. But teleportation was exceedingly risky.

"Float plane," he said easily, snagging his boxers off the floor and tugging them on. "There were no boundary wards on the hotel exits to circumvent, and a tiny rune attached to your bag yielded the location of your room."

I wanted to grin back at him, to tease him about keeping magical tabs on me, but I still couldn't tear my gaze away from him. I was using him to anchor me. Again. Not that Aiden minded. In fact, I had no doubt that was exactly why the sorcerer had shown up unannounced.

Or…

A lick of disconcertion ran up my spine. I ignored it. "Christopher had a vision?"

Aiden shook his head sharply. But then he shrugged. "Well, not that he told me. He was trying to cast cards for Samantha when I left. Or, more specifically, for Amanda, I guess."

Christopher didn't want to leave the property just to be trapped in hotel after hotel as Samantha and Daniel followed up on yet another lead they'd uncovered about Bee. But that didn't mean the clairvoyant didn't want to help. And he wasn't the only one. Kader Azar had promised to look into Bee's disappearance himself, though he hadn't come through with anything substantial either. And while he might be a total asshole, I would trust the elder sorcerer over Daniel's contacts any day.

"I feel like I'm just...piloting myself," I blurted, pressing my face into the bed. "Like I'm some sort of impostor, but inside my own skin."

"Emma..." Aiden whispered, stepping closer to run his hand down my back.

"Bee can do that," I said, deflecting whatever platitude the sorcerer was about to offer me. "Hollow out a person, control them. To varying degrees."

"To...you?"

I blinked. "No. Not that the Collective didn't make her try. But either Bee can't fully subsume the mind of one of the Five, or some part of her couldn't be forced to do it. No matter the punishment."

Aiden fell silent.

And now I'd ruined a lovely moment by bringing up the Collective and the reality of the Five's upbringing. I rolled over, sitting up so I could thread my fingers through Aiden's hair for the second time. But he was already reaching for me, already kissing me with all the emotion he'd caged up, all the emotion backing all the words he wanted to say.

Regrets that weren't his to hold, sorrow over what his father had done to us.

"Stay?" I whispered between kisses, lightly sucking on his bottom lip as I waited for his answer.

"I had this whole excuse worked out. The last gift I wanted Opal to have before the induction ceremony arrived about fifteen minutes after you left, and I was going to leverage it into staying." He smoothed his tongue across my lip, barely making contact. "But the truth is I just…missed you. And I barely got twenty-four hours with Opal. And—"

I silenced him with a deeper kiss, followed by some distracting caresses—at least until Paisley let out a heavy undulating sigh from the bathroom. Not loud enough to be heard outside the room, but pointed nonetheless.

I parted my lips from Aiden's just enough to call out, "Uninvited guests have no say in the retreat's activities. You can always return to the property."

The demon dog quieted instantly.

Aiden laughed silently, his bright-blue gaze playful. "I can stay out of sight."

"Pearl Godfrey probably knew the moment you set foot on the property. Even without boundary wards." I raised my voice to include the sulking demon dog in the bathtub. "Both of you."

"She's that impressive?"

"She holds her magic so tightly, I had to touch her to feel just a hint of it. Vibrant, electric. All the hair on my arm stood up."

Aiden grunted, impressed.

"Neither of us can participate in the coven activities with Opal, but we can still…" I shrugged, not certain why it all suddenly meant so much to me. It was as though each word, each moment, each decision I was speaking, breathing, making was weighted with a heavy expectation.

My own expectation?

It had to be my own. Because when did I let what others thought dictate my actions?

Except…for what Aiden thought. And Opal.

"What if I'm not good enough?" My voice cracked, and I couldn't meet Aiden's gaze. "I feel like…my instincts are on overdrive, but they're all leading me in the wrong direction. I can't barrel through this, intimidating people into doing what I want them to do." Namely, to not oppose me adopting Opal. Aiden and me. "Can I?" I asked hopefully.

"You are fucking magnificent, Emma," Aiden snarled, sounding actually angry. "And you and your home are what Opal wants, for herself."

"Yes." Relief flooded through me. I was acting like an idiot. I already knew that Opal had made her choice. "Yes. Us."

"Us," Aiden echoed, his tone moderated again. "Let's walk the beach."

I climbed off the bed without further prompting, snatching up my underwear, and straightening my dress and my bra. My hair was all askew as I padded through into the bathroom.

A small self-contained balcony created an exterior seating area against the cedar-silled bathroom windows. And now that I was upright, I could see that there actually wasn't a path near our room. So someone would have needed to skulk through the garden beds to look inside.

Good to know. For future moments of tangling tongues and limbs.

Though Opal was going to be sleeping on the pullout sofa in the living room area. So further romping would need to happen clandestinely. Not that I minded sneaking around.

Paisley was sprawled in the soaker tub, still in her pit bull aspect but much, much larger than she ever should have been while off the property. I assumed the dog bed was in there with her, though I couldn't see it. The tub was situated against the windows as well, giving it a lovely view of the beach beyond a couple of towering evergreen trees.

The demon dog regarded me with slitted red eyes. Clearly peeved.

"We had this discussion," I said, quickly washing myself a second time with a warm washcloth, then sliding on my underwear and making final adjustments to everything else. If she stuck to her large pit bull aspect, Paisley's magic shouldn't tweak any of the finely tuned witch senses we were going to be surrounded by over the next three days. But someone—most definitely including Pearl Godfrey—would notice if Paisley walked through shadows or crossed through dimensions in the vicinity. "You agreed to stay home with Aiden and Christopher."

Paisley huffed, deliberately turning her head away from me to set her chin on the rim of the tub where it met the deep cedar windowsill. Her head was so big she had her nose pressed against the glass. The candle Aiden had alluded to was sitting in the center of the sill.

The aforementioned sorcerer leaned in the doorway, smirking. He'd found a light-blue T-shirt that did ridiculously glorious things for his tanned skin and his bright-blue eyes. A pair of waterproof sandals dangled from his hand, as if he planned to carry them but not bother putting them on. At least not while heading out to the beach.

Paisley angled her head just enough to flick a forked blue tongue in the sorcerer's direction.

"Oh, it's my fault, is it?" he asked, amused.

"Well, you did break the verbal contract, sorcerer," I said chidingly.

Aiden shrugged. "I slipped through a minor loophole. At the most."

I deliberately gestured to Paisley lounging in the tub. "Apparently, it was a large enough hole for a demon dog to wander through."

Aiden huffed a laugh.

Paisley dropped her too-wide mouth open in an exceptionally toothy grin, chortling along with the sorcerer.

I sighed, running my hands through my hair in a half-hearted attempt to smooth it back into a tidy low ponytail. "Did you at least bring your leash and collar?"

Two black tentacles snapped out from Paisley's neck, holding the items in question.

"Fine," I said, pretending to be completely put out even though I was almost deliriously happy to have both Aiden and Paisley with me.

When had I become so…weak?

At least, the members of the Collective would certainly have thought me so.

I locked eyes with Aiden. "Let's go find our girl."

He reached for me, twining his fingers through mine and tugging me from the bathroom. Paisley followed tight on our heels, slimming down to a less prodigious size. I grabbed my own sandals from where I'd left them by the front door, and we crossed into the hall together.

Weakness was relative. And what the Collective thought of me hadn't mattered in many, many years now.

DESPITE CHRISTOPHER AND I HAVING LIVED ALONG the California coast for almost five years, I had never seen a beach quite as breathtaking as the one stretching out from the hotel's forested grounds. Based on the dampness of the wet-packed gray sand even near the log-strewn shoreline, the tide was currently quite low. Huge white-capped waves crashed relentlessly on the beach. Each one sent out a long wake across the sand, deep enough to soak anyone walking the midshore up to their ankles or even calves if they didn't retreat.

The ocean here could be deadly. I had read all about rogue waves while researching the area, almost canceling the trip at one point based on the lack of exit route options and the chance of Opal being snatched up from the shore and whisked away before I could grab her back.

Not that I had mentioned it out loud to anyone. Those sorts of debates were best kept internal, to not open myself up to a ridiculous amount of annoying teasing from Christopher and Samantha about being overprotective.

A brisk wind hit us the moment we cleared the shelter of the hotel, whipping my ponytail around.

I laughed involuntarily, flinging my arms out and digging my toes into the sand as all the wild magic barely contained in every grain of that sand, every ocean-smoothed rock, every broken seashell, rose up to dance around my ankles.

"There is so much power here," I cried, forgetting to moderate my tone. I didn't normally feel magic aside from that of other Adepts, and the tide of it was delightfully intense. Wild, natural magic. Nothing malignant or even potentially dangerous. "Do you think this is why the Godfreys hold their annual retreat here? Or maybe they've infused the area with their power over decades of coming here?"

Aiden didn't answer me, so I spun to him, arms wide, dress caught in the breeze. My dark sorcerer was watching me. His expression almost pained, though he was smiling. Smiling as if it hurt to look at me, but he never wanted to look away.

I knew exactly how that felt.

I reached for his hand, but he completely closed the space between us, enclosing me in his arms and pressing against me roughly as he laid a blistering kiss on my lips.

I sank into the embrace, just letting the moment—and the wild magic—surround us, hold us. As if welcoming us back, even though I'd never been on this beach or in this town before.

"Wow," a young voice said, close enough that I could hear actual awe. "That's...I didn't think people actually loved each other quite that much. You know, outside of the movies."

"You get used to it," Opal grumbled. "They do it a lot."

Aiden eased his hold on me, grinning against my delightfully swollen lips. Then he flicked his gaze over my shoulder. I pivoted slightly, still in his embrace.

Opal and Juniper were grinning at us like two little imps. Two powerful imps. The magic imbued into the very ground around us delighted in the young witches' presence as well. I could practically see it.

With her halo of gold- and silver-streaked dark-brown curls wild in the wind, Opal rested one hand on her hip, then pointed at Aiden critically. She was still grinning madly, though. "You're not supposed to be here!"

Reluctantly stepping to the side, Aiden threaded his fingers through mine as he smiled down at his adorable accuser. "I missed you."

"You missed Emma, and—"

Behind us, Paisley stepped out from some bushes she'd been lurking within. Rhododendrons, I thought. Broad shoulders rolling, leash dragging behind her, the demon dog lowered her head and made a beeline for Opal.

Juniper squeaked—a sound just short of a scream—at Paisley's sudden appearance, clasping her hands together. A whisper of power gathered within her fingers.

Apparently, the fifteen-year-old's sense for magic was acute enough to read something other than 'dog' even on a first sighting.

Opal flung her arms out gleefully, though. "Paisley!"

Snuffling agreeably, the demon dog presented herself to the little witch for pets and kisses. Then she deliberately glanced over to Juniper. And smiled.

Even in her regular pit bull aspect, and even with only a single row of teeth, that smile was intimidating.

"Oh," Opal cried, as if she'd forgotten something terribly important. "Paisley, this is my new friend Juniper. She's a year ahead of me at the Academy, and she hasn't picked a specialization yet."

Juniper huffed, loosening her hold on whatever defensive magic she'd been calling forth, and covering her reaction to Paisley's abrupt appearance. "Most of us don't pick until the end of our third year, dream walker."

Opal's grin was unrepentant. "Juniper, this is my friend Paisley."

Juniper raised her eyebrows slightly, presumably at a dog being introduced as a friend. But then she held out her hand, palm down, for Paisley to sniff without a hint of fear. Apparently, the teenaged witch could ignore her instincts far better than I could—even when those instincts were completely correct, since Paisley actually was a dangerous creature. Or maybe being surrounded by the coven was just that comforting. As was her trust in her burgeoning friendship with Opal.

"Apparently we don't rank an introduction," Aiden murmured to me, still grinning.

"Before Paisley?" I laughed quietly.

"She's beautiful," Juniper said, trailing her fingers over Paisley's head. "Kelly will definitely want to meet her. She specializes in animal husbandry. Is she yours?" She looked at Opal, brushing her windstrewn blond hair away from her eyes and frowning slightly. "Your familiar?"

Opal shrugged. "Paisley is part of the family."

The demon dog returned her attention to the little witch, her cropped ears flicking expectantly. Opal rescued her leash from dragging in the sand. "Do you want to see the surfers?"

Paisley chuffed agreeably.

Juniper blinked, then grinned. "She understands you!"

"Of course she does." Opal took off toward the crashing surf with Juniper and Paisley bounding alongside her, the demon dog mimicking the behavior of some of the other dogs arrayed along the beach.

"Just watching!" I cried after them, following at a more sedate pace.

Aiden laughed quietly. At me.

I threw him a look. "What? Being cautious about rogue waves and the undertow is tactically sound."

The sorcerer shook his head, still grinning. "I would never question you, Emma."

"But…?"

He snorted. "But…you felt the magic as easily as I can. No witch comes to harm on this beach. Not from natural causes, at least. How many years has the Godfrey coven held their annual retreat here? I'd thought it odd of them to gather so far from their base of power in Vancouver, but…" He swept his free hand forward, not finishing the thought.

Ahead, Opal, Juniper, and Paisley were playing some game that involved running up to the edge of the surf as it retreated, then dashing back as the next wave hit, racing to avoid the wake.

Magic prickled up my spine. And it had nothing to do with the beach or with the mostly dormant blood tattoos adhered to my top four vertebra.

Aiden's shoulders stiffened. His grin faded as he scanned the area.

I looked back toward the shore.

About a half-dozen meters away, closer to the forest and the hotel than the surf, a large raven was perched on a rotting wood pylon drilled into the beach, a remnant from a dock perhaps. The corvid's eyes glinted, reflecting an orange-red, catching the sunlight.

"What the fuck?" Aiden whispered, having followed my gaze.

The raven was so striking, so completely out of place that a few tourists were stopping to take pictures of it. Confirming that it could be seen by nonmagicals, at least when it wasn't perched on its mistress's shoulder.

"One of the witches has a familiar," I said.

Aiden's jaw tightened. "Which one?" With all the extensive research he'd done on the Godfrey coven, he wouldn't be happy he'd missed Mercury.

"Mercury. She's a visiting member. From the Dunkirk coven," I said, still watching the raven. I would have sworn it was watching me in turn, though I was slightly too far away to tell for certain. "Actually, she seemed displeased that she'd been summoned to the coven gathering."

"Mercury Dunkirk," Aiden said, his tone low and thoughtful. I knew that the moment we got back to the hotel room, he'd be gathering whatever information there was to be had about the witch. "That's seriously arrogant, even for a witch, to have a familiar out in plain view in the middle of the day."

"Because hurting or killing a bonded familiar can be used to weaken the witch?"

Aiden grunted, listening but still utterly focused on the raven. His sense for magic was far sharper than mine. And though he claimed that the ways of witches annoyed him, he was also extremely thirsty for any and all magical knowledge. Not addicted to magic, as he'd once worried, but certainly on the edge of obsessed.

"The familiar bond can be exceedingly useful with both magical and mundane applications," he said, almost begrudgingly. Narrowing his eyes at the raven, he slowly turned his head as if trying to track its focal point. "From power amplification or dispersal, to sight sharing, to simply being an early warning system. But…"

"But?"

"A raven isn't a typical familiar. Even crow familiars are unusual. Most witches prefer the independent, inherently sneaky, and morally flexible nature of cats when choosing a compatible companion."

"So surprising," I said, not at all surprised.

Aiden huffed a laugh. "Rumor has it that one of the Myers witches bound a wolf centuries ago."

"Why does that sound like the beginning of a morality tale?"

He nodded grimly. "The wolf eventually went mad. Or maybe it simply objected to having its will bound. It killed the witch, plus wounded at least a half-dozen of the coven before they managed to put it down. It was no longer simply a wolf, after being tied to a witch. Then harnessing some aspect of her power when it killed her."

The raven shifted its gaze, swiveling its head in the direction of Opal and Juniper. Spying on them rather than me.

And on Paisley.

The demon dog wasn't bound to any one of us, at least not as a witch bound a familiar. Still, she couldn't turn against any of the Five, according to what little info Samantha had managed to access about her breeding program from the data she'd collected before we'd taken down the Collective's compound. We'd been bred to handle tech, bypassing the problem of how most magic eroded electronics and machinery, but the physical hard drives that Samantha had loaded with the Collective's onsite storage had taken a lot of damage.

The demon dog hybrids, of which Paisley was the only survivor after our rampage through the compound, had been tied to all of us through magic and DNA from the moment of their conception.

Paisley had been created in a test tube.

Just like the rest of the Five.

"Emma?" Aiden asked, frowning.

I shook my head. Paisley wasn't a wild wolf roped into service against its will through some sort of one-sided familiar's binding. In my limited understanding, that sort of binding loosely echoed the magic witches wielded to summon demons from their dimension, forcing them into service. As Silver Pine had with her greater demon—a creature I had ultimately turned against the black witch with ease. Because it had already been eager to feast on its summoner. Its master.

"No sentient creature should be bound unwillingly," I said finally. "Not even if they're bred for that specific purpose."

Aiden squeezed my hand. "You never were bound, remember?"

"Well, not to the Collective."

"The other four are more bound to you than vice versa," Aiden said, seemingly plucking thoughts from my head though our connection wasn't telepathic in any way. "And they have plenty of freedom to roam. Even if, given the choice, they'd continually prostrate themselves at your feet."

I snorted. "The only way Samantha is getting anywhere near bowing down before me is if I put her there."

Aiden grinned. "Well, maybe that's just me."

Shoving away dark thoughts of just how capable I now was of bending sentient beings against their will, I leaned into Aiden. "You haven't been on your knees for some time, sorcerer," I teased.

"Had you given me a momentary reprieve a short while ago, amplifier..." He grinned at me wickedly, running his fingers up my bare arm. "Instead of just having your way, I would have been utterly, dreadfully happy to oblige."

"Emma!" Opal cried. Her shout was gleeful but more than a little concerned.

I spun toward the surf, already running.

Paisley had somehow acquired a surfboard, and was trying to drag it into the pounding surf while also climbing on top of it.

Knee-deep in the water, Juniper was watching her with both hands clamped over her mouth.

Opal was jumping up and down next to the other young witch, the waves nearly knocking her over, one after another. "Not like that!" she snapped, half-laughing and half-lecturing as she made a grab for the nose of the board Paisley was trying to mount. "You're too heavy!"

A male wearing a half-wetsuit was striding down the beach toward the trio, his focus intent, though he wasn't close enough for me to see his expression.

Aiden was already moving to intercept the new-comer with an easy smile plastered on his face and his hand extended. An offer to shake hands, not an overture to casting a spell.

I closed the space between me, the witches, and the demon dog, wading into the roiling surf. I made a show of grabbing Paisley's collar and 'helping' her out of the pounding waves. She chortled, playing along.

Opal and Juniper rescued the surfboard, drag-ging it back toward Aiden and the surfer, who didn't seem particularly distressed now that he was chat-ting with the sorcerer. Aiden could be as charming as he was deadly, so I wasn't terribly surprised that he could so easily smooth over the oddity of having a surfboard stolen by a pit bull.

"You're soaking wet," I chided Paisley.

She snapped at my hand playfully.

I lowered my voice. "And for future reference, the waves are strong enough that they should have knocked you over." I hit the word 'should' hard.

Paisley eyed the crashing waves, our ankles getting more and more buried in the sand under the onslaught. Then she snorted dismissively.

I tucked my hand under her chin, forcing eye contact. "Opal could have gotten hurt."

Paisley blinked up at me, then over at Opal. Who was apparently in the process of interrogating the surfer about where she could rent a board and what he would recommend for a beginner.

Paisley pressed her nose against my wrist, clearly apologetic.

"I know," I murmured. "I would never hurt her either, but we have to remember she wasn't...bred like us."

Paisley leaned against my leg for a moment. Then, still dragging her leash, the demon dog prowled across the wet sand to join the rest of the group.

For some reason, instead of immediately following, I glanced back up the beach, noting that the raven had left. Or at least relocated.

Mercury Dunkirk hadn't seemed particularly friendly with the Godfrey witches during tea. Perhaps she was using the raven to keep an eye on all of us?

Ocean and Burgundy, the other young witch from the library, had joined Aiden and the girls by the time I decided to do so myself.

Loosely grouped together, we wandered up the beach, Opal with Paisley's leash in hand, while the witches chattered about the retreat's lectures and classes and what they were going to take. Opal was particularly enthused about household charms, because she hated having to keep her room at the Academy clean. Juniper was eager to hear Pearl lecture about various types of circle work, then take a practical class with Scarlett in the afternoon.

And I tried to just breathe in the moment. To enjoy the astonishingly beautiful surroundings and the feel of my hand linked with Aiden's.

Even I knew—since the arrival of Aiden, since Opal—that moments like these were rare and should be cherished. After a literal lifetime of avoiding attachments, of hiding away under the pretense of keeping Paisley and Christopher safe, I was in full view and prepared to fight for what I wanted.

And I wanted…more.

More of this, of these moments.

"OH, EMMA!" LANI CALLED OUT FROM FARTHER UP the path that led to the inn from the beach. She was standing at an intersection near Mercury Dunkirk, as if they'd just been in the process of passing each other. No raven in sight. "I was just coming to remind you that I have that hot stone massage now."

The girls were trailing behind Aiden and me, Opal still walking Paisley on her leash.

"Sounds lovely," Mercury said. Her attention was trained on the intuitive, her tone far more inviting than it had been at tea. Friendly even.

"I hope so," Lani replied, though without really looking at the British witch. She'd put her hands on her hips and was shaking her head at Aiden, her tone playfully chiding. "You aren't supposed to be here, Aiden!"

"I couldn't stay away." He grinned at her.

"I get it." She laughed, winking at him. "I'm going to be late! I'll meet you all for dinner in about two hours? Your room."

"I'll make sure we're ready," I said, trying to sound friendly myself but not at all managing it. Not with Mercury in the vicinity.

Lani laughed under her breath, flicking her hazel eyes in Mercury's direction, then shoving her hands in the pockets of her shorts. "You know, Emma, if you actually looked at your phone occasionally, I wouldn't have to run around looking for you."

"I've heard that before."

She snorted, then lifted up on her tiptoes as if to peer around us. "Will you remind Ocean?"

Aiden fished his phone out of his back pocket, making a show of texting even though Ocean was only a meter or so behind us, chatting away with Burgundy while Juniper and Opal hung on their every word.

"Done!" the dark-haired sorcerer proclaimed.

"Hilarious," Lani said, heavy on the sarcasm. She shook her head again, waving as she spun away and took off up the path toward the main building of the hotel.

Mercury was watching me with her pale blue eyes. Wolf eyes, as Lani called them. She took in Aiden's and my entwined hands with a slight smirk. Then she looked behind us, toward the girls. Practically blocking our path.

"A dream walker," she said to me in her clipped accent. "The Dunkirk coven is well known for its dream walkers. Yet you choose the Godfreys for your foundling."

I considered decapitating her.

I didn't even need my blades. I could just—

Aiden squeezed my hand, amusement rolling off him.

Right. Witch games.

"The Godfrey coven is the most powerful in the world," Aiden said mildly. "With a variety of magic users."

Mercury sniffed, eyeing Aiden for a brief moment, then turning her attention back to me. "The Godfreys are…powerful, yes. But they are a young coven. The Dunkirk roots stretch back—"

"Why aren't you in London, Mercury?" Aiden asked pointedly, completely interrupting her pitch.

Mercury sniffed again. "I wouldn't expect a sorcerer to understand the importance of maintaining relationships between covens."

"Just as you wouldn't understand an amplifier allowing her daughter to make her own choices," I said.

"I certainly wasn't suggesting…" Mercury flicked her fingers offishly.

But before she could continue, Opal popped up beside me. Literally. She was still bouncing, buoyed by all the magic under our feet. "Talking about me?" she asked pertly.

"Mercury was just outlining all the reasons she thinks you should go to London," Aiden said, still with that smooth, mild tone.

"I was just suggesting some reflection…" the British witch said huffily.

"Yep," Opal said. "There's a family of dream walkers in the Dunkirk coven. Generational magic." That last was said as if a direct quote from one of her books or classes.

"See?" Mercury said, smiling at Opal.

"Two of the Dunkirk dream walkers teach at the Academy."

That wiped the smile off Mercury's face. "Of course they do." She abruptly changed the subject. "Opal, you must attend my lecture on familiars tomorrow afternoon."

I instantly bristled at the older witch's tone. Even more than I already was. No one told my Opal what she—

"I already signed up," the little witch said brightly.

"Well, good," Mercury said with a twist of a smile. "If I'm being forced to teach at all, I would prefer to have the brightest minds attending."

"We'll all be there," Burgundy said. The healer-in-training had come up with Juniper and Ocean to join us. The intersection that Mercury was still blocking was getting rather crowded.

The older witch flicked her gaze over Burgundy. And from her look, I gathered that the healer didn't measure up, because Mercury simply nodded, turned on her heel, and strode up the path toward the main building that Lani had taken.

The girls surged ahead of us up the other path. Paisley bumped her head under my fisted hand as she passed. I unclenched enough to pet her. Then I gave Aiden a look.

He laughed. "Witches."

I snorted. Apparently, I had misread Mercury—and her creepy raven's surveillance, both in the library and on the beach. It was Opal the British witch was interested in, for political reasons. The Dunkirk coven collecting power so the Godfreys wouldn't have it.

Thankfully, my little witch had already made her choice.

AIDEN SLIPPED MY PHONE INTO MY HAND WITH A sigh, brushing a kiss across my temple before he settled into the seat next to me on the small garden patio off our suite.

"Christopher is pissed. And apparently, he's been texting me his ire for the last hour or so."

I arched an eyebrow at the sorcerer. "Understandably."

He grimaced. Yeah, both he and Paisley had completely abandoned the clairvoyant, with Aiden's defection effectively giving the demon dog permission to leave the property as well.

Before I could scan the text messages that had accumulated while I was enjoying a walk on the beach and trying to not behead know-it-all witches, the phone vibrated in my hand as the aforementioned clairvoyant called, requesting a video link. I hit the green button, accepting the call.

Christopher's head and shoulders appeared on the screen. Whatever his mix of genetics, it had come with naturally tanned skin, as had Bee's. But having spent the bulk of the spring shirtless in the garden and orchard, he was an even deeper tan than Aiden now. His white-blond hair was currently slightly longer than he usually wore it. The clairvoyant's eyes were pale gray, not alight with the white of his magic. That was good. It wasn't a vision that had forced him to call instead of texting as usual.

"Paisley?" Christopher asked tersely.

"With Opal..." I made a show of tilting my head up and to the left. The muted voices of the younger witches filtered quietly through the open sliding door. They had gathered in the living room section of the suite.

"Are you..." Christopher frowned, taking in the area around me. "Are you reading?"

I raised the book I held higher into the camera's view—a text about empathy and empaths that Aiden had sourced for me. Unfortunately, it was lacking in actionable specifics and overabundant in pedantic basics that didn't apply to how I wielded my power. Or, more accurately, how I was relearning to wield my empathy like the weapon it suddenly was, rather than just an annoying latent ability. "It is supposed to be a vacation," I said.

Christopher chuckled. "And here I wasn't certain you understood the concept."

"Our entire life is a vacation," I said tersely.

That wiped the smile from his face. "So Samantha keeps telling me."

"You aren't required to involve yourself in their vengeance."

"I know," Christopher said softly.

He and I had had this conversation. Too many times. I loathed repeating myself. But Samantha and Daniel stirred up a lot of Collective shit—literally and figuratively. "If they've brought something down on Bee—"

"I know," the clairvoyant said, conciliatory. Interrupting my rant before I could ramp up.

I clapped my mouth shut, leaning back in the chair. As said, I hated repeating myself.

"Show me the view?" Christopher asked cajolingly.

I obligingly flipped the camera view and held the phone higher so he could see the beach beyond the hotel grounds.

"Wow."

Paisley shouldered her way out onto the patio. Aiden shifted his legs so she could situate herself between us, peering out at the view as well—and placing the top of her head in front of the camera to block Christopher's view.

"Paisley," the clairvoyant growled from the phone speakers.

The demon dog's ears twitched, but she otherwise ignored Christopher as she scanned the property with narrowed eyes. Looking for something? Sensing something?

I glanced over at Aiden, but his attention was buried in his own book about gemstone enchantment. He was studying spells for my wedding ring. Not that he'd said so, but I noticed the theme that had occupied the bulk of his research since I'd asked him to marry me, building on the work he'd initially done with the gemstones embedded into Christopher's shortsword and my own blades.

We had been waiting for Opal to return from the Academy before we set an official date for the official ceremony. But Aiden and I were already bound, not just by love and mutual respect, but also by invisible threads of magic. According to Aiden's magic-sensitive brother, Khalid.

I flipped the view of the phone so I could see Christopher again.

"I'd say I felt abandoned," he said with a huff. "Except it sounds just as childish in my head as it would out loud."

"Paisley will come spend the night with you," I said, making it an order for the demon dog. She was pointedly keeping her back turned to me, though she obviously wanted to be part of the conversation. "There's a formal dinner thing we have to attend with the witches tonight."

"And the induction ceremony tomorrow night," Christopher said.

"Under the Strawberry Moon," Opal chirped from behind me. Stepping out onto the patio, she hung her upper body over the back of my chair to get her face next to mine and on camera.

"Hello, little witch." Christopher's face brightened. As I imagined we all did whenever Opal entered a room.

"Hello, uncle mine," she said back in a singsong voice, grinning. "Are you coming up too?"

He pouted playfully. "Who would look after the chickens?"

Opal sighed affectedly. "Too bad. Some of the surfers are awfully pretty."

I blinked at her, then narrowed my eyes. "According to who?"

She just smirked at me. "Burgundy is taking us for ice cream."

"Off the hotel property?"

"Yes, but just across that main street. Where we saw those restaurants and stores right before we turned off."

I didn't remember seeing any stores or an ice cream place in particular as we drove in, but I had been pretty fixated on following the signage to the hotel property.

"Emma?" Opal asked tentatively. "I can bring back cones for you, Aiden, and Paisley."

The demon dog's ears flicked again. Ah, that was why she'd shoved herself between Aiden and me on the patio. She had overheard the witches' ice cream plans and was peeved because she wouldn't be invited. Couldn't be invited. Even if the girls were walking there and back, Paisley knew she couldn't go anywhere without me nearby. Well, without me or another one of the Five.

Clearly, though, that rule didn't count in the 'in between' while Paisley crossed through the demon dimension between locations. I had noted that particular bending of the rules—which had started when she was supposed to be in Europe helping Christopher and Samantha hunt for Bee—and allowed it. So far. But only because I'd deliberately set aside the responsibility of controlling the movements and choices of the Five years ago. And that included Paisley.

I glanced at Aiden, concerned about the younger witches' proposed expedition off the hotel grounds—yet not wanting to curtail what I assumed was a normal amount of freedom for a thirteen-year-old. I had no context or experience to draw upon, though. Aiden smirked at me knowingly, then held up a folded twenty-dollar bill between two of his fingers.

"I have money," Opal groused. Then she snatched the bill anyway. She bounced a little in anticipation but still peered at me questioningly.

I nodded. "There and back, please. And we have dinner in an hour and a half."

"Of course," she scoffed. Then she added with a wide smile, "Ocean has a spell to keep the ice cream frozen for longer!"

She skipped off as gleefully as she'd appeared. And I would have sworn she took a piece of my heart with her.

On the phone, Christopher was watching me with a soft smile.

I glared at him. "I can't quash her independence," I said. No matter that I had wanted, since the moment I'd rescued her in San Francisco, to bundle the little witch up in my arms and make certain she never had another moment of strife again. "She'll never come home on breaks if I do."

He laughed quietly. "You're exactly what she needs, Emma. A safe haven. The same for all of us, actually." He flicked his gaze toward Aiden.

The sorcerer nodded slightly, not looking up from his book.

Paisley shifted back, pressing against my legs.

"I just hope the witches... that one witch in particular... sees it that way," I murmured.

Christopher shrugged, seemingly indifferent. But his voice was abruptly underlaid with power. "Let them try to take her from us."

"It won't come to that," Aiden said mildly. "Ember already has the paperwork drawn up. This isn't even a formality. You'll now have the coven more involved in your lives than some of you would wish, but they aren't going to reject what Opal wants."

Christopher smirked at me. "Has he been repeating himself since he arrived?"

I grinned. "Not the entire time. His mouth was otherwise occupied earlier."

Christopher barked out a laugh. But before he could formulate a full response, magic flickered over his eyes and drew his attention away from the conversation.

I waited, achingly aware that Opal and the other witches had left the suite, and then the hotel, so swiftly that I couldn't feel their magic anymore.

"Opal is fine, Emma," Aiden murmured. "She's got a healer, an apprentice potion master, and the magic embedded in every aspect of this place with her." His attention was on Christopher, though. "What do you see, clairvoyant?" he asked teasingly. "I was hoping for salted-caramel ice cream."

Christopher laughed again, but his tone was remote. He shook his head, shaking off the vision. Though his magic still ringed his irises tightly. "Can't help you there, sorcerer. Just catching glimpses of

Samantha rampaging through some building under construction."

"Poor Fish," I murmured.

"Better him than us." Christopher tried for a playful tone that he didn't quite manage.

"We're going to be pulled into their mess soon enough," I said stiffly. I had always been clear that I wasn't interested in Daniel and Samantha's vendetta against the Collective. I saw no strategic advantage to potentially putting Christopher and Paisley in harm's way.

Christopher nodded, sitting back and shuffling his oracle cards. "It might be better to walk in willingly," he mused.

"Better for who?" I asked sharply, all but daring the clairvoyant to push me.

But he only shrugged. "I'm not sure yet, Socks."

My stomach hollowed, and I waited, letting him work through whatever his magic was showing him. He didn't speak. He didn't look up from the oracle cards he was twirling through his fingers, more by magic than skill.

Aiden had abandoned his book, all his attention riveted to the screen of my phone.

Christopher looked up, blinking, then grinning as if he hadn't let the conversation drop. "Call me back when you get your ice cream. You can take me for a walk on the beach before dinner."

I wasn't going to attempt to eat ice cream while holding a phone and having my hair at the mercy of the wind, but I just nodded.

If something was coming for us, Christopher would see it. But I had to let him work through it on his own. If I pushed, my influence might just overwhelm his senses, even remotely.

The clairvoyant met my gaze. "I can be there in an hour, if the flight schedule allows."

"Do we need you?" My throat ached.

"Rarely," he drawled playfully. "Call me back." Then he disconnected without another word.

"Did you see the cards he was holding?" Aiden asked quietly.

I hadn't. I'd only had eyes for Christopher. I shook my head. "Did you?"

"Just a glimpse," he said thoughtfully, grabbing his notebook from the table between us and paging back through it. Looking for his notes on Christopher's oracle cards, no doubt.

Paisley tried to sneak over the side of the patio. But she was rather large and the space rather too tight for her to be terribly stealthy. I grabbed her stubbed tail.

She glanced back at me over her shoulder, huffing indignantly. Then she swung her large head, scanning the branches above us with blood-red eyes. The trees appeared empty to me, both visually and magically.

I set my phone on the table and picked up my book. Pretending, if only to myself, that I wasn't already counting the minutes until Opal returned.

Vacation, I reminded myself. A beach, a book, and ice cream equaled a vacation.

The sound of large wings flapping drew all of our attention overhead.

"The raven?" I asked in a murmur, still not catching sight of anything but puffy clouds in the deepening blue of the sky.

"Witches," Aiden sneered. "Nosy and self-righteous. I believe I shall come to dinner with you." He returned his attention to his book, ignoring the pointed look I gave him.

Paisley pressed her shoulder to my knee.

"Sorry," I said. "The sorcerer I'll be able to pass off as an overprotective, controlling asshole. But the witches aren't going to believe that my pit bull needs to come to a buffet."

Aiden snorted, amused. "You could try to pass Paisley off as an emotional support demon hybrid."

Paisley narrowed her eyes—at the offending sorcerer, not me.

"Plus," I added, ignoring Aiden. "I think Christopher is lonely."

Paisley huffed, then once again turned her red-hued gaze to the hotel grounds and the beach beyond.

It had been years since Christopher, Paisley, and I had traveled. Since we'd been surrounded by so much newness. Other than the ill-fated Azar/

Myers family reunion a few weeks ago, we hadn't been around this many unknown Adepts since the compound. And even though I had no idea how much of that time with the Collective Paisley even remembered, I wasn't surprised that the demon dog's defensive instincts were firing as much as mine.

THREE

THE WITCHES HAD COMMANDEERED A PRIVATE ROOM with the same breathtaking view that the entire hotel appeared to boast from every west-facing window—for what I'd understood was supposed to be an informal dinner. A buffet was set along the wall to the far left, and the seating area was filled with plush chairs tucked around low, round tables. Despite how warm June had been so far, a fire was lit in a large stone fireplace, but it wasn't throwing off any heat.

Though I might not have been able to pick up such magic with my other senses, the blue tint to the flickering flames indicated a liberal application of witch magic. As did the way my ears had popped when we entered the room, crossing through an invisible sound barrier. A construct that caused Aiden's step to hitch with surprise, likely because it hadn't blocked all sound. We had clearly heard a low murmur emanating from the room as we'd approached, and the nonmagical staff came and went easily, clearing plates and carving a roast at the far end of the buffet.

"Clever witches," Aiden murmured as all eyes settled on him, Lani, Opal, and me. "A selectively filtering sound barrier. Impressive."

That was high praise from a sorcerer as powerful as mine.

The conversation among the gathered witches had paused for a breath, then resumed just as quickly. Ocean was already at the buffet and chatting with Olive, presumably about her hope for an apprenticeship.

"Opal!" Juniper cried from the near end of the buffet. She'd swapped her beachwear for a pretty green-print blouse, skirt, and sandals.

The schedule had indicated that the event was informal, but there wasn't a single pair of jeans in the group. Or much cotton, for that matter. Opal and I were in dresses—blue linen for me, matched with sandals, and an adorable dark-pink cotton dress for her, flaring prettily over her narrow hips and pink high-top sneakers.

Lani was wearing a silk tank top that showed off her impressive biceps, over flared pants that looked supremely comfy. And Aiden was pristinely pressed in a blue suit and white dress shirt. Layered with protection spells and featuring expanding runes on every pocket, of course. Because Aiden knew witches, didn't trust witches, not even at an informal buffet.

Pearl Godfrey crossed to greet us, raising her hand to meet Aiden's offered handshake without a moment of hesitation. He flashed her a charming grin that just slid right off the elder witch.

Now that was impressive. But then, I pretty much melted whenever Aiden even glanced my way, even after all these months of spending every waking moment together. And the sleeping moments as well.

Pearl kept hold of Aiden's hand, her head tilted thoughtfully. "Pearl Godfrey. You must be Aiden Myers."

"Aiden Azar," he replied smoothly.

That gave me pause, though I hoped my surprise didn't show on my face. I hadn't known that Aiden had decided to resume using his father's name. But after recent events, it wasn't at all surprising that he'd want to distance himself from his mother, and her coven. When Cerise Myers had tried to unleash the Hallowed on Kader Azar, she had almost killed Aiden in the process. Though I was fairly certain that it was the threat to me, to our life together, that he really couldn't forgive.

Pearl smiled at him knowingly. "Dramatic reveals usually come after dessert, sorcerer."

Aiden chuckled. "My apologies. I figured my presence was enough of a disturbance that I should just dive in."

So…he'd dropped the Azar surname as a test of some sort, and Pearl had instantly called him on it.

Adept power games. As annoying as always. Even when initiated by Aiden.

Pearl huffed, but appeared not even remotely displeased. Then she dropped the sorcerer's hand and turned to me. "Emma. There's a lovely fresh-caught sockeye salmon for anyone who doesn't eat red meat."

Oh yes, Pearl Godfrey didn't miss much. I hadn't been asked about any dietary restrictions when I'd RSVPed. Though perhaps Opal had?

"I'm sure it's lovely," I said stiltedly. Then I turned to Lani. "Lani supplies us with fish on occasion as well."

Lani nodded, smirking at me. Or perhaps at how awkward I was acting, but she accepted the deflection. "That's me. Mechanic and fisherperson."

Pearl laughed quietly. Then she gestured to a group of four witches in the far corner that included Scarlett and Kelly. "I'd love to introduce you, Lani. I don't believe you've had a chance to meet everyone yet."

Lani nodded, still smiling quietly. Pearl turned back toward the witches, two of whom I hadn't met yet myself. They were holding small plates of what I assumed were appetizers and laughing quietly among themselves.

Lani followed the elder witch, winking at me over her shoulder. As she went, she crossed by Mercury Dunkirk, who was alone at a low table near the fireplace. Alone because she appeared to have pushed all the other chairs away.

Mercury's familiar had apparently not been invited to dinner. Which wasn't surprising, given how Scarlett had been pissed that the raven had already made an appearance at tea. The British witch watched

Lani with narrowed eyes and a slight smile—assessing, not malicious.

Lani must have said or done something as she passed, pausing just for a moment, because Mercury's smile widened and she chuckled, her light-blue wolf eyes flashing. Admiringly. Brushing back the short lengths of hair that had fallen forward over her temple, Lani continued after Pearl, already nodding as the elder witch introduced her to Kelly.

I frowned at the interaction, not pleased that Lani had drawn the attention of a witch who was most definitely a snob when it came to the amount of power other Adepts wielded. Opal was seemingly a prize to be snatched away for her coven. Burgundy had barely been acknowledged.

His gaze on me, Aiden laughed, so quietly it was barely a rumble in his chest.

"What?" I snapped in a whisper.

"Flirting."

My frown deepened. "You're flirting?"

His laugh sharpened. "No…" He nodded toward Lani. "That's what flirting looks like. Nothing nefarious about it."

I lifted my chin, turning away from the sorcerer so he'd know I was miffed at him, then crossing to the buffet where Opal and Juniper were discussing every item before they decided what to put on their plates. Happily, I could see some salad and asparagus on Opal's plate already, because the end of the buffet appeared to be filled with cheese and bread.

The dream walker ate what was put in front of her, but left to her own devices…well, I'd seen her spreading a thick layer of butter on bread on more than one occasion and tried not to freak out. When I failed at reining in my reaction, the little witch would add jam and cheese and call it perfectly nutritious. Jam and cheese!

Aiden allowed his fingers to slide down my arm, then followed me to the buffet. He was still smirking.

I knew what flirting looked like. I watched TV. Okay…fine. I watched *Downton Abbey*. But being in a room full of witches was making me feel like every single one of my nerve endings was on alert.

I could, however, admit that Lani was an adult. She could flirt with whomever she wanted.

"I'm allowed to be concerned," I muttered out of the corner of my mouth, picking up a plate from the end of the long, food-laden table.

Aiden hummed thoughtfully, picking up a plate of his own. "You were a moment away from draining everyone in the room."

"I wasn't!" I looked at him sharply.

He grinned at me unrepentantly.

Teasing.

Right.

That was a form of flirting as well.

I narrowed my eyes at the dark-haired sorcerer, not amused. Grabbing the salad tongs, I loaded what appeared to be a spring mix on one side of my plate. Neatly labeled dressings were set to the side, and that was a little bit of luxury I would happily embrace...maybe even to the point of trying more than one.

"Emma!" Opal called from behind me, waving me toward the table that she and Juniper were in the process of claiming.

Forcing a smile onto my face, I nodded even as my gaze flicked around the room, noting every single witch who had looked up at Opal's call.

Not a single narrowed eye or twisted lip in the bunch.

A tiny bit of the weight I'd been carrying around on my shoulders all day...well, honestly, more like ever since Opal had gotten the invitation to the coven gathering...lifted. I knew intellectually that the Godfrey coven wanted Opal as a member, that they might even need her, given that she and Juniper were currently the youngest witches in the room. Just as at tea, it was clear that more than three-quarters of the members of the Godfrey coven appeared to be in their forties or older.

But knowing something wasn't the same as feeling the truth of it. Which was a terrible lesson for a born-and-bred sociopath.

Aiden carefully placed some tasty-looking salmon lox on my plate, leaning close to murmur, "Let's go on a date tomorrow." His warm breath and more than a touch of magic shimmered across the skin of my jaw and neck.

"Where?" I asked somewhat offishly, not ready to forgive him his earlier teasing yet.

"A hike? With a picnic?"

I wrinkled my nose.

Aiden's grin widened. "How about sushi for lunch, then a wander through a few galleries?"

I smiled, just a little bit. I was still playing at being begrudging, after all. Aiden and I didn't really go on dates. We never really got the chance. And I would worry about Opal just as much from town, a few minutes' drive away, as I would if I stayed locked in the room, or even if I roamed the hotel all of tomorrow.

Aiden brushed a light kiss across my cheek. "I look forward to it, my amplifier."

My grin widened. I was always up for any distraction Aiden had to offer. Mostly because he and I were on the exact same page when it came to the care and keeping of Opal. Both of us possessive and controlling, and completely ready to throw ourselves in front of any hint of danger for the little witch—even while trying to acknowledge how much she could navigate on her own without interference.

As it should be. Because our own childhoods had never taught us that lesson.

AIDEN HAD INSISTED THAT WE TAKE A WALK AT SUN-set on the beach. Just the four of us, including Ocean. As family.

Any protest Opal might have made—mostly around wanting to stay in and play some sort of board game that Juniper and Burgundy were setting up—dissolved under Aiden's use of the word family.

I found Paisley's collar and leash in the suite, but not the demon dog herself. Aiden texted Christopher to confirm that she'd gone back to the property, but we hadn't heard back from the clairvoyant by the time we headed out.

Ocean and Opal ran ahead, sticking to the dry sand and taking selfies together with the spectacular orange-and-pink sunset filling the horizon behind them. The tide had risen from a few hours before, but apparently the surf was always high. Which made sense, given that the sea that spread out from the west coast of Vancouver Island was open ocean all the way to Japan.

"Rogue waves," I muttered, my gaze pinned to the girls.

Aiden slipped his arm around me, tucking me against his side. He didn't bother reminding me again that Opal and Ocean were witches, and that the magic that teemed from the very earth, the magic that danced around their ankles even now, wouldn't allow harm to befall them. Or at least none of the wild, natural magic that surrounded us would bring them harm.

I scanned the hotel property and the edge of the forest. A few of the other witches were farther up the beach. Scarlett's strawberry-blond hair was a bright sail in the wind, catching the last rays of the sun dipping below the horizon.

My own hair was probably brighter still. Aiden kept getting it tangled in his fingers—deliberately, I thought.

The warmth was leaching from the air and the ground more and more as the sun faded. Not in a nefarious way, just naturally. I snuggled a bit closer into Aiden and tried to simply shut off my mind for a bit. To allow the moment to soothe my overactive imagination, the instincts chafing me from the inside out.

Opal dashed out into the surf as Ocean filmed her with her phone. The dream walker shrieked, delighted, as she almost lost her footing under the onslaught of a wave. Then, dress and hair buffeted by the wind, she ran back toward the older witch and pulled out her own phone so Ocean could be filmed next.

Opal wasn't allowed to be on any social media sites—as per the Academy's rules, not mine. But the school had an internal system that students used to chat and post photos. I had a feeling that these short clips would be uploaded as soon as the girls got back to the—

Magic shifted to my left, emanating from the edge of the forested area between the houses that occupied the properties farther down the beach.

Paisley.

I turned.

And saw the raven.

Mercury Dunkirk's familiar was perched on a lower branch of a large moss-and-lichen-covered cedar tree. I wasn't close enough to guess the direction of the corvid's gaze, but—

"Fuck," Aiden snarled.

I was already running, the useless collar and leash jangling in my hand. Leaving the sorcerer in my wake as I crossed the beach far more quickly than a mere amplifier should have been able to. I could practically feel the attention of every magical being on the beach snap to me as I moved.

I was still too slow.

Paisley exploded out of the underbrush, shifting size as she leaped—from small enough to lurk undetected, to large enough to...

Well, to hunt large prey—

"No!" I shouted.

The damn sand was slowing me down. But the magically backed command rolled across the distance between me and the demon dog, actually causing her to flinch as she absorbed it.

Absorbed it.

And flung it off.

Disobeying a direct order.

Paisley smashed a paw the size of a dinner plate against the raven, easily knocking it out of the tree. Then she pounced on it, slamming it to the ground.

Aiden yelled from behind me.

The raven shrieked, sounding almost human as it lashed out with wings and talons and beak.

I was only a few steps away. "I said no!"

Ignoring me, Paisley's great maw opened. She was bleeding from several places on her face and neck. She chomped down on the raven, silencing its cries in one sickening, spine-breaking crunch.

I stopped running, moaning, "No…"

Then Paisley ate the raven.

Ate a witch's familiar.

"Paisley," I whispered. "You…that was so…"

Feathers and blood littering the ground around her, the demon dog locked her gaze to mine, looking intensely satisfied. Her eyes gleamed red.

"So reckless…" I said. "I am so disappointed in you."

Paisley lowered her head, ears pinned back. Then, with a disgruntled huff, she slipped back into the undergrowth and disappeared into the shadows.

Aiden caught up with me, then tromped farther into the forested area after the demon dog.

My heart was hammering in my chest. An over-reaction, perhaps but…but…

I slowly turned, spotting Scarlett making her way across the beach toward me. Her magic didn't feel quite so charming now.

Opal was standing a few meters away, as was Ocean. The little dream walker was gazing at me with wide eyes. Ocean had her hand over her mouth. But Aiden's sister met my gaze, then placed her hand on Opal's shoulder to draw her away.

Aiden stepped out of the forest, tracking the teens as they headed back toward the hotel. "What the hell was that?" he murmured, switching his attention to Scarlett as she approached. With the wind against us, hopefully she couldn't hear us. "I thought Paisley couldn't disobey a direct order."

So had I. "I guess that depends on how she interpreted my 'no.' "

Scarlett came to a stop in front of me, scanning the trees, her magic simmering in her eyes and hands. That she was looking for the demon she'd just caught a glimpse of in the woods, I had no doubt. Paisley had taken down the raven with a swift burst of extreme violence, but a witch of Scarlett Godfrey's caliber didn't miss much. A witch with a seat on the Convocation…

The Convocation.

If adopting Opal came to a vote, Scarlett wielded one of the thirteen votes I needed. My heart was still hammering.

"I thought I saw…" The strawberry-blond witch didn't bother finishing her statement. She cast a gaze over her shoulder at the other witches heading our way, warning them off with a firm shake of her head.

"Yes." Aiden stepped forward, partially shielding me with his body. He was going to try to smooth it all over. Except witches didn't really like sorcerers, and Aiden wasn't the issue at hand. I was. And my ability to provide a safe home for Opal.

"Paisley," I blurted.

Aiden's entire body stiffened. Then he pivoted slightly, wiping the surprise from his face. Hopefully before the strawberry-blond witch saw it.

"That was Paisley," I said, meeting Scarlett's steady, blue-eyed gaze. "Our Paisley. Eating Mercury Dunkirk's raven."

Scarlett pressed her lips together, running a hand back through her hair and neatly looping it into a loose bun with a touch of magic. "Right, well. We knew of the dog, of course. Opal adores showing off pictures of her. Though we weren't certain you were bringing Paisley until you changed your reservation."

So we hadn't been fooling the witches for one moment. Not Pearl or Scarlett, at least. Their file on us was probably just as thick as the one Aiden had put together on the Godfreys. All the research they had to have done between me requesting guardianship of Opal and inviting the dream walker to join the coven. They knew Opal's background, of course. But also everything about her first year at the Academy, and everything they could find out about Emma Johnson and Aiden Myers.

With my history a complete blank, right up to the first time I used my passport to cross an international border.

Scarlett sighed, then shook her head ruefully. "That raven is…was a loathsome creature. It gave me the creeps every single time Mercury trotted it out. I'm sorry it discomfited your Paisley. But well…this is a bit of a mess."

Aiden pulled his phone out of his pocket, showing it to me. I nodded, understanding, as he stepped to the side, making a call rather than texting.

"Paisley, unfortunately, has developed a taste for magic...any magic, really, but more so when she perceives it as..." I kept my tone even, as if having a demon dog as a family member was completely normal.

"Malicious," Scarlett supplied.

"Yes. I...I'm not certain she had ever come into contact with a familiar before, but I think...well..."

"Mercury's been spying on all of us," Scarlett said. "I've had to stop myself from blinding the bird twice already." She laughed a little wryly. "It can't track Pearl at all, and my mother refuses to share her secret."

"The benefits of being the coven leader," I said neutrally.

Scarlett pinned her gaze on me. And no matter how beguiling her magic was, there was nothing soft about it now. "You don't want to make an enemy of Mercury."

"She's dangerous?"

Scarlett shrugged delicately. "For you? I doubt it."

"For Opal?"

"No! No. Nothing like that. But your...Paisley."

"I'll go apologize."

Scarlett grimaced. "She'll likely demand retribution."

"Financial?"

"Yes. She'll take the complaint to Pearl."

"That's fine…" I swallowed. "That will be…fine, right?"

Scarlett glanced over at Aiden. The sorcerer was having a muttered conversation with Christopher. I caught only a few words over the wind. Juniper's aunt, Olive, was waiting with her back to us a couple of meters away. The wind stirred her long, lightweight orange dress. The other witches had dispersed, some back out onto the beach and some toward the hotel.

The strawberry-blond witch stepped closer to me, lowering her own voice. "Good riddance, I say. But the coven leader will still have to be…neutral."

"But…Opal…" I trailed off, not quite able to speak the question, to give voice to my fears.

Scarlett looked surprised. Then she gently touched my shoulder. A caress of her magic, most likely meant to be comforting, tingled across my skin. Unfortunately, it couldn't penetrate my resistance to any and all magic, my layers and layers of natural shielding. Well, 'natural' as in not needing to be actively wielded. But like most of my power, that shielding had been unnaturally obtained.

"Opal is a gift," Scarlett said gently. "The coven doesn't take such gifts for granted." She stepped away, laughing as if I'd just said something funny. "You'd be surprised by the things that have happened during coven gatherings. This is simply…well, more than a blip, because I gather binding a raven is…rare…" Scarlett curled her lip derisively, but then instantly wiped the expression from her face.

She really hadn't liked the familiar. Or perhaps it was all familiars, or the magic needed to bind them. Witches were rather prejudiced against blood magic, or anything even verging on blood magic.

"It won't happen again," I said lamely.

Scarlett's lip twitched. "I don't suppose it will. As far as I know, Mercury only has the one raven." She glanced around her. "Though if you see a hairless cat prowling through the retreat..." She shivered. Just slightly, but I caught it.

"A sphynx?" Aiden asked, rejoining the conversation.

Scarlett nodded.

The sorcerer caught my gaze and shook his head—confirming that Paisley hadn't yet returned to the property.

"Mercury Dunkirk has a sphinx?" I asked, completely flummoxed. "I thought they were mythical?"

Scarlett blinked at me.

Aiden chuckled. "It's a breed of domestic house cat."

"Another diabolical creature," Scarlett said. "Googly-eyed. Not that I'd hold that against it. But...too intelligent." She shook her head. "I'll let Pearl know what I saw. That your Paisley was defending her people."

That was a generous assessment of the situation.

Scarlett smirked at me. "Mercury should have known better. She's a snob and a sneak. And that is the last nasty thing I shall say. I have a reputation to uphold, after all." She flashed a wide smile backed by a blast of pure charm.

Thankfully, that rolled off me as well.

"You wouldn't happen to know her room number?" I asked as the witch made to step away.

She grimaced. "Must you…confess…tonight?"

"She must have felt it…doesn't the death of a familiar hurt or weaken the witch?"

Scarlett snorted. "Mercury Dunkirk doesn't bond her familiars in any way that might detract from her own power. She's not that kind of witch."

"Still, it might be better to avoid a public confrontation," I said. I wanted this dealt with now, so it didn't linger over me. I wanted Opal clear of it.

Scarlett sighed. "She's staying in the main building. Away from the rest of us. Room 304."

"Thank you."

Then the strawberry-blond witch stepped over to join Olive, who was still waiting for her. Together, they headed back to the hotel. Aiden and I watched the witches until they were out of earshot.

"What do we say?" I asked Aiden. "Mercury will have sensed her connection being severed, right? Even if it didn't hurt or weaken her. And…to maintain their bond in any sort of functional, practical way…say, for spying…wouldn't Mercury need to be on the beach herself? Or at least very near?"

"I don't know." Aiden sighed. "I would have presumed that she at least saw the whole thing through the familiar bond. If the raven was actively spying for her at the time of Paisley's attack. But if that were the case, then I would have also expected Mercury to show up immediately to avenge the loss."

Delayed panic streaked through me. We didn't need the witches asking questions about Paisley. Well, more questions. Questions we'd have a hard time answering. And I didn't want to have to prove I could control the demon dog, rope her to my will. Bind her even tighter than any witch bound a familiar.

Aiden touched my cheek lightly. "You heard Scarlett. This won't impact the adoption."

"I also heard her refer to her mother by her first name, several times now."

Aiden nodded. "I caught that too."

"So Scarlett Godfrey might not speak for the coven…" Another lick of panic shivered through me. I tried to ignore it. Unsuccessfully.

Aiden pressed his hand to my face, his touch solid and grounding. "Scarlett wouldn't make statements if she couldn't back them up. She's her mother's scion."

"There's…" I swallowed. "I keep overreacting, don't I?"

"No."

"No?"

"Yeah, no. You react exactly right."

I just grinned at him. "Maybe you aren't the best judge of the things I do."

Aiden laughed huskily. "I am a bit…invested. But also…eating a familiar isn't great." He grimaced.

"I can't imagine what a Dunkirk witch is going to ask for as recompense."

He tucked my hand into the crook of his elbow, and we started up the beach toward the hotel. The last vestiges of the sunset faded from the ever-darkening deep-blue sky.

"We can pay," I said. "Money means nothing compared to…well, just about anything else."

Aiden nodded, but his gaze was remote, thoughtful. "There was something off about that raven."

"Like…something different from other familiars?"

He nodded. But instead of elaborating, he pulled out his phone and checked his text messages again.

"You're worried about Paisley?" I snorted, anger and frustration overriding my own concern. "I've seen her eat worse."

"Yeah," Aiden said, his attention firmly elsewhere. "I'm just going to put out a few feelers. I don't know any witches who bind familiars personally, but Sky or Ocean might."

"Ammunition," I said. "I understand."

He flashed me a grin.

And if we walked more slowly than normal through the hotel grounds toward the main building and Mercury Dunkirk's room? Well…I'm not sure anyone would have blamed us.

STANDING BEFORE MERCURY DUNKIRK'S HOTEL room door, even with Aiden at my side, made me pause. And run through my conversation with Scarlett in my head. Again. Honestly, it was probably the third or fourth time.

Would it be better to keep my mouth shut?

I glanced at Aiden.

His expression was neutral, but he offered me a smile. Patient. Content to follow my lead. In this instance, at least.

"Paisley?" I asked in a murmur, glancing up and down the empty hall. As with the secondary building, wood flooring and casings, cream-colored walls, and statement art dominated the decor throughout the hotel's main building.

Aiden tugged his phone out of his pocket, obliging me. Because the chance that he'd missed a text from either Christopher or Opal—who was back in our suite, having relocated the board game gathering with Juniper, Burgundy, and Ocean—was highly unlikely.

But my dark sorcerer opened the messages app and scrolled through his texts nonetheless. Nothing recent.

"She knows you're pissed," he said.

"Or she's having trouble digesting a magical fucking raven," I snapped, still seriously annoyed. Enough to swear about it.

I knocked on the door before I could hesitate long enough to think it all through for a fifth or sixth time. I never hesitated once battle lines had been drawn, not even if I hadn't chosen that battle for my-self. I backed my people. And, as tiny as the group that had claim to my heart or protection was, it included Paisley. Of course and always.

Aiden casually slid his hand into his suit pocket, ready to pull any of the spells that were only a finger-tip away from him these days. He kept his magical arsenal well stocked and locked away in the heav-ily fortified safe in his study—and via his magically imbued pockets, he could pluck any premade spell or weapon from that safe at will. He didn't angle his shoulder in front of me, but it had taken a while for me to break him of that impulse.

No one answered my knock.

It would have been tempting to pretend that Mercury wasn't within—except I could hear some-one moving around. And Aiden's more refined senses for magic likely stretched beyond the door. So back-ing away would have seemed cowardly.

I might have been feeling off, even out of sorts, but I wasn't a coward who couldn't take responsibil-ity for someone else. Someone who should have been under my command. But as was slowly dawning on me, though I hadn't wanted to treat Paisley like a pet, I had obviously given the demon dog too much free-dom to make her own decisions.

Either way, I should have acknowledged her distress earlier—anxiety, even—and sent her back to Christopher without allowing any argument.

I raised my hand to knock a second time.

The door swept open.

Mercury, cinching one of the hotel's plush robes around her waist, narrowed her ice-blue eyes at me, then Aiden.

"I'm sorry for disturbing you—" I began.

"Emma?" Lani said.

Quickly grabbing a tank top and underwear from the floor and tugging them on, the intuitive tumbled free of the rumpled bed that was tucked just at the edge of my peripheral vision. Her hair was mussed. Her lips...

I glanced at Mercury, who was also in a state of...well, having been rather thoroughly kissed. At the very least.

"What's wrong?" Lani asked, swiftly approaching the door.

I was staring. I was completely and utterly thrown, and not recovering at all quickly. Had Mercury Dunkirk tried to kill me in that moment, I probably wouldn't have seen it coming.

"Aiden?" Lani ran her hand through her hair, starting to panic. "Opal?"

"She's fine," Aiden said soothingly. "We're sorry to have interrupted."

Mercury was smirking at me, knowingly.

Anger, and not only at myself, flushed through me. I narrowed my eyes at her. "Your raven," I snapped.

"Oh?" Mercury met my glare with one of her own, her British accent clipped. "If such trifles bother you, amplifier, then might I suggest—"

"It's dead."

She snapped her mouth shut, looking from me to Aiden, then back at me. I couldn't figure out if she was surprised, or just very good at controlling her reactions.

No one spoke for a moment. Then Mercury pressed her hand to the doorframe, making a show of lowering the wards that she'd placed on the interior jamb. Wards I hadn't felt from outside the door.

Dark, dark-blue witch magic flickered over her eyes as she triggered some ability. Then she inhaled sharply, as if pained.

I still wasn't certain if she was feigning or being wholly transparent, but her own wards had apparently blocked her sense of her familiar. At least while she was focused elsewhere, such as on a new lover.

"It was…" I corrected myself. I wasn't here to make excuses. "Paisley ate it. The raven. On the beach."

Lani groaned quietly.

Mercury lifted her chin, tension lining her jaw. "Paisley?"

"The pit bull," Lani said, her tone gentle. "You saw her playing on the beach with Opal and Juniper, remember?"

Mercury exhaled sharply through her nose. Angry. As expected. "A pit bull?" She sneered doubtfully. "Managed to kill my familiar?"

"And eat it," I said, not quite certain why I needed to add that little detail, or with quite so much relish. Technically, I was the one in the wrong. Perhaps I just had too little practice apologizing.

"The coven leader has been informed of the incident," Aiden said smoothly.

"By you?" Mercury asked derisively.

"Scarlett Godfrey."

That gave Mercury pause. Well, she took a moment to absorb the information, at least. "I'll demand reparations."

"Of course," I said. "I'm...sorry."

"You should be!" she snapped. "Though...it's doubtful that a mere amplifier could possibly understand the complexities of binding a familiar, let alone a raven."

Lani frowned. But at Mercury, not me. "A mere amplifier?" she echoed, her tone tight.

"Again," Aiden interjected, "though the raven was stalking us, and Paisley was only doing her job, the fault is ultimately ours. We will be happy to discuss reparations tomorrow with your coven leader."

"Pearl Godfrey isn't my coven leader," Mercury said. The statement seemed to be more of a reflex than a condemnation. Perhaps because her attention was now trained on Lani, who had stepped back into the room.

"You understood what I meant," Aiden said coolly.

Lani scooped up her pants and sandals, then strode back toward us.

Mercury opened her mouth to speak to the intuitive, but Lani crossed between Aiden and me without even pausing to get dressed.

Aiden stepped farther into the hall as well, leaving me facing off with Mercury.

The older witch flushed angrily, met my gaze, and raised the wards over the doorway again. "Tomorrow, then."

I nodded.

She shut the door in my face.

I turned to look up the hall. Lani was tugging on her pants with Aiden only a few steps away. A frustrated anger sparked off the intuitive as she thrust her feet into her sandals, easily picked up by my errant empathy.

Lani looked up as I approached, grimacing. "I'm sorry."

"What could you possibly be sorry about?"

"I...I just..." She sighed heavily. "I have terrible taste."

"I doubt Paisley ate the raven because of you...and Mercury."

Aiden chuckled quietly, stepping ahead of us down the hall with both hands in his pockets now. The chuckle informed me that I was misreading the situation somehow.

Lani sighed again, wrapping her hand around my arm as we followed the dark-haired sorcerer. "Paisley is terribly possessive." She lowered her voice. "But also, that raven has been bugging everyone all day. There was no way Paisley wasn't picking up on that. Like Aiden said, I wouldn't be surprised if that's why she...well, killed it."

"That's not the main issue," I said quietly as we stepped into the stairwell.

"What's the main issue, then?" Lani asked, sounding a little amused.

"She didn't follow orders. And now she's disappeared."

Lani nodded, smiling slightly. "She's hiding out because she knows you're disappointed?"

I huffed.

She rubbed my arm lightly. "You take too much of this on yourself, Emma. We all make choices, even Paisley. We all then have to deal with the consequences of those choices. You can't fix everything."

"I'm not trying to fix everything," I grumbled.

Lani hummed doubtfully.

Aiden glanced back at us with a sharp grin.

I glared at them both. Then I pulled the phone I pretty much never used out of my pocket. Just in case I'd missed a text message.

Nothing.

"At least the sex was pretty good," Lani said mournfully. "But I guess I should have known that anyone who ran around with a creepy raven was an asshole."

Aiden laughed.

Energy shifted on my spine, a glimmer of Christopher's power simmering under my skin. His range had broadened, if he could reach for me from almost three hundred kilometers away.

Which wasn't surprising. No matter how careful I was to not amplify him unless we felt it was necessary, Christopher had lived in close proximity with an amplifier for over eight years now. And my contact with the Hallowed had seemingly upped my own amperage. Seemingly because that power—the power I'd been born with, not stolen—had always been available to me, the Hallowed had simply carved new pathways through my system, through my brain. And once carved, such things tended to be permanent.

A message appeared on my phone. I'd still been staring down at it. Like I knew Christopher was about to reach out.

Like maybe I'd been stealing power from him as well.

Shaking off that dark thought, I opened the text. I wasn't leeching power from my Knox. I had simply felt him reach for me.

>No Paisley. You?

Not yet. We're heading back to the room.

I glanced up from the phone, seeing Aiden and Lani waiting on me. But then a picture came through. An oracle card. A black-inked botanical drawing of a sprig of sage, with the intention Wisdom written under it.

My stomach hollowed.

"Emma?" Aiden asked.

I turned my phone to him. "Wisdom."

He nodded, reaching for his own phone. "I thought I saw him flipping the basil card earlier."

"What does that mean?" Lani asked quietly.

I stared down at the picture on the phone, then tucked the device away in my pocket. Aiden would pick up the conversation with the clairvoyant. "Wisdom…" I said, trying to answer Lani's question without coloring it with my own interpretation. "Intuition. Potential. And mystery."

"Right…and why are you and Aiden freaking out about it?"

"The sage adds other attributes. Protection. Insight. Longevity."

Lani huffed. "I'm still not getting it. None of those things are bad."

"It's not great that Christopher is seeing anything in his cards. Anything at all."

"He doesn't often see rainbow and candy canes?" Lani grinned.

"If he does, he doesn't feel the need to text me an image of the card that he's using as a focus."

We had traversed the hall and the stairs to the main floor, and were heading toward the front entrance before Lani picked up the conversation again. "Scarlett mentioned that there's a workshop tomorrow afternoon I might enjoy." She hesitated, glancing over at me as we crossed through the door that Aiden was holding open for us. "About setting a focus. That's what Christopher does with the cards?"

"Yes. Well, same idea."

A slight breeze stirred my dress around my knees. Though the bulk of his attention was still on his phone, Aiden absentmindedly brushed his hand down my back as we crossed through the moonlit grounds of the hotel, keeping to the low-lit gravel path that led to the secondary building.

"What is it exactly, Emma?" Lani asked in a murmur, her arm still wrapped around mine. "What bothers you about that particular card?"

"Wisdom," I said, looking straight ahead but not really seeing anything in particular. "Paired with the attributes of sage…it's not a card that Christopher has pulled when touching on my power."

"I…I don't know what that means."

"Christopher was focusing on me when he pulled the wisdom card."

"But…that's good, right?"

The hollow feeling was back in my stomach again. Actually, it had never left—just gotten heavier. Suddenly I wanted Opal. Aiden was trailing behind, texting with Christopher, so I wanted Opal in my sights, within my reach. I shoved the irrational thought away, focusing on the conversation.

"Wisdom," I said, "is not something I'm known for."

"Emma," Lani scoffed.

I glanced at her. "I'm not being self-deprecating. When you're constantly under the gaze of a clairvoyant, it's best to know yourself, to not overestimate your abilities. I am not wise. Or intuitive. I don't have the patience for games or mysteries."

Lani went quiet for long enough that the sound of the crashing surf dominated the night until we reached the side door to the secondary building. "The sage..." she murmured as Aiden stepped in front of us to open the door. "You said that means protection as well. And you have that, Emma. You have so much of that, you could bottle it and make a killing on it."

I wasn't totally sure what Lani meant. Except yes, I could make a killing of just about anything I did. I had been born and bred to be a killer, after all.

The intuitive touched my face lightly. "Emma?"

I tried to smile, but she winced a little in response, so I gathered there was nothing nice about the expression.

"It's the combination," Aiden said, finally looking up from his phone. "And our core being currently splintered...Paisley unaccounted for, Christopher at home alone, Samantha in Europe, and us here. That's the concern." He settled his soul-piercing gaze on me. "Christopher says he's never pulled the wisdom card while doing a reading before. Not in a single or a triple draw. But he's certain it's for you."

"He was reaching for me when he pulled it," I said.

Aiden nodded, looking grim.

"I still don't get it," Lani said. "We all grow into wisdom. Didn't you say that potential was part of that?"

"Christopher only uses the cards as a focus," I said, trying to be rational. "They become something else in his hands, but the wisdom and sage in relation to me…" I met Aiden's gaze again. "Someone is playing a long game? With me. But I don't play. I act. So…the cards might be telling Christopher that there's something coming, some threat that I need to protect myself or someone else from, that I have to…not immediately react to?" I shook my head. "That's not going to happen. I don't hesitate. If I hesitate, someone gets hurt."

Aiden grimaced. "That's Christopher's interpretation as well."

"Someone from your past? Or…" Lani lowered her voice, glancing around us. "One of the witches?"

"Could be," I said, stepping through into the hall and picking up my pace.

"Could be?" Lani echoed, close on my heels. "Could be which one?"

"Exactly."

Lani huffed. "Well, that's not helpful at all!"

Aiden laughed, the warm sound filling the hollow in my belly. Not completely. But enough for me to flash a smile back at him over my shoulder.

Lani huffed a second time, though a little more playfully. "I hate this magic shit."

Aiden slung his arm across her shoulders and pulled her into an awkward sideways hug. It was a difficult embrace to pull off while practically jogging after me.

Lani batted at his chest playfully. "Don't make it worse, sorcerer."

"Ah, am I tweaking your delicate witch sensibilities, Lani dear?"

"Oh, please. The only thing you tweak in any way that annoys me is Emma's gear shift."

Aiden burst out laughing.

Lani thumped his chest this time. "That's not what I meant!" She twisted out from under his arm, then jogged to catch up to me. "Men," she muttered under her breath.

I smiled at her. And as I did, I realized that even with Paisley still unaccounted for, Mercury seeking reparations, and my concern about what the fallout might mean for my adopting Opal...

I somehow felt...a little better. A little more like myself.

Because of Lani. And not for any magic she could wield. Just because she was...a friend. A friend by choice. Hers and mine.

"Don't worry," I said. "I have a habit of thwarting Christopher's visions before they have a chance to occur."

Lani barked out a laugh. "And only coming from you, Emma, is that not a brag."

FOUR

I'D GONE TO BED ANXIOUS, WOKEN UP ANXIOUS, AND eaten breakfast anxious. It wasn't a natural state for me. But thankfully, Opal's exuberance—and her ongoing discussion with Aiden and Ocean about the mending, circle work, and dual-casting classes she'd signed up for—kept me from randomly grabbing people and interrogating them as to whether they'd noticed a demon dog skulking around the hotel halls.

Paisley still hadn't returned, or at least she hadn't made her presence known, by the time I was sending Opal off to her first spellcasting forum. Yes, a forum. Apparently, the entire coven met for overview sessions about various magical applications in the mornings, then split off into individual group sessions in the afternoon.

Witches needed to sign up for the afternoon practical application sessions, and Aiden had struggled to not continually grin as he'd helped Opal decide what topics would best benefit her during her second year of studies at the Academy. I couldn't figure out if it was the organizational skills of the witches or Opal's own sharp focus on her future that amused the sorcerer more. The witches, most likely. Because Aiden simply adored Opal and was constantly indulging her with anything magical she deemed worth her attention.

I just wanted Opal to be happy. As long as she seemed happy, content, I wasn't going to worry that she was pushing herself too hard. She had a choice. She knew she had choices. I had no idea what my childhood would have been like had I had those same choices, so I wasn't going to curtail the little witch.

The door had just clicked shut behind Ocean, Opal, and Lani, who had decided to see what the fuss was all about until it got boring. Her words, not mine. Then Aiden had himself pressed up behind me, hands sliding up from my waist to cup my breasts.

I gasped, then immediately shimmied my ass back against him, as if I could actually get closer. I couldn't—at least not without removing a few layers of clothing. But I was always happy to try.

He groaned, kissing my neck, which I arched and twisted to give him better access.

"I thought the date was supposed to come first?" I asked breathlessly, trying to tease.

"We have hours before lunch." Aiden smiled, then captured my earlobe.

I shuddered under his ministrations, and he took that as the 'yes' it was, sliding his hands down my arms, grabbing my wrists, and guiding my hands to press against the door.

"Oh, I see," I purred. "No touching."

He hummed agreeably, stepping back slightly to press the side of his foot to my ankle, which prompted me to widen my stance. Then he slipped his hands up under my dress and fingers into my underwear without further words or directions.

Finding me more than ready for him, he cursed under his breath. Then the first thick rope of magic twisted between us—a mutual and unbidden sharing of power.

I obligingly pressed my hands and forearms against the wall, sticking out my ass, already panting quietly as my deadly sorcerer dipped and flicked his finger over the sensitive nub at my very core. Or at least it felt like the center of my being when he was touching it.

Then he was unzipping his jeans, bunching my dress around my waist, and slipping his hardness into me from behind with a groan. Lightly pinning me against the door, he muttered, "Even when I try to go slow, amplifier..."

"I know, sorcerer," I purred. "The feeling is always mutual." Then I started to move back on him, setting a fast pace that had him grabbing for my hips and cursing again.

More power rode those curses. And loosened from my normally rigid hold as pleasure twisted between us, my own magic flowed, cementing the invisible bonds that we didn't need any piece of paper to authenticate.

I CAVED AS WE WERE WAITING FOR LUNCH ON AN outdoor patio overlooking a small marina, giving in to my simmering concern for Paisley as I actually dialed Christopher.

Aiden shifted into the chair beside me and hit the button to initiate a video call as we waited for the clairvoyant to answer. Then the sorcerer took off one of his copper rings, giving it a quick spin in the middle of the table to cast an invisible barrier over us. Something to mute sound, I presumed, given the way the magic momentarily pressed against my ears.

Christopher answered the call, taking a moment to switch over to video. The white of his magic had nearly swallowed his light-gray eyes, but he blinked, and it ebbed slightly.

"Socks," he growled. "You know I hate it when you call."

"No one is dead," I said.

Aiden gave me a look that I didn't address, my attention riveted to the clairvoyant. "Paisley?"

"She was on the property when I woke this morning."

I sighed, more pissed than relieved. "You could have texted."

He shrugged belligerently. "The wards shifted again while I was eating granola. I assumed she was heading back to—" He stilled as his magic flooded his eyes again, then faded almost as quickly as it had come. "Zans," he said, clarifying where his magic—and his full attention—was currently focused. Not on Paisley.

Christopher still insisted on calling Samantha 'Zans' even though she'd expressed her distaste for the childhood nickname ever since he'd dubbed her with it when we were very young. After she'd almost killed Bee, slitting the telepath's throat in multiple places with the shredded remains of a metal cafeteria tray. But even though Bee had forgiven the almost-murderous tantrum the instant she could speak again, Christopher hadn't. Actually, neither had Fish. Or I.

"In Europe? That's a long way for your magic to reach."

"Yeah, hence everything being cloudy."

"The cards?" I asked, already knowing he'd be using his oracle cards to sharpen his sight.

"I thought you didn't want to be involved," he said mockingly.

I didn't answer.

The clairvoyant hissed, then shook his head. "Sorry, Socks. I occasionally forget... what conversation we're having."

"I know," I said stiffly, loathing repeating myself. "I told you I'd help find Bee after the coven gathering. If necessary."

He sighed. "I know, I'm sorry."

"Cards?" I prompted. Again. "More sage?"

He grunted. "Basil, mostly. But I think that one's pointing at Zans, not you."

Basil in traditional herbology indicated prosperity, protection, and happiness. The witch who'd designed the oracle cards to my specifications had paired that herb with the strength intention. Perseverance, courage, patience, and compassion.

Samantha was strong, all right. Even courageous. I wouldn't have thought that the other attributes suited her particularly well, though.

Christopher frowned. "Be nice."

I snorted. "Did you lay eyes on Paisley while she was there?"

"She kept to the barn."

To eat, most likely. We kept a freezer and a fridge there, stocked with raw and frozen beef for the demon dog. Lately, she'd been mowing through racks and racks of ribs.

"But I imagine she knows she screwed up," Christopher continued. "She'll come to you, Socks. Groveling for forgiveness as we all do when we disappoint you."

Aiden stiffened beside me. At Christopher's tone, no doubt.

"Don't make this about your issues with me," I said coolly. "Just because you feel left behind."

"Like the child I am," he said mockingly.

I just waited.

Again.

Christopher growled under his breath. "I'm fine. And you didn't need to schedule people to pretend to drop in to check on me. Jenni has been here twice already."

"That wasn't my doing." I might have mentioned we'd be away, of course. But the RCMP officer and coyote shifter Jenni Raymond wasn't under my command. And as far as I knew, she hadn't reignited her sexual relationship with the clairvoyant either. "Plus, Aiden was supposed to be there."

I shouldn't have added that last part. I knew it the moment the words were out of my mouth.

Aiden chimed in, refocusing the conversation. "We're just worried about Paisley. If we have to track her down and magically tag her…"

"She won't like it," Christopher finished for the sorcerer. "None of us would."

Aiden nodded.

We had actually discussed the possibility of summoning Paisley if we needed to—like a summoner might call forth a demon. Whether it would work was purely suppositional, but the idea made me a little sick. Okay, a lot sick.

Christopher glanced in my direction, grimacing through another flood of his power.

I waited, but he just shook it off, took a deep breath, and shuffled his cards. He split the deck, shuffled again, then did a fancy flipping trick that left the basil card face up on top.

He frowned down at it.

"If the basil is meant for us?" I asked, seeing if I could prompt some clarity from him.

Christopher shook his head. But then he spoke slowly. "If it's you, then...you just need to keep moving forward, keep your focus on your goal. Making a good impression and coming home with Opal."

"No one is in danger?" I asked.

"You're surrounded by a coven of witches, Emma," Christopher said crossly. "They're technically wooing you. Right, sorcerer?"

Aiden grunted agreeably.

"Us," I said.

Christopher smiled, suddenly radiating happiness that shoved away the last vestiges of his power. "Us." He nodded to himself. "If you have to track and tag Paisley, then do it. You know if any of us were in trouble, we'd want you to bail us out just the same."

"She's a...she's not my pet."

"Neither are any of the Five, Emma," Christopher said gently. "But we are under your command. Your protection." He flipped up the basil card, filling the screen of the phone with it.

Protection. Happiness. Perseverance.

"I thought that wasn't about me," I groused, trying to be playful and not pulling it off.

Christopher snorted. "Everything comes back to you, Socks."

"Us," Aiden said sharply.

"Yeah," Christopher said. "Us."

"Text us the moment Paisley sets foot on the property again," I said.

"I understand my orders," the clairvoyant said stiffly.

"I don't think you do," I said darkly.

He blinked. A thick white line of magic suddenly lined his irises. "I'm with you, Emma. Always. I just get a bit…untethered when we're apart. If Paisley comes to me again, I'll keep her here."

I nodded, then ended the call. I scowled at Aiden. "Why am I always more pissed off after a conversation with…well, anyone? Or anyone but you or Opal?"

Aiden laughed, plucking up the still-spinning copper ring and sliding it on his finger just as the server approached with our lunch. The sound barrier bubble over us dissolved with a quiet pop.

"You think Christopher is playing games with you," Aiden said mildly, straightening and crossing over to the other side of the table.

"He's not?"

"He's at the mercy of his power. We all are."

"We all learn to control our power," I snapped back—fully aware that after recent events, I wasn't really in any position to claim perfect control myself. But Christopher hadn't had to tangle with an immortal entity, so he didn't have my excuse.

Not that I would ever claim to need an excuse. Not out loud, at least.

"And Christopher has learned, with you and the other four to balance him." Aiden tapped the back of his neck to indicate he was referencing the blood tattoos on my own spine.

I sighed, ceding the argument. The power tying Christopher to me was practically dormant at that moment, and the other three tattoos were completely inactive. But I had lots of things to distract me from dwelling on that empty feeling. Christopher didn't.

The server placed our miso soups and first rounds of sushi in front of us—salmon and tuna sashimi for Aiden, and a California roll with real crab for me. As Aiden chatted with the server quietly, I thought about my own behavior for the last day or so. About how out of sorts I'd been feeling.

Maybe, just maybe, the blood tattoos grounded me as well.

And that was certainly an annoying realization.

Because I'd spent the last eight years trying to keep those bonds at bay, going so far as to banish the other three—or so Samantha would have put it. And just as I wasn't a big believer in fate or destiny, I didn't like even contemplating what ifs…

What if I hadn't demanded that the Five go their separate ways eight years ago?

Would I have found Opal? Met Aiden?

Just the idea of not having my dark sorcerer and my dream walker in my life made me feel cold and empty inside.

I remembered that feeling, even from when I'd been surrounded by the other four. I never wanted to live that way again. So…was there a middle ground where I got to keep Aiden and Opal, yet not fight the binding of the tattoos quite so much?

I sipped my miso and tried to focus on the moment. The soup was salty and almost too hot—perfect for grounding me. If only for a brief time.

AFTER FINISHING LUNCH AND POKING AROUND A couple of the galleries in town, I finally admitted to myself that I couldn't focus on anything but the Paisley problem. I wasn't even angry anymore. I just wanted the demon dog safe and glued to my side, even if that meant taking her with me to the meeting with Pearl the next day. Or rather, the inquiry.

"We should head back," I said as we walked along the main street of Tofino. The art in the gallery we'd just stepped out of was already just a blur of bright colors in my mind's eye. I had barely been able to focus on the whole room, let alone the individual pieces.

Aiden, proving he was just as distracted as I was, instantly pulled out his notebook and fell into step with me as I turned us back toward where we'd parked the car.

A quick glance informed me that the dark sorcerer was attempting to sketch a complicated rune. While walking.

Yeah, I wasn't the only anxious one.

"Is that to track Paisley?"

He grunted in the affirmative, skirting the Mustang and climbing into the passenger seat without looking up from his sketching.

I started the car, checking my mirrors before I pulled away from the curb, seeing that someone was already waiting for my parking spot. The meter still had almost two hours on it, so bonus for them. "We'll need to start at her last location," I said. "Or at least the last place we saw her."

He nodded. "And I'll need blood."

I nodded back. Paisley had been injured, however slightly, during her attack on the raven. That meant we might find some blood spatter in the same area.

I drove the Mustang back to the hotel while Aiden continued to sketch. Ocean, Lani, and Opal were all occupied in various afternoon workshops, assuming that the part-time intuitive hadn't bailed yet. And if she hadn't, perhaps she was soon to be a full-time intuitive?

Aiden and I didn't bother even entering the hotel, simply parking the car and taking the path that led to the beach. Heading for the last place we'd seen Paisley at the edge of the forest. Aiden was still sketching, replicating the rune he'd already crafted on two more pages—three spells for us to trigger.

"It didn't rain last night," I murmured, scanning for signs of the scuffle that I hoped had survived the eighteen or so hours since the demon dog had eaten the raven. Aiden grunted, acknowledging my obvious observation.

The beach behind us was filled with surfers, swimmers, and sunbathers, but no one was in the immediate vicinity. A few sets of footprints were scattered nearby, which wasn't a surprise. The witches had presumably checked out the area after we'd left, as I would have. I just hoped they hadn't cast any spells that would interfere with Aiden's tracking. Leaving the sorcerer with his head bowed over his notebook, I circled the area, looking for blood in the sand, on the cedar tree, and on the undergrowth.

"Nothing," I said, frustrated.

"It'll have dried," Aiden said soothingly. "Hard to see on the darkly colored bark and the deep green of the plants." He flipped back a few pages in his notebook and tore a different rune free from it. Crumpling the page in his right hand, he flicked it outward. The paper combusted without a single word from my powerful dark sorcerer, sprinkling a layer of almost imperceptible ash all around the nearest tree.

As the ash settled, a glimmering hint of dark-blue magic appeared in multiple places.

I leaned in close, gazing at and below the lower branch where Mercury's familiar had perched. "Probably the raven's blood?"

"Likely." Aiden tore one of the three tracking runes from his notebook, pressing the center of it to the marked locations on the tree trunk.

I stepped to the side, where the edges of a broad-leaf bush glimmered. "Here." I broke off a stem, offering a glowing leaf to Aiden. "Might be more blood from the raven. It happened so fast…but

Paisley did step back through into the shadows here…" I gestured toward an area of churned dirt and mangled undergrowth between the trees.

Aiden took the leaf, rubbing the dried blood his first spell had highlighted into the center of the second tracking rune.

Then both of us crouched, eyeing the remaining spots that had been highlighted by Aiden's spell. I ran the confrontation between the demon dog and the raven back in my head. Well, the execution, really. Trying to assess where Paisley might have bled.

"All of this could be the raven," I said.

Aiden nodded. But then he pointed to the tree, about a half a meter from the base. "Let's take that smudge. Paisley was slashed on her face, right?"

I'd been closer to the brawl than he had. "Yes. And her left shoulder. You think some might have spattered the tree as she shook her head?" As she broke the raven's back, actually.

Aiden stepped forward, pressing the page that held the third tracking rune to the tree.

The other residual was quickly fading. And as soon as it rained, or even if the tide got high enough to spread sea mist all over the area, the rest of the faint magic here would wash away.

"Do you think it's fresh enough?" I asked Aiden. The magic that ran through the blood of any Adept faded quickly once removed from that person or creature.

"Should be. But we're not only tracking by magic residual. The runes should track DNA, flesh, and bone as well."

"Anything infused with blood."

"Yes."

I grinned at Aiden. "Tricky, sorcerer."

He huffed. "Don't praise me yet. Let's see if it works."

We straightened. I slipped behind Aiden's right shoulder, both of us facing the forest. Ceding the lead only on this specific occasion.

"Let's just hope Paisley didn't immediately slip dimensions when she took off after eating the raven. That would put her well out of the spell's reach." Aiden crumpled the first tracking spell in his fist, holding it tightly. Power welled within his hand.

How Paisley crossed through shadows, seemingly teleporting, wasn't something we completely understood yet. Aiden thought that she might simply be stepping into the demon dimension at will, then projecting herself forward from there—back to the property, or keying specifically onto one of the Five. Though the demon dog hadn't been able to key in on Bee.

I was also fairly certain she could slip shorter distances, using the shadows but keeping to our own dimension. But we hadn't confirmed either supposition, because while the demon dog was happy enough to play around with Aiden as he tried to assess her abilities, she could become capricious if she got bored with his tests. Or if the treats he offered weren't to her liking.

"One of the three spells might at least pick her trail up if and when she returned to this dimension, though," I said hopefully.

Aiden grunted noncommittally, then released the crumpled spell with a flick of his fingers. It flashed before us, more felt than seen—to my senses, at least.

Then, nothing.

The sorcerer angled his head, as if he could see something. He crossed deeper into the forest with me at his heels.

Well, this was going to be annoying. It was one thing to let Aiden take the lead—and completely another to be a redundant participant in a hunt.

I tugged my phone out of my dress pocket.

No text messages.

Not allowing myself to grumble about the situation—at least not out loud—I dutifully followed my sorcerer.

AIDEN LOST THE TRAIL ALMOST IMMEDIATELY. BUT then casting the second tracking spell twisted us in the other direction, taking us along a series of quiet forest paths that eventually cut back around to the hotel. That trail disappeared again near the exterior door that led to our room, so Aiden cast the third tracking spell. That blood rune drew us past the reception area, then skirted the main building into an area of slightly more manicured gardens. They were still full of wild indigenous plants and a ton of moss and lichen, but had been groomed into what appeared to be smaller, deliberately cleared areas.

The function of those areas became clear as Aiden's final spell fizzled out, and we picked up the low murmur of a voice from ahead.

A woman with an English accent.

We slowed our pace before we barreled right into a small group of witches, keeping slightly back in a stand of evergreens so as not to disturb the ongoing session. The sound of the ocean was muffled. By a spell no doubt, because I could still see the crashing surf through the trees to our far left.

The group was presided over by Mercury Dunkirk. I barely stopped myself from hissing in disappointment. Aiden and I shared a grimace instead.

His tracking spells had worked. Unfortunately, it was the raven's blood we had collected, not Paisley's, and it had directed us back to the familiar's master. That left little doubt that Mercury tied her familiars to her through blood magic—and that the British witch was an idiot to have let the raven wander as it willed, if its blood could be used to track her. Of course, someone would have to be willing to perform blood magic, sacrificing that familiar to get to the witch. And if she'd been behind strong wards, Aiden's tracking spells might not have worked.

Scarlett Godfrey was standing with her arms crossed at the back of the otherwise seated group, tucked between cedar trees. The strawberry-blond,

charisma-laden witch was mostly blocking the narrow path that led to the seating area, and was wearing
a light silk tank top over a perfectly pressed skirt, all
in shades of blue. Her arms were crossed, and she
sparked with energy, as if she was angry, though her
expression was neutral.

I caught sight of Opal and Ocean perched on
log stools at the front of the group, directly in front
of Mercury. The British witch, barefoot and dressed
in what appeared to be a multilayered linen tunic
over capri pants, had what I was guessing was a cat
perched on her shoulder.

I was guessing because the feline looked more
like some kind of imaginary goblin taken from one
of the children's books the Five had used to learn
to read. Its bat ears and slanted, bulbous eyes were
far too big for its pointed face. And it was hairless,
its dark-gray skin speckled with blobs of pink on its
underside.

"Now," Mercury was saying. "Some witches
might suggest otherwise, but the tightest binding, of
course, is always blood based. Infallible if done right."
She waved her hand offishly. "Yes, you can woo with
food offerings and moon spells, but it is the unpre-
dictable nature of an animal that makes them such
brilliant hunters and trackers. And feeding your—"

"Thank you, Mercury," Scarlett said, clapping as
she stepped forward. "But unfortunately we've run
out of time, and the girls need to move on to their
next workshop."

The cat goblin leaped off Mercury's shoulder, twining around her ankles and twitching its tail.

Mercury huffed. "We've barely gotten started. I wanted to end with a practical demonstration—"

Scarlett, beaming from ear to ear, gestured toward the small group. "Let's all thank Mercury and move on. Quickly, quickly!"

"Thank you, Mercury," the witches chorused.

Opal's voice was sweeter and brighter than the rest. Though perhaps only to my ears. Then the witches all stood, leaving Mercury glaring at Scarlett.

One of the older witches, Olive, grinned at the scion of the Godfrey coven as she passed. "The girls?" She laughed. "I'm older than you by half a decade!"

Scarlett flashed her a smile.

Olive turned to the group, calling out, "Those of you signed up for foraging follow me, please."

Three witches immediately followed Olive, including Opal and Ocean.

"And Kelly is doing her spell knitting workshop on the lower level." Scarlett gestured slightly to the left of Aiden and me, where a secondary path cut back to the hotel. All but one of the other witches departed in that direction, leaving only Burgundy, the healer in training. And Mercury.

Burgundy had brand-new pink streaked through her light-brown hair, likely either from Ocean's spell work or an earlier class. She stepped up to Scarlett, grinning. "I'm with you. Can we go over soothing tinctures again?"

Scarlett nodded, but her gaze was still fixed on Mercury. "I want to work with bandages this afternoon." Burgundy grimaced, though the expression was playful. "But give me a moment with Mercury, please."

Nodding while biting her lower lip, Burgundy glanced back over her shoulder at the Dunkirk witch. The goblin cat was grooming itself by Mercury's right ankle.

Yeah, the Godfrey coven wasn't going to be happy about Mercury casually inserting talk of blood magic into her workshop about familiars. Even I knew that witches of the light didn't like to play with blood or demons. They considered such things a one-way trip into the darkness.

I didn't disagree.

I also didn't interject when Aiden used blood in his training with Opal. He was exceedingly clear about what applications he thought were worth the possible risks, and he watched the young witch closely. But even my dark sorcerer wouldn't be pleased with his daughter being taught binding spells based in blood. Binding spells meant to subjugate a target's will, assuming I had properly grasped what Mercury had been about to suggest before Scarlett cut her off.

Burgundy's eyes lit up as she stepped around Scarlett and spotted Aiden and me hovering in the background. "Oh, Emma!" She stopped herself from barreling toward me to acknowledge the sorcerer. "And Aiden, hi."

Scarlett turned, eyeing us with a slight frown. Apparently, she hadn't heard us or felt our presence, likely because we were all surrounded by so much magic. Plus Aiden was rather skilled at masking himself when he wanted to do so, and I held everything that made me so ultimately terrible as tightly as I could. So much so that it was second nature, though I'd had to work at reinforcing that hold after the Hallowed. Over and over again.

"Hello, Burgundy," the sorcerer said, amused. Then he stepped forward to murmur something to Scarlett. She nodded stiffly in response, and they both glanced over at Mercury.

The other witch huffed, tapping her foot and drawing the goblin cat's attention to her red-painted toenails.

"Um, Emma?" Burgundy asked, grinning tentatively. "Opal thought you might be able to lead a demo tomorrow...there's a free slot at 3:00 P.M. On the application of amplification in spellcasting. My friend Gabby is also an amplifier, but she...I mean, I've worked with her before, and she's brilliant, but she doesn't come to the retreats, so not many of the others have had the same chance. A few of us are working on larger ongoing projects, and a careful application of...um, amplification...would...I mean, it could help. Right?"

She finally took a breath, allowing me time to respond.

"Yes."

I was all in. Even if I had to go way out of my comfort zone, I would do anything asked of me to help cement Opal's position in the coven. I also had no problem playing the part of a regular amplifier. My other abilities might continually leak, but I wasn't going to accidentally start draining or beguiling someone during a practical demonstration.

"Yes! Really? I know you don't have to...you aren't technically a member of the coven...and honestly, Pearl pretty much ordered me not to ask you, but..." Burgundy shrugged, grinning broadly. "You were standing right here."

I laughed quietly, suddenly liking the healer in training. A lot. It was bold of her to approach me when her coven leader had told her not to. "I can only amplify people, though. Not spells."

"Oh, I understand! Same as with Gabby. But we do these individual projects...like goal setting, you know? Some of us might just need a tiny boost to master the spells. And working with an amplifier is totally different than pulling magic from a circle. Like, in a battle, you have to work with the allies you have, and not be so overwhelmed because you haven't practiced with every resource you could when the opportunity presented itself that you falter."

I blinked at her, having no idea what battles a coven healer would expect to find herself in the midst of...or had already been involved in?

Burgundy flushed. Then she bit her lip, casting her gaze somewhere around my shoulder. "Maybe...it's silly..."

"No. It's not silly. It's very practical. Maybe we should work with more actionable spells rather than your projects. Things that a witch would need to call upon quickly, even without a circle to draw from. And if your amplifier friend, or another amplifier, was in the group, they could be the boost needed."

"Like…a sleep spell maybe?" Burgundy said excitedly. "Normally, that's used for healing, but it could be used offensively if boosted, like you said."

I nodded. "Or for the other witches, a stun or confusion spell."

Burgundy bounced on her heels, then noticed Scarlett watching her with an amused expression. She laughed, then took off at a jog. "I just have to grab my kit from my room, Scarlett!"

The strawberry-blond witch laughed quietly. Then she turned back to eye Mercury.

The British witch sniffed derisively. "A coven needs to use all its resources, Scarlett." She waved toward me. "Even your junior healer understands that."

"Emma, Aiden," Scarlett said, quietly but firmly dismissive. "Will we see you at dinner?"

"Of course," Aiden said, stepping back toward me.

Allowing Scarlett to brush us off, we crossed down the path together. But we could still easily hear Mercury as we left the witches behind.

"Why ask me to speak if you don't want my expertise?" she said coldly.

"The Godfreys don't condone blood magic," Scarlett snapped.

"Tell that to whoever erected the wards around that bakery of yours," Mercury snapped back.

I glanced at Aiden, who shook his head. Then we were too far away to catch the rest of the argument.

Nothing in Mercury's perspective was a surprise to me, of course. The Collective had trained the Five—literally from the womb in my case—to use all the methods at our disposal. If blood magic offered power, the morality of using it wouldn't have remotely been a factor. But that certainly wasn't the childhood I wanted for Opal. So if that meant siding with the judgemental witches, I would do so.

Well, mostly. I did have a demon dog to find and protect.

"The meeting with Pearl has been set for 2:00 P.M. tomorrow," Aiden murmured, confirming my assumption of what he'd been speaking of with Scarlett. "The coven leader does general office hours when she's not teaching during the retreat."

"We should take Paisley with us."

"Really?"

"I don't like the cards Christopher is pulling. Sage. Wisdom. Basil. Strength."

"You usually wait for something a little...with a little more clarity from the clairvoyant before acting on it."

"If someone is playing a long game with us," I snarled quietly, "then we'll play those cards to our advantage."

"Protection," Aiden murmured thoughtfully. "That's doubled between the two cards."

"Yes. So…we'll protect. And thwart any attempts at being undermined. The witches will accept Paisley, and we'll make reparations. Because they desperately need Opal."

Aiden's lips quirked.

"What?" I snapped.

He allowed his grin to fully manifest. "So fierce, my amplifier."

I laughed, surprised at my husky tone—and how quickly I still responded to my deadly sorcerer. "What are you going to do about it?"

He opened his mouth to reply, but I spun away and took off down the path.

Aiden lunged for me, his fingers slipping through my hair.

Keeping my pace in check and sticking to the more private paths so our chase wasn't misconstrued, I didn't let the sorcerer catch me until I found the perfect moss-covered tree.

It was my turn to do the pinning, and I didn't want my sorcerer's skin taking any damage in the process.

Christopher could try to track Paisley from the property as a next step. He had access to items she touched daily, which might make a more effective base for a tracking spell. Presumably, the clairvoyant had already checked in with Samantha to determine whether the demon dog had joined her in order to avoid me.

But Aiden and I could take a slight break.

Fifteen minutes max.

Similar to taking an early-afternoon tea…but without the tea or ginger snaps.

FIVE

WHEN A TEXT MESSAGE FINALLY CAME THROUGH, IT wasn't the one I'd been waiting for—namely, an update from Christopher. And yes, I was pacing the hotel room by that point. I was thankful that Aiden, who had pulled a few books via his suit pockets from his library at home, was focused and steady as usual.

If Christopher's tracking spells fizzled, as our second and third attempts had done, we were going to try to summon Paisley. But even Aiden, as dark a sorcerer as he'd been bred to be, hadn't ever actually summoned a full-blooded demon, let alone a demon hybrid. So he was unsure of how to do so safely—and without binding Paisley to his will. Or to my will, though it was unlikely that I'd be able to trigger the summoning spell with my own magic.

Aiden had been making notes, texting his contacts, then going back over both notes and texts to craft a summoning spell for almost two hours.

And yes, we were procrastinating. Hoping that the demon dog eventually just went home to Christopher or showed up back at the hotel.

The text was from Samantha. And unless she had Paisley, I didn't even remotely want to hear from the telekinetic. I didn't want to be pulled into whatever mess she and Fish were in the process of making under the guise of tracking down Bee.

>*I need the dog.*
>*Paisley.*
>*Fish still hasn't surfaced.*

"I thought Samantha and Daniel already met up?" I asked Aiden.

The dark-haired sorcerer didn't look up from the pentagram he was sketching in his notebook. "They did, last night. Well, last night their time. They're in Russia somewhere...or Ukraine?"

"Apparently not," I muttered, typing out a response on my phone.

I thought you were already with Daniel?
>*He didn't make it back to the hotel last night.*
And you're only texting now?!
>*He left the bar with someone else. Voluntarily.*
So you were drinking while on a mission.
>*You are such an asshole. We're allowed to have lives.*
Not if you then need to involve me.
>*It's the damn dog I'm trying to involve! You think you'd give a shit about Fish being missing.*

And now you're contradicting yourself. Is he fucking around, or is he missing?

>I don't know why I even bother with you.

>Why do you even have a phone?

Christopher forced one on me.

>Are you going to send Paisley or not?

I stared down at the request, seriously loath to admit that I wasn't actually in contact with the demon dog. I had assumed that Christopher would have been keeping Samantha updated. And even if I knew where Paisley was, the demon dog didn't seem to be in the mood to take orders from me—let alone requests from Samantha, who Paisley still hadn't fully forgiven for treating her like a dog.

Not.

>Screw you, Emma.

Text Christopher next time. I'm busy.

>You're always too busy for any of us.

I'm trying to finalize Opal's adoption.

The three little dots indicating that Samantha was typing flashed on my screen. Then there was a long pause—probably the telekinetic deleting her response. Then a new message appeared.

>Right. Sorry. I forgot. That is more important.

I blinked down at the message, completely surprised at Samantha's sudden ability to think of anyone but herself. I couldn't even pretend she was being sarcastic, because she adored Opal.

I'll ask Paisley to find you when I see her next.

>*See her next? Christopher said she was with you.*

Ah, that was why I was fielding text messages. The clairvoyant definitely hadn't been forthcoming.

It's possible that she's avoiding me.

>*She's in trouble? With you? This is because you're such a hard-ass, Socks.*

>*Though I would have thought it impossible for Paisley to ignore you.*

Which is why she hasn't been in my vicinity since last night.

>*You don't think she's hurt, do you?*

No. Keep me posted about Daniel.

>*Really?*

No. Keep Christopher posted.

>*That's more like it.*

Samantha ended the conversation with a string of emoticons, or emojis, or whatever they were called. I didn't bother deciphering the symbols. If it wasn't important enough for actual words, then it wasn't important enough for me to read.

Aiden was frowning down at the sketch of a pentagram before him—one of five options he'd devised, though I couldn't discern the differences he'd presumably embedded within each one. Then the sorcerer lightly retraced the footprint of the summoning spell he was working on, over and over again. Thoughtfully.

Worried.

"You don't think Paisley's hurt, do you?" I asked. Not liking the thin, needy quality of my tone, but not able to take it back once I finally voiced the concern.

"No," Aiden said, immediately reaching for me. He rubbed my arms lightly.

"The raven…I know Paisley hunts. I mean, we've paid for two of the Wilsons' cows, though only the first was a sanctioned kill…but a…a familiar is imbued with magical properties…and…"

I sighed, not bothering to complete the thought. Aiden knew what was worrying me, even without me vocalizing it, and sometimes I just couldn't. The words got stopped up in my throat. Doing, acting, wielding my magic or my blades was so, so much easier than hanging around a hotel room and waiting…waiting…waiting…just like this damn adoption—

"Emma…" Aiden said gently.

I tensed.

Aiden firmed his tone, became matter-of-fact. "Paisley ate those flowers that were somehow tied to the Hallowed. You said she ate the spikes that the mystic's twin black witches used to anchor their spells." He was referring to Chenda, the self-styled Mystic of the Golden Peninsula. Another of the Collective's former members. "And I've personally seen her swallow and spit out heavy-duty curses. She attempted to eat one of the Cameron coven grimoires that I obtained rather…well, illegally, depending on who's interested in enforcing the sale of black magic items."

"What?! When?"

Aiden huffed. "She was pissed that I wouldn't let her cast one of the animation spells."

I inhaled. Deeply. "What did she want to animate?"

Aiden made a dismissive noise in the back of his throat. It sounded like it was loaded with guilt.

I stared him down.

"That chick... that little pullet that Christopher had to put down."

"It might have had Marek's disease," I seethed. I had hated that we'd had to put down one of the chicks we'd hatched in the spring. But it had been limping and lethargic, and something like Marek's could spread through the entire flock. "It was in pain!"

"Well, had the demon dog managed to reanimate it, I guess it wouldn't have been in pain any longer."

I glared at him. "Not funny, sorcerer."

"Emma," he said placatingly. "I didn't let her try."

"But you let her read the damn grimoire!"

The door to the suite burst open, hitting the stopper hard. Then Opal barreled into the living room area, grinning widely and streaming magic in her wake. "Guess what we learned today!" She opened her palm, revealing the broken pieces of an ash-white sand-dollar shell. "Watch!"

Aiden touched my shoulder lightly, acknowledging the fight we were in the process of having but wanting to set it aside for the moment. I didn't want to be fighting in the first place. I was doing so only because I was so tense.

As one, we stepped forward to peer down at Opal's hand. By unspoken agreement, we were trying to not upset the young witch. So until we'd exhausted all the means of finding Paisley at our disposal, Opal didn't need to know how concerned we were about the demon dog.

Most likely concerned for absolutely no reason. Paisley got into sulks all the time.

She just didn't usually do so while off the property. Or after disobeying a direct order from me.

I shoved that thought away, focusing on the present. Which, I reminded myself, was exactly where I wanted to be.

A whisper of power writhed around Opal's hand. She screwed up her face. Then, with a quiet grunt of concentration and a push of energy from the little witch, the sand dollar's shattered pieces sealed together. Loosely.

Panting gleefully, Opal looked up at me. "It's a variation on a healing spell! If I practice, soon I'll be able to do it without any cracks."

"Brilliant," I said, giving in to the impulse to gently touch the ends of her curls.

Opal bounced on her heels, grinning madly and glancing between me and Aiden. "Dinner?"

"Yes. And then you need to get ready for the induction ceremony." Then I added teasingly, "I believe there was some meditation prep?"

Opal's smile faded slightly. "Right."

Her abrupt reluctance was palpable. And concerning. "Has something happened?" I asked. "With the witches?"

She shook her head. But she turned the cracked sand dollar over in her hands instead of meeting my eye.

My heart squelched.

I knew it. I knew that I would end up being an obstacle for the little witch. Or Paisley with the damn raven.

"No," Opal said quietly. "Everyone has been really nice."

"Do you not want to join the Godfrey coven?" I asked.

Aiden crouched, settling his hand under Opal's elbow. "We can keep looking for the right fit. Maybe the Sherwoods?" The Sherwoods were technically Opal's coven by blood.

"No, no! I like the Godfreys. I just…what if I'm not accepted…by the magic, I mean?"

"Explain," Aiden said. It wasn't a question. I could feel his rising anger even without touching him, though he kept his expression and voice neutral. Sorcerers and witches were traditionally at odds. Aiden was witch-born, but he certainly wouldn't accept any of the coven members making Opal feel even an iota of rejection.

"You feel it? On the beach? All the magic?" Opal blinked her wide, far-too-serious eyes at Aiden. "You feel that, right?"

"I do."

"I'm…I'm not sure it likes me. That power." Her gaze flicked to me, as if she was worried about admitting anything, any shortcoming in front of me. But Aiden was a safe confidant.

I had to swallow that. To understand that he and I played different roles in Opal's life. She needed the structure I provided. But I couldn't bond with her over spellcasting like Aiden could.

I touched her shoulder and led her over to the couch, curling up on one end myself. Aiden followed. Opal wedged herself between us, then awkwardly tugged the throw off the back of the couch to burrow underneath it.

The sorcerer met my gaze over her bowed head, grinning. I brushed my fingers across the back of his hand—he had his arm slung along the top of the couch, over Opal. The happiness rolling off him was almost overwhelming. He wasn't worried about the conversation at all.

So…this was normal…

Opal having doubts about herself, and coming to us about them, was perfectly normal. So normal that it made Aiden blissfully happy.

I grabbed onto the emotion rolling off the sorcerer and stole a bit for myself. Opal pushed back into my arms a little more, twisting to face Aiden, and that purloined happiness expanded into a tiny ball of lightness in my chest.

"What if I'm not good enough?" Opal asked the sorcerer earnestly.

"At spells?" Aiden asked. Though I knew by the way his fingers twined through mine that he'd heard the true intent behind Opal's question, and was just giving her a moment to clarify. "You're in the top five of your year."

"Top three," Opal interjected with a sniff. "Jack Fairchild and I are technically tied, but he didn't miss so many days of school."

I stifled a smile at her—interesting and self-serving—math.

"So…" Aiden said as he also swallowed a smile. "Good enough how?"

She squirmed slightly. "Like…I'm different. I had to…do things…before I found Emma."

"And…?" I smoothed my hand down her arm, hoping the touch of my magic was as comforting as I intended it to be.

"And…maybe I'm dark," she mumbled.

"Am I dark?" Aiden asked gently.

She shrugged, not looking at him.

"So…yes?" he asked, smiling.

"Emma calls you her dark sorcerer."

I actually felt myself blush at that. Aiden flashed me an almost feral grin. "That's, ah…" I cleared my throat. "That's a…love thing."

"A pet name?" Opal asked.

"Yes. Because if Aiden were truly dark, he wouldn't be able to find space in his heart for you, for me…for our life together."

"So, love is the opposite of darkness?" Opal tilted her head up at Aiden, asking for his clarification.

"Balance is what we all try to achieve. Especially those of us with darker pasts. Those of us who have done things to survive. But yes, I think I would have been lost to the darkness if I hadn't found Emma to anchor me. And you."

"What about Kader?" Opal asked, her tone almost sly. As if she was actively trying to look for loopholes in Aiden's logic.

"What about Kader?" I asked, my own tone on the edge of dangerous.

But Opal ignored me, waiting on Aiden's answer.

He grimaced. "My father has done some truly evil things."

"But he loves you."

"So he says. But our actions dictate who we are, truly. Not our words."

Opal hummed thoughtfully.

Aiden touched her knee, and she released her hold on the sand dollar to slip her hand under his. "The magic here dances in your wake, my darling daughter," he said gently. "It will rejoice when you take your place among the coven tonight. It will welcome you in all its ancient wildness, all its purity and light, under the full moon in the darkest hour of the day. Because it will only be reflecting those aspects of yourself."

"Do you understand?" I said, a little breathless at Aiden's words, his proclamation.

"Balance," Opal said, completely abandoning the sand dollar and finding my hand.

"We walk between the light and the dark," Aiden said. "Occasionally dipping off the path, but always striving to self-correct. With our focus both on the life we are striving to live, the present, and on what we want for our futures."

"Yes," I said, squeezing Opal's hand. "We do our best. We try to make decisions in the moment, knowing what we want our future to look like."

"So…I'm not tainted?"

"Who said you were tainted?" I asked in a low, vicious snarl.

"No one!" Opal squeaked. "I mean…I overheard some kids at the Academy talking about necromancers and black witches…and I…I might be a black witch. What if I'm a black witch? The coven will find out tonight, won't they?"

"You aren't a black witch," Aiden said gruffly. "I hate the fucking conditions that witches put on everything!"

"Not helpful," I chided without heat.

He huffed angrily.

"Emily said all necromancers go dark," Opal continued, speaking of another of her friends from

the Academy. "Jack and I didn't care. And honestly…"
She glanced at me, worried. "I really don't care."

"Opal…" I really didn't like the way she was
looking at me. "Are you planning to go around mur-
dering people in cold blood?"

"No!"

"Well, then?"

"That's it?"

"Yeah, that's it."

"What if I do other things?"

"Like what?"

She huffed as if exasperated. "Like eat someone's
familiar!"

"Is that what this is about? Paisley eating the
raven even though I told her to leave it?"

"No." And now she was being belligerent.

I had to quash another smile. God, sometimes I
just loved her so much. She was so perfect. Powerful
and intelligent. Fierce, loyal.

"But…" she added. "Paisley is part demon. She
is literally half dark."

"And you think demons are inherently evil?"
Aiden asked.

Opal blinked at him. "Aren't they?"

"I've never had a conversation with one," he
said, grinning at her. "So I'll reserve my judgement."

Opal threw her hands up in the air. "You're not
helping!"

I slid off the couch, kneeling before the dream
walker and taking her hands. "You are not evil. You

are not inherently dark. You aren't even half and half. You are whole and amazing. You are everything that has happened to you, yes. But you are also everything you are going to do in this world, including being a family with me and Aiden. And Christopher and Paisley."

"And Samantha," she added.

I pretended to internally debate the notion. "Yes, all right. And Samantha. Plus whoever else you choose to love. The Godfrey coven is lucky, so, so lucky that you want to join them. They will back you magically. And Aiden and I will back you with everything else."

Opal had screwed up her face, trying not to cry. But I had to finish what I needed to say...without tearing up myself.

"I love every part of you. There is nothing you can ever do that would make me turn away or leave you. Even if you ate someone's familiar."

Opal laughed wetly.

"Same," Aiden said gruffly.

"And...if the magic rejects me tonight?" she asked.

"Impossible," I said.

"But you don't believe in impossibilities." The little witch sucked on her upper lip.

"If...impossibly...something goes off during the induction ceremony and the magic rejects you tonight, the coven will accept you anyway."

"Really?"

"Oh, yes, my little witch," Aiden said. "You are that valuable."

"And we will love you either way." I tilted my head playfully. "Actually…maybe you'd be more interesting if the magic did reject you, dream walker."

"Emma!" she squealed, giggling.

I grabbed the blanket. Then, moving too quickly for the little witch to track, I cocooned her within it and tossed her into Aiden's waiting arms. He playfully held her in place while I tickled her.

She writhed and screeched, laughing.

Then I gathered her into my arms and pressed a kiss to her forehead. "I love you, Opal mine."

She wiggled her hand free from the blanket and pressed it to my cheek. "I love you, Mom."

I set her on her feet before I dissolved into tears, joy threading through me—with just a tinge of that terror that I felt whenever Opal called me Mom—and she pressed a kiss to Aiden's cheek.

Then, freeing the rest of herself from the blanket and setting her hands on her hips, Opal declared, "We only have a little more time for me to show you all the other things I learned today, because after dinner, Ocean is coming by to do my hair as soon as she finishes streaking hers."

"We are all yours," Aiden said, the words infused with heady emotion.

So I snuggled next to my dark sorcerer on the couch, smiling so much that my cheeks hurt, as Opal gave us a point-by-point rundown of her day. And I didn't once feel like an impostor. Like I was just posing or pretending to be someone I wasn't.

STANDING BESIDE THE FULL-LENGTH MIRROR SET ON the inside of one of the closet doors, Ocean smoothed her hands down Opal's royal-blue cloak one last time. Witch magic followed in the wake of her light touch. I couldn't see any remaining wrinkles, but Ocean had arrived utterly determined that we were all going to be 'beyond presentable' for the induction ceremony, then had spent the last two hours making certain of that.

Apparently, Aiden's sister was delighted with what she'd seen of the Godfrey coven in the last twenty-four hours, and had 'plans.' I doubted the Myers coven was going to enjoy the unfolding of those plans, but it also wasn't any of my business.

Ocean had hemmed Opal's custom-ordered cloak earlier in the evening, but it still swamped the dream walker's tiny frame over the simple black shift dress she wore beneath it, her legs and feet bare. And that was even with her halo of gold- and silver-streaked curls—extra curly and springy due to a liberal application of witch magic delivered via one of Ocean's hair tonics—adding an extra three inches to her height.

I was fairly certain that Ocean was using Opal to show off her cosmetic potion talents. Just a little.

And Aiden's smug look informed me that he was well aware of it as well.

Opal flicked her bright-blue eyes up to meet my gaze in the mirror. "It's okay, right?"

I forced myself to smile widely, finding that the heady emotion I was struggling to keep at bay was actually somewhat relieved to be given even a simple outlet. "Perfect."

Ocean was similarly cloaked, though hers was a rich cream in color. She and Opal both wore their hoods down, but Ocean had explained that all the witches except Juniper and Opal would be hooded for the ceremony.

Ocean's sheath dress matched the cream of her cloak and fell to her ankles. When she'd pulled the cloak on after doing both her and Opal's hair and makeup—only a light shimmery lip gloss for the little witch—I realized for the first time how much she looked like her mother, Cerise. The elder witch preferred to be swamped in shades of cream at all times. Apparently, it was the Myers coven color of choice.

The royal blue of the Godfreys was much more flattering.

And who was I all of a sudden? To be even remotely interested in, or have any opinion at all of, such things?

"I have something for you," Aiden said gruffly.

Opal spun around, her cloak flaring around her prettily. "Gimme, gimme."

Aiden, in a pristinely pressed light-gray suit, knelt on one knee and pulled a square wooden box out of his suit jacket pocket. Mahogany, I thought, inlaid with golden oak. A box that couldn't possibly have fit within that pocket without a liberal application of magic. "I know you've already picked out some options for your grounding stone."

Opal nodded. "I brought all three I found in the garden."

"And any of those would be a powerful choice, especially because the farm is your chosen home."

"But also because Emma has walked the earth there for years," Opal said earnestly. "And Christopher and you and Paisley and now Samantha."

"That is a hell of a power base," Ocean muttered, amused.

"Yes..." Aiden cleared his throat. "But...the Myers witches use crystals that are tuned to their magic."

Opal glanced over at Ocean. The older witch nodded, pulling a pale blue gemstone from her cloak pocket. It was cut but only smooth polished, and about the width of her palm. "Aquamarine. My birthstone. It was my great-grandmother's. She passed away right before my induction ceremony."

Aiden offered the box to Opal, holding it out to the dream walker in both hands.

She stepped forward, her expression serious as she opened the box and peeked inside. Her eyes widened, and she looked up at Aiden. "Really?"

"It's a fourth option, if you want it."

She reached into the box with both hands and pulled out a large amethyst cluster. A deep-purple stone with reddish tints.

Ocean made an appreciative noise.

"Amethyst," Opal whispered.

"How does it feel in your hands?"

"It…it hums."

"That's good!" Ocean exclaimed.

"More than the stones you chose from the property?" Aiden asked.

Opal nodded, her expression still very solemn. Maybe a little overwhelmed. "What if…what if I lose it?"

Ocean laughed. "You can't."

Aiden cast a slightly peeved look at his sister. Not liking her amusement, I thought.

"But…it's…something like this is really expensive, right?" Opal asked, still cupping the crystalline cluster in both hands.

"It was…a significant investment," Aiden said carefully. "In your future."

"The induction ceremony will involve you claiming the crystal," Ocean said, laying her hand on Opal's shoulder. "Even if you accidentally leave it behind, you will always be able to find it. Some really powerful witches can just call their grounding crystals to them."

"But…" Opal sounded like she was on the verge of crying. "What if someone tries to steal it?"

Aiden pulled a black velvet pouch out of the bottom of the box, holding it up. No, not black. A deep-purple velvet. "I've spelled the pouch."

Opal grinned tentatively. "And you'll teach me how to renew the spell."

"I will."

"You don't want anyone else to touch the stone after you claim it," Ocean said. "So the pouch is perfect. I only use mine in formal settings, like tonight, so I just leave it in my cloak pocket." She made a show of dropping it back into a pocket practically hidden in the generous folds of her cloak.

Someone knocked at the door.

"That's Lani," Ocean said, spinning to answer it.

Aiden touched Opal lightly on the shoulder. "You can use one of the stones from home."

She met his gaze steadily. "You researched this for me."

"I did."

"You found the best gemstone you could."

"It's from a witch in Thunder Bay, Ontario. Canada. A Myers witch, whose family has been involved in mining amethyst for decades. So the stone took no damage when harvested, and collected no malignant energies from touch or during transport. It is as close to pristine as it would have been had you been an expert lapidary and plucked it from the earth yourself."

"Ready?" Lani called from the doorway. She was wearing a simple teal linen dress that fell to her ankles. No cloak, as she was merely an observer, as were

Aiden and I. "The witches are already gathering and heading for the beach."

Opal carefully tipped the amethyst cluster into the velvet bag, cinched the silk drawstring ties, and pressed a kiss to Aiden's cheek. "Thank you, Aiden!" Then she practically skipped down the short hall, the velvet-bagged crystal swinging from her wrist as she joined Ocean and Lani.

Aiden bowed his head, absorbing the moment. Then he stood and met my gaze. I reached up, running my fingers across his once-again clean-shaven jaw, then weaving them back into his hair. He pressed his forehead against mine, breathing steadily.

"I…I just don't want to overly influence her magic," he said gruffly.

"I don't think we have to worry about Opal finding her own path, taking the opportunities that are right for her," I murmured. "She found her way to us. She demanded to stay. I'd never have her out of my sight if I had the choice."

Aiden laughed quietly. "Same."

I shrugged, trying to be the lightness the sorcerer currently needed. I knew, even without being able to read his mind, that thoughts of his own childhood and everything Kader had crafted him to be were heavily influencing his mood and actions.

"But she also chose the Academy," I said. "And now the coven. Opal knows what she wants. And we'll be with her when she falters, when she needs a moment to regroup, when she needs encouragement—"

Aiden covered my mouth with his own in a fierce, demanding kiss. I allowed myself to curve into his hard hold, welcoming him, anchoring him.

The door clicked back open.

Ocean muttered, "They're doing it again."

"Emma! Aiden!" Opal cried from farther up the exterior hall. "We can't be late!"

Aiden broke the kiss, laughing quietly.

"See?" I whispered. "If anything, she dictates to us."

Aiden hummed thoughtfully, his smile full of joy as he threaded his fingers through mine and started for the door. "Let's go witness our little girl become a coven witch."

I tried to reply, but the words got all tangled up in a sharp well of emotion. All I could do was grip his hand tightly and just hold on. Just hold him and accept the moment, as I could a blow or a wound, and still keep moving forward.

Sometimes loving a person as fragile as Opal made my chest ache as badly as the residual from taking a death curse. But I would never trade that pain for an easier time. Not ever.

SIX

"STRAWBERRY MOON," OPAL WHISPERED, GAZING UP at the bright full moon in the dark, slightly cloudy sky. We had just stepped through the edge of the forest onto the beach. It was almost midnight.

The witches had given Opal a detailed map of the series of paths we'd taken from the hotel, leading us farther down the beach than we'd explored earlier, near an outcropping that looked to be accessible only at low tide. The maps hadn't been all that necessary in the end, as we could have just followed the tiny pinpoints of light that flared along the edges of the path as the younger witches led the way through the mossy forest—light-blue witch lights reacting to their inherent magic.

The tide was about halfway up the beach, the surf still throwing its long, white-capped wake across the dense wet sand. A steady pulse that seemed inevitable, even relentless.

I ignored that weird thought, focusing on the gathering of cloaked figures a few meters farther along the beach, keeping to the drier packed sand. The entire coven, I thought, counting even more witches than I'd seen at either the tea or the dinner. Apparently, attendance was mandatory for the induction ceremony.

Everyone was barefoot, including Ocean and Opal. Lani and I had removed our sandals to step onto the sand. Aiden might have been the only one on the beach wearing shoes. All but four of the witches wore the same royal-blue cloak as Opal.

Juniper, grinning madly and clad in that same blue, scrambled over to us. I could feel magic sparking off the young witch in a gentle effervescence. The raw, wild power under our feet rose to meet each of her footfalls.

She grabbed Opal's hands and squealed quietly, trying to contain herself and doing a terrible job of it. "Ready?"

Opal grinned back. "Ready."

Ocean stepped around us, touching Opal lightly on the shoulder as she passed. She was the only witch wearing cream, but three other witches standing on the edge of the main grouping denoted their other-coven status with cloaks of dark green, red, and navy blue. As Ocean neared the visiting coven members, she tugged her own hood up over her head, completely obscuring her face.

The goblin cat poked its head out from underneath the witch swathed in dark green, batting playfully at the hem of Ocean's cream cloak as she slipped into place. So the Dunkirk color was green. Mercury didn't bother acknowledging Ocean, but the witch in red and the witch in navy both turned to greet her. Not that I could hear any conversation over the crashing of the waves.

"What's with the different cloaks?" Lani asked Aiden.

"Royal blue is the Godfrey coven." Aiden touched my shoulder lightly, halting our forward progress to keep us a couple of meters back from Ocean and the other visiting witches. "Dark green for Dunkirk. Navy for Cameron. And I believe the red is a Medici witch. All covens that hold seats on the Convocation. With Ocean in attendance, that's representatives from six of the thirteen seats present to witness Opal's induction."

Lani laughed quietly. "You don't have to sound so smug about it, Aiden. And your math is off. Five different colors. Five seats, not six."

"You're forgetting your cheat sheet, Lani," Aiden said, highly amused. "Scarlett currently holds the thirteenth seat. That's two for the Godfreys."

Lani snorted playfully.

My gaze settled on Pearl Godfrey as the royal-blue-cloaked witches all shifted forward to form a large circle, standing with at least a meter between each of them. She stood just back from center of that circle, her cloak bearing some sort of silver design woven into the edges and hem, presumably distinguishing her as the coven leader. Her hood was still back. Her long, wavy silver hair was unbound, catching the moonlight.

Unlit white pillar candles were arrayed around the witches, set into the sand. A smaller circle of four candles was set closer to Pearl, in white, red, blue, and green. Elemental candles, Opal had called them. Pearl stood next to the green pillar. Green for earth.

A royal-blue-cloaked witch turned and beckoned toward Opal and Juniper. I caught a glimpse of strawberry-blond hair and a hint of a smile, but Scarlett's hood otherwise obscured her face.

Juniper tugged Opal forward with her, but my little witch turned to look back at me.

I smiled, though it was the last thing I felt like doing.

Opal reached back for me. Juniper took a few steps forward, but then waited. The dream walker wrapped herself around me, pressing her cheek to my chest and gripping me as hard as she could.

"You don't have to do this," I murmured. "If you don't want to."

Opal shook her head. "This is the best thing I can do…" She peered up at me, her blue eyes already rimmed in the even brighter blue of her witch magic. "This is how I protect us."

Something cracked in the center of my chest, flooding my system with a phantom pain. An emotional response, mixed with a spike of adrenaline. I chided myself internally, struggling to stop myself from simply snatching up the little witch and fleeing into the dark forest.

The little witch who'd chosen me. Chosen us.

Aiden pressed his hand against my lower back.

"Like we talked about," Opal continued. "That day? On the bench by the river? About me going to school and becoming so strong that no one could ever ignore me again. Ignore what I wanted. Right?"

"No one is going to stop me from keeping you," I said, my voice hard, and nowhere near the tone I ever wanted to use when addressing Opal. But I couldn't seem to soften it. And the words were wrong as well. But they were the only ones I had. "You belong to me. I protect you."

"I know." She shrugged. "But this will help. Allegiances are important. Plus..." She squinted her eyes thoughtfully, as if recollecting something. "It's better to know who might come for you. To know their weaknesses and strengths."

I narrowed my eyes at her. "That's not..."

"Got to go!" She released me, grabbing Juniper's hand. Then together, they ran toward Scarlett, kicking up sand behind them.

Lani stepped up to my left, her hands deep in the pockets of her long dress. Her attention was riveted to the witches, but if anything was tweaking her senses, she didn't mention it.

"Weaknesses and strengths?" Pressing my shoulder to Aiden's, I leaned closer to him. "Where is she hearing that sort of garbage?" I didn't bother with knowing my enemy. I just dealt with each threat the same way—quickly and definitively.

Well, except for the threats that were blood related to someone I loved. Then I was forced to withdraw. But that unfortunate hindrance was relatively new.

"My father," Aiden said darkly. "That's my father's garbage she's quoting." He grimaced. "Though for those of us who can't simply drain the people who annoy us with a single touch, it is a fair truth."

"I don't have to touch someone to drain them," I said silkily.

Aiden flashed me a grin, but it faded as he returned his attention to the gathering of witches.

"Opal hasn't met Kader."

"That we know of," he muttered darkly.

"But...the contract you made him sign...in blood. It covered any contact with Opal."

"It did."

"Then..."

He looked at me, then sighed. "It didn't include her reaching out to him."

"But...she..."

"Is ridiculously clever."

Opal was clever.

"And very, very skilled at getting what she wants," the sorcerer added.

"She's a survivor," I said stiffly.

"Yes," Aiden said. "And she's nowhere near as powerful as the family she wants to be part of."

"She's thirteen."

"You and I know that. But she's just coming to understand that the more knowledge she has, the better chance she has of survival, because she has to wait and train to gain magic, power. A relationship with my father—"

"Isn't going to happen," I snapped.

Aiden nodded, looking down and casting his face into deep shadow. He swallowed, then just said, "Of course. As you wish."

I opened my mouth, then realized I had nothing to say. I reached for his emotions instead, trying to figure out if I'd upset him.

But Pearl Godfrey's voice whispered across the beach, carried on magic. "We begin."

All the candles on the beach flared except for the white and the red pillar set before the coven leader.

The hooded witch I'd identified as Scarlett Godfrey directed Opal and Juniper through the outer candles, leading them toward the unlit pillars. White for Opal, representing the element of air. And red for Juniper, representing the element of fire.

Scarlett paused before the already-lit blue candle. Blue for water. All the other Godfrey witches were in place, each before one of the white pillar candles, forming a larger circle that encompassed the smaller elemental circle. Pearl stood at the connection point with her back to the pounding surf. The four visiting members stood outside the larger circle, directly opposite the coven leader. Official witnesses of some sort. With Aiden, Lani, and me as lesser observers. Which made me realize that Juniper didn't have any other family members present, except her aunt and sponsor, Olive, who was among the cloaked Godfrey witches.

"Connected circles?" Lani asked Aiden quietly. "Using a circle to focus casting was mentioned in a couple of lectures today, but nothing like this."

Aiden nodded. "This is a consecutive design. Pearl at the peak of the smallest circle, which also includes Scarlett, Opal, and Juniper. Pearl is the anchor point. And if you drew a line in the sand, you'd see that they also stand within the larger circle, framed by all the other witches. Those two circles meet under Pearl's feet."

He then gestured toward Ocean, Mercury, and the two other visiting witches, all of whom were now holding lit candles. "And the visiting members, the witnesses, stand in a smaller circle. We can't see it from here, but I assume it's been etched in the sand and loosely looped into the larger. So when Opal is inducted, she's tied directly to Pearl, Scarlett, and Juniper, then through Pearl to the rest of the coven. But only a minimal tie to the visiting members. Enough that they could cast together but not share magic."

"So..." Lani's voice was so quiet I could barely hear her over the surf. "Coven members can't harm each other?"

Aiden shrugged. "Anything is possible, of course. But they'll hesitate to hurt another coven witch because it will have repercussions. Both magically and through Pearl. Covens draw their power cooperatively...and for the Godfreys specifically, they draw a lot of it, given what I can feel from this location alone."

Aiden flashed his teeth at me in something that wasn't quite a smile. "You've found our little witch the most powerful coven in the world. And that's not even counting the nonwitches."

"Opal chose," I said stiffly. Not acknowledging that I had factored what little I'd known of the Godfrey coven into the decision to move to Lake Cowichan in the first place.

Aiden just smirked at me.

I ignored him, fighting the urge to grin back.

Pearl smiled at the two young witches before her. Juniper was almost as tall as the elder witch, but Opal was still tiny. In my eyes, at least. Then the coven leader invited them to light their candles with a flick of her fingers. With her hood still back, I could clearly see Pearl's lips moving, but I couldn't hear the words.

"Silencing spell?" I asked Aiden.

He snorted. "Damn secretive witches."

"And maybe possible mundanes in the area?" Several large houses were tucked into the forest that lined the shore of the long beach, but only a few of those properties—no doubt outrageously expensive—had any lights visible from where we stood. It was moments from midnight, and according to Lani, local surfers preferred to get an early start before tourists flooded the area.

Aiden chuckled. "The entire forest, every pathway, is layered with spells to turn back the mundanes. The circles are sealed as well."

And I had walked through it all without even noticing. So had Lani.

Aiden chuckled quietly.

I gave him a look, and he raised both hands, palms out. But his grin widened. The sorcerer was enjoying himself. And with so much magic at play, I wasn't surprised. I spared a glance for Lani, but she seemed unaffected.

I narrowed my eyes at the gathered witches, trying to see through all the magic I could feel to figure out what they were doing to induct Opal. Watching for anything I didn't like.

Aiden leaned in and whispered against my neck, "Goddess of mine."

I shivered, and not just with desire. Then I continued to ignore him as Opal cupped her hands around her candle and coaxed it to light without a word or a rune. I couldn't see the magic she commanded, but I grinned at the effortless result.

She had lined up every candle in the house two nights ago for a last round of practice—with Aiden and Ocean critiquing her technique. Because apparently, it wasn't just about lighting the candle, but the ease with which she did so.

Juniper snapped her fingers above the wick of her red pillar. The candle flared, then guttered.

Opal visibly held her breath, exhaling in a rush when her new friend's candle recovered, blazing with light.

Grinning, both girls turned their eyes to Pearl. She reached her hands toward them, and they each took one, then joined their own. Scarlett was left out of the even-tighter circle that embrace created. More magically muffled words fell from the coven leader's lips. A wind born of the wild energy that gently thrummed under our feet stirred Pearl's long, silvered hair, until I swore I could see crackles of blue energy between and around the glossy tresses.

The candles of the outer circle flared. Magic rose and fell, as if all the coven witches were chanting to its rhythm, or perhaps conducting that rhythm. But with their hoods up, I still couldn't see much of their faces.

Pearl released the girls' hands and reached back for her own hood, pulling it up. Not enough to obscure her face, though. For the briefest of moments, I swore I could see that blue lightning twine around her forearms and wrists and between her fingers.

I glanced at Aiden.

He nodded, not taking his gaze off the ceremony.

Opal and Juniper pulled their grounding stones out of their cloak pockets, each holding her stone before her chest in both hands.

More talking, the girls seemingly echoing back whatever Pearl was saying.

The amethyst began glowing in Opal's hands. So much so that I caught the little witch's glance at

Juniper's mostly white quartz stone. It wasn't anywhere near as luminescent.

Aiden's grin was wide and smug.

I knocked him with my shoulder playfully.

He rubbed his arm, feigning being hurt, but still couldn't stop himself from grinning. His magic was so bright in his eyes that it almost obscured them. "Only the best for my girls," he said.

Pearl reached forward, placing her hands over top of Juniper's and her grounding stone. They exchanged more words. Then the elder witch tugged Juniper's hood up and over her head. The young blond witch was grinning like mad, having a hard time staying still.

The magic the coven had pulled forth made me want to dance—and I never danced, not unless I was wielding a sword—so I understood that impulse.

Pearl then reached for Opal, wrapping her hands around the dream walker's wrists rather than covering the amethyst cluster as she'd covered Juniper's grounding stone.

Aiden hummed thoughtfully, even more pleased.

"It would be bad to touch the crystal, even for the coven leader?" Lani asked quietly. Though she understood as little of it as I did, she was obviously studying every last nuance of the ceremony.

"Not bad. It's just that Pearl doesn't want to disrupt the power already contained there," Aiden said. "Opal doesn't need any help tying the amethyst to her magic. Claiming it."

Opal was echoing whatever Pearl was saying now. The magic that had been undulating around the circle seemed to condense, quieting for a moment.

"The vows of fealty," I muttered, recalling the brief outline Ocean had given us about a typical induction ceremony. For the Myers coven, at least. I was still displeased about any vows being exchanged.

"You want to give her everything you can," Aiden said gently. "Inducted into the Godfrey coven, she can go anywhere in the world with their protection. When we can't be there...or even when she doesn't want us at her back. Say, at the Academy. She is now a Godfrey witch with the most powerful amplifier in the world as her mother. She'll have her choice of classes, of specialties, of position within the coven and our world. She'll have other Adepts at her feet."

"If that's what she wants," I said.

He laughed quietly. "Yes, always."

Pearl drew Opal's hood over her head.

The magic that had quieted now thrummed even fuller than before. Because that magic, that seemingly bottomless energy, was tied to the power of a dream walker. Fledgling or not.

"Maybe she wants to stay with us, at the farm," I said stiffly. "After she graduates. Maybe she'll want that."

"Maybe," Aiden murmured doubtfully.

"I'd never hold her back," I said, acknowledging the shadow of the lie even as I voiced it. Oh, I wanted.

I wanted to hang on to Opal, to keep her close and cherished. But I would never cage her.

Aiden threaded his fingers through mine. "As much as we'd both like to…"

I leaned into him, just for a moment. Another acknowledgement of those needs that we shared, of the darkness that we both actively shoved away every day.

The candles went out. All at once.

Then Scarlett threw her hood back and stepped forward, grasping the girls' shoulders and smiling down at them both.

The other witches broke ranks, mingling and chatting as they created a loose line behind Scarlett to formally welcome Opal and Juniper into the coven.

"That's it?" I asked Aiden. "It's done?"

"It's done."

Well…that was a little…underwhelming.

Aiden's shoulders stiffened. Then he cocked his head to the side, listening to something I couldn't hear. He released my hand and slowly rotated, taking in the beach, the crashing surf, then the forest behind us.

Pearl abruptly stepped away from the circle, from the witches she'd been chatting with.

The two witches who'd been collecting the candles paused, one still crouched over, one in the process of dropping a candle in her satchel.

I couldn't hear anything over the crashing of the surf. I couldn't feel anything beyond the wild power undulating under my...

That energy had shifted.

Again.

The rhythm was more...chaotic.

I wasn't usually sensitive to such things, but—

"Emma..." Aiden growled. His baseball bat suddenly appeared in his hand, borne there all the way from the property by unvoiced command. The runes etched over every centimeter of the wood flared with dark-blue energy. The dark-haired sorcerer's eyes blazed with his power in a matching hue.

Sandals abandoned, I was already running.

Even before Aiden finished whatever warning he was about to give, I was already running for Opal, leaving the sorcerer in my wake.

"From above!" Lani yelled.

My step hitched because I'd forgotten about the intuitive, but Opal spun, seeking me out with her wide eyes bright with power. I dug into the sand and increased my pace.

The attack did come from above.

Silent and borne on wings.

No reactionary cries rose from the gathered witches as I dashed through their ranks. No, they all remained cool with their feet firmly planted, snapping shimmering light-blue shields around themselves and their neighbors.

I would have been impressed, except I only had eyes for Opal. A magical barrier of slightly darker-blue power snapped up, covering the entire main circle, including me, but I was already reaching for the little witch. She was clutching her amethyst crystal in one hand and Juniper's hand in the other.

Multiple somethings hit the shields overhead. But I didn't bother to look up.

Pearl was issuing orders, calm and steady.

I could feel smaller explosions of power beyond the witch shield—Aiden wielding his bat.

"What are those?" Juniper screamed, her gaze fixed overhead.

"Seagulls?" Opal set her wide eyes on me. "Emma? Can seagulls go rabid?"

I didn't answer her. I simply grabbed her forearm and started dragging her back toward Aiden. The little witch towed Juniper in her wake.

The other witches let us pass.

Beyond the main shield, the dark-haired sorcerer was grinning madly. He was completely un-shielded as he almost casually swung his bat at what indeed appeared to be dive-bombing seagulls. But up close, they were much larger and sharper beaked than regular gulls, with beady red eyes that I suspected might be magic at play rather than naturally occurring in seabirds.

Two strides from the edge of the circle that Aiden was keeping clear—but still within the witch circle—the sand under our feet started to churn.

Small mounds appeared, then exploded to disgorge crabs of all sizes and shapes.

Both Opal and Juniper shrieked. I snagged Juniper's forearm, worried that Opal would lose hold of her friend if she tugged too hard.

Scratching and nipping, the crabs swarmed our bare feet and ankles.

Well, that made the decision easy.

I yanked the young witches beyond the nebulous protection of the crab-infested circle, braving the dive-bombing seagulls.

The witches were chanting softly in unison. Not a single one of them had broken rank and fled. But I would wait to be impressed until after I got the girls to safe ground.

As I ran for Aiden, I had no idea if we were truly under coordinated attack, or if this disturbance had just been inadvertently called forth by the powerful induction ceremony. And if it was an attack, I had no idea who it was directed toward, as it was seemingly focused on all the witches at once.

Reaching Aiden, he snapped a shield around the three of us with a flick of his fingers. And was still lazily taking out any seagull stupid enough to come too close.

"Show-off," I muttered, grinning at him despite the oddness of the situation.

He laughed, darkly delighted, power spilling all around him. Juniper's gaze snagged on him, and her jaw dropped and stayed down. The sorcerer was magnificent.

I spared a glance over at Ocean and Lani.

Mercury Dunkirk was holding a shield over both of them. Ocean looked rather put out—so I gathered she was trapped within that shield and feeling useless. Lani met my gaze, then just shrugged as if this sort of thing happened to her all the time.

I laughed. I couldn't help it.

The witches' overall shield shifted, becoming denser. It was a safe guess that it was being anchored deeper and deeper into the earth in an attempt to stop the flow of crabs.

A mound appeared by our feet. Then two more. Another wave of red-and-brown-shelled crabs exploded up through the sand.

"Meet you at the hotel?" Aiden asked.

I nodded. Then with the crabs already swarming the shield the sorcerer was holding over us, I tugged the girls with me back to the path, keeping my pace slow enough that I wasn't just dragging them. Aiden's powerful shield moved with us.

"Wow!" Juniper cried, speaking to Opal. "A mobile shield?"

"Yep!" Opal said proudly.

Leaving the dry sand, the grabby crabs, and the weirdly possessed seagulls behind, we skirted a few weathered logs that delineated the edge of the beach. Then we hit the trees, and the forest closed around us. The moonlight barely penetrated the thick, heavy-limbed evergreens. The packed dirt was cool under our bare feet, but I remembered that the path turned into a boardwalk up ahead. I hoped the girls wouldn't get any more scratched up than they already were.

"Was that…is that unusual, Emma?" Opal asked quietly.

I slowed my pace, noting both girls attempting to gaze back at the beach. "I would think so."

"Maybe they were drawn to the magic?" Juniper asked, nearly tripping over her own feet. "That was a lot of magic. More than I've ever felt before."

"Eyes forward," I barked, scanning the darkened forest. Both girls flinched, but they obeyed as I drew them onto the boardwalk and kept moving steadily forward. With the attack seemingly localized at the beach, getting the girls away was clearly the best move. But until I had Opal tucked away behind Aiden's wards and in a room I could easily defend, I wasn't going to pause to pontificate.

The witch lights that had guided us to the beach didn't flicker on to illuminate the way back to the hotel, presumably because we were shielded. Realizing belatedly that I might have been clutching Opal and Juniper too tightly, I loosened my hold on the girls' forearms. They tucked their grounding stones away in their cloak pockets and shifted to hold my hands instead.

Aiden's shield flickered and died. I'd have to tell him how impressively long it had lasted. But with it down, I realized that the heavily treed area around us was strangely silent. So still that I could hear the swish of the girls' cloaks around their ankles.

It was after midnight, but I would have thought there might have been some nocturnal creatures active in the underbrush. Mice, rats? An owl hooting?

Juniper raised her free hand, and a tiny pinpoint of light appeared in her palm.

"Oooo, nice," Opal whispered.

"I can only hold it," Juniper admitted. "I can't get it to hover above us yet."

We reached the end of the first section of boardwalk pathway, stepping back onto cool, hard-packed dirt. Juniper's witch light barely penetrated the dark, muffled forest. I slowed my pace further, tucking the girls closer into me.

"Keep the light behind Emma," Opal whispered to Juniper behind my back. The tiny blue light shifted slightly higher, as if Juniper had set it on top of her shoulder or head.

Energy clawed up my spine. More of a knowing rather than anything carried by magic.

I stopped walking. Listening intently as I reached out with all my other senses.

I was far enough away from the beach that the ongoing situation there was barely a blot of amorphous power signatures. Though I could still parse Aiden's muted magical signature from among the witches.

"Emma?" Opal asked in a hushed whisper.

Juniper's grip on my hand was actually starting to hurt.

I slowly pivoted, keeping the girls tucked against my legs.

Something was stalking us.

And it wasn't human.

Or at least it wasn't a human imbued with magic, because it wasn't twigging my magical senses.

No. It was the sudden deadness of the air. The even deeper quiet weighted with...a malignant intent.

I was going to need my hands free.

"Hold hands," I murmured.

Opal raised both girls' already-joined hands into my peripheral vision. I nodded, pivoting to face the path leading back to the hotel. We were still a fast ten-minute walk from the grounds. "Grab hold of my belt."

The girls loosened their grip on my hands and transferred it to my waist, bunching the fabric of my linen dress.

"Stay behind me," I said, moving forward at a steady but unhurried pace. "Stay with me. No matter what. Don't leave the path."

"Always," Opal whispered. She jostled Juniper promptingly.

"Okay," the other young witch whispered.

The smooth-packed dirt path quickly gave way to another short section of boardwalk, set up presumably to stop the natural habitat from being too badly trampled in places, or perhaps to raise the path over marshier areas. But even my enhanced eyesight was being challenged among the aged, tall evergreens, despite the filtered moonlight and Juniper's weak witch light.

My feet hit smooth dirt again. It was slightly damp this time. Not great for my footing if—

The attack came from my right.

I felt it—a rush of air and a brush of energy—and turned into it, shoving the girls behind me.

A large body slammed into me, driving me a step back.

Red-rimmed eyes.

Thick claws.

Sharp teeth.

I got my hands around a furred, muscled neck as what felt like four limbs clawed me, shredding my dress. Then my eyesight caught up with my other senses.

I was grappling with a canine of some sort.

Juniper screamed, her reaction delayed. She dropped her hold on me.

"No!" Opal shouted, still gripping me but pulling against Juniper's attempt to flee.

A large, jagged-toothed maw made an attempt to bite my face off. I dropped my hold on the beast's neck, then quickly snatched its jaw when it lunged for me a second time.

I tore its jaw apart, flinging the lower half away into the undergrowth.

Juniper screamed a second time. I could feel her fighting against Opal's hold. The dream walker was still clinging to me with one hand.

The beast backed off a few steps.

It still hadn't made a single sound.

I couldn't feel any magic from it.

I reached my right hand out for one of my black blades, focusing all my intention on visualizing it settling into my waiting palm. Though I wasn't certain that it would come to me at this distance. Aiden was powerful, but I wasn't terribly skilled at triggering his spell work.

The creature flung itself at me, unable to bite and likely already bleeding out, but still somehow not retreating.

The hilt of a blade settled into my hand.

I stepped slightly to the side and brought the magically sharpened shortsword down across the creature's neck. Decapitating it.

The head spun away. The body fell to the ground, blood gushing across my dress, bare lower legs, and feet.

It stank. Unnaturally so.

I kicked the corpse to the side of the path, hoping that tucking it far enough into the bush would hide it until the witches could clean up after me. Then I punted the head in after the body.

I still couldn't quite tell what it had been in life. A large dog? A coyote?

Juniper was on the ground, breathing raggedly, but no longer fighting Opal's hold.

The dream walker slumped against me. I wrapped my free arm around her as best I could while still scanning the forest.

"On your feet," I snapped at Juniper.

Opal reached back for her friend, helping her up.

Two more canine creatures shot out of the dark underbrush to my left and slightly behind me. They were aiming for the girls.

I pivoted to block their path, catching another flash of reddened eyes. My second blade settled into my free hand, even though I hadn't consciously called for it.

Juniper screamed, a sharp, strangled sound. Terrified.

Then she ran, taking the little pinpoint of witch light with her.

Opal shouted, then—wisely—stuck with me.

Not letting them get anywhere near my little witch, or get around me to pursue Juniper, I made quick work of the two new beasts. Definitely coyotes this time. I didn't stick around to dissect them or the situation, though, simply passing one of my blades to Opal and shoving the corpses into the underbrush.

The black blade was almost too large for the dream walker to carry, let alone wield. But my sheath didn't have a recall spell on it, and I didn't have the time to put together a makeshift one. I grabbed the dream walker's hand and took off after Juniper.

A pinpoint of blue drew us off the main path, through some scratchy, tangled vines that might have been wild blackberry or salmonberry. We crossed around the wide base of a huge, moss-covered cedar tree.

On the other side, Juniper was burrowed between two large roots.

Clutching her ankle, she blinked up at me with a tear-streaked face. "I screwed up."

"We keep moving," I said calmly. "We'll debrief back in the room."

Opal crouched down, peering at Juniper's ankle. "Broken?"

Juniper shook her head, getting her quiet sobs under control. "I don't think so, but…but…I can't walk on it."

I passed Opal my second blade, my stomach going oddly sour as I did so. I ignored that trepidation, or fear, or whatever it was, and scooped up Juniper in my arms.

"Wow," she cried. "You're so strong—"

I shifted my hold on her, slinging her over my shoulder. She grunted as her breath whooshed out of her. I likely could have been a bit gentler.

I took one of my blades back from Opal, waiting until the dream walker had her hand fisted in my dress again. She blinked up at me with bright-blue witch magic rimming her eyes. I wondered what, if anything, she could see in the dark. I couldn't take the time to comfort her, though.

I turned us back toward the path, and we walked through the still-silent woods until we found hard packed dirt and turned again. Silence encased us until I finally spotted lights ahead. Then the corner of a building came into view.

Magic shifted behind us.

Magic I'd been waiting on all day, practically two days now, to feel.

I turned, a chastisement already on my lips despite the relief flooding through me.

"Paisley!" Opal cried, loosening her hold on me and darting off the path into a small moonlit clearing.

The demon dog had paused, still deep within the shadows. Her eyes glowed red. Her form was larger than it should have been when in the company of strangers.

Without any other hint of danger or wrongness, my heart started thudding in my chest.

Opal dashed to Paisley. "We missed you! Where have you been?"

Every single one of my instincts started screaming, in one overwhelming voice. I gently set Juniper on her feet, keeping hold of her.

"Emma?" she whispered to me.

Paisley took a few more steps out into the open. Her red eyes remained pinned to me. Her upper lip curled to reveal both canines, but she was silent. No chortling. No playful snorting.

And her magic…

I had never really felt it so acutely, presumably because Paisley just…was. She was unique, and her power was embedded in her every cell. But now I could feel that power roiling around her, and—

Opal threw her arms around Paisley's neck.

The demon dog didn't react. Her gaze still trained on me.

I gently pushed Juniper to the side. She hopped on one foot until she could steady herself against the nearest tree.

Opal was still chattering to Paisley, but I couldn't hear the words over the blood rushing in my ears.

I raised my blade. Opal was still holding onto my second weapon, her hand so small that it didn't completely cover the glowing blue gemstones set in the hilt.

I finally found my voice, along with my footing. "Opal," I snapped. "Step away from Paisley."

Opal lifted her head from Paisley's neck, frowning back at me. "What?"

I was too far away.

Something was very wrong.

And I was too far away.

"Step back…slowly."

Paisley still hadn't acknowledged the little witch. She hadn't chuffed or asked to be petted.

Everything slowed down, like it did before I exploded into action. Before I fought like nothing else mattered but the mission, the end results.

I could hear Juniper's slightly pained breathing.

I could see Opal's confusion, her arms slowly dropping to her sides. My second blade, dangling loosely from the little witch's fingers.

And I could sense the malignant silence that surrounded the demon dog. My constant companion since I'd rescued her from the Collective. Since we Five had slaughtered all her brethren, inadvertently or not. Since she'd been bred to be a killer, a tool, just as I had been.

Opal took a half step back, gazing at Paisley with her brow furrowed. Her witch magic still encircled her eyes. She reached for Paisley, rubbing her fingers over, then under something looped around the demon dog's neck.

"What is this?" she muttered, dropping my second blade. Then, holding what appeared to be a dark rope tied around Paisley's neck, she rubbed the fingers of her other hand together, frowning. Her eyesight was still somewhat compromised despite the bright moonlight.

"Is this…blood?" Her head snapped to me. "Emma!?"

I reached out with my free hand, wary of stepping forward. "Cross to me. Slowly."

Opal huffed. "Paisley's hurt."

"I see that. Step to me. Then I will assess—"

Every single one of the demon dog's black tentacles snapped out from her neck, creating a massive writhing mane. A dark-tinted energy flared, then flickered as if electrified between those tentacles.

Juniper stifled a scream.

Still ignoring Opal, Paisley took a step forward. Her head lowering, ears pressed back, red gaze fixed.

Stalking.

Stalking me.

I raised my blade, my chest aching. No, my heart aching. "Paisley. Stand down."

Opal. Stupidly brave Opal ran her hand over the demon dog's shoulder, over her back haunch. Then she looked at her palm. "You're hurt!" she cried. "That's...that's not rope!" She gestured toward the loop around Paisley's neck.

A loop indistinguishable from the demon dog's own skin in the dark.

"I'm giving you a direct order, Paisley," I snapped. "Stand down."

The demon dog shuddered. Then she shook her head, still eyeing me, but not moving any closer. For a long moment, I held her gaze steadily. I was alpha. She would bow to me.

Ever so slowly, and with what appeared to be great effort—maybe even overcoming a compulsion—the demon dog turned her head and fixed her gaze on Opal.

The dream walker's frown of confusion twisted into disbelief. She took a step back.

"Look at me, Paisley," I said, my tone low and dark.

Opal took another step, now angling toward me. She raised her hands, then she glanced toward the black blade she'd dropped when she'd investigated the noose around the demon dog's neck.

Paisley's big broad head swung toward me again, then back to Opal, then to me. And I saw the moment she came to some decision.

I leaped forward into a flat-out sprint. My power snapped out from me. A power, an ability, I'd sworn to myself I would never use on anyone, let alone someone I loved.

Paisley snarled at the blast of magic. The first sound she'd uttered since appearing. I tried to grab her, to hone that power into a rope with which to bind her. My new, mostly untested ability to control the emotions of others, and through that control their actions.

The dark-tinted energy ran through Paisley's tentacles again, momentarily shaking off my loose hold. Then those tentacles snapped to the side, surrounding Opal.

The dream walker had a moment to lock her gaze to mine, sudden realization flooding through her. "Emma?"

And then they were gone.

Just gone.

Paisley hadn't even stepped back into the deeper shadows.

My second blade lay in the dirt. The gems in its hilt had gone dull without Opal's witch magic to trigger their sharpening spells.

A terrible noise—part scream, part shout, part command—ripped through my throat. I slid to a stop in the dirt.

I pivoted, my senses thrown wide open.

Sensing nothing.

Nothing.

No sound.

No movement.

I couldn't feel Opal's magic.

"Emma?" Juniper whispered.

I had forgotten the other girl was with us.

I was just standing there, the fallen blade at my feet. My mind racing, unable to latch onto what had just happened.

Paisley had taken Opal.

Could…could Paisley even carry another person with her while teleporting…? And didn't she cross through the demon dimension…? Could…

Could…Opal survive that dimension—?

"Emma?" Juniper was hopping on one foot toward me, pain etched across her face.

Something about that pain, about knowing I still needed to function, to get Juniper to safe ground, cracked through the numbness threatening to immobilize me.

And then…anger.

So much anger.

Someone had attacked us.

Someone, by some means, had compromised Paisley.

And because I knew why, even if not yet knowing how, I knew who to blame.

No.

Not blame.

Eviscerate.

Right after she told me how to get my Opal back. And my Paisley.

I snatched up my second blade, pressing it into Juniper's hand. Then I scooped the young witch up, and I ran.

I ran back toward the beach, not caring that I was displaying speed and strength that wouldn't come naturally to a normal amplifier. I ran toward the witches I could still feel at the very edge of my senses. Toward Aiden.

After all, I needed a healer for Juniper, and a sorcerer to guard my back while I tortured a witch with the ability to bind familiars against their will. A witch who had clearly decided to play with what she'd deemed easy prey—a mere amplifier.

Yes, it might have taken me a little time to figure out I was being played with. Even taunted, assuming the raven had been a setup from the beginning. But I wasn't stupid.

Anger was usually an utterly useless emotion, but I was going to enjoy unleashing it on Mercury Dunkirk.

SEVEN

I PRACTICALLY EXPLODED OUT OF THE FOREST AND onto the sand, Juniper a silent weight in my arms. Farther up the beach, Aiden straightened from examining the corpses of seagulls and crabs that littered the area, already spinning toward me with his hand flung out and a spell on his lips.

I looked beyond him, noting small clusters of witches, paired off to examine and clean up the results of a summoning that had only one logical origin.

Mercury Dunkirk.

The British witch with the ice-blue eyes was even farther up the beach, gesturing expansively as she spoke—or rather argued—with Scarlett and Pearl.

I continued running, toward Aiden now, watching as his hand lowered and a frown creased his brow. Watching as his gaze flicked behind me—and taking in that Opal wasn't with me. Seeing how his bright-blue power flooded his suddenly fierce gaze.

"Emma?" a witch called to me as I raced past.

I almost ignored her, but Juniper touched my cheek lightly. "Burgundy can heal my ankle, Emma."

I had scared the wounded witch in my arms. Had scared, and was still in the process of scaring, Opal's new friend.

I pivoted midstep, rounding on Burgundy, the healer, so quickly that she squeaked and stumbled back. She recovered quickly, though, magic already flowing out to her fingertips as she reached for Juniper. "It's your leg?"

"Ankle," Juniper said. "Sprained, I think."

I was offloading Juniper into Burgundy's arms before my brain caught up to my actions—at which point, I realized that a healer in her early twenties couldn't actually support the entire weight of a fifteen-year-old witch who was only slightly shorter than her.

I shifted Juniper awkwardly so she could settle down onto the sand, realizing that I had pulled the rest of the witches' attention to me now. Aiden was only a couple of steps away with his bat back in his hand. Half the runes etched into its length had been drained.

"It's broken," Burgundy said. "I'm going to need my premade spells. I can't heal something like this without—"

I shoved my hand in her face, and she blinked up at me. "There's going to be more blood tonight, healer," I said, my voice sounding deadened even to my own ears as I shifted my attention to my far right. Homing in on Mercury.

The British witch—the animal mage—stiffened, then glanced back at me. The movement appeared involuntary, as if she'd felt my intent all the way across the beach. The goblin cat was peeking out from under the low hem of her dark-green robes again.

Scarlett followed Mercury's gaze. Her frowned deepened as she took in the sight of me standing over Juniper and a crouched Burgundy.

The healer slipped her hand in mine as Aiden stepped up beside me. I amplified Burgundy quickly. Not as hard and fast as I could have, but as swiftly as possible without overwhelming her. Hopefully.

She gasped. Her fingers flexed in mine, and I loosened my grip to let go. She firmed her grip. "I'm fine. Thank you. I'm fine. It was just…sudden."

I kept my gaze locked to Aiden, who was examining me as if he could see what he needed to know written on my face. He flicked his gaze downward, then stilled.

My dress and legs were splattered with blood, my feet caked in dirt and sand.

"Opal?" Aidan gasped involuntarily.

"Coyote," I said darkly.

"Three of them," Juniper whispered. "Attacked us in the woods. There was…there was something wrong with them."

I felt her glance up at me, so I tried to offer her a reassuring smile.

She flinched.

"I'll take care of it," I vowed.

"I know you will," the teen witch said, pure belief threaded through her words.

Burgundy was patting my hand, lightly but insistently. In a way that let me know she'd been doing so for some time. "I'm good, Emma. That's good."

I wasn't thinking completely clearly. As it turned out, anger wasn't a terribly manageable emotion. Not for me.

I released the healer, then plucked my second blade out of Juniper's grasp even as I was walking away, heading for Mercury. Aiden was tight to my side.

Burgundy, panting quietly, called, "Thank you!" after me.

"Tell me," Aiden growled quietly.

"Paisley's been compromised. She took Opal."

"Took?"

"I'm fairly certain she was supposed to grab me."

"Supposed to…" Aiden touched my elbow, perhaps attempting to get me to stop for a moment, to communicate clearly.

But I wasn't capable of that. Not now, not yet. I slowed my pace, though, noting the other witches turning toward us, tightening around their coven leader—and as a result of her proximity to Pearl, shielding Mercury from direct attack.

"What do you mean took?" Aiden murmured. "As in they could be back in the room?"

I slowed further, suddenly confused. Could I have misinterpreted what had happened in the forest with Paisley?

No.

I shook my head. "She'd been bloodied. Leashed somehow."

Aiden snarled, "You think it's one of the witches?"

"I know it is."

He opened his mouth, and I knew he had more questions. I knew he needed answers. But I also knew myself and what I was capable of. What I needed to do, and how quickly. I shook my head again, hoping he understood.

He swallowed harshly, nodding once. Then his expression blanked. He became the cool, formidable dark sorcerer that he'd been bred to be, and slipped a step behind me on my right. Ready to shield me, back me, without any more questions.

I turned to take in the scene before me. The gathered witches. My black blades loose in my hands, lowered but always ready. And all my power on display.

My breeding wasn't something I could switch off like Aiden could, but normally I kept it muted while around judgemental strangers.

Not tonight.

Screw the witches.

I didn't care one bit who I scared, or who tried to stand between me and—

"Mercury Dunkirk!" I snarled.

A few of the witches flinched. Witches who had reacted calmly and effectively when being attacked by suicidal seagulls and raging crabs. I was that much more terrifying.

I shoved that unhelpful thought away.

Nothing mattered but Opal. I would terrorize the entire world to get her back. I'd slaughter anyone who laid a finger on her, who—

"As I already told the others," Mercury said in her clipped British accent, clearly already peeved. "They were attracted to all the magic Pearl was throwing around. Such a display from the coven leader—"

"Enough chatter, witch." I took a few more steps toward her, Aiden silent and deadly at my back. "You've had your fun, your retribution."

The witches standing between me and Mercury shifted. Involuntarily, I thought. Their magic-filled gazes were flicking between the sorcerer and me.

"Chatter!" Mercury huffed indignantly. "How dare you accuse me of—"

Pearl stepped between me and Mercury, the witches parting around her without a verbal or visual cue. Scarlett was a step behind, guarding her mother as Aiden was guarding me.

"This isn't how we air grievances in a coven," Pearl snapped. Not a single strand of her hair was out of place, but I knew she was already riled. I knew because I could feel her potent magic—magic I hadn't been able to catch even a hint of before. "With sharp blades and unsubstantiated threats."

"Opal is gone," I snapped back. "Nothing stands between me and my child, Pearl Godfrey. Not even you."

Pearl frowned deeply.

"Gone?" Scarlett echoed. "What do you mean?"

"Taken," Aiden snapped. "By someone who can control animals through blood magic."

A murmur of whispers and power ran through the gathered witches. Then as one, they parted, literally forming a path between Mercury and me.

Aiden.

A cool flush of relief ran through me.

Aiden always knew the right words to wield. I caught sight of Ocean and Lani to the far left of the main group, holding hands. Aiden's sister would protect Lani.

"State your evidence," Scarlett said crisply. She had positioned herself directly across from Pearl, both of them centered on the aisle the witches had formed.

If I wanted to lay hands on Mercury, I'd have to move past every witch on the beach to do so.

"Paisley has been compromised," I said, slowly lifting my blade and pointing it at Mercury.

"Paisley?" one of the other witches asked in a murmur.

"Her skin was flayed, and then spelled into a collar with which to control her." That was some quick guesswork, but this wasn't my first time facing off against a black witch who wielded blood magic to compel.

Mercury was grinning at me, not even bothering to deny anything. Her arms were casually crossed. The goblin cat had somehow appeared on her shoulder, though I hadn't seen it make the jump. The creature seemed completely disinterested. As if I wasn't a threat.

"I was there…" A voice piped up behind me. Juniper. The teen witch stepped up to my left, keeping to the side but not limping. Burgundy was hovering beside her, but then she joined the ranks of the witches on the left, slipping in beside Kelly.

Juniper's voice was quiet, yet easily heard despite the thundering surf. The witches must have cast a noise barrier when I'd confronted Mercury. Or, more likely, there had already been one in place, covering a chunk of the beach. And I had just walked right through it, casually showing off my abilities without even knowing it.

I hadn't fooled a single one of them. Not from the moment I'd joined them for tea.

Olive, Juniper's aunt, shifted from among the witches where she'd been standing with Scarlett, beckoning for her niece. But Juniper simply squared her shoulders and lifted her chin, speaking to Pearl.

"I saw everything. Everything exactly as Emma says."

As one, all the witches looked to Mercury.

"What proof do you have of my involvement, amplifier?" Mercury said silkily. "An eyewitness to the actual event proves only that the event happened."

"I'm sure the corpses of the coyotes will provide the coven with more than enough residual magic to tie the event to you," I said, equally as cool outwardly, though my emotions were raging within.

"Coyotes?" Scarlett asked. "Like the seagulls and crabs?"

At my side, Juniper shook her head. "No, different. They...there was something wrong with them. And their blood smelled...bad."

Mercury scoffed. But more in amusement than denial.

Juniper's voice strengthened. "I can take you there. Emma tucked the bodies out of sight, if you need the proof right away."

Scarlett motioned toward Kelly and Olive. But before they broke away to follow Juniper back to the path, to the proof the coven needed, I took another step toward Mercury. Then another.

I wasn't waiting for the coven to verify my claim—that Mercury had hurt Paisley because the demon dog had eaten her raven.

"I'm not interested in proof. I already know," I said, slipping tendrils of my power toward Mercury. Paisley had broken my hold because I'd hesitated. I had questioned myself. That wouldn't happen again. "I also know that you didn't want my Opal, did you?"

Mercury chuckled, low and dark. Still not even remotely denying my accusation. The goblin cat dropped from her shoulder to twine around her ankles again, in and out from under the hem of her dark-green cloak, practically indistinguishable next to the wet moonlit sand. Except for its eyes. They reflected red.

"You wanted to exact your own revenge," I said. "For the raven. Not the promised reparations." I took another step closer, my right blade raised, my left lowered at my side. "But kidnapping a child doesn't set the balance right between us. No matter what the witches decide when they've gathered their evidence."

Those aforementioned witches remained a silent, steady presence on either side of me, all their attention trained on Mercury. Listening to every word, every accusation that passed between us.

But the British witch only smiled at me. Indulgently. "Shall I tell them who you really are, Emma? Do you think they'd stand against me...for you?"

I frowned, pausing midstep. Mercury was suggesting...that she somehow knew me? Was she...connected to the Collective?

I shoved the thought away. I wasn't interested in playing a game with the smug witch. "I will tear every last bit of magic from you."

Aiden's power roiled around the baseball bat, around his free hand. Spilling over the sand to slip around my ankles and thread through my own unleashed energy.

"Drop by drop," I said, still stalking forward.

The witches shifted, those nearest Mercury peeling back a few steps, widening the mouth of the corridor they'd held while assessing the situation. Leaving the field open for me. And Aiden. I could feel the dark sorcerer's anger, hot pulses of energy against my right shoulder, neck, and face. And he hadn't even watched Mercury's little game unfold in the forest. Unfold and then go sideways when her hold on Paisley had slipped.

The compulsion wearing thin, perhaps? Or was the programming to obey me, or any of the Five, just that strong in the demon dog?

As I assessed the distance to Mercury, I realized that the tendrils of power I sent for the witch were impeded by an invisible barrier. Licking up against it, looking for cracks. "And before you slip into unconsciousness," I said, "never to regain your magic, you will tell me what you've done to my—"

"Do you think she'll survive?" Mercury asked musingly, plucking up and petting the cat. The creature didn't appear to be enjoying her caresses. "Transportation through the demon realm. I knew it was a risk, even with you—"

I lunged.

Aiden hit the invisible shield between Mercury and me with one of his exploding runed spells.

The shield cracked.

Mercury's eyes widened with the first hint of fear.

I brought my blade down, cutting through the rest of the barrier spell she'd erected. Energy thrummed under my palm, then died, telling me that

I'd exhausted the sharpening spell Aiden had embedded in one of the gemstones.

No matter.

That was why I dual wielded.

The goblin cat screeched.

Power pulsed out of Mercury. I braced for a hit, but it was aimed toward the roiling surf, not me.

Aiden pivoted, responding to an attack from the right, but I only had eyes for Mercury.

She stumbled back, managing to avoid the tip of my second blade. I'd been aiming for her shoulder. Unfortunately, I needed to question her, not decapitate.

The witches were shouting. The ground thrummed with magic under my feet.

Magic...and the passage of something very large...not footsteps.

Ignoring it all, I dropped my spent blade and reached for Mercury, already roping my power around her. She was still holding fast to her personal shield, but it wouldn't take more than a moment for me to break through and lay my hands on her skin.

Aiden's power exploded behind me, as though he'd just hit something very large with his bat.

He grunted. Pained.

I risked a look back.

Three huge creatures had rolled up out of the surf. Dark skinned, long necked, huge bodies...and flippers? The creature nearest to Aiden had taken a magical blow from the sorcerer's bat that was still smoldering across its neck and shoulder.

Mercury threw the goblin cat at me. It hit my head, clawing for purchase and howling.

Another pulse of power burst from Mercury as I tried to stop the cat from scratching out my eyes, wrapping it in my power to quell it. Again, though, the witch's spell wasn't directed at me.

The nearest creature bellowed, shaking off the blow that had momentarily stunned it. The two others answered, the sound loud enough to box my ears. The ground shuddered under them as they charged.

Not at me. Not at the witches, many of whom had remained on the beach to fight while they covered the retreat of the others.

But at Aiden.

I tossed the hissing and spitting goblin cat to the side. Mercury had danced out of my reach.

She couldn't run as fast as I could, though.

But Aiden couldn't take on three creatures at once.

I turned and ran to my sorcerer. He was standing his ground between me and the closest charging creature, bat at the ready—but none of the runes were lit with power. He had drained its remaining reserves already, against the seagulls and crabs, and now the second attack.

Thick conduits of my power, redirected from Mercury and the goblin cat and transformed to fuel rather than drain, got to him first. I was already amplifying the sorcerer before I'd even closed the distance between us.

Aiden straightened under the amplification onslaught even though I was fairly certain he was hurt, channeling as much magic as he could into the bat before the creature got within striking distance.

He stepped to the side. Not enough to actually avoid the huge flippered feet, but enough to clear the bulk of the creature's body. It was way, way too quick for its size and shape.

A sea lion, I realized. A bull.

Three bull sea lions.

Aiden brought the bat up under the sea lion's chin. Power exploded—every last charged rune discharging to back the blow.

The sea lion was actually thrown back. Not enough to flip it—it had to weigh a literal ton—but enough to shove it off its front flippers.

It fell forward into the sand, its head only a half meter away from Aiden's feet. It didn't move.

I'd closed the distance to Aiden, tangling him in my power, feeding more and more into him even as I wrapped my hand around the back of his neck. My sorcerer took every last drop of that amplification, muttering under his breath and funneling it all into his baseball bat.

The second bull sea lion bore down on us.

We weren't going to be quick enough.

Then the creature shuddered. Convulsed. And collapsed. All before Aiden could even finish refueling his bat.

A cheer rose from the witches hidden from my view behind the bulk of the two downed sea lions. So much magic was roiling around me, I hadn't even felt the coven attacking the second creature, let alone bringing it down.

That left one.

Already running toward it, I called my second blade back into my hand—the recall spell still active, even if I'd exhausted the sharpening spell. The blades were sharp enough that even with just my strength behind the blow I should be able to cut through—

The third creature abruptly tried to halt its forward progression, scrambling in the sand but sliding forward nonetheless.

But not because it was afraid of me.

No. As with the coyotes in the forest, these creatures were no longer controlling their own actions…

The sea lion bellowed, the sound confused and even pained. It swung its large head side to side, blinking black-orbed eyes.

Shaking off the compulsion…

I spun back to where I'd left Mercury.

She was gone.

"Aiden!" I shouted, running to where I'd left the British witch, tracking her footprints in the sand.

The dark sorcerer was at my side an instant later. We ran together, racing up the beach, past the site of the coven ceremony. And as we neared the edge of the forest, he touched my elbow, silently requesting to lead.

I slowed my pace, trusting his senses.

He snapped up a shield around us, and we stepped into the undergrowth in silence.

Lights became visible only a short distance later, revealing a house that had been wholly hidden within the trees. A mansion, really. Millions of dollars of real estate masquerading as a beach house.

Three more steps, and we hit a gray-bricked path that led to the front door.

It was hanging open.

"Fuck," Aiden muttered under his breath.

Every light was on in the house despite the fact that it was way after midnight. Quiet music drifted out the open front door as we approached.

We stepped inside. I glanced around, noting nothing of the decor. Just that there weren't any immediate threats in the vicinity. Without hesitation, likely following residual magic that I couldn't sense while behind his shield, Aiden continued to the right.

An archway opened up to a huge living room. The source point of the music.

Bodies littered the floor.

Mundanes. Not Adepts. Most looked as though they were sleeping. Or under a compulsion spell.

Three of them had been arrayed into a make-shift circle in a cleared space in the center of the room. Those three had been sliced open from sternum to genitals.

They'd been having a party.

Enjoying some music and conversation with friends.

And then Mercury Dunkirk had entered their home and ended their lives. Because she'd been fleeing before me. And from the coven.

Aiden dropped the shielding spell, carefully stepping over the tangled limbs where the others had fallen, to pace around the slaughtered mundanes. His face was a granite mask.

"A teleportation spell?" I asked, my voice thin, reedy.

Aiden crouched, then pressed his fingers into the intermingled blood that had collected at the center of the circle of bodies. Not a drop had flowed in the other direction. He rubbed his bloody fingers together, nodding stiffly.

Magic.

Blood magic.

"But…" I whispered. "They're mundanes…aren't they? How…how could—"

Witch magic shifted behind me. I whirled, bringing my blades into play and almost decapitating Scarlett and Kelly.

Scarlett leveled a censorious look at me that I actually felt, then stepped past me to survey the room. Kelly stayed in the foyer, her eyes wide. She wasn't knitting anymore.

I closed my eyes, momentarily quelled by my own unkind thought.

"Oh my God," Scarlett murmured from behind me.

"Yes," Aiden said. "A teleportation spell."

"We're going to need Pearl," Scarlett said, apparently speaking to Kelly, because the other witch touched me lightly on the shoulder, then pivoted and jogged out of the house.

I thought the touch was meant to be comforting. And I was momentarily thrown by the witch's capacity to reach out to me, even after seeing just a small part of what I was capable of on the beach.

"We only crossed along the path and directly through the entranceway...to here." Aiden's voice tugged me back to the reality I was obviously attempting to disassociate from. Trying to stop myself from accepting responsibility for...more ragged slashes in my already mangled soul. So...many...bodies.

"No matter." Scarlett's tone firmed, all business now. "We'll do the entire house and property." She crouched next to the nearest mundane, a brown-haired woman with an upended glass of red wine still loosely held in her hand. "Just knocked out. That's...that's something to be thankful for."

Aiden carefully stepped his way back to me, holding out his now-clean hand. The spent baseball bat was still clutched in his other hand.

Scarlett straightened, glancing from Aiden to me. "We can attempt to track her. Mercury. Before we clean up the...spell."

Spell. That was a lovely way to gloss over human sacrifice.

"She's mine," I said darkly. "Ours." I locked my gaze to Aiden's, trying to see nothing but him, nothing but the magic cloaking his eyes. Just for another moment. Before reality had to be acknowledged.

I had let Mercury Dunkirk get away. And people had been murdered to cover her retreat.

"The Dunkirks will demand—" Scarlett began.

I narrowed my eyes at her.

She twisted her lips, then nodded. "You don't care."

"I don't care."

"The Godfrey coven will back you."

"I doubt that very much." I turned away before she could say anything else. I needed to be moving forward. I needed to get to Opal.

Because if Mercury Dunkirk would go so far as to compel or even enslave Paisley, then set up an elaborate attack with three sea lions held in reserve, then slaughter innocents to get away...

What would she do to my Opal?

Panic gripped me—and I had no immunity to that, no natural resistance. I felt it trying to drag me down, but kept moving.

Out the door.

Down the path.

Gripping Aiden's free hand.

"I need Christopher."

"Yes," Aiden said.

"I need Christopher now."

"Yes," Aiden said again, his phone in his hand instead of his bat. A ring was already emanating through the speakers.

The line clicked.

"Opal," I cried, barely holding back a sob. "Knox! My Opal."

"I'm already on my way." Christopher's voice was harsh over the speakers. "Try to wait for me, Socks. And…Aiden?"

"Yes, Christopher?"

"I'm driving your SUV. The flights cut off hours ago. I need you to keep Socks calm so I can actually continue to see my own reality."

"Just get here," Aiden growled, ending the call.

Together we stepped into the forest, hand in hand. And though Aiden had to have questions, had to have made some observations, we didn't speak.

I wasn't certain either of us was capable of exchanging words anymore.

I TRIED NOT TO PACE AS AIDEN SILENTLY CROUCHED over the third coyote corpse I'd dragged out from the underbrush for him. We had lined them up along the path—after I'd had to take time to search for the heads—which had forced the few witches who'd finished the cleanup on the beach and were now returning to the hotel to step around us.

Magically drained and visibly tired, none of the members of the Godfrey coven paused to chat, though Scarlett, Pearl, Kelly, and Olive—among others—were reportedly still at the house.

Burgundy, still teeming with the power I'd fed into her, had herded Juniper away when the younger witch tried to stay to help us. And I'd sent Ocean and Lani to check our rooms and then scour the hotel for any signs of Opal or Paisley.

I would have checked myself, except I already knew it was a waste of time.

Aiden tore yet another rune sketch from his notebook, crumpled it, and tossed it on the third body. As he'd done with the first two.

I—yet again—fought down an urge to scream, frustrated and angry and so...so scared. I had never felt fear on this level. Everything I'd done, every death at my hands, every death I'd faced and thwarted—and I had never felt such terror.

I couldn't rant at Aiden's need to be meticulous. His questions to me had been few and carefully posed. I wasn't articulate even under normal circumstances, so I couldn't fault him for wanting to gather as much evidence as possible.

I would have just cut through whatever lay between me and the little witch, even understanding that was verging on reckless. Especially if I was dragging Aiden and Christopher with me. Especially if I had to face Paisley again, to get through the demon dog to rescue Opal.

It would be prudent to understand how Mercury's control over animals functioned before all of that happened.

So… I was pacing, and Aiden was conducting his own investigation instead of questioning me. Instead of asking how I could possibly have let anything happen to our little witch, our daughter.

I dropped into a crouch, my head buried in my hands, digging my fingers into my hair as I held back another scream.

I wasn't certain I could do this.

I wasn't certain I had the capacity.

Aiden grabbed my shoulders and dragged me to my feet, wrapping me in a hard, intense hug. I would have needed to exert myself to break his hold. If I wanted to break his hold.

"Why aren't you blaming me?" I whispered, my voice ragged.

He squeezed even tighter. "I blame Mercury," he snarled viciously. He pressed his lips to my temple, hard and fierce. Nothing sweet about his touch now. "I blame the goddamn coven for not having her under control."

Something inside me loosened at his tone, that anger that echoed mine. I sagged into him, unexpectedly enough that he stumbled slightly before firming his footing.

"Tell me again," I demanded against the warm skin of his neck. Aiden had been talking me through his own thoughts as he'd pieced them together, but in my present state of mind, I'd barely taken it in. "About the teleportation spell. About what you saw on the beach, and how that's different from what you see here with the coyotes."

He inhaled deeply, as if trying to get his own emotions under control. I was only a breath away from crying myself, but some part of me knew—even though such a thing had never happened to me before—that if I started crying now, I'd never stop.

"I'll have to check with the witches to confirm...probably Kelly, who also works with animal husbandry. But the first two summoning spells on the beach, using the wild magic and the power called forth by the induction ceremony, seemed...spur of the moment. As if Mercury saw the opportunity to create chaos and took it." Aiden loosened his hold on me enough to smooth the hair back from my face with one hand, then settle his hand gently across my throat.

"She didn't have an exit strategy," I said.

He nodded, grimacing. "She didn't think she needed one."

"Because she thought that between the coyotes and Paisley, she'd achieve her objective with no one knowing."

Aiden ran a hand through his hair, sighing heavily. "Distract the witches, force you into the forest...setting aside the quandary of how she knew you'd get the girls off the beach..."

"The crabs were a localized threat. And..." I met his gaze sadly. Apologetically. "She knows who I am."

"She thinks she knows," Aiden said stubbornly.

My throat was threatening to close up again. I had to stay focused. "Explain more."

Aiden huffed a sad laugh. Then he swallowed harshly and turned his attention to the coyotes. "These creatures are different."

"I didn't know that one witch could bind multiple familiars."

"They can't. Not as far as I know. But Mercury had two. The raven and the cat."

"And the coyotes...?" I gestured toward the corpses. "And...she also bound Paisley somehow?"

"These," Aiden said grimly, "aren't coyotes. I'm not even sure that they ever were purely coyote. Which is why we need to do this..." He ripped out another page in his notebook, crumpled it up, and flicked it toward the corpses. The spell exploded in midair, then rained embers down over the dead creatures, setting them instantly on fire.

Pretty magic.

Powerful. And terrible.

The fire burned fast, yet put off no heat. The corpses crumbled to ash.

"You don't want the other witches seeing them?" I whispered. "Because of...because you don't want them knowing about this sort of magic?"

Aiden raised his hand over the ashy remains. Dark-blue power whirled under his palm, and the ashes dissipated into the undergrowth, borne on a wind I couldn't see or feel. "I can't block against a reconstruction. Even attempting to do so would make it seem like we had something to hide. This will just read as politely cleaning up after ourselves."

The sorcerer snagged my hand, and we started back toward the hotel. But even as happy as I was to be finally moving forward again, he hadn't actually answered all my questions.

"Why, Aiden?"

He glanced back at me. "I'm no expert. I have people I can contact though…like…my father."

"Your father doesn't deal in blood magic."

He laughed grimly. "But he knows all about it. He knows people who do…and who deal with demons."

Memories of red eyes flashed in my mind. And not Paisley's. "You think…?"

"The seagulls, crabs, and sea lions were bespelled," Aiden said, biting off the words as the corner of the hotel came into view. "By a powerful witch."

"Powerful enough to harvest the life force from mundanes."

He nodded stiffly.

"But the coyotes…weren't just bound by blood or black magic?"

"It's fucking black magic all right. No one would dispute it." Aiden guided us around the building and through the side entrance.

He wanted us in our room, I realized. Before he told me everything he was thinking. I let him lead me. I let him unlock the door, fruitlessly reaching out my senses for any hint of Opal within the suite. But the little witch wasn't anywhere near enough for me to feel.

Aiden shut the door and triggered the runes he'd placed around it before we'd gone to bed the first night.

Then he half-turned to me, looking down, his expression tense.

"Tell me," I whispered.

"The coyotes have demon magic in them," he said. "Maybe simply from being fed demon blood...but maybe..." He looked up and pinned me with a soul-aching gaze.

"Maybe..." I echoed. "Some sort of hybrid."

Demon hybrids. Like Paisley. And unless there was another player who we hadn't yet uncovered, they were under Mercury's control.

"It doesn't have to be related," Aiden said. "Maybe it's just an odd coincidence."

"No," I said, my tone empty. "It might have started out as a coincidence, but it turned into a connivance. That's why she was so calm about Paisley eating her raven. She knows who I am. She knew from the start. So she knows who Paisley is...what Paisley is."

Aiden shook his head, pacing the few steps that the hallway would allow. "I still don't see how that equates to trying to use Paisley to grab you."

"I don't know. I don't care." Pulling my phone out of my pocket, I strode deeper into the room. I needed to shower and to find some clothing not splattered in demon hybrid blood. "But we're going to need access to Samantha's notes."

Aiden trailed behind me, his phone also in his hand. "You think Mercury Dunkirk is a…was a member of the Collective?"

"I doubt she used that name if she was." I paused to send a text message to Samantha.

Call me. I need to know what you've uncovered about Paisley's breeding program.

"But," I continued, stepping into the dark bathroom, "even if she was only working for the Collective, or for a member of the Collective, it was enough for her to recognize me, then Paisley, by sight."

I dropped my phone on the bathroom counter and stripped. Aiden did the same. Our shower was efficient, with each of us buried in our own thoughts. We didn't exchange a single intentional caress. Not until I'd shut off the water, my hair dripping wet, and Aiden cupped my face in his hands and kissed me fiercely.

No other point of contact, just lips and tongue. His stubble was already growing in, enough to prickle, to help keep me in the moment.

He pulled back slightly. "I don't blame you."

"I hesitated."

"To avoid hurting someone you love. Paisley."

"It won't happen again."

He pressed his forehead to mine and sighed. "I know, Emma. But—"

I turned away, breaking his hold and opening the glass door of the shower before he could finish the thought. "I don't want to be placated, Aiden. I don't want to be soothed."

"Okay," he said gently.

I glared at him, yanking a dry towel off the rack. "If she wants me, she won't hurt Opal." I said it like I believed it. I needed to believe it. "So she can have me." I smiled, vicious and sharp.

Pain etched across his face, Aiden smiled back at me, seeing me as I was and loving me just the same. "I'm with you."

"I know."

EIGHT

RED-HUED EYES BLINKED AT ME, SEEMINGLY HOVER-ing just above the railing of the small balcony off the corner of the bedroom. They were too small and too close together to be Paisley, though my heart had done a weird, pinched squelch when I first spotted the spy.

Between fielding text messages, Aiden and I al-ternated pacing the living room, then the bedroom. Or rather, Aiden's contacts seemed to be messaging him back—he was accumulating pages and pages of notes—while my phone remained mostly silent. Pre-dawn light was just barely tinting the sky. Ocean and Lani had given in about two hours ago, heading to their room to sleep.

Which was fine because I already knew I was leaving them behind. Lani could get Ocean home in the Mustang. And Ocean would be the go-between for the witches and us before that.

No responses from Samantha.

No recent texts from Christopher. And I was trying to keep my attention, and therefore my magic, away from the clairvoyant. Driving Aiden's SUV in the dark over roads he didn't know wasn't going to go well if he kept getting dragged into visions of my future.

No matter how much I wanted to know that those visions of me included Opal.

I opened the sliding door of the balcony and was unsurprised to find Mercury's goblin cat perched on the railing. It blinked its too-large eyes at me, the hint of red fading.

"More spying?" I drawled. "Why not just come to me yourself, Mercury?"

The goblin cat shivered. Then, almost inexplicably, it mewed, quietly plaintive.

I huffed. "I'm not letting you in. I'm not an idiot."

The cat bobbed its head encouragingly. I had a feeling that was the sort of thing a cat would do to encourage petting—just before skewering the idiot who'd fallen for the ruse with its wickedly sharp claws.

Proving how big a pushover I really was, after closing the sliding door, I snagged two dry towels out of the bathroom.

Aiden watched me, clearly bemused, as I took the towels to the door, opened it, and dropped them unceremoniously to the ground right by the threshold. I then closed the door again, though not all the way. The cat couldn't get into the room, but it could make a nest by the door and maybe leech a little heat while doing so.

I turned my back on Mercury's familiar, arms crossed.

Aiden was grinning at me.

"It didn't ask to be bound to a black witch," I snapped.

He made an attempt to quash his grin, failing. Then he raised both hands placatingly. The forefinger and middle finger of his right hand were stained with ink. "Unless Mercury is still in the area, I don't think she can use the cat to spy on us. And Ocean and Lani have scoured the property and the immediate vicinity. I'd guess it got left behind."

"After trying to scratch my eyes out," I grumbled.

"Actually, it confirms something for us. That Mercury is far enough away that her familiar can't sense her."

"Fine," I snapped. "Good."

He grinned. "Maybe you've beguiled it, my amplifier."

I didn't answer because his joking about beguiling just reminded me of what I hadn't done. Reminded me that I hadn't used every tool at my disposal—specifically, my new ability to weaponize my empathy—to quell Paisley.

I stupidly hadn't even trained that power, not yet having anticipated a situation in which I'd need it.

A heavy silence fell between us. Again. We had been struggling out from underneath it for sips of air and sanity over the last few hours.

I glanced over my shoulder. The goblin cat was curled into the towels, half underneath one. Its head was turned away, the round of its shoulders nearest to the slight opening in the door.

If it wasn't spying, I had no idea why the damn thing had come to me. An uncomfortable thought occurred to me though, and I voiced it because I would truly do anything for Opal. Even if it scoured away the last vestiges of my soul. "Can we use the cat's tie to Mercury? To track her? If we don't get a location from Samantha?"

Aiden frowned. "Possibly. Depending on whether it was the raven's blood tie that led us to Mercury. But that just might have been a side effect of my tracking rune, not a reliable result. A witch might be able to do it. Kelly, maybe."

Except Kelly Godfrey wasn't about to perform sacrificial magic on an animal for just a glimmer of a chance that she could use Mercury's familiar bond to track her. I didn't even need to know her at all to know that.

But the problem that was currently stopping us up, even as we waited for Christopher, was that while we could source as many addresses for Mercury Dunkirk as we could find, including through Pearl Godfrey, that didn't mean we'd find where she was keeping Opal. We couldn't afford to end up guessing where to go and spending time getting to that location, only to have chosen wrong.

"If she were a normal villain," I snarled, "she would have tried to lure us to her by now."

"As far as I've been able to assess, none of the villains involved with the Collective were of a normal caliber," Aiden said, far too calmly for my liking.

But then, I needed him steady while I imploded. That way, we could trade off.

We had already proven we couldn't track Paisley. At least not easily. Most likely because she'd actually crossed out of our dimension. And if she'd transported Opal the same way—

A terrible pain lodged itself in my chest. I pressed my hand against it, actually bending forward.

"Emma…" Aiden whispered, pained as well.

"No," I snarled, forcing myself to straighten. Hands clenched at my sides, I paced. "Someone has to know something. I need…I need—"

Energy shifted across my spine. An intense, welcomed tingling. And I ran for the door, feeling the power grow—the connection reestablished and more powerful for having been so thinned for days—with each step.

Aiden jumped up behind me, following. But I was down the short hall and throwing open the door before he'd made it through the living room area.

Christopher was a few steps beyond the door, dressed in worn light-blue jeans, a simple black T-shirt, and combat boots. I refused to allow myself to contemplate why he'd taken the time to lace up boots he never wore before heading for us. His eyes were blazing so brightly white against his golden skin that I couldn't discern his expression.

But it didn't matter, because I was throwing myself into his arms and breaking…

Breaking…

Splintering into little pieces…

He crooned and caressed my hair, then was forced to practically carry me back into the room.

And I was crying.

Ragged, jagged sobbing, full of terror and frustration.

Magic thundered around us. I was probably hurting the clairvoyant with my outburst, but I couldn't let go of him. We crumpled to the floor together, Aiden managing to get the door locked behind us, and I clutched at Christopher's T-shirt while he rocked me in his arms.

I cried.

I never cried.

Okay, I *rarely* lost myself in grief. But I was really, really making up for that all now in a terrible flood of tears and snot and so…much…magic.

Aiden snarled under his breath, and I realized that he was trying to hold a shield around us, to keep my outpouring of power hidden from all the magically sensitive witches currently occupying nearby rooms.

"Knox…my Knox," I sobbed.

"I know, Socks. I know."

"I lost her. I lost our girl. After I promised." I sobbed, almost screaming, hurting myself now, feeling as if each word was ripping through my chest, my throat, my face.

"No, Socks." Christopher gripped my shoulders, trying to make eye contact.

But I couldn't look at him. I didn't want to see his grief…

I didn't want to know what he might already know.

What his magic had shown him that had sent him running to Aiden's SUV and driving to Tofino before even checking in or telling us that he was coming.

The blood tattoo that bound me to him, bound our magic to each other, was burning, writhing with energy. I was inadvertently amplifying Christopher. Recklessly so. Hurting him, triggering him. If I continued, I might burn him out, possibly damaging his ability to navigate his visions.

I was acting like a child.

Like a coward.

I had bottled it all up so much that now I couldn't seem to stop the tsunami of rage and grief. The self-pity.

A creature crawled into my lap. It had crossed through Aiden's boundary shield. It had walked right through the damn glass doors.

The goblin cat.

I stopped crying—and then started hiccupping and shuddering with residual emotion.

Christopher shifted back, blinking as if trying to see the damn cat through the magic that clouded his eyes. "Who is this?"

The cat stretched up on its back legs like a gopher. Then it smacked me. Across the cheek. No claws, but a surprising amount of strength.

I reared back, completely shocked.

Christopher barked out a laugh.

"You fucking asshole," I howled, actually touching my cheek like the idiot I was.

Flicking its hairless tail, the asshole goblin cat curled in my lap and began to purr. Loudly.

Christopher was still laughing. Louder and louder, clutching his belly and everything.

I blinked up at Aiden. My eyes felt swollen. My nose was filled with so much snot that I had to breathe out of my mouth. "It walks through walls?" I asked numbly. "And magic?"

"Apparently, it's not just a familiar," he growled. "And apparently, you've tamed it."

I glanced down at the cat in my lap. It blinked up at me, still purring, seemingly in competition with Christopher for who could make the most noise. "That's very creepy. Why would it come to…?"

I thought back to the beach and all the magic I had tried to snag Mercury with. All the power I hadn't tested and trained as well as I should have, because I hated using it.

I hated compelling people into believing I was some sort of goddess. But I had tried to quell the cat, to stop it from scratching me.

"Damn it!" I snarled.

Christopher was struggling to get his laughter under control. "Another disciple."

"It's a black witch's familiar," I snapped.

Christopher blinked rapidly, his magic finally condensing to a thick ring of white around his irises. "Not anymore."

"So much for sacrificing it to use the familiar bond to track Mercury."

Christopher raised both eyebrows. "That was an option?"

"Maybe." Aiden rubbed his chin.

"No," I snapped, desperately needing a tissue. Or possibly an entire box. And now I had a dull, heavy headache. As far as I could tell, not having a plethora of data points for comparison, crying made me feel worse, not better.

But I couldn't get to my feet yet. Couldn't move forward yet.

I needed to know.

I reached for Christopher. He placed his hands in mine as if he'd anticipated me. And, knowing his magic and how it worked, he had. He was probably reliving this exact moment, only now in the present instead of in his mind's eye.

"Tell me," I said. "Tell me Opal is alive."

"She's alive."

A tiny shiver of relief ran through me. Not enough, not nearly enough, but something to hold onto. "Tell me she's going to stay that way for as long as you can see."

Christopher's sight was most reliable for about forty-eight hours. But on occasion and under the right magically imbued circumstances, he could see much further.

"Paisley is protecting her," he said, his tone far too serious. "From the witch."

"Mercury wants to…kill Opal?" I asked, my throat tight. I wasn't really a coward. I had just experienced a momentary blip. So I needed to know.

Christopher shook his head. "I'm not tuned into the witch. Just Opal. I can't even get reliable glimpses of Paisley."

"Mercury is Collective," Aiden growled. "She'd know how to ward against a clairvoyant."

"What?!" Christopher cried. "The Collective?"

"Not confirmed," I said. "We haven't heard from Samantha."

The clairvoyant went to pull his phone from his pocket, but I grabbed his hand back. "Tell me you know where Opal is."

He grimaced. "Not yet. A room. No distinguishing features."

My heart thumped oddly in my chest, but I ignored the feeling for the sake of moving forward. "Tell me you see me finding Opal."

He swallowed, hard. "I will. I will see that."

"Tell me...something..." My voice cracked. The blood tattoo on my T3 vertebra flared. I was asking too much, pushing too hard.

Christopher cupped my face in his hands. "I see you and Aiden gazing at each other lovingly, eyes brimming with magic, surrounded by power. You're wearing a silky ivory-colored gown, with a black rose tucked in your hair. And Opal is holding your hand. I've seen this moment many times over the last few weeks. And I saw it again only a couple of hours ago."

Opal had been gone for more than a couple of hours. The vision of Aiden and I getting married was Christopher's proof of life.

I choked out a sob, managed to stop a second one, then nodded stiffly. "Thank you, oh clairvoyant."

Christopher smiled, the expression pained. Then he pulled his phone out of his pocket, stood, and stepped around me while already dialing a number and pressing the phone to his ear. The time for text messages had passed.

Aiden crouched in front of me, a box of tissues in hand. I grabbed a handful, wiped my face, and blew my nose. Noisily.

Aiden glanced down at the damn goblin cat. It was now stretched out like my crossed legs were some sort of plush lounger. "You've collected another stray."

"No..." I touched his face lightly, knowing without surfing his emotions that he was hurt. Possibly because I'd broken down with Christopher, not him. "It's me who was lost without you. Without all of you."

He kissed me gently. Then again with more heat.

The cat hissed. Nastily.

I broke the kiss and tossed the cat out of my lap. It sniffed at me snottily, but then just curled its body around the corner leading into the living room, looking back as if waiting on me.

I met Aiden's gaze. "You know what we need to do next."

He twisted his lips ruefully. "Interrogate Pearl Godfrey. But even though Mercury's only claimed visitor rights with the coven, Pearl might not want to give her up. She'll want to take care of the situation herself."

"No…" I touched his shoulder. Already sorry for what I was going to ask him to do. "We need to talk to your father."

Aiden's face blanked. "But he'll…he's not going to give us answers for nothing."

"I know."

"What…what are you willing to…" He trailed off without fully voicing the question.

How far was I willing to let Kader Azar into our lives? What freedom would I give up for Opal?

"Anything, Aiden. He can have anything. As long as I get Opal back. And Paisley."

He nodded. His eyes were deeply shadowed. But then he nodded a second time. "We're stronger than him."

I smiled tightly. "Yes, we are."

CHRISTOPHER HAD SEQUESTERED HIMSELF OUT ON the deck, seemingly watching the dawn slowly kiss the rolling surf while shuffling his oracle cards over and over. Judging by the amount of power pouring off him—all inadvertently amplified by my breakdown—he was more than likely navigating multiple future timelines. Trying to find our way to Opal.

His shoulders tight and his expression grim, Aiden was setting up the iPad in an odd corner of the main living room area. I'd barely paid any attention to the space, which was little more than a stub of a hallway that didn't actually go anywhere. I assumed now that it was supposed to be a tiny reading nook. Aiden had dragged a side table into the cramped space and placed the iPad screen so it displayed only the upholstered chair. He'd changed into a clean suit after our shower—navy blue with a crisp white shirt, no tie, and heavily layered with protection spells.

It took me a moment to understand that Aiden was trying to limit what his father would see when and if we got through to him. The sorcerer had suggested calling, but I'd insisted on the video feed. I needed to see Kader when I questioned him, and I actually didn't want to invite the intimacy of having his voice in my ear.

"Are you worried about him being able to track us?" I asked.

Aiden shook his head but didn't answer verbally as he touched every item in the nook. For the third time, even though they were already placed where he presumably wanted them.

"Aiden," I said as gently as I could when all I wanted to do was tear down anything and everything that stood between me and Opal. Logic was still keeping that panic at bay, but just barely. I had to know what needed to be rent asunder. I had to at least be pointed in the right direction.

"Five more minutes, please," the sorcerer said without looking at me.

I gave him his five minutes, but only because a quiet knock drew me to the door. I could feel Ocean and Lani in the hall beyond.

The moment I opened the door, Ocean had her arms around my neck, squeezing before I'd even gotten a good look at her. I met Lani's gaze over the younger witch's shoulder.

"Nothing?" the intuitive asked. She'd thrown an overly large lightweight sweater on over leggings. Her dark hair was mussed, and dark circles occupied the hollows under her eyes.

"Christopher's here. Opal's alive."

Ocean pressed her face into my throat, swallowing a sob. Then she released me to push into the room, her bare feet slapping lightly on the granite tile of the hall.

Lani reached for me, and though I normally didn't touch her—not wanting to involuntarily amplify a power that I still wasn't certain she wanted to wield—I took both her hands in mine.

"I can't figure it out," she whispered, emotion clogging her throat. "I'm...how did I not know that something was going to happen?"

My chest constricted, but I just shook my head, not really capable of having any sort of rational conversation. Not about Opal at least.

"Isn't that how my stupid, useless magic is supposed to work?" Lani dropped one of my hands to wipe at her face, a little harshly. Mad at herself.

We were all mad at ourselves, I realized.

We weren't supposed to be this fallible.

Lani cried quietly. "I even tried a circle with Ocean this morning, after she did another spell and wandered all around the grounds...where Opal was yesterday, she thought. Same as last night." She squeezed my hand. "Emma...you could amplify me. I'm supposed to be able to find things, right? Like with that weird swamp. You could use me like that again, right?"

"But you already knew something was wrong that time," I said, carefully working the connections through in my head. Thinking about how Lani had found me at Grant farm. "You'd already come to the property looking for me."

"Yes. But you used me to..."

I shook my head. "Maybe your power only works for things you can effect."

"What do you mean?"

"Maybe it has to be something you can fix, Lani."

Her expression crumpled. Her grip was so tight it was actually beginning to grind my finger bones together. "Emma," she gasped, "I don't want to be useless."

"I'm not going to amplify you for no reason, Lani. You don't want that, beyond this moment. Right?"

Her hazel eyes brimmed with tears, but she sucked in a breath and tried to compose herself. "Tell me what I can do."

Ocean appeared at my side. "A packed breakfast," she said with firm intent. "Christopher says they're going to need to move soon. And we two can't stay here, in the room. He's picking up too much already from Emma and Aiden."

I hadn't thought of that—that too many Adepts would cloud Christopher's sight. And the Godfrey witches would be up and moving soon enough, though I had no idea how long it had taken them to clean up Mercury's midnight slaughter.

I should have thought of it, of protecting Christopher's mind. But I wasn't really here, in the present. Not wholly. A huge hunk of me had been torn away when Paisley took Opal, and I...I...was barely holding onto the ragged edges.

Both Ocean and Lani were looking at me, their eyes brimming with unshed tears. I'd lost the thread of the conversation, so perhaps they were waiting for me to answer...something. Tell them something.

"Breakfast." Lani cleared her throat, looking at her watch. "The little cafe down the hall opens at six. Let's get an order together while we wait."

"Did you check on the beach and the mundane house?" I asked Ocean, my voice as strained as my mind. I had to get all the pieces of myself together before confronting Kader. Otherwise, he'd take what was left of me, and I wouldn't get what I needed.

No.

Stop it.

Stop being ridiculous. It was a mission.

Mercury Dunkirk couldn't take me on the best day of her life. And she definitely couldn't take Christopher, Aiden, and me together.

Ocean's expression was twisted, her gaze downcast. She must have answered my question, but I hadn't heard.

"Are the witches done?" I growled, sounding angry. Though only at myself.

Ocean nodded grimly. "The bespelling of the mundanes took hours."

Those without magic were actually quite resistant to having their minds and memories altered.

"Pearl took the memories of the survivors back about five minutes, then muddied…everything else. Since it was a party, hopefully no one will notice if they're missing any time or specific memories."

"And the three people Mercury slaughtered?"

Ocean sighed and swallowed. "If it worked, the witches…made the others think that one of the three murdered the first two, then committed suicide after knocking everyone out with some sort of gas. They called the mundane police in."

A triple murder-suicide.

Lani's body language was tense, fists clenched.

Ocean looked at her sympathetically. "Making the dead just disappear and completely wiping the memories of the survivors would have been more invasive."

"Even if they had a powerful telepath," I added. "They might have left more bodies on the floor. Or turned some of the mundanes into walking corpses." Taking and then rewriting memories from anyone was a delicate business. Even for a telepath of Bee's caliber.

"So I've been told," Lani said, clearly displeased.

"It wiped the core of the coven out," Ocean said. "They'll be sleeping for hours yet. That might be good...if...you know."

If more bodies were about to join the massacre Mercury had started. Just by my hand, my blade.

Ocean touched my elbow. "Aiden's ready for you. I hope you know what you're doing, Emma."

No one wanted to give Kader Azar any more power than he already wielded over all of us. Because he was Aiden's father, I couldn't just kill the sorcerer Azar and be done with it. Especially given that there was an odd chance that all of Kader's power—and therefore all the responsibilities of overseeing the Azar cabal—would be transferred to Aiden upon Kader's death. A sorcerer wielding the level of power that Kader had accumulated could trigger that sort of magical inheritance upon death. And Ocean had only recently discovered that her entire life had been financed by Kader, including the trust fund that allowed her to focus on her studies.

Also, there was the outstanding tricky bit about a death curse, which Kader had indicated he was all too willing to release against his entire bloodline should he be murdered.

"I always know what I'm doing," I said to Ocean, my tone cool.

She grimaced. "I didn't mean—"

Lani touched her shoulder. "We have our orders. Breakfast."

"Right." Ocean practically lunged at me, kissing my cheek. "I'll see you and Opal at home. We have a wedding to plan!" Then she was dragging Lani down the hall before the intuitive could add anything.

I let the door close and just stood in the quiet of the hall for one self-indulgent moment. I was about to do battle with the sorcerer Azar. But words had never been my best weapons.

"Father," Aiden said stiffly from the living room area. "Thank you for setting up the connection so we could speak."

I didn't hear Kader's response, but I wasn't going to let Aiden stand alone before his father. I pushed away from the door and strode forward.

AIDEN HAD JUST ENOUGH ROOM TO STAND SENTRY behind me, arms crossed and expression blank, though I could feel the conflicting emotions roiling around him without a single touch. My dark and deadly sorcerer wanted to hate his father, but that hate was all tangled up in also wanting to make him proud. Aiden needed to prove that he was powerful enough to be an Azar, despite his mix of witch and sorcerer blood.

I didn't understand. Or rather, I couldn't rationally empathize. I'd never had a single parental figure, and my still-unknown mixture of DNA was what made me so powerful.

What I could understand was being a parent. Even if I had only the barest of inklings of what that meant for me, I knew what it meant for Opal.

It meant I would always rescue her. I would always stand between her and harm. I'd always be hers.

And it made no difference that Kader's gaze had turned calculated when I sank into the chair Aiden had set up before the iPad, sticking one of the earbuds in my ear so I could hear the elder sorcerer. I would make him act like the parent I wanted to be. Even if I had to threaten him. And then follow up on those threats.

The irony being that I didn't think a single other of the Azars would act against me if I came for Kader. And I wouldn't come alone.

If I lost Opal, I would gather the other four, and the Five would rampage the world, tearing down everything that stood between us and vengeance.

I shoved that bloody thought away—because I wasn't losing Opal. I tuned back into whatever Kader was going on about. Aiden had decided that he wanted his father as far in the dark as we could leave him, so I'd asked about Mercury Dunkirk and Paisley's breeding program first.

"The witch who was wasting our time on those demon hybrids wasn't a member of the Collective." Kader was as casually dressed as I'd ever seen him, in a lightweight beige linen tunic with a short, stiff collar open at the neck, exposing his deeply tanned skin. The lack of a suit made me wonder what time zone he was in, though not enough to worry that we'd woken him. He projected boredom, seemingly a little put out that he'd been summoned to talk about things he deemed beneath himself.

Kader was a sly bastard. But he wasn't fooling me.

"She was simply an asset," he continued. "I would never have allowed demon DNA to be introduced into your pristine code, Emma."

Behind me, Aiden stiffened at that dig. Except I knew Kader actually thought he was complimenting me, flattering me. I reached back beside the chair, settling my hand on Aiden's calf before he could short out the iPad with a retaliatory burst of magic.

Kader's dark-brown gaze shifted, following the movement of my arm. Then he smirked as if delighted that he'd gotten a rise out of his youngest son.

I leaned closer to the iPad, making certain I filled his screen and blocking out his access to Aiden.

"But you knew everything there was to know about your assets, Kader. You wouldn't have worked with them otherwise."

"None of the witches who worked with the Collective claimed any coven affiliation," he said offishly.

"Don't make me threaten you," I said coolly. "You know I always follow through. And my doing so would hurt more than just you."

He huffed, tapping his long, unadorned fingers on the table before him for a moment. "Why now? I was under the impression you didn't care, Emma. That you were content in your life. Why start asking questions now?" He fixed me with his dark-eyed gaze. "Is something wrong with Paisley?"

"If you know," I said quietly, "and you think you're playing me, I will tear down everything you've built."

"Yes, yes. And murder me." He sighed affectedly.

"Oh, no," I said, smiling. "I'll keep you alive. And then I'll let the other four play with you as they will."

Kader's jaw clenched. Then his expression smoothed into that perfect blank slate that was an Azar trait. He even managed to mute the spark of anger in his gaze. Had I been in the room with him, I knew I wouldn't have been able to feel a drop of either magical power or emotion from him.

"I thought we were past all this nonsense," he said.

I was tired of talking.

"Paisley has been compromised," I said. "She has Opal. I need to know if this is bigger than simply…the demon dog overriding her programming."

Kader narrowed his eyes at me. "Where are you?"

"At the Godfrey coven retreat. They inducted Opal last night."

The sorcerer Azar sniffed derisively. "And your new friends cannot help you track—"

"I need your help, Father," I whispered. Finally giving him what I knew he wanted from me. An acknowledgement of his claim on me, outside of the hierarchy and history of the Collective. Even a hint of an emotional attachment.

Because all of Kader Azar's children loathed him to some extent, and he wanted a legacy.

Me. And the Five.

"I need to know everything you know about Mercury Dunkirk. And if she was connected to the Collective, I need to know in what capacity, and what to expect when I go after her. I need an address. Give me locations, and I can have Christopher focus his sight."

"You have the clairvoyant with you?" Kader asked. His tone was sharper now, engaged. But he didn't wait for an answer before continuing, "I'll reach out to my former colleagues…those who have survived the telekinetic's and the nullifier's spree of vengeance. I'll email Aiden all I have right now, then text as new information comes in."

Christopher stepped around the corner. "A ferry. Not as large as the one we travelled on from the mainland to the island. I see you on a ferry, Emma."

I glanced back at Kader. "We're about to be on a small ferry—"

"Midsized," Christopher corrected.

"Midsized," I said to Kader. "Let us know if you find any probable locations for Mercury that can be reached by ferry from Vancouver Island."

Kader nodded. His attention also partly divided. I realized he'd muted his sound, and could see him giving what appeared to be brusque orders to someone offscreen.

A little bit of relief twined through me. As idiotic as it was to rely on Kader Azar, I felt relieved that he was at least willing to help.

Christopher crossed to me, knelt beside my chair, and threaded his fingers through mine. He pushed the iPad back so he occupied the screen alongside me.

Kader looked at the clairvoyant for a long while, studying him. Then he looked at our joined hands. The sorcerer Azar smiled, bright and brilliant, and reached for his screen—to turn on the speaker, I presumed. "Christopher."

I would have you know me. The first time I'd come face-to-face with Kader Azar, rescuing him from the rogue shifters who'd kidnapped and tortured him under the direction of Silver Pine, Chenda—aka the Mystic of the Golden Peninsula—and his own son Isa, he had looked at me the way he looked at

Christopher now. He'd asked my name, and I'd told him that I was simply a designation.

That had angered him. But maybe not for the reason I'd always assumed.

The clairvoyant inclined his head, though he wouldn't have actually heard Kader without an ear-bud. His light-gray eyes were rimmed with bright white. He'd never met the architect of the Collective.

"Father," the clairvoyant said.

Aiden sighed heavily.

Kader nodded, just once. Then he went immediately back to business. "Aiden will have everything I have on hand now. I'll text as soon as I have a possible location. I can be with you in less than twenty-four hours."

"That's not—" Aiden started to protest.

Kader simply disconnected the call.

Aiden stalked out from around the chair and table, turning back toward Christopher and me. Confusion and disbelief etched across his face. "You didn't bargain."

"What would you have had me say no to?" I asked, settling into that cool rationale that always overtook me before a battle. "For Opal. What line would have been too far, too much?"

Aiden shook his head. He opened his mouth, then shut it.

"He could have had anything, Aiden," I said quietly, squeezing Christopher's hand. "I could endure anything. If it meant I got Opal back."

"Yes," my Knox said.

"We," Aiden said, his voice suddenly rough. "He can have anything if it means *we* get Opal back."

"Yes."

A notification popped up on the screen of the iPad—likely the email Kader had promised.

And that was all Christopher's power needed to grab hold of. That was the key to unlocking the visions that had just been waiting to manifest.

"Welcome to Westview ferry terminal," the clairvoyant gasped. His hand spasmed in mine as he tried to navigate whatever his magic was telling him.

Aiden snatched up the iPad, fingers flying over its surface. "Powell River," the dark and deadly sorcerer snarled. Then he clasped his hand on Christopher's shoulder. "It's an hour and a half by ferry from Comox. A three-hour drive from here. Just point me in the right direction, my brother. Get me close. I'll get us the rest of the way."

"By tracking Mercury?" I asked, momentarily confused.

Aiden smiled, smug and focused. "Tracking Opal. She's currently wearing no less than five tracking runes. Plus I can home in on the resonance of the amethyst cluster. I took an imprint."

Christopher barked out a laugh. "And Emma? How many ways can you track our amplifier, sorcerer?"

Aiden didn't even bother to look embarrassed. "Three. But I have to renew the runes every three days or so. Even when they aren't touching Emma's skin, her magic eats away at them."

Still laughing, Christopher rolled to his feet. "We'll need gas before we hit the highway." He glanced back over his shoulder at me, his eyes blazing white. "And Socks needs to sleep."

I sprang to my feet, a ready snarl on my lips—both at the order and at the suggestion that I was less than ready to move out immediately.

Aiden raised his hand. "Opal is our dream walker, my love. She's obviously reaching for you."

And Christopher had seen as much.

"You could be a little clearer, asshole!" I called after the clairvoyant as he crossed farther into the suite.

He didn't answer. Though if it weren't Opal we were so desperate to retrieve, I assumed he would have shot something snarky back. Most likely about my own generally abysmal communication abilities.

Aiden was watching me, all sharp-eyed and brooding. Waiting for me to chide him about sneakily tracking Opal and me. About his rampant possessiveness.

Except that would have been seriously hypo-critical of me.

I closed the space between us, threading my fingers through the thick but silky hair at the back of his neck. Up on my tiptoes, I hovered my lips over his, just breathing him for a moment. He was tense under my touch, coiled and ready. Not to attack me, but to lash out at anything else. A not-uncommon reaction after any interaction with Kader Azar.

"You already said we couldn't kill your father," I murmured.

"The death curse." He ghosted his fingertips up my bare arm.

"But that doesn't mean we can't…keep him."

Aiden reared back slightly, not enough to break my hold, but enough to force eye contact. "He didn't impose terms…"

I grinned, wide and fierce. "Which leaves a lot of leeway…on both sides."

Aiden laughed huskily, shaking his head slightly. "And…I underestimated you."

I shrugged playfully. "I'm not good with words. I can see why you thought I got caught up in his boring rhetoric, in his feigned indifference."

Aiden snorted. "Only you could find my father boring."

"He wants you in his life," I said. "More than anything else."

"Not just me."

I nodded because I couldn't dispute Aiden's assessment of his father's motivations for helping us.

"You deliberately mentioned all five of you!" he said accusingly.

"Bait."

He swooped in to bite my lower lip. A slight chastisement—for worrying him, I thought—that quickly turned into a heated moment of need and fear we unleashed on each other.

Aiden pulled away first, pressing his forehead to mine. "Some bindings are hard to sever, once reinforced."

I kissed him lightly. "I'm not interested in severing any bonds, Aiden. I want Opal safe. I want Paisley safe. Your father's minor hold can be easily mitigated."

Aiden grimaced slightly, but didn't offer further argument.

With our suitcases already packed and the clairvoyant collected, we were out the door only minutes later. Lani and Ocean, carrying two brown paper bags that looked as though they held way more food than we could possibly need, met us halfway down the hall.

The younger witch was pale, her eyes reddened as she silently wrapped her arms around Aiden's neck and just held on for a moment.

Lani touched Christopher on the shoulder as she passed him one bag. "Eat the fried-egg sandwiches right away. They're still warm."

The clairvoyant kissed her lightly on the cheek and exited into the parking lot. The white of the magic pouring out of his eyes would become incapacitating if he was surrounded by any more Adepts. Hours in the tight confines of a vehicle with Aiden and me wasn't going to be easy for Christopher to navigate either.

A text message pinged through on Aiden's phone, and he broke his embrace with his youngest sister to pull the device out of his pocket. Three more pings were heard before he too was stepping out after Christopher without another word.

I took the second bag of food from Ocean and pressed the keys to the Mustang into Lani's hands.

"I feel like I really messed up, Emma," Lani whispered. Her throat sounded raw. "Was...was Mercury trying to get to you through me?"

I shook my head. "I don't know. And I don't care. It has no impact on my...our relationship either way."

Lani nodded, stepping back and wrapping her arms around herself.

Those hadn't been the right words, the right sentiment. But I would have to figure that out after I got Opal back. "Take care of each other, please," I said gruffly, turning away quickly to follow the sorcerer and clairvoyant.

Ocean threaded her arm through Lani's. "Don't worry about us, Emma."

I left them, crossing through the parking lot and climbing into the back seat of Aiden's dark-burgundy Mercedes SUV. The sorcerer had already backed it out of its parking spot.

Messages were still pinging through on everyone's devices. Aiden had turned the alerts on so he wouldn't miss a single thing, and Christopher had commandeered my own phone since I sucked at checking it. But with each brain-piercing ping, I grew slightly more concerned...just slightly...about how deeply I was allowing Kader Azar to embed himself into our lives.

I had all but destroyed the Collective once before, though. And they would never be able to hold me again. Because I had Opal and Aiden to protect now, not just Paisley and the other four.

And Kader Azar knew what I was capable of, what he'd bred and raised me to be. So he would come at me far, far more subtly the next time.

WHILE AIDEN DROVE, CHRISTOPHER SKIMMED ALL the info that Kader had emailed. It was seriously thin, mostly single-line reports from the department that Mercury had indeed run for the Collective—focused on the breeding of demon hybrids. The bulk of it was in code, including the names of the department heads, even Kader and Chenda. The Mystic of the Golden Peninsula, who had claimed to be Christopher's mother, who had attempted to quell me using the bonds that tied me to the Five, and who had been bound from doing further harm to us herself. On paper, at least.

"I don't think that Mercury is the Chemist," Christopher muttered from the front seat.

"Kader confirmed that," I said, somewhat pissily. I hated discussing the Collective. "She was just one of the Collective's employees."

"I must have missed that part of the conversation," the clairvoyant practically snarled, "since only you and Aiden were wearing headphones, and you haven't deigned to illuminate me on the finer details."

I opened my mouth to rip into him about using his vaunted sight if he wanted clarification, but Aiden skillfully interrupted before a fight could truly explode.

"The Chemist?" he asked without taking his gaze off the road. I could see him checking each sign obsessively, watching for our next turnoff even though he had the GPS programed to get us all the way back across the island, then farther up the east coast to the ferry.

"Zans and Fish think they've identified all the main members of the Collective," Christopher said, "except two. One is someone codenamed 'the Chemist.' Based on what I can read of these internal memos...Mercury provided the magic, the demons, and the animals, but the Chemist sliced the genes. Mixed the DNA. They would have also been the one to do the mixing of the genetic makeup of the Five."

Aiden grunted. "Using donations from other Adepts, including my father. And Chenda, the mystic."

"And Silver Pine, I assume. Though wasn't there some inference that she was a newer member?"

The question wasn't specifically directed at me, so I didn't answer it.

Silence fell.

The SUV chewed up more road.

Christopher shook his head, scrubbing a hand across his face. "I need Zans's help to break the code.

But as best I can piece together, Paisley's litter was the only successful demon hybrids to have come from the program."

Which meant that either Mercury had continued the program on her own—or that her familiars weren't necessarily full demon crossbreeds. Normal creatures fed demon blood and flesh maybe? Though in my experience, both were rather acidic. As in the melting of skin and bone sort of acid.

The lack of information Kader had bothered to retain about Mercury's department only reinforced the disdain the elder sorcerer had for that particular branch of the Collective. His disdain for anything other than the building and breeding of uber-powerful Adepts. Building, breeding, and controlling.

Except the controlling part hadn't worked out for the Collective with the fifth generation of their creations. Or, more specifically, the choice to use an empath as my surrogate had undone the Collective's control. Because even when wielded by a recovering sociopath like me, empathy could apparently become a catalyst for the mass destruction of over a hundred years of research, and the focused intent of at least a half-dozen powerful Adepts.

Not that I bothered keeping track of the members of the Collective.

I left that to Samantha and Fish.

Christopher had forwarded everything, including the texts that kept pinging through to Aiden's phone, to Samantha, but we still hadn't heard back from the telekinetic.

I forced myself to stretch out in the back seat, to try to sleep. I had eaten the breakfast sandwich Christopher forced upon me while it was still warm, not even tasting it enough to know what it contained.

Aiden continued to break all the speed limits heading for the ferry.

Christopher's power shifted almost imperceptibly around him in the front seat. He put the phones away and pulled out his oracle cards, but his power didn't intensify.

I couldn't sleep.

I desperately needed to sleep, and I couldn't.

"What if Mercury has her warded?" I said, speaking into the silence swamping the interior of the SUV. Normally I had no issue with the quiet. But nothing was normal that morning. "What if Opal can't reach through to my dreams?"

"She'll find you," Aiden said. "She's strong, and you two are connected, bound by magic and love." He flicked his eyes up into the rearview mirror, though I wasn't certain how much of me he could see at that angle. "And you'll talk her through how to claim any wards of Mercury's for herself."

"I remember," I said belligerently. Aiden had talked me through the specifics of having Opal claim any offensive ward while I was stuffing food in my mouth and not tasting it.

"She uses the crystal as an anchor—"

"I remember, Aiden!"

My dark sorcerer fell silent.

I squeezed my eyes shut, breathing through a well of panic. "I'm sorry."

Aiden reached back and squeezed my knee. "I love you. I love Opal. I love our life together. Nothing will stop me from getting you to her."

"I know."

"Thanks for the inclusion, sorcerer," Christopher muttered.

Aiden laughed quietly.

And some of the tension eased. Just enough for me to breathe slightly deeper.

I tried meditating.

Yes, I was that desperate.

But I wasn't built to sleep during high-pressure situations. I was built to push forward, to keep those around me moving and focused. I was built to take energy when I needed it, not grab a nap to refuel. All of the Five were built that way and trained in that mindset. To push forward until our bodies shut down, even though our minds might be compromised far more quickly.

I had dragged my Knox through jungles, through deserts. Through foreign city streets that he never saw with his actual senses, streets that I doubted he even retained any memory of passing through. With his power pouring from him, his mind subverted so that only his body still functioned, still moved by rote, still anticipated what was coming at us. What was coming at me.

During those sorts of missions, just as with breaking out of the compound, it was often only my ability to focus, to remain alert, that got us through.

"Socks," Christopher whispered quietly from the front seat.

I couldn't see him, likely hunched forward over the iPad and various phones. But I was apparently triggering him, triggering his sight, and not in a focused way.

"A sleep rune?" I asked Aiden without hope.

He reached back through the seats, squeezing my knee again. "It might block Opal from reaching you."

I nodded, an odd desperation that I'd never actually felt before clawing at my insides. "Every time I close my eyes, I can see...I remember the look that Paisley gave me right before she snatched Opal."

Mercury had somehow commanded Paisley to grab me. But why? I still had no idea. I was neither a demon nor an animal. Even as a former member of the Collective, Mercury neither had use for me nor the ability to contain me.

"She..." I swallowed a spike of emotion that would only lead to tears if I let it free. "Paisley realized something...that I was too powerful to grab? That she wouldn't be able to hold me, let alone transport me? But she also knew...despite whatever Mercury had done to her..."

Aiden was squeezing my knee again, fiercely enough to leave bruises. And I accepted the pain, welcomed it as a focal point.

"Paisley realized…" Aiden said, his own voice clogged with emotion, "… that you would follow Opal."

"To the ends of the earth," Christopher added.

"To the depths of hell," I whispered, agreeing.

"We're going to give Mercury Dunkirk more than she ever thought she could want," Aiden said.

Christopher laughed quietly, though likely at something his magic was showing him, not the present conversation. "Yeah, if the black witch thought she could use Paisley to get to Emma, she's going to be shocked when we all show up on her doorstep."

"She doesn't know…" I murmured, staring up at the ceiling of the SUV. "For all her taunting on the beach, Mercury doesn't know about Christopher. And I doubt she knew about me or Paisley. Not until she saw us."

"For a sloppy plan, it was still too effective," Aiden snarled.

Christopher huffed. "The Collective didn't foster weakness, sorcerer. Not even in its employees, never mind its founding members."

"No…" Aiden squeezed my knee gently a last time, then withdrew his hand. "Weakness wouldn't have survived any induction my father would have overseen."

"You do realize that he stepped into the position, right?" Christopher said. "He's too young to have been a founding member of an organization that stretches back over a hundred years, as far as Samantha has been able to track."

Aiden glanced at the clairvoyant. "I didn't realize that. So...he took over the position?"

"Maybe even expanded it or focused it," Christopher said with a shrug. "But yeah, he's not the—"

Something landed on my stomach, hard enough that I lost my breath with a whoosh. I snatched the creature by the neck, only refraining from tearing off its head with my bare hands when I realized it was Mercury's goblin cat. It hung in my hold, clawed toes barely taking any of its weight.

And blinked at me.

Christopher had twisted around in his seat. He started laughing. "Stowaway!"

"Some clairvoyant you are," I said snottily.

That insult only incited more laughter.

Even Aiden was grinning. "Some sorcerer I am. I didn't even pick up its magic."

"It's muted underneath Emma's. Everything is," Christopher said, though without heat.

I released the cat. It turned around a few times, then settled onto my stomach. Aiden glanced back, highly amused—mostly in response to whatever expression was etched across my face. Disbelief? Mixed with wariness.

I was not a cat person.

But then again, I wasn't a demon dog or chicken or mason bee person. And that had all kind of sorted itself out around me.

The little goblin closed its bulbous eyes and started purring. A warm engine of comfort.

Christopher laughed again in quietly knowing fashion.

I knew that if I let him, the clairvoyant would spout something idiotic about fate.

Still…I shifted the sweater I was using as a pillow and closed my eyes.

The clairvoyant reached back along the side of the seat, only able to touch my shoulder without twisting farther around. His power pulsed lightly against my skin. "Breathe," he said. "We're with you. I'll see you finding Opal. I know it. Breathe. Sleep."

I breathed.

I sank into the feeling of Christopher's power. It wrapped around my shoulder and neck, slipping down my spine and pooling on my T3 vertebra. I focused on that awareness, filtering out all other sound and motion.

Except for the damn goblin cat.

So I let the unwanted stowaway lull my other senses. Its purring, both heard and felt, settled into my skin, and my brain finally gave way and shut down.

I WOKE—OR RATHER, I BECAME AWARE—WHEN GENtle fingers brushed across my cheek. Opening my eyes, I connected with orbs of sky blue slashed through with brown nearly the same color as her skin.

"Hello, my little witch," I whispered as I touched her cheek. So that for a moment, it was just the two of us—me lying on some wood floor and her hovering over me. The halo of her hair shut out the rest of the world.

"Found you," Opal whispered. Then a terrible sob racked her tiny body in a horrible expulsion of pain.

But when I reached for her, she shook her head and squared her shoulders resolutely.

I let my arms drop. But unwilling to completely let her go, I settled my hand over hers. She let me offer her that little comfort.

A rippling snarl emanated through the otherwise empty room. A malicious sound I had never heard before and hoped to never hear again. Because the underlying voice was unmistakable.

Paisley.

The room lost its solid edges.

Shuddering with the effort, Opal closed her eyes and breathed deeply. The room—the dreamscape the young witch had pulled me into—solidified, and I could see a window cased in wood, a brick fireplace on the far wall. Both of which were barred by metal and no doubt by magic.

I could work with a fireplace. Because fireplaces came with chimneys. And chimneys were bold beacons on the top of a house that led directly down to the room that housed the fireplace.

"Why are you smiling like that?" Opal asked.

"Because I'm coming for you," I said. "And no one…no person, no magic, no demon, and no building…can stand against me."

Opal took a shuddering breath. And for the briefest of moments, her eye appeared swollen, the side of her face bruised.

I shot up, grabbing her shoulders and inadvertently knocking the goblin cat off my stomach with the motion. Yes, apparently the creepy creature had made the transition into the dream with me.

The hairless cat yowled discontentedly. I ignored it, bodily moving Opal closer to the window, to the only light source, then peering down at her.

Her skin was pristine. Both eyes unbruised.

"Opal!" I growled.

She hunched her shoulders, almost curling into herself. "It's nothing, Emma. It's noth—"

Anger fueled by frustration rolled off me, along with a tsunami of power. "I will destroy everything she loves," I vowed darkly. "I will make her watch as I dismantle her life, and only then will I drain her, drop by painful drop until—"

The room became hazy around me.

"You're destabilizing the connection, Emma," Opal snapped pissily.

Damn it!

I sat down right where I stood, crossing my legs and closing my eyes. I felt the firmness of the floor under me, then the wall at my back. I yanked on my power, gathering it all into me.

Purring like an utter moron, the goblin cat settled in my lap. I was too busy reining myself in to push it away.

It had nothing to do with any growing affection or connection.

It wasn't even a real cat. Not in the dreamscape anyway.

"Wow." Opal hunkered down in front of me. "Impressive."

"Everything I do is impressive," I said, my lips twitching as I repressed a smile.

She grinned at me, flashing her crooked eyeteeth.

I struggled to not melt into a pool of frustrated despair.

How had all this reactionary emotion become my life? I loathed it. Except…I couldn't really loathe it, since it came with Aiden and Opal.

"Tell me," I said brusquely, making it an order because I needed focus—and because the dream walker needed to know she was going to be okay.

Opal nodded. "I'm in a house. I think. It's tall. Like maybe I'm on the top level. Not a corner. I can see the forest and green-covered mountains. And…that's it."

"Paisley brought you there?"

Opal shrugged, her gaze downcast. "I woke up in the room." She swallowed. "Mercury was really mad to find me here."

"She hit you."

Opal blinked at me, then nodded reluctantly.

I held onto my anger. Barely.

"It was maybe a good thing?" Opal whispered. She tilted her head as if listening.

I fisted my hands, then realized I was doing so and relaxed them. I might not have been able to project outward calm, but I could try to not be completely unhinged. For Opal's sake.

Then I heard that vicious snarling again. As if the sound was filtering through from Opal's reality, and she could hear it subconsciously even while she was sleeping. To reach me.

"How was Mercury hitting you a good thing?" My tone was stiff. Hard, even, but I couldn't soften it.

"It broke some of her hold on Paisley."

Seeing Opal hurt had allowed the demon dog to regain some autonomy. "How much?"

Opal wet her lips. "She won't let Mercury hurt me, but she...she's still not herself. She won't let me touch her, help her."

"I'm coming."

"You know where we are?"

"Christopher sees you." I couldn't lie to her. "Glimpses. And when we get close, Aiden will be able to track you."

"Even through wards?"

I touched her face gently, just below where I'd seen the bruise. "Nothing will stand in our way. That's what you get for choosing us. The bad and the good." I frowned slightly. "The room is warded?"

Opal nodded.

I allowed a grin, full of fierce pride, to encapsulate my face, letting the moment soothe a tiny section of my ragged soul. "Look how powerful you are, dream walker."

Opal blinked at me, confused. Then a tentative grin bloomed on her face, "Maybe Mercury forgot about the dream walking? So she didn't ward against it?"

I shook my head. "She knows. Any wards she had on the room would have been altered when she realized she was holding you. She's just not powerful enough to counter you, to dampen our bond." I held out my arms.

Finally giving in to the need to be comforted, Opal climbed into my lap. Instead of taking off, the goblin cat simply shifted into the young witch's lap, so that I was cuddling both of them.

The snarling sharpened, deepening in intensity.

Opal's gaze flicked to a door that hadn't been there a moment ago. "I can't stay with you much longer. Paisley needs me. Needs me awake. Otherwise, she really…freaks out. And then…" She sobbed. "Mercury hurts her. Really bad."

I wrapped my power around her, aware that I couldn't actually amplify the little witch in a dream. But desperately needing to give her everything I had to give until I could get my actual arms around her. She was so brave, fearing for Paisley when any other child would be—

I shook my head. Opal hadn't been a child for a long time. That childhood had been snatched away by her birth mother's death and the things she'd been forced to do to survive.

"You're coming, right?" she asked in a whisper. "I'll tell Paisley...I...I asked her to go to you, to lead you to me, but...first she wouldn't leave me, and then..."

"And then?"

"Mercury hurt her so much...I don't think that she can walk through the shadows anymore." The young witch radiated a pain that was all emotion.

I inhaled deeply, and my subconscious finally remembered the prep Aiden had run me through. "Opal. Do you still have the amethyst cluster?"

"Yes." She smiled smugly. "Mercury can't take it away from me." Her smile faded.

That was why the black witch had hit her. She had tried to force the dream walker to hand over her grounding crystal.

"Why?" Opal asked.

"Because you're going to claim the wards on the room."

"To break out?"

"No. You'll take them for your own, to keep Mercury out."

"Aiden...Aiden told you how to do that?"

"He did. And I'm going to tell you."

"Okay." She nodded, then tilted her head slightly, listening again. "Maybe I can figure out how to let Paisley in first…"

My stomach soured, and I almost told her no. Almost ordered her to leave the demon dog, almost told her Paisley could take care of herself.

Except that wasn't who Opal was, and it was better to help her than hinder her.

"Emma? I'll be safer with Paisley in the room with me."

I shoved my panicked response away. Opal was at ground zero with Paisley. I had to trust her assessment of the demon dog's mental stability. Plus…if Mercury was torturing Paisley…

I tamped down on another almost overwhelming surge of anger, tempering my response. "Maybe. But you have to be careful to not leave any holes for Mercury to exploit."

Opal shifted off my lap, still holding onto the madly purring goblin cat, its red-hued eyes fixed on me. She pulled the amethyst cluster out of the pocket of her cloak. "I promise…" Her voice hitched. "I'll do my best."

"You always do, my Opal."

"Tell me what to do."

The room had almost faded away by the time I ran through the last of Aiden's instructions with Opal. I clung to it, to the dream, to the image of her for as long as I could.

And then I woke up in the reality of the back seat of the SUV, with loudspeakers overhead announcing the loading of a ferry. We were in line at the terminal, waiting to drive on. The goblin cat was still asleep on my stomach, breathing almost silently.

I turned my head and met Aiden's gaze. He'd likely felt my magic shift as I woke. "She's okay. Opal…she's going to be okay."

He nodded, his face etched with suppressed anger.

"Paisley?" Christopher asked from the front passenger seat.

I closed my eyes, hearing the echoes of that snarling—the vicious, deadly sound of a desperate creature in pain. "Alive," I said, my tone flat. "But we need to keep moving."

Christopher sighed, his head bowed forward. "That's what I thought."

A heavy pain settled on my chest. I sat up, careful to not dislodge the goblin cat, in an attempt to shove the emotions away. Both my own and what I was suddenly picking up from Christopher.

He had seen something while I was sleeping.

Something about Paisley.

She wasn't going to make it.

"I'll step right," I said quietly. Then I firmed my tone.

I could thwart Christopher's visions. I had before, and I would again.

It wasn't an ego thing. It was a power thing. A me thing.

"I'll step right instead of left."

Christopher looked back at me through the seats, his eyes rimmed with simmering power and unshed tears. "Okay." He nodded and offered me a sad smile. "I believe, Fox in Socks. I always believe in you."

The car in front of us pulled forward, and Aiden shifted the SUV into drive, following.

I handed Christopher the goblin cat. It snarled and hissed quietly, but didn't protest the change of venue for long. And my Knox needed the comfort. I had already amplified him far too much, so he was going to have to take that comfort from the creepy cat who had decided we belonged to it.

"It needs a name," Christopher said, handing me a bottle of water.

"We're not keeping it," I said testily.

"Right." Christopher's power shifted across the blood tattoo on my spine, but he kept whatever his magic had shown him to himself.

We drove onto the ferry in silence.

Less than two hours away from the dream walker now. Just as long as we weren't heading in the wrong direction.

NINE

CHRISTOPHER HOPPED OUT OF THE FRONT SEAT barely a breath after Aiden shut off the SUV. The clairvoyant was opening the back door and practically pulling me out even as other vehicles were still loading behind and around us.

"I'm fine here," I snarled at him, displeased at the skin-to-skin contact he was forcing on me. "And you'll be better away from—"

"I see you upstairs, at a table by the window."

"Doing what?" Still peeved, I climbed out of the vehicle and tried to smooth out my dress and hair. Not that it mattered if I looked rumpled. I just hated drawing any attention, judgemental or not.

Christopher looked away from me, outright refusing to elaborate. And normally, I wouldn't have pushed. Normally, I let him decide what he wanted to tell me. The clairvoyant had his own rules when it came to sharing visions. His own feelings about what could or couldn't, what should or shouldn't, be changed. But I was in a terrible mood.

As in, I wanted to tear the world asunder. I knew in the dark, tattered depths of my soul that I had that capacity. And if I lost Opal…

I might just drag Aiden down that path with me. Aiden and Christopher. Zans, Fish, and Bee.

I folded my arms across my chest and refused to budge.

Aiden skirted around the SUV. The damn goblin cat was perched on the sorcerer's shoulder, looking around as if it already owned the place.

Well, that was going to draw much more attention than a rumpled sundress.

Christopher snorted at Aiden, eyeing the cat and then turning his light-gray gaze on me. His power was a mere whisper of energy, even from the blood tattoo embedded into my spine. He wasn't being triggered, wasn't lost in multiple possible futures. He had clear sight.

I just leveled a look at him. Still waiting.

The ferry wasn't full, most of the passengers already filtering up to the seating areas on the upper decks, or to grab breakfast or coffee.

The clairvoyant grimaced. "I don't know…all right?"

"How important can it be, then?" I asked. "I'm not hungry, and I'm tired of talking. You and Aiden are going over everything Kader has sent." Even those text messages had slowed as I'd taken my precious moment with Opal while I slept. The sorcerer Azar had yet to uncover a recent location for Mercury Dunkirk, but I suspected what little information he had sent was fueling Christopher's sight. And that was all I needed to find my little witch.

"Listen to me for once in your goddamn life," Christopher snarled quietly.

"Watch your words, asshole," Aiden snarled back, actually shifting so his shoulder was partly in front of me.

Christopher stepped up, into Aiden's face. They were practically the same height, the clairvoyant only slightly shorter. "You don't stand between me and Socks, sorcerer. Ever. Married or not. Bonded or not. That's not your place."

Power boiled around Aiden's hands, around his rune-etched copper rings. "Step back." Like me, the sorcerer had been a breath away from wanton destruction since we'd discovered Opal had been taken. Unlike me, he hid it a lot better.

Christopher actually puffed out his chest, actually moved closer. But then the goblin cat perched on Aiden's shoulder swiped at the clairvoyant, scoring claw marks across his cheek.

He stumbled a step back, hand going to his face in stunned surprise. His golden skin was speckled with blood in four thin lines.

The goblin cat leaped off Aiden's shoulder onto the top of the SUV. Then—purring insanely loudly—it began licking its paw and its claws clean.

I could actually feel the tiny sparks of Christopher's magic it was consuming.

Aiden was having a difficult time not outright smirking.

The cut on Christopher's cheek healed almost instantly, and he dragged his gaze away from the goblin cat to me. Before he could open his mouth and say anything to further aggravate me—presumably something about how much the cat suited my personality—I turned and met the goblin cat's eyes.

It stiffened, lowering the paw it had been cleaning.

"No," I said firmly. "Though the clairvoyant forgets it himself sometimes, we don't harm each other in this family."

Christopher stiffened behind me, his power condensing even tighter around him. But he wisely kept his mouth shut.

"Do you want to stay?" I asked the goblin cat.

It lay down, settling over its front paws and bringing its eyes almost even with mine. Then it blinked.

"Never again," I said. "If you need blood, you may hunt within reason. But never from anyone under my protection. Never again."

The goblin cat batted a paw toward me, playfully.

I reached up, and it gently curled its claws around my forefinger.

Christopher muttered something under his breath. Cursing, I presumed. But when I turned my gaze back on him, he simply scrubbed his hand through his hair, sadness etched across his face, heavy on his shoulders.

"Why?" I asked gently. Well, gently for me. "I could try to have another nap, to check on Opal."

The clairvoyant shook his head. "I see you. And I know you need to be there. For…" White magic flared across his eyes, and his breath hitched for a moment. "To find Opal…quickly. The quicker the better, Socks. We don't have time for Aiden's tracking spells now."

The dark-haired sorcerer barely swallowed a moan of pain, drawing Christopher's attention. The clairvoyant clapped Aiden on the shoulder, then when the sorcerer responded in kind, drew him in for a hug.

"I'm sorry," Christopher whispered, his gaze locked to mine over Aiden's shoulder. "Will you let me lead? Just for a little while?"

For the briefest of moments, every instinct I had when it came to the clairvoyant flared to life. That he needed to be protected. That he wasn't to be trusted. And, fundamentally, that we didn't believe in the same things.

Specifically, I didn't believe in what Christopher would willingly sacrifice in the name of what he believed to be fate and destiny.

"Yes," I said.

Aiden and Christopher parted. The clairvoyant stuffed his hands in his pockets, head bowed, as he turned toward the stairwell. The dark-haired sorcerer pressed a kiss to my temple, breathing me in as I stepped past him. I threaded my fingers through his and pulled him with me.

"Guard the vehicle, please," I said over my shoulder to the goblin cat currently pretending to be asleep on the roof of the SUV.

"Don't let any of the mundanes see you," Aiden added. Then a few steps later, he said, "So picking up strays is going to be life with you?"

I gave him a look.

He flashed me a devastating grin meant to knock me onto my back and charm me out of my panties.

I smirked at him, reminding him nonverbally that even if I disliked games, it didn't mean I couldn't subvert the parameters for my own means. Specifically, him pinned under me. Or even better, pinned against the stairwell wall, with me on my knees before him and him begging for mercy.

Aiden laughed huskily.

"Time and place," Christopher called from halfway up the stairs in front of us. "Time and fucking place. Like I already don't have enough in my head."

CHRISTOPHER LED US TO A TABLE, THEN REDIRECTED me with a flick of his fingers when I went to sit across from him. Placing me next to him, on the aisle. The clairvoyant directed his attention out the window, and Aiden went off in search of coffee.

"Now what?" I muttered. As far as I could sense, there wasn't a single other magical signature on board the entire ferry.

"We drink tea," Christopher said mildly, his power at a low simmer—aware but not triggered.

Except I didn't just sit and drink tea. Well, okay—I did, but only when I wanted to. But I sat there as asked, and I would wait. Because I had to trust Christopher. At least when it came to Opal.

Aiden returned with coffee for himself and Christopher, and hot water for me. I looked at him questioningly. He tugged a reusable tea bag out of his pocket and slid it across the table to me.

I shook my head at him. But willing myself to accept the offered distraction, I raised the loose-weaved bag to my nose and inhaled. Lemongrass, ginger, orange peel, and a hint of licorice and black pepper.

"Lemon ginger," I said, lips twisted into a smile despite my resolve to remain in an utterly pissy mood until I had Opal back. Aiden had packed me tea from home and tucked it away in the safe in his study, just so he could pull it out of his pocket at the perfect time.

"One of your favorites in the morning." The dark-haired sorcerer pinned me with one of his soul-searing looks. "I'd offer you sugar..."

"But I don't add it to this tea." I dropped the tea bag into my hot water. My heart was hurting, even as I tried to smile at my dark sorcerer. If I was being completely rational, it was actually the muscles of my chest, and therefore my breathing, that were constricted due to a chemical reaction to Aiden's sweet gesture. It felt like pain, though. Mostly because I couldn't feel any joy. Not without Opal.

"Why don't you ever smolder like that in my direction, sorcerer?" Christopher complained teasingly.

Aiden huffed a laugh.

And freed from the intense moment, I capped my to-go container, then reached for one of the three devices the clairvoyant had arrayed on his side of the table—his phone, my phone, and Aiden's iPad. I needed to set a timer, not wanting to oversteep my—

A woman paused next to the table. She'd been crossing toward us, but since I hadn't registered any power signature or apparent threat from her, I hadn't paid any attention.

She stopped just out of my reach.

Because Pearl Godfrey wasn't an idiot.

The three of us just stared at her. She could have slaughtered us all, had she been so inclined, because I had no doubt she had the power to do so.

The head of the Godfrey coven flicked a slightly disapproving gaze from me to Aiden, lingering for a moment on Christopher. Then she rested her indigo eyes on me.

I still couldn't feel a drop of magic from her.

"We haven't all been introduced," she said, voice clipped and again with a sharp edge of disapproval.

I had never taken orders well. I'd never had a parental figure, let alone one that I actually wanted approval from. Yet Pearl Godfrey made me...react.

"My brother," I said. "Christopher Johnson. Clairvoyant."

Pearl nodded at Christopher.

"Pearl Godfrey, head of the Godfrey coven, chair of the witches Convocation," I said, not daring to actually turn my head enough to look at Christopher.

"Pleased to—" Christopher started to say, but Pearl cut him off with a flick of her fingers toward Aiden.

I froze for a moment, waiting for whatever spell she'd released to hit.

I actually froze.

Me. With all my violent survival skills.

But it wasn't magic the elder witch was wielding. It was a nonverbal command. And Aiden followed it dutifully, ceding the chair across from me to Pearl and sitting next to the window instead.

Pearl sat, her gaze on me steady. Waiting, but patient.

"Why didn't I see you?" Christopher blurted. "I'm...I'm pretty impossible to block."

The tiniest of smirks lit up the elder witch's eyes. Gently, she uncoiled the gossamer lace scarf she had curled around her neck, exposing the oddest necklace I'd ever seen. A series of thin gold chains with what appeared to be charms hanging from them. Except the charms were eclectic. An ancient gold coin, a diamond-studded ring. A piece of smooth blue sea glass, a bit of china…?

"Alchemist…" Aiden breathed, seriously impressed.

Pearl laughed just once, sharply delighted. "Not me, sorcerer. My granddaughter. She is that and more."

That and more. The weight of that seemingly benign reveal was heavy with intent, despite the lightness of Pearl's tone and the broadening of her smile.

I glanced at Christopher—not a hint of his magic in his eyes.

Pearl Godfrey wore an object of power around her neck that allowed her to move through the world as if she were a mundane. It no doubt simply harnessed and amplified a power the elder witch already wielded—but still, it was the *why* that was more disconcerting. What power did Pearl Godfrey wield that she felt the need to keep it so well tucked away?

Or was it simply that she was precisely what her titles already proclaimed her to be? The head of a powerful coven and the head of the witches Convocation. And able to pull all the power from all those connections—likely more power than she could ever need.

I wasn't certain I'd truly put that together before.

Not only was Pearl as strong as every witch bound to her, but she could presumably pull power—or perhaps share power was the more witch-appropriate way of putting it—from the other uber-powerful witches of the Convocation…who were in turn connected to their own covens.

The idea was staggering.

And it was in that moment that I completely understood I was facing exactly what I'd been bred and trained for twenty-one years to take down. More specifically, to place myself and the rest of the Five between the Collective and threats of the magnitude Pearl Godfrey represented.

She could wipe the Five from the face of the earth without even opening a single vein or summoning a horde of demons to do her bidding.

But witches of the light didn't slaughter indiscriminately. Witches of the light stepped in to correct such bad behavior.

Christopher threaded his fingers through mine, resting our joined hands on the table. His power flared down my spine almost searingly, settling into a low simmer on my T3 vertebra.

Pearl's gaze dropped to take in our clasped hands, then flicked up. Sensing the clairvoyant's power, and my reaction to it. The elder witch's eyes narrowed slightly—as if she'd just confirmed something she already knew, rather than widening in surprise.

I expected her to unleash a battery of questions. Perhaps condemnations.

Instead, she simply said, "Tell me everything."

So I did.

The Collective.

The Five. Who we were.

What we were capable of.

I told the elder witch every last bit of everything, including our ongoing connections to Kader and to Chenda. What had happened with the Hallowed and Haoxin, the guardian dragon.

Because I would do anything for Opal. And that included following where Christopher had led us—to the ferry, to that very table.

"Will you help us?" I whispered when I was done, suddenly feeling epically weary, but just a little bit lighter. "Knowing who we are?"

Pearl regarded me coolly. "It was never about you, Emma. You can clearly take care of yourself. It's Opal I won't let Mercury hurt. No Dunkirk comes into Godfrey territory and snatches one of my witches."

Pearl reached to her side, opening something I couldn't see. Then she pulled a leather portfolio the size of a thick magazine or catalog out of thin air.

Aiden grunted, clearly impressed. But also starting to get a little bit pissed about it.

I flashed him a grin I didn't know I was capable of producing. He laughed, shaking his head.

Pearl offered the portfolio to me.

I hesitated for the briefest of moments. If the portfolio was spelled, I couldn't feel it. And though I could take a lot of hits, I wasn't certain I'd ever faced the sort of wallop that Pearl Godfrey could wield.

"It's just a portfolio," she said, a slight snap to her words.

So I took it, setting it on the table before me. Then I just looked at her. While it might have been instinctual to follow the older witch's commands, it didn't come naturally. I could feel my resistance growing as each moment passed.

And because I gained immunity to most magic fairly quickly, that told me that my acquiescence had something to do with Pearl's power, at least in part, even though I couldn't feel that power. A different sort of manifestation of the charisma that her daughter Scarlett wielded so effortlessly, perhaps.

Pearl smirked, settling back in her seat. She crossed her ankles, straightening a crease in her linen pants with a flick of her fingers and a flicker of her magic. "You will find that very little surprises the Godfrey coven, Emma."

I opened the portfolio, revealing what appeared to be a stack of charcoal sketches. One edge was ragged on each, as if the drawings had been torn from a wire-bound sketchbook.

I was immediately caught, ensnared, just staring at the first sketch I'd revealed.

Christopher gasped. His hands jerked, as if reaching for the portfolio involuntarily.

I raised my hand, holding him at bay.

The black-and-white sketch was…us.

The four of us, seated at this very table, by this very window, traveling by ferry to rescue Opal. Me across from Pearl. Christopher beside me, across from Aiden. Even our hot drinks on the table and Pearl's necklace were detailed.

"An oracle?" Christopher breathed.

"Yes," Pearl said matter-of-factly.

"That's how you knew to be on the ferry?" I asked, my voice sounding far away, detached.

"That. And I had an associate uncover the existence of a property early this morning, held by the Dunkirk witches. Just outside Powell River."

My heart hammering in my chest, I passed the top sketch to Christopher, carefully examining the next. Then the rest.

They were of me, all depicting scenes from my recent past. With Silver Pine's greater demon in the forest at the edge of the Grant farm. Floating within a maelstrom of power, demons and the partially destroyed Grant house in the background when I'd implemented the Amplifier Protocol. Holding the cracked vessel that had contained the Hallowed.

And three sketches with Opal. Holding her, gazing across at her under a tent of blankets...

Except...that had been a dream...

How...was that possible...?

The second-to-last sketch depicted Christopher alone. Just his face, upturned, and his eyes bleeding magic. Three oracle cards hovered around him—ginger, rose, and strawberry. The reading he'd gotten over and over that had heralded Aiden's arrival in our lives.

The final sketch of the set was different. Hazier, as if the oracle wasn't quite certain what, or in this case, *who* they were seeing.

I knew who he was the moment I uncovered the sketch, though his back was turned and his face was in profile. The breadth of his shoulders was unmistakable. As were the four blood tattoos on his upper spine.

"The oracle requests an introduction," Pearl said.

"With me?" I asked, not looking up.

"No." She smiled tightly, then leaned over and deliberately tapped one perfectly manicured, peach-painted, blunt fingernail on the sketch. "With the man in that drawing."

I met her gaze, trying to keep my expression neutral.

"He's one of yours. One of the Five."

That wasn't a question, so I didn't answer. Pearl Godfrey knew exactly who we were. Had clearly known for almost a year, perhaps even since Christopher and I had passed through Vancouver on our way to Lake Cowichan. She'd kept an eye on us, through her oracle. And had let us be.

"She will not harm him." Pearl smiled again. "Rochelle believes he is her…brother, of a sort. But that the connection between them isn't clear, neither genetically nor magically." She narrowed her eyes at the upside-down drawing. "She says the resemblance to her grandmother is striking."

Christopher snapped his head to me, clearly struggling to continue ceding the conversation.

I nodded, suddenly feeling far more in control of the situation. Pearl wanted something from me. That I understood. That I could navigate.

"We can send a picture of the sketch…" I glanced at Christopher promptingly.

The clairvoyant took a photo of the sketch with his phone. And, when Pearl didn't stop him from doing so, he began to grab shots of the others.

"I can pass on Rochelle's name and affiliations to Daniel," I said, promising nothing.

"That's all she asks." Pearl nodded brusquely. "If he won't come to her in Vancouver, she'll go to him. She seems to have reason to believe that he's been looking for her grandmother."

I narrowed my eyes, rapidly thinking through the implications of that. Thinking about the only people I knew of who Daniel had been hunting. "She's one of the Collective, then."

"Perhaps. You will know that better than I. Or Rochelle. I believe she and her grandmother have had very little contact." Pearl paused thoughtfully. "A conversation for another day, perhaps."

I nodded, part of me itching to examine each sketch again, over and over. And another part wanting to burn them, along with the portfolio.

Avoiding either extreme, I passed the now-empty portfolio to Christopher. Having finished taking pictures of them, he tucked the charcoal sketches within it and slid it back to Pearl, clearly reluctant to let it go.

Pearl smiled tightly again, then went back to business. "I've confirmed just in the last hour that in addition to the residence she maintains just outside Vancouver, Mercury Dunkirk also maintains an overly large house on an overly large piece of property on the coast. Apparently, she co-opted the property from another witch in the Dunkirk coven, then had the house built three years ago. Two years after she applied for guest status with the Godfrey coven. The Dunkirk coven, interestingly, disavowed Mercury without question and without trial about thirty minutes ago."

"And how did you come by this information?" Aiden asked tersely.

"I have a trusted associate digging through Mercury's finances, after they paid a visit to her other property. And, of course, I've spoken directly with Emerald Dunkirk, the head of the coven."

"And the Vancouver property is empty," I said. It wasn't a question.

Pearl smirked. "A front for my biannual visits, perhaps. But once focused, my investigator, Jasmine, is hard to shake. The connection to the property outside Powell River was made with ease. I then had a local contact drive by, confirming active warding, but not the actual presence of Mercury. Or Opal. I knew of Mercury's work with her animals—"

"And demons," Aiden interjected.

Pearl's lip curled. "Yes. That has become apparent. But either Mercury's warding is far more impressive than I realized, because I haven't gotten a hint of anything disturbing during my visits to her other home. Or she conducts her other…experiments elsewhere."

"Or she cleans up well," Christopher said.

Pearl sniffed dismissively. "I certainly don't call ahead. I will go with you to the property. I will get you through the wards if Mercury doesn't allow us access." She scanned each of us, her expression cool. "And then I will clean up any mess you make."

A TEXT CAME THROUGH FROM KADER ON AIDEN'S phone while we were following Pearl Godfrey's vehicle along a stretch of gravel road barely wide enough for a single car. Not a logging road, but definitely not a main thoroughfare. Aiden had almost taken off his side mirror on the low boughs of evergreens three times in the last ten minutes. If there were houses among the trees, they couldn't be seen.

It had been just after 10:30 A.M. as we'd driven off the ferry onto the rugged west coast of the BC mainland. Following Pearl, we'd cut straight through the tiny town of Powell River near the terminal within a few minutes, not that I'd been in the mood to take in the view.

I glanced at the screen. "GPS coordinates." Then I passed the phone into the back seat for Christopher.

Tension hardened Aiden's jaw, and for a moment his hands and his magic tightened on the steering wheel. "If it's the correct location…"

"I know." Despite the fact that Pearl Godfrey was in the process of leading us to Mercury—with all of us hoping the witch had retreated to her Sunshine Coast property—if Kader also supplied us with the means to rescue Opal, then we'd be beholden to him.

For Aiden, who thought his father already had too much control of far too much of my life, that would be a concern. I wasn't bothered in the least, though. Because for some odd reason—or twist of fate, as Christopher would say—Kader Azar needed me more than I needed him.

I had seen it in the way the elder sorcerer had looked at Christopher as well. Everything Kadar Azar had created, every life he'd deliberately ushered into this world, had disappointed him, like the overly magically sensitive Khalid, who Kadar had tried to shape into a combat sorcerer. Or they wanted to usurp him, like his eldest son, Isa. Or they had been murdered, like Isa's siblings.

Everyone except for me. And I was the key to the rest of the Five. Or at least I was in Kader's eyes.

Christopher grunted from the back seat.

"We're almost there?" Aiden asked grimly.

"Yep. Looks like there's only one entrance—" The clairvoyant sucked in a harsh breath as his power exploded across my back, radiating from the blood tattoo that bound us to each other.

The phone hit the floor.

Christopher moaned. A quiet, pained sound that cut straight through me. Because he had learned at a very young age to weather his visions in utter silence.

I was out of my seat belt and awkwardly climbing between the front seats and into the back before I'd made the decision to move. The decision to interfere. Because this was too important to just ride out, to ignore what Christopher was seeing.

Aiden grunted as the vehicle swerved, dipping off the road briefly before the sorcerer got it back under control.

By then, I was grasping Christopher's face, pulling his gaze to meet mine while pumping power into him. He gasped again for a completely different reason, rearing back from me even as his hands latched around my wrists to hold on to me. To maintain control.

The white of his magic poured from his eyes, obscuring his other features.

"Opal?!" I cried—breaking every single rule that I had about working with the clairvoyant, amplifying him without permission while he was already in the grip of a vision. And in pushing his power, I was likely straining his mind, his grasp on reality.

"No." He panted, a violent shudder running through him. "Paisley. Oh, oh…Paisley!"

I inhaled deeply, settling into myself. And then I spoke—not to Christopher, but to the power that coursed through him.

"See me, clairvoyant."

His gaze snapped to meet mine. The power that had been whiting out his features condensed until it filled just his eyes in a dense layer of magic.

"See me, clairvoyant," I said again, softer but no less intensely. "I will not allow any harm to come to Paisley. See me, believe me."

"I believe you, Socks," Christopher said sadly, mournfully.

And his tone told me everything I didn't want to know.

That it was me, not some random harm, that would take Paisley's life.

My heart stuttered. I drew Christopher to me, pressing my forehead to his. He loosened his grip from one of my wrists and slid his hand around my neck, under my hair, dipping his fingers down my back to press the blood tattoo that bound his magic to mine.

I loosened my hold on his face, already knowing that he'd probably bear bruises from how tightly I'd grabbed and held him. I slipped my hand around his neck, but I didn't have as far to go. My power, my blood, was imbedded into his T1 vertebra. And I never touched it. I never amplified it directly, skin to skin. Unless I had to.

He shivered under my touch.

"See me, clairvoyant," I murmured.

"You'll do what you have to, Socks," he said, his voice ragged.

"I'll do it differently this time."

Christopher shook his head, our foreheads almost grinding together where they were still pressed. "Some things are set. And you will never allow…any of us to be a danger to…anyone else."

My heart was hammering in my chest, knowing, knowing what Christopher was seeing. "I'll make a different choice. Now that you've seen me one way, clairvoyant, see me another way. See me make different choices."

He shook his head sadly. Then he tipped his face up to mine, brushing a kiss across my lips. "I love you, Emma. Always."

He dropped his hold on me, shifting away from me as much as possible, practically pressing against the SUV door to get away from me. To get away from my magic.

I tightened my hold on my power, drawing it inward and making certain no part of me touched any part of Christopher. I needed him functional to see me through to Opal.

Sadness poured from the clairvoyant. Deep waves of grief. For something that hadn't even happened yet.

Anger welled—my own emotion, shoving back the onslaught of Christopher's emotional pain. Pure undiluted anger.

Not frustration. Not confusion or a sense of being overwhelmed, but pure, bright anger.

I met Aiden's eyes in the rearview mirror. I wasn't certain what he saw in my gaze, but he flashed me a vicious smile, all teeth and deadly intent.

And something very different sang in my heart, stretched through my limbs as if just awakening. "No one tells me what to do," I said, my voice oddly melodic.

Christopher's head snapped to me, but I kept my gaze locked to Aiden's in the mirror.

"Not the Collective. Not the power embedded in the blood tattoos. And certainly not fate." I laughed, the sound light, almost chiming, as it filled the vehicle.

"I know," Aiden crooned darkly. "I know, my goddess."

Smug and filled with certainty, I finally shifted to meet Christopher's gaze. "See me now, clairvoyant."

He swallowed harshly, then just bobbed his head.

The anger that had fired through me banked slightly at that acknowledgement. And I climbed back into the front seat, pausing to lay a blistering kiss on Aiden that forced him to slam on the brakes.

Up ahead, Pearl Godfrey pulled off the road, which continued to stretch out through the forested landscape. She parked in front of a gate visible from the road but set back within the trees.

"You're going to need your bat, sorcerer," Christopher said from the back seat.

"Already loaded," Aiden said, sounding almost peaceful.

I opened my door as the SUV slid to a stop behind Pearl's car. The elder witch was already striding up the short drive to a set of industrial steel gates. A matching fence, easily two meters tall and topped with barbed wire, shot off in either direction through the trees, mostly hidden from sight of the road.

My feet hit the ground. Two steps away from the SUV, I could already feel the power humming from the fence and gate—both actual electricity and magic.

But it had nothing on the power that now radiated off Pearl Godfrey.

The elder witch was standing otherwise sedately, staring at what appeared to be an intercom wired to a freestanding pole.

"Have it your way, Mercury," she said as I approached.

Aiden and Christopher were only a couple of steps behind me. The clairvoyant had brought his sword, and my sheath and blades were dangling from his left hand.

Pearl pivoted back to us. "I'll subsume the wards, then open a doorway for you," she said, her voice heavy with the same power that blazed from her eyes and crackled through her fingers.

"Subsume?" Aiden echoed doubtfully. "You just announced our presence—"

"My presence," Pearl corrected sharply.

"Mercury knows we're here. We have to move quickly. We don't have time for you to—"

"You are here by my leave, sorcerer. Allow me to—"

"Opal is my daughter," Aiden snapped. "Not even you could keep me from her."

Pearl huffed, then flicked her hand offishly. More blue-tinted electric magic jumped and sizzled between her fingers. She turned her piercing blue gaze on me. "Emma?"

"Subsuming is better than simply tearing through?" I asked, trying to be rational.

The elder witch nodded, then took in Christopher over my shoulder with a wry twist of her lips. "Care to enlighten everyone else, clairvoyant?"

Christopher grinned charmingly. "First, tell me how you know?"

Pearl stretched an arm toward the fence, tilting her head thoughtfully. "I'm already tapped into the wards. I can feel what they contain. Feel what must continue to be contained as you pass through."

Aiden grunted, impressed despite himself.

I'd also had no idea that Pearl was already skimming the property wards. Without a circle or runes. Just by merely stepping onto the land.

"Mercury is tied to you," I said, putting the connection together.

"Lightly," Pearl said. "I wouldn't allow her in my coven otherwise."

"She can't turn against you?" Aiden asked.

Pearl grimaced. "She can try. But I gather that you will be keeping her busy." She looked at Christopher with that slightly superior smirk. "Am I correct, clairvoyant?"

He grinned at her. "You already know you are, Pearl."

She sniffed. "Sorcerers are the doubtful sort."

Aiden huffed, exasperated.

But before he could retort and hold us in the moment any longer, I said, "I can amplify—"

"No, Emma," Pearl said dismissively. "You might need all your reserves. This will not overly tax me." She winked at Aiden playfully. "Watch and learn, young sorcerer."

Christopher chuckled.

Pearl turned to face the gate, toed off her sandals, and bowed her head.

I took my sheath and blades from Christopher, strapping them on across my back.

For another moment, nothing happened.

Then the few strands of gray hair that had worked their way out of Pearl's bun lifted up as if touched by a wind I couldn't feel, and power crackled around her.

She lifted her head, raised her arms, and that gathered magic shot out of her hands as streams of crackling energy. Lightning strikes of power hit the previously invisible property wards, crackling over their surface.

More and more power shot from the head of the Godfrey coven, thickening, deepening those first strikes and sharpening them. The ward pulsed in response, undoubtedly trying to repel Pearl.

But as I watched—all the hair on my body becoming electrified and standing on end—Pearl's strikes wove themselves into the wards. A flush of blue appeared, washing over and deepening in color as it radiated outward, following the fence line.

Aiden swore in that language of the Azars. But the vicious-sounding words had been rendered almost sweet and awestruck by the time he tapered off.

The metal gate slid open, just enough for a single person to pass through. It had moved seemingly of its own accord—and in doing so, had established Pearl's dominion over the property wards without any other words needed.

And that was good enough for me.

Because the time for words had passed.

I strode forward. Christopher tucked himself tight on my heels as Aiden brought up the rear. As we'd practiced numerous times.

"Have fun." Pearl chuckled, not looking at us as we stepped around her. Her voice radiated outward, almost as if it was carried through the wards. "I'm buying the ice cream on the way back. Opal will love the little cafe at the ferry terminal."

I didn't answer, but the crazy clairvoyant blew the elder witch a kiss.

As soon as Aiden stepped through, the gate slid shut behind him, the wards sealing over. I didn't bother looking back. I also didn't bother ducking off into the trees to hide or obscure our approach.

I would walk straight up the drive and find the chimney that would lead me to the room where Mercury was holding Opal.

The British witch might have been stuck in a lab during her time with the Collective. She might have had little to do with the Five. And she might therefore have no idea what she'd unleashed when she compromised Paisley.

But that didn't mean I'd mitigate my blows. Because Opal and Paisley were mine to protect.

And the witch who had hurt them would see me coming—should see me coming—all the way until my blade was at her throat and her lifeblood was pouring over my feet.

I was inescapable now.

For Mercury Dunkirk, I was her fate written in all the bloody deeds that she'd committed in the name of power. For the Collective and for herself.

And she would lose every drop of that power she'd so greedily collected—that she had likely sacrificed many lives to obtain, even beyond the animals she threw at me to slaughter, and the mundanes she'd used to fuel her teleportation spell.

She would lose it all to me. Because taking power, siphoning that magic from a person until they were merely a husk, was exactly what I'd been bred to do.

"See me now," I whispered up the gravel drive and into the towering trees. "See me as I truly am."

Christopher's fingertips ghosted over the back of my neck, his magic rising to answer mine.

The first attack came from both sides of the drive, exploding out of the trees with fangs and claws and malicious intent.

TEN

AIDEN THREW UP A MOBILE SHIELD AND CALLED forth his baseball bat as Christopher and I dealt with the first wave of Mercury's creatures. The shield was a design the sorcerer was still in the process of perfecting, allowing us to partially pass through it to deliver a strike, then step back within. Daniel would be seriously jealous of my sorcerer's prowess.

Aiden could hold this particular shield for about ten minutes before he started draining the energy stored in his copper rings, then the bat. But we'd never practiced with it while being pummeled by witch-controlled creatures from all sides. So I didn't take the time to properly investigate what we were fighting, or how Mercury was controlling the horde that had fallen upon us. I simply picked up my pace and physically drove us forward up the drive.

Not terribly nuanced of me. And almost disrespectful to use the elegant spell that Aiden had wrought as though it were a simple battering ram.

A mixture of canines and other large predators—all sharp teeth and claws, all seemingly ravenous—crashed into Aiden's shield. Each attacker slid off the magical barrier to one side for one of us to decapitate.

I had tried letting the first few rabid creatures simply be shoved away, but they then attacked from behind. And since we didn't know how many hits Aiden's shield could take under these extreme circumstances, I took the creatures down systematically—trying to not think about Paisley, or even the goblin cat, and all the life I was destroying, as I did. All the lives that Mercury had already stolen.

Mercury's horde wasn't marked by enough magic for me to pick it up. And none appeared to be demon hybrids like Paisley.

They died under my blades just the same.

As a massive cedar-and-river-rock-sided house came into sight, I noted its five rock chimneys with a burst of anger. Finding the room in which Mercury had caged Opal wasn't going to be as easy as I'd first assumed. A few niggling thoughts wormed their way through the steady, sharply focused haze that always took me through battles such as this one—though on the Five's missions, we would usually have been inundated by full-blooded demons.

The first thought was that, having subsumed Mercury's wards, Pearl Godfrey was now effectively holding the black witch hostage on her own lands. And us along with her.

And the second thought—a possible clue as to why Mercury had tried to use Paisley to kidnap me—lay scattered all around us as we paused to stare up at the house. There were still no other obvious demon hybrids among Mercury's horde. At least none of Paisley's intelligence, independence, or skill.

So did that mean the witch couldn't produce them? If so, what made Paisley special? And did it have anything to do with me?

I shoved both concerns away.

As powerful as she was, Pearl Godfrey couldn't hold against me, let alone the three of us. And I didn't care about Mercury's possible motives.

I wanted Opal. In my arms. In the next few minutes.

Otherwise, I was amplifying the fuck out of my dark sorcerer and letting him tear every fucking thing down.

Everything.

Christopher rolled his neck and shoulders, likely cementing himself in the here and now rather than wherever my blood-soaked intent had just taken him in his mind's eye.

"Report," I barked, staring up at the house. Mercury's horde had thinned enough to safely allow them to pummel against Aiden's shield for a moment.

Christopher's eyes were full-on white. He inhaled, settling his shoulders and magic further, not ready to speak.

Aiden was breathing heavily behind me. Without looking away from the clairvoyant, I sheathed one of my blades, then reached back for the sorcerer to amplify him.

Instead, he grabbed my hand and slipped one of his copper rings onto my forefinger. It was slightly loose, but almost immediately, I could feel a tug of energy from it…

Pulling me toward the house.

"Good," Christopher said, his gaze on our still-joined hands. "I see you in a long hall, likely the second floor. Blades out, but all the doors are closed to you."

"Closed to me?" I asked, confused by the phrasing. No door was truly closed to me. I could muscle my way through most cages of mundane origin.

"Opal subsumed her own set of wards?" Aiden asked, grinning as his breathing evened out.

Christopher flashed him a smirk. "Is that what you had her do? With the amethyst cluster?"

Aiden wiped his brow. "Glad to hear it was successful."

"She's here?" I asked, not entirely certain I wanted the answer.

"What does the ring tell you, goddess mine?" Aiden murmured.

I raised my hand, feeling that tug toward the house again. A viciously edged grin swamped my face, that joy feeding rather well into the anger I'd enveloped myself within.

"Let's keep moving, then," I barked, reaching for my sheathed blade.

Christopher settled his hand on my shoulder. "You're going in alone. Or at least separate from us. At first."

I glanced back at Aiden. His expression was impassive. He already knew. This had been part of some conversation he and the clairvoyant had already had. While I was asleep?

Anger uncurled in my chest again.

I didn't like being played. Not by Christopher, and certainly not by anything he would call fate.

"You still don't trust me," the clairvoyant said sadly.

Before I could answer, Aiden was kissing me. A hot yet gentle kiss that had me curving into him, yielding to him—while I pumped power into him at the same time, of course.

He laughed huskily, then bit my lower lip lightly. "The wards are thinner over the second-floor windows."

"Shoddy casting," Christopher muttered.

"Or Mercury just isn't all that skilled in that particular type of witch magic," Aiden said without looking away from me.

He kissed both corners of my mouth, then my forehead. "Heed the clairvoyant, my darling, and bring both our girls back." Then he deliberately dropped his hands from me, stepping back and wiping all expression from his face.

Before I could speak, could question either of them further—because splitting up was always the wrong choice—the door to the house banged open, and three beasts prowled out, shoving at each other and destroying the doorjambs in their effort to be first through. Their sickled claws hooked into and then pulverized each concrete step they traversed down into the graveled front yard.

"Aiden…" I said—realizing it was possible I'd been wrong about what level of demon hybrid Mercury could produce. Their dark skins were smooth, hairless. Not scaled like some demons. Lions perhaps? But they had fangs and definitely something else unnatural mixed in.

Except I couldn't see any nuance in these creatures. No stalking or sizing us up. Just barreling forward to their targets.

"We're going to be just fine," Christopher said coolly. Then he nodded toward the house—specifically, toward a second-floor balcony with a sliding glass door.

"Need a boost?" Aiden asked teasingly, though his gaze was fixed on the incoming creatures, his expression blank.

"I can arrange my own," I said as haughtily as I was capable of being. "Enjoy the show, sorcerer mine."

I took off, racing toward Mercury's three beasts. The creatures' red eyes bled with magic, but not a hint of intelligence.

Mercury had held them in reserve. Why? Because she didn't have control over them?

The nearest beast lowered its head like a bull, bellowed, and charged me. The other two followed with echoes of that same cry.

Not lions, then.

Buffalo?

Or, even harder to believe, rhinoceros?

I had no idea how any of that worked. Except that it probably involved a petri dish and multiple demon summonings.

I leaped over the head of the first beast—short-sighted of it to lower itself for me. It reared back, but it didn't have the canine dexterity that Paisley had, so it couldn't easily twist back to follow me.

It did, however, suddenly have spikes the length of my forearm all around its thickly scaled neck. So these creatures were shapeshifters to some extent, like Paisley. I landed on its back, grabbed a spike with my free hand, then slid my blade as far as I could reach around and into its neck. One of Aiden's sharpening spells exploded, then died under my palm, but the black blade sliced through the creature's thick hide nonetheless.

The second beast had gone for Aiden and Christopher, no doubt lured away from me in some fashion I didn't want to know about. Aiden wasn't as squeamish about using blood magic as his father was. Kader liked to be tidy along with being deadly. And since he only grew more powerful with age, he had that privilege.

The third beast charged me—or, more specifically, it charged the creature I was now in the process of flaying along its spine.

I sheathed my blade only a moment before the third creature rammed into the first. I timed my jump, using the hit to propel me back toward the house.

Then I was twisting in midair and grabbing hold of the bottom of the balcony. A sharp jolt of pain feathered through my shoulders, but at least nothing popped.

Christopher cheered exuberantly.

I levered myself up enough to grab the railing and get a leg up, slightly embarrassed that I couldn't simply pull myself by my arms alone. I'd grown soft. Well, softer. In body, at least.

Below me, the first creature slammed into the house. Energy vibrated through the wards at the hit, but the structure didn't seem to take any damage. The third creature tore into the first.

Yeah, Mercury might have successfully bred them, but she didn't have any control over these beasts.

The second creature was taking hit after hit from Aiden, but its hide looked fairly impervious to magic. I had to keep moving, though. The ring was steadily tugging me forward.

I turned my back on Aiden and Christopher, feeling as though I was leaving a chunk of my heart behind me, even as I pushed forward to collect another already missing section. Two missing sections.

As Aiden had noted, the wards were thinner over the sliding glass door. The balcony was just deep enough that I could put a good amount of effort into a sharp front kick focused on the locking mechanisms of the door.

I cracked the glass, but it took two more kicks, one kinetically fueled by a vertical jump, to shatter the wards and step through into what appeared to be a sparsely furnished bedroom. Bare mattress, bare bureau, no pictures on the walls. One interior door.

I shut out the sounds of battle in the front yard, though I was aware that the third beast had joined the second in attacking the sorcerer and the clairvoyant. And that Mercury hadn't yet made an appearance.

The doorknob turned easily under my hand, and I stepped out into the hall beyond. The ring tugged me to the right.

I let Aiden's tracking spell guide my footsteps. Not bothering with any attempt at being clandestine other than the natural prowess with which I'd been built. Which had come with everything else I'd stolen.

I wasn't that much different than the creatures in the front drive, after all.

I was just a sharper-honed weapon. And I wielded the powers bequeathed to me through blood and sacrifice with a tiny measure of intelligence.

AS I TRAVERSED THE UPPER HALL, EVERY DOOR I passed was shut tightly—and the sparseness, the empty feeling of the house, became more and more apparent. Even stifling. White-painted walls, no baseboards or casings. Everything was basic, functional. As if Mercury had bought an unfinished home and paid someone to slap on a bit of paint, basic door handles, and simple fixtures.

At what I assumed was the center of the house, the hallway exited into an upper walkway that looked down into the main foyer. The front doors—steel reinforced on the interior—hung off their hinges, the previously mangled doorjambs now smoking. But with a dark-blue magic, not fire. Aiden's magic.

Linoleum flooring only reinforced the feeling that Mercury had simply bought a shell of a house, then not bothered finishing it. That flooring was splattered with various pools of dark-tinted ichor, actually eating through the linoleum in places. Demon blood. Or at least hybrid demon blood, though Paisley's blood wasn't corrosive.

No signs of Mercury or any of her creatures, though.

I heard shouting from beyond the trashed doors, pausing long enough to discern Aiden's voice but not the words. Spells, presumably, in that language that the Azar sorcerers all defaulted to when casting or when emotionally heightened.

It took a ridiculous amount of willpower to not rush down the stairs and out into whatever fight was continuing to take place in the front yard. Staying on task wasn't usually an issue for me. In fact, the rest of the Five often disparaged my ability to set aside exterior concerns and focus on the mission. But divided between Aiden and Opal, I was struggling. Emotionally.

There wasn't a choice, though. Opal would always come first. Because Aiden could take care of himself.

I allowed the runed copper ring to tug me away from the landing, continuing along the upper hall. The fact that I was crossing unmolested through Mercury's domain wasn't lost on me. I doubted that Aiden and Christopher had her that distracted.

The witch wanted me to achieve my end goal. Which meant there was something else she had waiting for me.

In the second wing, the decor just gave up all pretense of being any sort of home. The hall was lined with exposed drywall, uncased doorjambs, and plywood flooring. The doors—too many punctuating the walls now to be decently sized bedrooms—were constructed out of steel and shimmered with witch magic.

All of them were closed to me, as Christopher's vision had shown him.

And I didn't bother with a single one of them, not even the few where I was certain I could feel something, some creature, shifting on the other side. I followed the tug of the ring instead, trusting Aiden's magic.

And if Mercury was luring me down to the end of the hall? If she had the means to open all the doors behind me at once? And release whatever creatures were still contained within? Effectively trapping me?

Well, I'd already seen a window in the dream walker's mind. And barred or not, all windows could be used as egresses when necessary. Especially by the likes of me.

Except I doubted that Mercury's plan for me was quite that simple. Because I already knew, without him breathing a word, what Christopher had seen. The trap the black witch had laid within the creature that she would no doubt claim as her greatest accomplishment. Just as Kader claimed me.

Paisley.

The steel door blocking me from Opal was the second in from the end of the hall on the left—so facing the back of the house, as expected given the forested mountain view the dream walker had mentioned. I could actually see the studs framing the door in the gap at the edge of the drywall, which meant that if it hadn't been for the magic coating the door and the walls alike, I could have easily kicked through the drywall and insulation.

I wrapped my hand around the door handle, noting the addition of exterior latches on this door—none of which were locked into place. Magic danced across my palm, twining around my fingers. Witch magic.

But not Mercury's power.

A grin swamped my face, and heady relief rushed through me. "Opal!" I called, hoping that the steel and the magic didn't block sound as well as entry. "Open the door!"

I couldn't just tear through the wards. I mean, of course I could breach the wards with physical and magical brute force. But not without hurting the little witch.

And now I knew why the latches on the door were undone. Mercury must have tried to enter and been repelled. Otherwise, she would have double-secured the physical fortifications.

"Come on, little witch." I pressed my palm against the center of the steel door. "Open up for me. I'm taking you home."

The power securing the door shifted, as if Opal might have placed her hand on the other side, stirring her magic. Maybe trying to read me, my presence, through it?

I heard a muffled voice but not clear words. They sounded…doubtful?

I loosened my hold on my power, not entirely certain that would help Opal identify me. My voice should have been enough…

"Prove it," the voice said—shouting now, but still muffled through the magic.

I could hear her most clearly through the gap around the door, so I shifted to my left, practically pressing the side of my face to the raw drywall.

"It's me, dream walker. Feel my magic."

And then I remembered…

Opal had already been kidnapped by someone posing as her mother.

When first at the Academy, while under the care of a foster mother, Opal had known in her heart that her birth mother hadn't miraculously come back from the dead to claim her. But the impostor—Ruwa, Aiden's ex—had played on the young witch's needs…on her dreams. Ruwa had attempted to break a life-debt bond she'd made with Isa Azar by binding herself to a demon. She used the power she gained from that binding to shape shift, but unlike most shifters, she could replicate human forms. She had also been able to absorb enough of someone's magical signature to fool even my senses. For a moment or two, at least.

Opal didn't answer me for a long moment. Then she said, "Tell me something only Emma would know."

Momentarily stymied, I paused, actually eyed up the wall in front of me, and considered just kicking through it. I hated playing games, and proving I was who I said I was really felt like some sort of game…

Except this was Opal. And Opal didn't need me scaring her.

I couldn't bring myself to hurt the dream walker in any way, not even for the briefest of moments.

"Emma?" she asked, her voice hollow.

"I'm here," I said. "I'm just trying to think of something that no one else would know." What moment had I shared with Opal that no one could…

San Francisco.

I cleared my throat of a sudden clog of emotion. "I…I don't know if this counts, but…I remember the first time I saw you…across that containment spell, the pentagram."

"Other people were there too," she said belligerently.

I laughed. My little witch had been kidnapped by Mercury and struck at least once, then locked in a barred room. Yet she was still so full of…life.

Yes. Life.

That was what I'd seen when I first set eyes on her. Her life force draining out of her…and I couldn't bear to watch it happen, not then, not ever.

"Everyone who was there is dead now," I said mildly. "Including Ruwa."

She grumbled something I didn't catch, then added, "Keep talking."

I quashed another round of laughter. I never wanted her to think that I was laughing at her, rather than in pure relief, pure joy.

"There was a moment," I said obligingly. "When I thought about tearing through the barrier that the sorcerers were fueling with your lifeblood. I could have freed myself easily."

"But you didn't."

"No. I was worried that I would hurt you, so I took a moment…and I'd never taken a moment before in my life…to try to assess the spell, the runes painted onto your skin. And you met my gaze."

The barest of whispers filtered through to me. "I remember."

I was crying now, recalling the moment, the fear, the turmoil, and all the things that I'd had no capacity to navigate then. "You were dying," I said. "But you were so full of life. When Christopher and Paisley arrived, I didn't even notice what I had to do to get to you. I couldn't even tell you who'd been in my way, who I had to drain, until you were in my arms and I was filling you with everything I had to give you."

I swallowed a sob. "It...I regretted every moment of handing you over to Ember's team, but I knew I couldn't keep you safe...and now...now..."

The door latch clicked, then Opal was throwing herself into my arms, and I was on my knees, one blade dropped to the floor as I clutched her too hard, crying.

"I'm sorry," she sobbed into my neck. "I'm sorry. I should have listened to you. You gave me an order, and you were right, and it wasn't your fault."

It took a moment for her words to filter in around her sobs and my overwhelmed senses. I pressed fierce kisses to her head, then her temple, pulling back so I could smooth my hand over her face, wiping away her tears.

"This is not your fault," I said firmly. I kissed her forehead, and she slipped her arms around my neck.

"Bad things just happen?" she asked quietly, resting her head on my shoulder.

I rocked her lightly, smoothing my hand down her back as I reached for the quiet simmer of her power and added my own to it, gently amplifying her.

Aiden would talk it all out with our girl. He'd know what to say. But I could give her this, my strength. My touch and my strength.

A low warning growl filtered up the hall from the direction I'd come.

Opal stiffened in my embrace, turning her head but still resting it on my shoulder. "Paisley," she whispered.

I had already known, even without looking. I could feel the demon dog's power, even more darkly tinted, more twisted, than it had been in the forest.

"I had to lock her out," Opal said mournfully. "She...she wouldn't let Mercury hurt me, but then...Mercury got the door open and made Paisley come out to her and did some...something..." Her voice cracked, and she pressed her face into my neck again. "When Paisley came back, she...I couldn't let her back into the room. I just knew...I knew Mercury had hurt her too much. That she didn't remember me."

My heart felt like it was cracking open, spilling pain throughout my system.

I firmed my grip on Opal, reached for the blade I'd dropped, and got to my feet with the little witch wrapped around me. Then I pivoted, getting a good look at Paisley.

The demon dog was...altered. As big as a lion, her shoulders practically brushed each side of the hallway. Her eyes seemed to bleed red instead of simply glowing. And half of her wild mane of tentacles dragged on the ground around her front feet. Injured. Maybe even beyond repair.

Paisley dropped her head, a low, keening snarl rippling through her. Anger mixed with pain.

But not mindless anger like that of the rhino hybrids Mercury had unleashed on us in the front yard. Not yet.

Blood dripped from the rope tied around Paisley's neck. It was thicker than before, possibly braided. I knew that if I could see Paisley's back haunches, she'd be missing more skin. Wounds that weren't closing over despite her natural healing ability.

She stalked forward.

I set Opal on the ground, not taking my eyes off the demon dog.

Her upper lip curled back, revealing a double set of sharply pointed teeth—some broken, some missing altogether. Blood crusted her gums.

Mercury had tortured her.

Anger rushed through me with such force that I actually swayed with it.

Paisley snarled viciously. Like I was triggering her.

"Emma?" Opal whispered fearfully.

I touched the little witch's shoulder. "Into the room, Opal," I said, surprised that my tone was firm, steady. "Seal yourself in."

"But…what are you going to do?" She glanced at the steadily approaching demon dog.

This was it.

This was the moment Christopher had seen…

The moment that had hurt him so much to witness that he'd actually moaned, even after such re-actions had been tortured out of him at a very early age.

This was the moment I had vowed to change.

And I had no idea how to change it.

Not with Opal's safety to take into account.

"Seal the wards," I told her.

Opal stepped over the threshold. "Already sealed."

I called my second blade into my empty hand. "Close the door."

Dark energy crackled through the active section of Paisley's mane.

"But…" Opal's voice broke. Then she whispered, "I understand."

The door shut with a tiny snick.

Another large piece of my heart broke off.

I firmed my footing, raising my blades. The hall didn't give me much room to play, but if I could get my hands on Paisley—

Except…

I didn't need my hands.

Not anymore.

I released my hold on my power, including everything extra I'd been struggling to keep at bay since my contact with the Hallowed. An intense wave of power rolled out from me, seemingly endless. It thundered through the hall and swamped the demon dog.

Paisley snarled and snapped, writhing.

I tried to grab hold of her, to compel her. To bend her to my will.

She went insane. Thrashing and howling. Uttering sharp keening barks…of terror.

I was scaring her.

Hurting her.

I let go.

I couldn't do it. I couldn't enslave Paisley. I couldn't do that to anyone…

The demon dog fixed her bleeding eyes on me. She got her footing, lowered her head and prepared to attack.

Tears slipping down my face, I raised my blades again.

I couldn't let Paisley kill me. And I had no doubt that whatever Mercury's original intent had been, the demon dog had been sent to kill me now. And Opal. Then Christopher and Aiden.

But she wouldn't get past me.

She couldn't get past me.

There wasn't any other way around it. Because my Paisley would have traded her life for Opal's in a second. Or Christopher's. Or mine.

I couldn't let her kill any of us.

She lunged.

I brought my blades up to meet her.

Because that was always how it was going to be.

Me.

My blades.

And the end of another life.

My power was still raging around me, everything unleashed, everything I'd been denying.

And then I just knew...

I knew what I had to do...

I had to step right. Right instead of left.

I had to cheat fate with the simplest of actions.

So instead of gutting the demon dog as she leaped over me, I ducked. And spun right.

Paisley blew past me, slamming into the end of the hall, then ricocheting off one wall, drywall and wood crumbling under the force of impact.

She scrambled to get her footing.

I pivoted to face her.

She lowered her head again. Another vicious snarl tore from her throat.

I dropped my blades.

And sat.

Cross-legged, my hands on my knees.

Paisley paced side to side, momentarily uncertain.

I closed my eyes.

And I accepted.

Everything.

I accepted the moment, and my inability to control it, to control the actions of others. I accepted my anger and my pain.

I accepted all that I'd been trying to hold at bay.

All the power that the Hallowed had riled up within me, loosened, amplified.

I had thought, early on, that the Hallowed still controlled some aspect of me, that it had burrowed itself so deeply within me that I would never be purged of it.

That was a fear-based reaction.

Fear of what I was ultimately capable of doing. Specifically, draining the power of others and keeping it for myself.

The Hallowed wasn't within me. But whatever it had been—an entity powerful enough that the guardian dragons had only contained it, not killed it—I'd absorbed some aspect of its power. The power wielded by an immortal entity that called itself the mother of the dawn.

Paisley shook off her doubt, nostrils flaring as she stalked toward me. Long claws shot out from her feet to score the rough plywood flooring.

Going completely against my training, against my instincts, I settled into the power writhing around me. I absorbed it as I would a blow or a curse. I absorbed it as I would when draining someone of their magic. It all flooded back into me, as if I'd opened up a hidden empty compartment and was letting magic rush in to fill that space.

Every one of the blood tattoos on my spine flared, as if they too had been revived and then amplified. I could feel my Knox nearest to me—his power on my T3 vertebra, yes, but also the thick rope of the binding that connected us.

I accepted that connection—truly accepted it for the first time—and actually felt it when Christopher responded in turn. Our power forever connected, me fueling him effortlessly despite the walls and wood and stone between us.

Then I felt Fish and Samantha farther away, feedback from touching them rushing back to me. And then Bee, but only thinly, as if she was hidden under layers and layers of protection spells. But never beyond my reach.

All the energy I pulled back into myself continued to condense around the tattoos. Then, as if using those bindings as anchor points, the energy spread farther down my spine and outward.

Like wings.

Invisible wings, thrumming with everything that made me Emma—the amplification, the empathy, and the strength—pressed against the walls, wider than the hallway.

I opened my eyes.

I met Paisley's gaze.

She was within striking distance—me to her and her to me. Yet she was transfixed by me.

I smiled, my heart full—weighted with love and acceptance.

"I love you," I said, my voice heavy with power. Tremendous, intense, and wholly me.

Paisley unleashed a keening wail, yipping and crying. She settled before me and lowered her head onto her paws. I reached for her, both with my hands and with the great, invisible wings I'd somehow manifested.

I placed one hand on her broad head. She shuddered under my touch.

I wrapped my wings around her, cocooning her in my power.

Then I tore the bleeding rope from around her neck.

Paisley screamed, trying to muffle her response.

I began pouring power into her. Following some instinct that felt a little creepy even in the moment, I fed her the rope constructed out of her own skin and Mercury's magic.

Paisley gobbled it up, licking my hands clean. Then she rose, shrinking down to her large pit bull aspect as she pressed her face to my neck, just as Opal had done.

I smoothed my hands down the demon dog's back, then said teasingly, "I told you eating magic was going to get you in trouble."

She huffed through my hair. And the wounds on her haunches finally stopped bleeding. She'd managed to tuck the dead tentacles away, so hopefully they would heal as well.

"Emma…" A reverent-sounding Opal spoke up to my left. "You…you have wings…"

I reached for her, cuddling her against me and giving in to the impulse to amplify them both at the same time. Opal slipped one arm around my neck and the other around Paisley.

"Thank you for taking care of me," the little witch said. And she might have been talking to either or both of us.

Paisley wouldn't meet her gaze, though. And when Opal released her, the demon dog stepped away from the little witch, briefly meeting my gaze, then dropping her still-reddened eyes.

"We love you," I said.

Paisley didn't respond. And I found myself hoping that I hadn't actually compelled her in my fear that I would have to put her down. That I hadn't forced her to acquiesce, simply swapping Mercury's control over the demon dog for my own.

I shoved the thought away—to be investigated later—and stood, realizing halfway through the process that I still had invisible wings, and they were really awkward.

I visualized tucking them away, as I would with my power when it was raging around me. They didn't dissipate but folded in, snug up against my back. Smaller, but not fully absorbed back into me.

Not for the first time, I reflected that it might have been a good idea to question the guardian dragon, Haoxin, when she'd appeared to toss the Hallowed back through that golden portal. Because as much as that entity had learned by inhabiting my body and wielding my power, I had absorbed something from it as well.

And that *something* came with wings. Thankfully, they appeared to be mostly invisible. Unless the person gazing at me could see magic.

As Opal was currently doing, still more than a little awestruck.

I didn't like being looked at that way at all.

"Come," I said gruffly, picking up both my blades and sheathing one across my back. The wings were unaffected by the sheath and the blade. "We should go help Aiden and Christopher." I also had no idea where Mercury was lurking. Unless she'd run.

Opal slipped her hand into mine, not at all scared of me. Paisley pressed her shoulder into my thigh. And something settled in me a little bit more.

ELEVEN

ALL THE DOORS ALONG THE HALL THAT HAD BEEN previously closed hung open as we passed back through the house. Mercury had apparently emptied her cages, but had called her creatures away rather than sending them against me, presumably in preparation for her final stand.

Whatever that was.

Based on the putrid stink filtering past those open doors, Mercury hadn't treated her creatures well. After glancing through the first few to make certain we weren't going to be blindsided, and noting the piles of feces and rotting food within, I stopped looking.

It was the ragged nests tucked in the corners of the otherwise empty cells that had bothered me the most. The creatures that Mercury had created, or re-made, or whatever the hell she was doing, had been sentient enough to want a safe spot. A bed. They'd torn up drywall and plywood and whatever else they managed to find…and how many of them had I killed?

I hadn't bothered counting. I'd just carved my way through. To Opal. To Paisley.

Opal made a mewing sound, and I released her hand to tuck her head against me. Then I kept walking. Paisley was a silent, battle-scarred specter at my side.

The house wards had fallen. The front doors were completely missing now, just a massive hole where they'd once stood. More half-animal/half-demon bodies were strewn across the concrete stairs leading out into the front yard.

I held Opal a little tighter, but I didn't cover her eyes. She'd been worried that she might be a black witch because of the things she'd done to survive, and she needed to see what happened when an actual dark power was allowed to fester and grow, hidden or not.

Mercury Dunkirk might never have done anything with her horde had she not set eyes upon Paisley and me, but that wasn't a responsibility I could carry.

Christopher and Aiden were facing off with Mercury a few meters from the front door. She appeared to have contained herself in a circle constructed out of fallen canine creatures, two scaled wolf-like beasts sitting at her heels. Aiden's bright-blue gaze had fixed on Opal the moment we'd stepped out into the open, and a pained sound—half sob, half growl—tore from his chest, his very being.

Heedless of the black witch, Opal broke from me and ran for the sorcerer. He met her halfway, snatching her up and just holding her. His blue gaze was pinned to me over her shoulder.

"I'm sorry," she cried over and over again. Needing absolution from both of us.

Aiden just clutched her, appearing lost for words. Perhaps for the first time since I'd known him.

Paisley's head lowered as she homed in on Mercury.

The witch hadn't turned at our approach, instead sneering at Aiden and Opal. "Cute."

Paisley paced around the other side of Mercury's horrific circle of corpses. I saw the moment that the black witch realized she was being stalked. Her back stiffened, and she looked back—but at me.

I wasn't the biggest threat in the yard, though.

Not at this moment, at least.

Christopher lowered his shortsword slightly, reaching for Paisley as she passed. The demon dog ignored him completely. No eye contact, no grinned greeting. Her red eyes remained fixed on the witch who had compelled her. Had forced her to kidnap Opal. Then had tortured her when she wouldn't allow any harm to come to the dream walker.

I reached Aiden and Opal. He was murmuring to the little witch now, something lyrical in that language that was all his own. She had quieted, her head on his shoulder. So it might actually have been a calming spell.

I wrapped my arms around the both of them, already pumping my power into them. Aiden's reserves were as low as I'd felt in a long time. I could see the corpses of two of the rhino hybrids behind the sorcerer, still smoldering with his dark-blue magic. It appeared that Christopher had also managed to decapitate them. Mostly. Doing so would have completely drained the sharpening spells in the gemstones embedded into his blade.

"Emma," Opal said, sounding a little squished, "I'm really full. So full."

Aiden laughed, weary and sounding on the edge of being out of control. He was bleeding in a few places, but his suit had taken the bulk of the claw and tooth strikes. So many that I doubted it was salvageable.

"Let's go home," I said, easing my hold on Opal and forcing myself to stop amplifying her. I continued pumping power into Aiden, though, even as I reached my hand toward Christopher.

The clairvoyant crossed to us, as if he'd just been waiting for an invitation. He grabbed my hand, accepting the power I pumped into him even as he leaned forward and pressed a kiss to Opal's cheek.

"I'm sorry," she mumbled sleepily.

"Stop," Christopher said. "You have nothing to be sorry for."

"I didn't follow orders," she said slightly belligerently. As if she wasn't going to be talked out of taking responsibility for her actions.

I swallowed a smile, noting Aiden doing the same.

Christopher huffed. "Well, we've all done that. Even Emma. Of course, she's usually saving someone's ass at the time."

Opal giggled. But even with as much power as I'd pumped into her, she was rapidly losing her battle to remain awake. Aiden's calming spell was likely helping with that.

"Home?" Christopher asked, glancing over at Mercury. "All of us?"

He was asking whether or not I was going to stay behind, or to ask him to stay behind, to deal with Mercury.

"Yes," I said firmly.

Aiden pivoted and walked away, just like that. He had gotten his arms around Opal—it must have devastated him to let me enter the house alone—and he was done.

So was I. The Godfrey coven could deal with Mercury and the aftermath. The coven would exact a far more painful punishment than any quick death I could deal. And, oddly, I had no problem with ceding that trial and judgement…

Perhaps Christopher's wisdom card had been drawn with me in mind after all.

With my evolution in mind? Though the wings being part of the equation was a little annoying, I could accept the…serenity that came with the mere idea of following Aiden and Opal, going home, and leaving the blood and death behind.

"What?" Mercury asked mockingly. "The great and powerful Amp5 walking away?"

I spared the black witch a glance.

Paisley was still pacing her circle. Three of the demon dog's tentacles had appeared, and she was using them to test the boundary ward Mercury had erected around herself.

"Paisley," I said gently. "Will you come home with us?"

Mercury snorted. "You might have tamed the dog, Emma, but she will always be my creature."

"Just like Emma and I are the Collective's creatures?" Christopher asked mildly.

Mercury took that for the warning it was, quieting, then tilting her head thoughtfully. "I didn't want any of this, clairvoyant. You can see that, can't you?"

"My backsight isn't terribly sharp," Christopher said offishly. "And I certainly don't want it focused on you."

Instead of deterring Mercury, his response seemed to galvanize her. "As soon as I saw Emma on the beach, with the dog..." She nodded dismissively in Paisley's direction, not looking close enough to see that the demon dog had rather subtly shifted a few of the corpses that Mercury had used to seal her protection circle. "I knew she had to be the key. The amplification paired with her—"

"No!" Christopher shouted.

Heedless of the clairvoyant's warning, Paisley attacked Mercury's corpse circle. Her jaws and front

paws widening even before the rest of her transformed, she threw herself at the magic barring her
from her tormentor.

Mercury stumbled back a step. Then with a flick
of her fingers, she released the final two creatures at
her command.

One scaled wolf took Paisley by the neck while
the other tore at her exposed belly. They rolled across
the yard, snarling viciously—terrible, terrifying
sounds I knew I never wanted to hear again.

I lunged forward, both blades in my hands and
Christopher at my side.

Paisley got one of the beasts off her, tossing it
toward us. We both fell on it, blades flying. Mine was
still sharp enough, though Christopher's was a little
duller.

The demon dog got her back legs up under the
wolf-creature that had her pinned, just as my blade
sliced open the neck of the first one.

"Left!" Christopher shouted.

I spun left. The clairvoyant stepped with me.

Paisley flung the wolf-creature off her—it would
have taken us out at the knees—and Christopher and
I lunged to finish it off, turning our backs on Mercury.

The white of the clairvoyant's magic flooded
his eyes, and he stumbled, getting a claw swipe
across his face for his inattention. Blood spurted, the
scent—and likely Christopher's magic—riling the
final creature further.

Only then did I realize that some of the creatures Mercury had been bleeding out for her protection circle were still alive. And they were coming for us, clawing their way across the gravel, guts dragging behind them.

The black witch was chanting something, a silver knife in her hand, blood dripping from a cut across her forearm. Her gaze was pinned to me.

"Paisley," the clairvoyant moaned, barely avoiding a second swipe from the black-scaled wolf.

I shoved myself between him and the creature, decapitating it swiftly—and using up the last of my blade's sharpening spell.

Then I turned to deal with the creatures that were slowly and painfully clawing their way toward us.

Mercury was smiling at me. "Just think of how powerful we'll be together, Emma. With your amplification and my ability to—"

She had turned her back on Paisley.

Despite her still-healing wounds, despite the fresh ones the wolf creatures had inflicted, the demon dog had clawed her way next to the witch.

Paisley rose on her back legs, tore through the boundary between her and the witch with her front claws, and tried to rip out Mercury Dunkirk's throat.

"Stop her, Socks!" Christopher shouted.

I moved.

Mercury screamed. Then she hit Paisley with something dark and malignant—a spell thrown in desperation and fueled by all the blood she'd already spilled.

Paisley stumbled back, tripping on her own intestines.

But I was there, between them, shoving Mercury harshly to the side and taking her place.

Paisley's maw opened, all jagged teeth. She clamped down on my shoulder. Searing pain shot through me.

I stumbled. But instead of going down, I wrapped my arms around Paisley, hugging her to me.

She immediately released me, mewing in pain and trying to twist away.

I held her tighter, blood pouring down my shoulder, soaking the remnants of my sundress and coating my skin. "I've got you," I said, panting in pain. The demon dog's fur was slick with her own blood, and I was having a hard time keeping hold of her. "You've got nothing to be sorry for."

Mercury scrambled to her feet beside me. Her hands flashed forward to hit us with some spell.

I turned, hoping to take the brunt of it on my back.

Then Christopher skewered the black witch through the chest.

Paisley sagged in my arms, heavy enough—even for me—that I fell to my knees.

Mercury parted her lips to speak, her gaze still fixed on me, not Christopher. But only blood burbled out.

"I may have punctured a lung," Christopher said calmly, withdrawing his sword.

Mercury fell to her knees, then keeled over. Around us, the last of her half-dead creations slumped to the ground.

I cradled Paisley as best I could, pumping power into her as my own wound healed over. Slowly. Even half dead, the demon dog had a potent bite.

Christopher crouched next to us, first inspecting my shoulder, then laying his hand on Paisley's head. "I'm sorry. But there would have been no coming back," he said to her, his eyes a clear light gray.

"She wanted to eat Mercury?" I asked, already knowing the answer.

Christopher sighed sadly, nodding once. He didn't like killing people either, which was why he would have walked away with me. If Paisley had let us.

She blinked up at me.

I shook my head at the demon dog. "No people. No black witches," I said sternly.

A lone tentacle rose from her otherwise invisible mane. It flicked over my shoulder and arm, scouring my blood away and cleaning the wound she'd made with tiny zaps of energy.

"Paisley," I prompted. "No people."

She blinked again, maintaining eye contact, steady and true. Her eyes shifted back to dark brown, the red bleeding out.

I let her go. Christopher and I helped her gain her feet, but it quickly became apparent that even though her wounds had sealed over, she couldn't walk. Christopher had to help me lift her onto my shoulders. Even in her smaller form, she was hefty.

We left Mercury Dunkirk bleeding out among the corpses of her creatures, heading down the drive to where Opal was waiting for us with Aiden. The sorcerer would have already briefed Pearl Godfrey. At least, about the parts he knew about.

She would also know that we'd tried to walk away.

"Was there anything in the house?" Christopher asked.

"Like what?"

He hummed for a moment. "Things that Zans and Fish might want."

"Well, I guess they should have been with us," I said haughtily. "Or you can go back."

"No," he said quietly, laying his hand on Paisley's head as we walked. "I'm where I need to be."

We continued in silence toward the end of the driveway. Aiden came into view beyond the open gate. The goblin cat, tiny at that distance, was perched on the roof of the SUV. Pearl Godfrey was a few steps away, her phone to her ear. Calling in a cleanup crew, I presumed.

"Should have been with us…" Christopher said quietly, repeating my own words back to me. "Does that mean you'd let them come home? All three of them, once we find Bee?"

I just looked at him steadily, and he held my gaze. No hint of magic in his eyes. I grinned, wondering if he ever hated that about me. Not always knowing what I was going to do. Or worse, watching me thwart the fate to which he was so devoted.

He laughed quietly.

Then I crouched to let Paisley slide off my shoulders, encouraging her to walk the rest of the way to the gate—slowly. As we neared Aiden, the demon dog picked up her pace, pressing her head under his hand when the sorcerer reached for her. Aiden gently ran his hands over her shoulders, avoiding all the freshly healing wounds.

My heart ached a little. In a good way.

Maybe the demon dog would be okay.

I stopped walking, turning slightly toward Christopher, but keeping my gaze on Aiden and Paisley. "I'll think about it."

He smiled.

I stepped away, but he leaned into me and whispered, "Such pretty wings, by the way."

I started, realizing that somewhere between Christopher taking down Mercury and me hefting Paisley up on my shoulders, the wings had dissipated.

Maybe right around the time I'd subconsciously realized I didn't need access to all that power. Didn't need to be so primed and ready to unleash, at least.

I threw Christopher a look.

He grinned unrepentantly. Then, walking backward a few steps, he called, "Hey, Paisley! Emma beguiled you a friend."

Behind him, the demon dog turned to look at me, her jaw hinging open in a big smile full of double-rowed sharp teeth.

"Not for eating!" I blurted.

The demon dog chortled. Her voice was ragged and rough.

I huffed as Aiden and Christopher chuckled, and I closed the space between us, muttering, "And I didn't beguile it."

On the roof of the SUV, the goblin cat rolled over on its back and reached out for me—sharp claws shooting out to slice the air.

"The cat has six toes on its left foot," a sweet voice called from the back passenger seat. The door was open, and Opal was propped up at an angle that allowed her to see the mouth of the driveway. Aiden must have moved the SUV so that she could sit in comfort while they watched for us.

Various emotions flushed through me, lingering terror finally giving way to joy. Then settling into a warmth…

Into happiness. And I actually had to stand still and just absorb the moment.

Aiden threaded his fingers through mine, raising my hand to his mouth and pressing a kiss to my palm.

Opal blinked up at me, a smile blossoming across her face. "Oh good, you are you again."

I frowned. "I'm always me."

Opal stretched her arms over her head, clawing her fingers and putting on a creepy voice. "All shall love me...and despair. You know."

I blinked at her. "I scared you."

Opal huffed. "Of course not." She peeked up at me. "Okay, yeah, you are scary. Just, you know, the benevolent sort of scary. Like from the *Lord of the Rings* movies."

My frown deepened.

"Emma!" she cried, exasperated. But—happily—not at all scared of me. "We watched them during spring break!"

"A movie..." I said doubtfully, playing along.

The little witch just grinned at me, all sleepy and content.

Paisley stretched up to eye the goblin cat, her large front paws pressed to the side of the SUV. She had wanted a pet for a while now, and Christopher had been asking to get a barn cat. Though I wasn't certain that the hairless goblin would be interested in chasing lowly mice—

The goblin cat smacked the demon dog across the nose for her impertinence.

Paisley reared back, looking at me and then Aiden, totally affronted.

"Well," Aiden drawled, "you did just walk right into that one."

Paisley huffed, then shoved her way past us, climbing over Opal and into the back seat. The little witch giggled and protested at the same time.

I turned my head, just enough to capture Aiden's mouth with mine and explore it—warm and sweet. I stayed there long enough that my fingers ended up threaded through his hair, his hand gripped around the back of my neck, cradling my head.

We broke the kiss, then just stood in each other's arms, foreheads pressed together. A loud purring vibrated across the roof of the SUV.

"I think the goblin cat might be a pervert," Opal said, utterly earnestly from the back seat.

Aiden barked out a laugh. A quick glance toward the SUV revealed that Opal's eyes were closed, her head resting back and a slight smile on her face. Paisley's head was in the little witch's lap.

Christopher wandered back toward us, hands in his pockets. "Pearl would like us to wait with her for a few more minutes. She's got a cleanup crew coming, but just in case Mercury has some tricks left to play…"

"Do you see anything?" I asked.

He tilted his head, smiling softly. "You don't usually ask, Socks."

"For the safety of the coven," I said.

He smirked. "I don't see anything here. Home is another matter, though."

Aiden narrowed his eyes at the clairvoyant, whose smirk grew into a pleased, playful grin. "You aren't going to like it at all, sorcerer."

Aiden frowned. Then he groaned. "My father?"

Christopher laughed quietly, then swiped the goblin cat off the roof, cooing to it. "You need a name, my sweetness."

"Emma…" Aiden growled.

I shrugged. "You're the one who abandoned the clairvoyant all alone at home."

The sorcerer huffed.

But Opal's sweet laughter filtered out of the SUV—for a sleepy witch she had sharp ears—and an involuntary grin swamped Aiden's face instead.

And I got it.

Deep in my tattered soul.

I knew. Without using even a touch of my empathy. I knew how he felt.

WHILE WE WAITED FOR THE CLEANUP CREW, AIDEN texted Ocean, though I suspected she would have already heard the pertinent details from the coven. Opal reclaimed her orange backpack from among the luggage and found her own phone buried underneath all the other items I'd frantically stuffed in the bag back at the hotel while trying to keep myself from melting down, or more likely, going ballistic. She texted Juniper and let her friend know that both she and Paisley were safe.

Then we headed home.

BACK ON VANCOUVER ISLAND, WE STOPPED TO PICK up hot food for a late lunch. Carving my way toward Mercury's house, then getting to Opal had felt like it had taken hours, though it had really been only minutes. The expenditure of massive amounts of magic had a way of stretching time. Christopher sourced and then ordered take-out Indian food online, which ended up being delicious. The samosas were perfection, slightly crisp on the outside and warm and spicy on the inside.

The clairvoyant climbed into the back seat with Opal for the rest of the trip home, forcing me to drive so Aiden could grab a nap. Paisley was stretched out—snoring—in the back hatch, having gotten rid of all the luggage. I liked a lot of the sundresses I'd packed too many of, and seriously hoped that the demon dog knew where she'd tossed the suitcases. And that she could get them back when we arrived home.

I had just spotted the first sign announcing the distance to Lake Cowichan when I saw Opal snuggle into Christopher's shoulder in the rearview mirror.

"I knew it," she whispered. "I knew you were angels. Did you see Emma's wings?"

"We aren't angels, my little witch," the clairvoyant whispered back gently. "But we would do anything, even if it meant manifesting wings, to get you back and keep you safe."

Opal grumbled playfully. Then she grabbed her iPad and persuaded Christopher to play against her in some video game.

For the rest of the drive home, the clairvoyant's magic danced up and down my spine in a gentle caress. Informing me that he was seeing a lot of whatever was lying ahead for us.

I had never really felt his power highlight each blood tattoo in turn, slipping from one to the other. But perhaps the connection I'd felt when I accepted the power I'd inadvertently absorbed from the Hallowed was now something Christopher could access...and perhaps it strengthened his sight of the other three?

Either way, he didn't deem it necessary to mention any of it.

TWELVE

KADER AZAR AND THE MYSTIC OF THE GOLDEN PEN-
insula were sipping iced tea and nibbling on ginger
snaps on the front patio. Apparently waiting for us
while they markedly ignored each other.

With one foot set on the bottom stair and one
hand on Opal's shoulder, Aiden's eyes narrowed on
Kader, clearly seriously considering slaughtering his
father where he sat.

We had pulled through the front gate, which
opened at our approach, driven up the gravel drive,
and parked beside the barn. Not even remotely sensing that two of the architects of the Collective were
already on the property. Everyone—or at least everyone but Christopher—stumbled out of the SUV
unaware, sleepily content to be home.

Paisley had obligingly returned our luggage.
The Mustang wasn't back in the barn, but Ocean had
texted to say she and Lani were on their way.

The two surprise guests were seated as far as possible from each other as the patio would allow. Kader was in a slowly shrinking sunny spot in the left corner, wearing a light tan suit, one leg crossed over the other. Chenda, situated in the shade on the far right of the door, was swathed in an embroidered green silk gown with a high collar and short sleeves.

Whatever complex shielding they'd each held individually over themselves fell as we approached the steps.

Aiden opened his mouth, magic rising to his command.

Her senses slightly delayed, Opal screeched, utterly delighted as she dashed up the stairs. "Grandpa!"

Kader smiled broadly, setting down his iced tea on the table near his elbow. He reached out a hand for Opal, who grasped it. The dream walker then pecked the sorcerer Azar on both cheeks.

Aiden snapped his mouth shut, casting me a look full of dismay.

"You called it," I muttered.

He snarled under his breath, the words backed by a wallop of power.

"You didn't think I'd ignore my first grandchild, did you?" Kader said, smiling at Opal as if he cherished her.

Aiden scrubbed a hand across his face.

"Did you bring me an end-of-year gift?" Opal asked. "I was in the top five in all my classes."

"Of course," Chenda purred, inserting herself into the conversation.

Christopher threw his head back and laughed.

"I'm glad to see you recovered your missing foundling," the mystic said. Her tone was cool and poised, though the dark gaze fixed on Christopher was pained. Yet somehow also greedy. Needy? "I hope my information was valuable."

The clairvoyant huffed, taking as many of the suitcases as he could carry from Paisley. "We were already on our way."

Chenda smiled smugly. "Well, that is the way with your magic, isn't it? First, I found the information, then—"

"Pearl Godfrey led us where we needed to go," I said coolly.

"And we're here to make certain that need is never an issue again," Chenda said, just as cool. She nodded toward Kader—the gesture seemingly the smallest she could make and still acknowledge the sorcerer.

He smirked, then tapped his forefinger down on an empty spot on the table. Except it wasn't empty. A thick manila envelope had appeared under his hand. "I took the liberty of making a stop on my way here."

"After I made the arrangements," Chenda added.

Kader flicked his fingers dismissively, and everyone on the patio except Opal stilled. Ready for whatever spell the sorcerer was about to unleash.

Opal pounced on the manila envelope. "You got it!"

"I did," he said, smiling at her benevolently.

Opal spun around, clutching the envelope to her chest, her eyes shining brightly. "Emma! The adoption papers. We just need to sign."

"All of us," Kader said.

"Yes. All of us," Chenda said. "So no more unfortunate misunderstandings occur."

I looked at Christopher, not certain I'd caught all the nuances of the conversation. I could handle whatever Kader was suggesting. The Mystic of the Golden Peninsula, though...

Chenda had claimed to be Christopher's mother—in a more significant fashion than simply contributing to the mix of DNA that had gone into the genetic code of all the Five. I still wasn't entirely certain how the clairvoyant felt about that claim.

Christopher wasn't laughing anymore. But he also wasn't protesting, and his gaze was clear of magic. He had gotten me hit with a death curse the last time he'd paused to listen to Chenda—and the trust issues that had resulted between us lingered still.

"Let me do this for you," Chenda said softly. "What else is a lifetime of collecting power good for if I can't help protect your family?"

The clairvoyant's power flickered in his eyes.

Chenda stilled, all her cool disdain draining from her expression. Her deep-brown eyes were open, clear, as she simply waited for Christopher's judgement.

"It's Emma's decision," the clairvoyant finally said, settling his gaze on me.

"It's Opal's decision," I said. "She chooses her own family."

Aiden stirred beside me but didn't interject.

A broad grin swamped Opal's face as she bounced on her heels. "I pick the biggest, most powerful family I can get."

Christopher laughed, shaking his head.

"A perfectly calculated decision," Kader said approvingly.

Opal stepped up to me, her neck craned back. I leaned over her, and she whispered into my ear, "But mostly just you, Emma. You and me."

I swallowed what felt like my heart as I brushed my hands through her curls, settling them on her shoulders. "Yes, my darling dream walker. Yes."

She bounced again, then started tearing the envelope open.

"I'll get a pen," Aiden said, seriously peeved.

"No worries," Kader said smoothly, standing and pulling a pen out of his inner suit jacket pocket. "I have one of Isa's, primed and ready."

"Of course you do, Father." Aiden's tone was tense and hard.

But he'd called Kader 'father.' So that meant something.

Christopher brushed by us, carrying the suit-cases into the house. Opal followed on his heels. Paisley, who'd been uncharacteristically quiet while she watched the two interlopers on the patio and took in the conversation, trundled up the stairs, pressing her shoulder against me. She swung her large head from Kader to Chenda, then back again.

The demon dog was still hurt and weary. Barely healed wounds marred her gray-blue furred skin.

"You survived," Kader said, speaking to Paisley. "I would have expected nothing less."

"Indeed," Chenda said. "You are far too powerful for a silly black witch. Mercury always was obsessive."

"She never would have gotten half as far without Lindiwe Fourie," Kader said conversationally. " 'The Chemist,' as your Samantha calls her." The elder sor-cerer offered me a conspiratorial smirk.

I ignored it.

The mystic sniffed. "I disapproved of the entire department."

"But…Silver didn't," Kader said, his tone drip-ping with condescension.

And even I recognized a threat when I heard one. Chenda had helped Silver Pine and Isa capture Kader in LA. Where the sorcerer had been tortured, nearly drained of magic, before the Five had rescued him. A rescue that had resulted in Silver putting out an unsanctioned kill order on me.

Chenda simply huffed, straightened, and held out her hand toward Paisley. "After we all sign the adoption papers for Opal, we'll draw you a hot healing bath. You'll like that."

Paisley dropped her massive maw open in a sharp-toothed smile. Or perhaps she was contemplating eating the mystic despite my most recent edict. I couldn't chastise her for merely thinking murderous thoughts, though.

Then the demon dog trundled forward and pressed her broad head under Chenda's hand. The mystic's normally placid expression sparked with fury as she gently ran her fingers over Paisley's wounded flesh.

Then Paisley's tentacles whipped out, and she stole the entire plate of ginger snaps, eating it whole.

Kader snorted.

But Chenda threw her head back and laughed—a charming, chiming laugh that was achingly similar to how Christopher often reacted to the absurdities of life.

I reminded myself that she wasn't really his mother.

"The plate," I said to Paisley, understanding that the demon dog was striving for some normalcy.

Paisley deposited the empty plate back on the table with a flick of her tongue. Then, her large shoulders rolling under battle-scarred skin, she stepped through into the house.

Chenda picked up her iced tea and the empty plate, following the demon dog without another word.

The moment the patio was empty except for Aiden, Kader, and me, Aiden practically spun on his father.

Kader just waited, his expression blank in that Azar way that meant his thoughts and emotions were likely roiling. Though perhaps I was giving the sorcerer Azar too much credit.

"I was explicit," Aiden said through clenched teeth and a rigid jaw.

"Emma has already made the call."

"Emma can drain every last drop of your magic where you stand with no more effort than looking at you," Aiden snarled.

"Can she now?" Kader gave me that smile that I'd once thought was possessive. Because it was.

But it was also proud.

He looked at Aiden that way. A lot.

"That's not the point," Aiden said, trying to moderate his tone but already losing the thread of the argument. "Opal doesn't understand what you are."

"She understands," Kader corrected smoothly, "what I can be to her." He smiled at both of us. Slipping his hands into the pockets of his pants, and rucking up his suit jacket to do so, he stepped through into the house.

Aiden turned to me, an almost helpless look on his face. "Emma, Opal doesn't need the target painted on her back...she..." He swallowed, then closed his eyes and didn't finish what he'd started to say.

I answered anyway. "You once told me that her magic already made her a target."

"Yes."

"And that if I claimed her, I could protect her."

He sighed. "Yes."

"The more of us there are…the more of us who others fear…"

"Yes."

I closed the space between us, pressing up against the length of him, but not otherwise touching him. I dropped my head back to look into his eyes. And we just gazed at each other for a moment.

Then I whispered, "For Opal."

He nodded, though he wasn't even remotely happy.

I took his hand, and we crossed into the house together.

KADER HAD PICKED UP TWO CERTIFIED COPIES OF Opal's adoption papers from Ember Pine. I had no idea how he and Chenda had pulled it off—and hoped my lawyer hadn't come to any harm in the process. But neither point was appropriate to ask about in front of Opal. He'd also had Ember print out a third copy. For Opal to keep.

We laid all three sets out on the kitchen table. Opal, Aiden, and I signed the first two sets—aka the official legal documents. One copy for our records and one to be sent back to Ember, to be filed in whatever way made the adoption legal among the mundanes as well as the Adept.

Then, after Aiden and I signed the third set, Christopher carefully printed his name and signed beneath ours, adding 'Uncle' under his signature. Then Chenda signed, printing 'Grandmother' under her name. Kader with 'Grandfather' under his name signed last.

Sorcerer magic in the black ballpoint ink, courtesy of Isa, shimmered across the page—then adhered to that page, along with a touch of pure intent from each of the co-signers. A simple, binding declaration of that intent, of familial bonds claimed and pledged.

Opal's copy wasn't for lawyers or a court system. Rather, it was magically binding. The dream walker would never be alone or abandoned again, not even if something happened to Aiden and me.

I had already known that Christopher would step forward to care for Opal, as would the Godfrey coven. But now so would the Azar cabal and the Mystic of the Golden Peninsula.

I slid the papers back toward Opal. She took the pen and carefully printed Paisley's name on the bottom right corner. The dream walker claiming the demon dog as family, in a reverse of the earlier process.

Paisley had positioned herself at the young witch's elbow so she could watch the entire signing.

Opal screwed open the pen, realized it was a ballpoint insert, then blinked up at Aiden. The dark-haired sorcerer helped her crack the end of the insert so she could smear ink on the bottom of Paisley's right front foot.

"This just makes it official," she said solemnly.

I was crying now, and not giving a shit if anyone saw me doing so. Aiden's and Christopher's eyes were also damp.

Paisley blinked up at Opal, then pressed her paw to the paper where the little witch had printed her name. She left a perfectly inked paw print behind.

Opal looked up at me. "And Samantha can sign when she comes home? As my aunt?"

"Yes."

"Perfect." The little witch signed her own name, then blew on the ink, though there would be no smudging any signature spelled by an Azar sorcerer. She flipped the papers closed, held them to her chest, then burrowed into my arms for a hug.

Paisley pressed her shoulder against my leg. Aiden settled his hand on Opal's back, just gazing at me with—

Christopher's magic exploded in his eyes so suddenly that he grabbed the top of a chair to steady himself.

Then a text message pinged through on his phone.

Frowning, Opal fished the phone out of the clairvoyant's back pocket, glancing at the screen. "Zans."

"Emma," Christopher gasped, then shook his head to clear some of the magic clouding his sight of the present. "The message is for Emma."

Opal passed the phone to me.

I opened the text message. It was a video attachment.

I hit play.

Samantha appeared on-screen. The telekinetic was standing, feet planted, hands fisted at her sides, wearing only a thin tank top and panties. She looked as though she'd been in a massive fight—which was saying something, because all of the Five healed quickly.

She was glaring at someone beyond the camera, at whoever was filming. Next to her, slightly off-screen, Daniel was wearing only thin boxers and sporting multiple bruises in various stages of healing. Including odd marks on the inside of his elbow.

It took me a moment to recognize bruised injection sites.

It took a lot to bruise one of the Five. I wouldn't have thought being jabbed with any sort of needle could do it. Not unless Daniel had been mostly or even completely drained of his magic.

"Emma is so going to kick your ass!" Samantha snarled on-screen.

The video cut out, but not as if the recording had been stopped intentionally. More like it had been magically fried.

A second message appeared below. *I'll be in touch.*

Aiden swore under his breath.

Kader glanced at Chenda sharply. The mystic shook her head in quick denial.

I met Christopher's gaze. "Tell me."

"You're going on a trip," he said simply.

"It will be my last one," I said caustically. "Enough is enough."

Christopher—my Knox—smiled tightly. "You are always enough."

I cast a withering glance over Kader and Chenda. "Either you're with me or against me. There are no shades of gray anymore. No shadows in which you can linger to see what will happen when one of you pokes one of the Five."

They both gazed back at me, unblinking.

Opal pressed against me. "Samantha?"

I smoothed my hand over her shoulder, allowing myself to top up her already-too-full magical reserves just a touch as I did so. "The telekinetic is hard to kill."

"We all are," Christopher added.

"But I'm tired of people trying." I met Aiden's gaze. "It's past time to end it."

He smiled almost gently. "I'm with you, Emma. Always."

RECON
MISSION: BEE

MEGHAN CIANA DOIDGE

AUTHOR'S NOTE

Recon Mission: Bee is a novella in the Amplifier Series, which is set in the same universe as the Dowser, Oracle, Reconstructionist, Archivist, and Misfits of the Adept Universe series.

For Michael
Who would never abandon me in
the middle of nowhere.

Basil

STRENGTH

CONCERNED THAT WE HADN'T HEARD FROM HER IN over a year, Fish had dragged me all the way into the middle of Russia to follow up a lead on the whereabouts of our telepathic team member. Amanda, aka Bee. But what was supposed to be a simple reconnaissance mission—gathering intel so we could formulate a plan that might need to involve the rest of the team—went sideways within twenty-four hours.

Because even though the bonds that held we Five together in life were tied so tight that the death of one of us might mean the death of all...

I was apparently the only one who took the responsibility that came with those ties seriously.

I WAS FAIRLY CERTAIN I'D BEEN HIT BY A TRUCK. AND yes, I knew what actually being hit by a truck felt like.

My head was pounding. Every joint in my body ached. And in the moment between a deep sleep—okay, it was pretty clear I'd passed out—and surfacing into the gray morning, I couldn't remember where I was.

I did, unfortunately, know exactly where I wasn't.

I wasn't on the West Coast of Canada. The lack of magic tingling along my spine told me that instantly. But the too-soft bed, scratchy sheets, and stale air of the hotel room were big giveaways as well.

I wasn't where I wanted to be.

Not that I would ever admit that out loud.

Not while Emma was in hearing range. And the amplifier had hearing so heightened that it almost rivaled her superiority complex, so I kept my contentment over living under her roof to myself. Perpetually.

Or I would blame that feeling of rightness, and my need to stifle it whenever I was away from her, on the blood tattoo that bound us, magic to magic. Blood to blood and bone and sinew.

I tried cracking my eyes open, halfway hoping I was wrong.

I wasn't.

The room was just as gray as the triangle of sky I could see through the window while sprawled across the bed. I'd managed to remove my jacket, pants, and belt before passing out, at least. So I was slightly more comfortable in a black cotton T-shirt and boy shorts than I would have been otherwise.

Emma favored lacy underwear, even though she didn't need a bra any more than I did. And yes, I secretly coveted the pretty lacy things the amplifier hid under her thrift-store sundresses. But I'd never been able to force myself to buy any, to admit that I wanted anything pretty or sweet in my life. And I certainly wasn't interested in titillating anyone with that underwear, not in the way that Emma had her dark sorcerer panting after her.

I wasn't jealous.

I just honestly wasn't all that interested in being intimate with anyone who wasn't already embedded under my skin. Certainly not long enough to woo and then wed them. And…even then…I'd only climbed into Fish's bed, so many years ago now, because Emma had done so first. And where Fox in Socks went, we—Knox, Bee, me, and even Fish—were sure to follow…

Until she'd kicked us all to the curb.

And sure, that was a bit of revisionist history I had going on. But since it was all in my head, I could play the wounded party all I wanted.

Bee had been curvier than Emma and me. She'd needed a supportive bra around the age of twelve, and the Collective had provided the barest of essentials.

But then, we hadn't been bred for beauty.

We'd been bred for power.

And I was that.

Pure power.

Though I didn't feel particularly powerful this morning. Or perhaps it was early afternoon…

I turned my head, already knowing that the second bed was not only empty but hadn't been slept in at all. After dosing my whiskey with whatever witch brew he'd had in his flask too many times, Fish had taken off with a slightly older witch with pretty curves, bright-blue eyes, and the palest of blond hair.

I hadn't mentioned that the witch was wearing colored contacts. Or that she'd come on to me in the bathroom in the hopes of making it a threesome. Fish—Daniel, as I had to remember to call him in public—didn't need me forcing myself into his bed any more than I'd already done in the second decade of our lives.

As long as I was wallowing in a hotel room and being uncharacteristically honest with myself— thanks, witch brew—I could admit that I'd never really invited anyone to my bed. Any one-night stand I'd initiated in the last eight years never made it to an actual bed. Ever.

Because true sexual intimacy meant finding someone who wouldn't be scared of me after the ceiling or floor cracked when I orgasmed. Or the bed frame, for that matter.

So I didn't let go. Ever.

I kept my hands and my magic to myself and didn't really bother with even thinking about it.

Though Emma's and Aiden's sexual appetites made it necessary for me to play with myself far more often than usual.

No matter how many wards the sorcerer etched in their bedroom, he would never fully block the connection between our blood tattoos…

Still, I would take that if it also meant living under the same roof as Emma and Christopher. Being near two of the Five had me more settled in my own skin. A grounding I'd had no idea I was missing.

Anyway, that meant Fish got the one-night stand the previous night, not me. What I'd gotten was a raging hangover that had me acting maudlin, overly and annoyingly self-reflective.

I forced myself up, then onto my feet and shuffling the three steps to the bathroom. The tile and the walls were as gray as the room, but with age, not dirt. I got the cold water on—it took a second to sputter through the pipes—and liberally splashed my face. Grabbing and pressing a clean towel to my face, I managed to avoid the mirror.

I knew without needing to look that even my normally glorious dark complexion and dark eyes wouldn't be able to compete with whatever Fish had dosed me with. Bruises I could hide. Even blood. But if I felt like I'd been hit by a truck, then I knew I was going to look like it—dull skinned and red eyed. And I didn't need to wallow in my own misdeeds any more than I already had.

As Emma would have icily reminded me, I was on mission.

Not that I hadn't been a willing participant last night. Getting drunk, or even lightly tipsy, wasn't something any of the Five did easily. Our genetically amped-up metabolisms didn't help, of course. But we were also just too powerful to lose ourselves, even for a moment, without being in the company of at least one of the others.

And then Fish had left the club.

Asshole.

Though apparently I had made it back to the hotel on my own.

The window in the bathroom overlooked lower rooftops. While the buildings immediately around the hotel appeared to be service oriented, stout apartment complexes spread out beyond them toward a large city on the horizon. Maybe still Moscow. It had taken me more than twenty-four hours to travel to that Russian city from Lake Cowichan, British Columbia, Canada. Fish had been waiting at the airport, directly off his own flight. He drove. I napped. Because despite the ten-hour time difference, there was no way I was ever going to sleep while surrounded by strangers on a plane.

So now I seriously didn't know where I was, beyond being in Russia and on the outskirts of a major city.

I brushed my teeth, feeling a bit better for it. Then I snagged Fish's toothbrush and perched on the edge of the tub. The porcelain was gloriously chilly.

I forced myself to focus on the brush, on its individual tiny bristles.

Then I called up a lick of the power that was never more than the briefest of thoughts away, barely tucked underneath my skin. I carefully plucked one bristle from the toothbrush, holding it to hover before me.

Yes, with my mind.

I was a telekinetic, after all.

I plucked another bristle. Then another.

Delicate, precise applications of my power were far more of a challenge than tearing things apart. I could have pulled the entire hotel down on my head—and survived the experience—more easily than what I was currently trying to do.

It was also the perfect hangover cure. Something about using my magic so precisely drove the lingering toxins from my system.

So I plucked individual plastic bristles from Fish's toothbrush until it was bald. Then, still holding those bristles aloft in a gentle cushion of my magic, I turned my attention to the plastic handle itself, shaving it down one layer at a time.

After I had completely destroyed Fish's toothbrush, I delicately arrayed all its bristles and plastic shavings into a complicated mandala pattern on the bathroom counter. A little present for him when he returned, hopefully feeling as awful as I was. A nullifier of his power didn't carry around a flask of witch brew to indulge in unless it was strong enough that he'd feel its effects acutely as well.

Feeling far better, but now insanely hungry, I jumped into as hot a shower as I could coax out of the pipes, then dressed. I avoided wetting my hair, thankful that my halo of thick, dark curls had survived the night and the hangover with a minimum of attention.

Dressing in multipocket tactical pants and a fresh skintight T-shirt, I stole Fish's leather jacket. All in black, of course.

And yeah, I was going to hold a grudge about the hangover for a while. Probably months.

It had already been near dark yesterday when Fish pulled into the parking lot at the hotel. We'd lingered only long enough to toss our bags in the room, then walked to a club Fish knew for a late dinner. An Adept-only club. As in, only the magically empowered could even find the place, let alone eat and drink copiously there.

I hadn't minded the idea of drinking with Fish while we waited on the meeting he'd set up. But I was seriously peeved about being abandoned.

Not that I would admit it.

Making certain nothing jangled, even though my pockets were filled with as many small metal projectiles as I could carry—as always—I grabbed the key card from the top of the dresser, along with my backpack and laptop. Then I headed downstairs, where I assumed I'd be able to find some sort of meal.

I WAS JUST FINISHING A PERFECT BREAKFAST WHEN my phone buzzed in my pocket. The breakfast—made by special request because it was actually deep into the afternoon local time—consisted of fairly typical fried eggs and sausage, but was paired with a deliciously spicy and sweet hot tea and a number of small, fluffy, crispy-edged pancakes served with a sour cream topping and raspberry jam. The server spoke English far better than any stilted Russian I could have managed with the help of an app. He'd also been mostly absent after dropping off my food, which was a relief. Because I wasn't into small talk in any form.

Expecting a text from Fish, I found myself looking at a photo of an oracle card, right before it disappeared in the wake of a second text message.

A shiver of trepidation that only one of the Five could arouse in me tingled up my spine, reminding me that even Fish's tattoo currently felt almost dormant on my T4 vertebra.

Not that I needed reminding. Emma's tattoo on my T1 vertebra actually felt hollow, constantly empty whenever I was far enough away from the amplifier that it didn't shimmer, shift, and tingle under my skin. I'd gotten used to feeling that I was carrying around a black hole at the base of my neck after we'd torn down the Collective's compound—mostly because Emma had completely drained me of magic at the time, giving me a year of reprieve.

But then it had all flooded back.

All the power.

And none of the connection.

In those years we'd all spent apart—literally banished by Emma, ordered to set out in different directions, then to stay away from each other to make it harder for the Collective to track us—I often wondered if I was going slowly insane. Knox, as a clairvoyant, had needed to go with Emma to preserve his own mind. And maybe I was more like him than I'd known?

Being away from the amplifier was worse now, after living with her on and off for the bulk of the last four months. Even with Fish to anchor me. Though that asshole hadn't reappeared yet, and my lingering headache wasn't going away.

I shoved all my stupid, on-the-edge-of-dramatic thoughts away and opened the text messages.

The oracle card bore the picture of a black-inked basil plant. Or a basil clipping, at least. With the word 'Strength' printed under it.

An appropriate draw. If it was meant for me. Though all oracle cards had a flip side.

And when drawn by the most powerful clairvoyant in the world? Well, let's just say that being in Christopher's sight from the other side of a whole ocean and almost an entire continent was disconcerting.

The second text message read:

> *I'm not sure if this is for you or Emma.*

I texted back:

The basil means?

Emma had procured the oracle cards—twenty-two of them, similar to a basic tarot deck—from a witch who inked her magic within each card, then tied them to individual intentions. In Christopher's hands, those cards became something more. A way to sharpen a clairvoyant sight that had gotten only deeper while living in close proximity with Emma for the last eight years.

>*You've lost something.*

I sighed. That wasn't an answer, so Christopher was still refining whatever he was trying to see with the cards.

But…had I lost something other than Bee?

She was the reason I was I-don't-know-exactly-where in Russia. The only reason. We'd been on the telepath's trail for almost a year now, and I hadn't seen her face-to-face for over eighteen months. She was wily, and I had no idea why she didn't want to be found. But if we got a solid line on her, then Emma would join the hunt. And Bee wouldn't be able to hide from the amplifier even if she wanted to.

As long as she was still alive.

Bee had to be alive.

Dormant or not, I didn't think the blood and power of the telepath embedded under my skin would survive long after her death. Nor would I for that matter.

>*Yes?*

Fish is off somewhere, I texted, taking a guess at what else I could have 'lost.' I wasn't going to admit my longing to be in Emma's general vicinity...like, constantly. As long as I wasn't actually face-to-face with the amplifier. If we were close enough to lay eyes on each other, all we did was get on each other's nerves.

Emma thought I was jealous of her. Jealous of the position we'd put her in, and that she'd then rejected. Our leader. But that wasn't it at all.

I hated her solely because I loved her.

Because I'd been forced to love her, to pine for her. From the moment her power had been tattooed under my skin.

>*Care to elaborate?*

We're on mission, asshole. Why are you texting?

>*Do you need Paisley?*

Typical clairvoyant, not rising to my level of pissiness. *No.*

>*Are you sure?*

I considered ignoring him. Seriously. We were on a recon mission. On Emma's orders, really, though she was still trying to deny her attachment to any of us, except Knox.

>*Let me know when you need Paisley.*

Care to elaborate about the basil card?

>*I will when the time comes.*

I hate you.

>I miss you too.

Snarling, I tossed my phone on the table and jammed the final pancake in my mouth. It had grown cold.

I forced my attention, my focus, out the window and away from the clairvoyant. Honestly, Emma let Knox get away with way too much shit, coddling him for fear of losing him. Or, more specifically, for fear of him losing his mind, and then Emma losing him. Because haunted by visions they couldn't control, especially as their power grew, clairvoyants typically didn't have long lifespans. Often taking their own lives.

But none of the Five were typical. In any way.

I was seated right next to the window. The glass was speckled with dried raindrops. Months and months of dried drops. The cafe was connected to the hotel, but the decor was brighter than in my room, muted reds with some art hanging from the plastered walls. The day was still gray, though.

The guy in the black trench coat leaned against the brick-walled building across the street and lit his third cigarette. He was dark haired and broad shouldered, and I had momentarily thought he was Fish when I sat down and ordered. But he was older than Fish by at least a decade, and his features were rough hewn, his skin pale. Untouched by Fish's muted mix of Asian ancestry.

Not that any of the Five really knew what our heritage was. We'd been mixed up in a tube and brought into the world through surrogates. Still, my skin was dark enough to suggest that I had more Black or African ancestry than the others. Same with Emma, but at the far opposite end of the skin-color scale.

I tugged my laptop closer, opening the browser and doing a series of quick searches of what properties the basil plant brought to the Strength card.

Prosperity. Protection. Happiness.

Well, that was entirely unhelpful.

The guy was still lounging across the street. He hadn't spoken to a single person, though if he was watching the cafe or me, he hadn't actually glanced my way. Not that I'd seen. I also hadn't felt any magic from him. Granted, I wasn't the most sensitive of Adepts. I wielded a huge amount of energy. Continuously. I had literally been called chaos walking to my face, on more than one occasion, by more than one person. So it was possible that how I held my power blocked my other senses unless I was in close proximity.

Across the street—and with the glass of the window, parked cars, moving vehicles, and pedestrians between me and him—trench coat guy could have been one of the Collective. And I wouldn't know it until I was within lunging distance.

Except I knew he wasn't a member of the Collective. I had identified all but two of the main members from the copious amount of data I'd stolen from the servers in the main compound in Peru—right before we Five tore through and out of that compound.

And both of the unknown two identified as female, based on the scattering of pronouns I'd uncovered that didn't refer to Silver Pine, the black witch who'd tried to kill us, or Chenda, the self-proclaimed Mystic of the Golden Peninsula. The main members of the Collective had communicated mostly in code or used titles, including their signatures in emails and reports, but they let names and other info slip from time to time.

Fish had a line on the member we thought might be a sorcerer from Hong Kong or China. But the one code-named the Chemist, who'd been responsible for the actual mixing of the Five's magic and DNA, had eluded us so far.

The guy across the street could have been wearing a disguise, of course. But I probably would have picked up the amount of magic it would take to hold an illusion that persuasive in place over the course of the forty-five minutes I'd had eyes on him.

He was probably just waiting on someone. If he was still hanging around when I headed back to my room, I'd confront him. I was fairly intimidating even without putting on a power display, though I'd never mastered that bone-chilling expression Emma pinned to her prey right before she decapitated them. Or even when she was just thinking about removing their heads.

I'd been on the other side of that stare too many times to count.

I was way too preoccupied with thoughts of Emma today.

I blamed the hangover.

I continued researching the Strength card, as it would work in a regular tarot deck. It represented perseverance, courage, patience, and compassion.

I snorted.

Not me, then.

The card was clearly intended for Emma. Which was odd, because she was supposed to be at a coven retreat with her soon-to-be-adopted daughter, Opal. Which reminded me that I needed to route my return flight through Frankfurt or London, because I wanted to get the little dream walker a cool gift for making it through her first year at the Academy.

My phone was still sitting on the table, just beyond my dirty dishes. The blank screen mocked me.

Damn you, Fish.

I picked the phone up and texted the nullifier.

Where the fuck are you, asshole?

I regretted the neediness of my tone the moment after I hit send, so I added, *We're on mission.*

The contact we'd come all the way to fucking Russia to meet was Fish's. For all I knew, the asshole nullifier had left the witch's bed early this morning and headed off to the meeting without me.

Seriously, all the Five were assholes. Even me. But Fish was more accustomed to going it alone. Possibly a byproduct of his magic. He literally shoved everyone with a hint of magic in their veins away. Except Emma, of course—but only because the two of them wore each other's power under their skin. As all of us did.

That connection made us all stronger, more capable of working cooperatively, as the Collective had needed. But it had the unintentional side effect—or at least I thought it was unintentional—that none of our powers could completely overwhelm the others. As in, we couldn't kill one another. Not without also possibly dying or disabling ourselves.

Except Emma had demonstrated just a few months ago—by torturing me with the blood tattoo that bound me to her—that she might have discovered a loophole, even if only for herself.

I wasn't denying that I hadn't deserved it then. I had stupidly hurt the demon dog, Paisley. Badly. But was it any wonder that I hated Socks as much as I needed and loved her?

I gathered up my things, shoved them in my bag, and headed over to the cash register to pay.

By the time I hit the street, trench coat dude was gone. So I headed back up to the room.

To wait.

I was always waiting, wasn't I?

Waiting to be included.

To be utilized.

To be valued. By any of the other four.

We wouldn't even be looking for Bee if it weren't for me. No one else gave a shit that she might be in trouble.

Honestly, even Bee might not give a shit. Which would explain why she hadn't bothered answering any of my messages for almost a year now.

BY THE TIME THE SUN WAS THREATENING TO SET, just about nine o'clock local time, I'd identified a revolving guard of three switching out on a forty-minute rotation—and pointedly not looking up at the window of my hotel room.

I still hadn't heard from Fish. He hadn't returned. He hadn't answered my texts. And he hadn't been in touch with Christopher either.

I was assuming the three watching the hotel were Adepts, though I couldn't feel any magic in them from the third floor.

A forty-minute rotation was stupid, no matter that they approached from different directions, stayed on opposite sides of the road, and stood in slightly different places. Especially because the dark-haired, broad-shouldered, pale-skinned male I'd first spotted during lunch was incessantly smoking. If they'd been on a continual loop with at least five people, it would have taken me more than an hour to figure out I was under surveillance. Unfortunately for them, all the other buildings within a block were shorter than the hotel, so they couldn't surveil me from a neighboring window or roof.

The hotel room had a small table, presumably intended as a desk given that the phone had been on it. I had pushed it up to the window to set up my workspace, then opened the curtains as far as they'd go in an attempt to get more light into the room. But I still felt clouded in the all-pervasive gray, practically breathing it in. Wasn't it supposed to be summer?

The blood tattoos that bound me against my will to the other four of the Five were all dormant, though I kept catching the occasional flicker from my tie to Fish on my T4 vertebra.

It required a lot of effort to take out a nullifier of his power level. It was likely he was the most powerful nullifier in existence, plus he was pretty handy with sorcerer magic. All of the Five had an extra magical skill subset, except me. Christopher could wield some witch magic. Emma could wield just about anything she wanted to, as long as she'd drained that skill from another Adept. And Bee was far more than a simple telepath or mind reader. She was a manipulator.

But me? I couldn't cast circles or whisper spells. I couldn't screw with minds, or kill with a thought or touch.

I could move mountains, though.

Literally.

And I was okay with that.

It was conceivable that Fish wasn't actually missing. He could have just been off indulging. But him doing so while on mission would be highly out of character. I had actually been surprised that he'd abandoned me last night, drunk or not.

It wasn't impossible to take the nullifier out, but he'd have to have made himself very vulnerable. And again, if he was dead, I was fairly certain I would have felt it. Or that Christopher would have seen it, and not just that stupid basil oracle card he'd texted me.

So, my guess?

The petite, almost-too-pretty witch from the bar wasn't just a witch. Or she had some powerful friends—possibly the ones waiting for something outside. Waiting for me? Or, more likely, waiting to see who I was in town to meet.

Unfortunately for them, and my own boredom, I wasn't the point of contact for that particular meeting. The contact that had drawn us here was Fish's.

When darkness fully fell, I would find out just how powerful those stalking me were. Until then, I watched them, noting each and every flaw, noting any time one of them twitched or got distracted, while I made certain I was up-to-date on all the info that regularly trickled in to me from contacts all over the world.

DECIDING TO NOT IMMEDIATELY TANGLE WITH THE rotating guards out front of the hotel, and not knowing if the back exits were also under surveillance, I slipped up to the roof, disarmed the alarm with a touch of my magic, and stepped out into the still-cloudy night.

It was muggy. Ugh.

Keeping my hands free, I muffled the sound of the heavy steel door latching back into place behind me with another touch of power. The process was so ingrained that I barely thought about it. Though I did wait a moment to check that the alarm had rearmed itself before I stepped away.

If I threw too much magic at small electronics, I could fry them rather than just momentarily disrupt their signals. But living on and off again with Emma and Christopher for the last four months had forced me to focus the bulk of my constant training regime on smaller, more mundane tasks. The results weren't as satisfying as tearing down an entire building complex, but were actually more useful.

Also, we did lots of hand-to-hand combat. Because Socks still liked to kick my ass at least once a day.

The reason for my clandestine exit? It had become apparent to all of the Five that we didn't move through this world as unnoticed as we'd once hoped. And I wasn't referring to the remaining members of the Collective keeping a close watch on their creations. I meant the guardian dragons. The very beings that the Collective had created the Five to stand against if it had ever come to that, while they scurried off and tried to hide all their nefarious deeds.

I had honestly thought the dragons were pure myth. Then a guardian, apparently one of nine, popped in via portal to help Emma clean up Cerise Myers's mess a couple of months back. Aiden's mother had tried to use her son's blood tie to his father to murder him. In the process, she'd inadvertently released an immortal entity that momentarily possessed Emma—something that had called itself the Hallowed, and which had required the power of over a half-dozen witches and sorcerers to finally contain it.

Though according to Emma, that guardian had let one of the main architects of the Collective—Kader Azar, aka Aiden's father—off with a mere warning. So I seriously questioned the dragon's judgement.

That wasn't entirely the point, though.

The point was, the Zans I'd been when we broke free of the Collective's control had been eager to tear the rest of the world apart. That Zans would have confronted the first asshole she even presumed to be stalking her.

Because that Zans had nothing to live for. Though admittedly, I hadn't known that right away. Not until the magic Socks had drained to nothing had come roaring back twofold. Not until waking up hungover and alone in motel after motel, having no idea what city I'd just left or where I was heading.

Hunting the remaining members of the Collective had given me focus. Had brought me back into contact with Fish, and occasionally Bee. It still didn't fill the void, but it mitigated it.

Then, without another choice, I'd crawled back to Emma. For help. And I got a taste of the life she'd built. I sneered at it, of course.

Until I went away again and realized that all I wanted…all I needed…was that. Or something like what Emma painstakingly protected, even from the rest of the Five if necessary.

A home.

And maybe some horses.

Did I know anything about horses? Nope.

But the idea of breeding beautiful beasts was just appealing. And I wasn't going to read anything into that. Just like Emma would hit anyone with that look of death for daring to comment on her idyllic white-painted, red-roofed farmhouse, replete with barn and fruit trees and chickens.

So now, swathed in black, I avoided the confrontation I would have eagerly embraced before, and crept across the rooftop to peer over the far edge. Silent and stealthily—not my core strengths—because I wanted to go home after this mission. And that meant not drawing any attention until it couldn't be helped.

Of course, if someone had actually taken Daniel? If they'd harmed Fish? Well, I'd have to get in line behind Emma to exact vengeance. Yet another reason to keep quiet about it until I knew I needed help.

Emma might have spent eight years pretending the other three of the Five didn't exist, that we weren't her responsibility. But we'd always known that she would come for us, whether to rescue or to punish.

The blood tattoo on my T4 vertebra tingled again—my tie to Fish.

I waited.

It fizzled, telling me nothing except he had to be somewhere nearby. Within the immediate outskirts of the city, at least.

The hotel was taller than the neighboring buildings. I couldn't fly. But I could, however, jump. Rather nimbly, if I said so myself. And farther than the average person. By a lot.

The narrow alley below was empty but well lit. I would need to be quick.

I backed up a few steps, spotting a ladder lying to the side of what I assumed was some sort of mechanical room. Well, that made things even easier.

With a flick of my fingers, I tugged the ladder to me, breaking the chain that held it—that I hadn't seen in the dark—with a quick twist, and a hope that the sound of it dropping to the roof hadn't carried.

Even Fish would have sneered at me for that oversight, as slight as it was.

I was in my head.

I had been all day.

It was time to focus, to track down Fish.

I ran for the roof edge, the ladder hovering alongside me. I leaped, bringing it along with me. Allowing myself to fall a meter or so, I tucked the ladder under me, ran along its rungs and took another leap, making it down to the next roof and landing as softly as I could.

Keeping the ladder with me, I traversed a dozen more rooftops in the same way, moving in the direction of the Adepts-only club that Fish had taken me to last night.

His blood tattoo remained dormant. Like all the others.

I dropped off the last building at the corner of a block. Using my telekinesis to jump or drop was pretty much second nature after almost thirty years of wielding that power mostly unfettered. I tucked the ladder into a patch of scraggly bushes of some sort, then continued on foot.

It was impossible for any of the Five to sneak up on each other, not since we'd been branded with the tattoos at the age of fourteen. Ironically, for tattoos meant to make us all more powerful because they continually connected us to Emma's amplification, they also made it completely impossible to block any of the others magically. Fish had gotten the biggest boost after we'd been tattooed, because it meant that Socks could reach through his nullifying power and actually touch him without being dampened herself.

I was fairly certain that was why she'd crawled into his bed for the first time soon after. Not that Socks would ever admit to needing to be connected to any of us, least of all by touch.

But the range of the blood tattoos was fairly tight, and certain terrain and conditions—such as a city full of people and electronics—could limit that range further.

But in a smaller neighborhood, after dark? I should have been able to get a read on Fish fairly easily.

The single-lane streets were mostly empty of pedestrians, and most of the storefronts were closed except for the occasional cafe. The stout apartment buildings that lined either side of the street along the next couple of blocks were well lit, though.

No sign of my stalkers. I'd either eluded them, or they were actually waiting for someone else. Maybe for Fish to return. Or for his contact to arrive?

Eventually, the apartments gave way to a small warehouse district. I slipped steadily through the shadows, holding my power in a tight coil around myself. I could use my telekinesis as a personal shield, though I couldn't shield others as effectively as Fish could. Holding a perpetual personal shield while in enemy territory was always the solid tactical choice, because with my sense for magic lacking, I often found myself taking the first hit before I realized that another Adept was even near me.

It was exceedingly rare that any such attacker got in a second hit.

Fish's tattoo flared momentarily. Enough to slow my pace, then for me to tuck myself into the deep shadows at the side of a building to try to get a sense of direction. Then it went dormant again.

If I hadn't known better, I might have thought that a third party was somehow using my connection to Fish to lure me in. Except I was almost certain that wasn't possible. Because who even knew about the tattoos? And who would be powerful enough to first contain Fish, then to access our blood ties?

I continued on, picking up the first hints of residual magic as I neared what appeared to be a der-elict warehouse on the far edge of the district. Signs in Russian that I couldn't read were accompanied by a picture of a ship. As far as I knew, we weren't any-where near water, so maybe they'd once built ship parts in this complex? But the Adepts in this part of the city had gotten hold of the property at some point, and now it was a club. A gathering place.

I slipped through the ward line unimpeded. If I'd been a mundane, the magic would have presum-ably forced me to turn away. The building wasn't derelict on the other side of the boundary line. It was just perfectly nondescript. Gray on more gray, with the windows painted over.

Hands stuffed in the pockets of the oversized leather jacket I'd stolen from Fish—and therefore with easy access to a half-dozen ball bearings—I followed the residual magic to the side entrance. It tickled my nose slightly, like breathing in static. I tugged open a large, unmarked steel door. With my mind, not my hands.

Another tingle of static filtered out to me, then I crossed a sound barrier, and music blasted over me instead—American pop. From the nineties, I thought, though I really knew nothing about music.

About a half-dozen people were dancing to the far right under strobe lights. A long, well-lit, mir-ror-backed bar lined the far left wall. The lounge area where they served food spread out between the two. At first glance, it was less busy than it had been the previous night, though we'd hit the bar only after eat-ing a late dinner.

Plus, certain aspects of the evening before were still rather blurry.

I flicked my gaze up to take in the behemoth bouncer—and I was tall enough that it was rare for me to have to look up at anyone. A shifter of some sort. Most likely a wolf. They were the dominant shifter type. But he was bigger than any werewolf I'd ever met.

His nostrils flared, confirming I was an Adept. Though I shouldn't have been able to get through the door if I didn't hold any magic.

I flashed my teeth at him in a quiet display of dominance. I hadn't even bothered looking at who-ever had staffed the door yesterday, since Fish had been in the lead.

He snorted, pleased. Dark wavy hair fell over his wide forehead, long enough to brush his seriously bushy eyebrows. His skin was pale, as was the case for just about everyone I'd seen here the previous night.

Bear, maybe? Wolves got pretty pissy at the slightest provocation.

"I'm looking for someone," I said, pitching my voice just over the music but trying not to outright yell. A shifter's hearing, wolf or not, was sensitive. Daniel had spoken some Russian last night, but then had quickly switched to English. Adepts, being a small percentage of whatever population they found themselves in, were generally multicultural. But En-glish was a fairly common denominator, even in a club in the middle of Russia. "We were here together last night."

He grinned, not leering but definitely interested. "Let me know if you don't find him. I'd be happy to fill in."

I raised my chin offishly. "He's my...brother." Fish and I looked nothing alike, but simply calling him my brother would let the bouncer know how pissed I'd be if something had happened to him—say if shakedowns were typical for the club. Not that Fish would ever fall for something so mundane.

The bouncer's grin widened, but then he just nodded toward the bar. "I just got on shift. Bette's been here since opening. She was tending bar yesterday as well."

I gave him a look that had him pivoting to watch me walk to the bar. Not because I was sexy or even pretty, but because I was dangerous. And I had to be twigging all his senses.

Apparently, he liked dangerous.

Scanning the dance floor and then the lounge area for any familiar faces from last night, I stepped up to the bar between two stools, catching my reflection in the mirrored wall behind the rows of liquor bottles. As had been true the night before, I was the only dark-skinned person in the club. Hell, maybe even in this entire part of the city. I never expected to blend in, but I'd gotten accustomed to larger, more diverse populations. The Adept typically weren't prejudiced about race. They divided themselves by power. Shifters, witches, sorcerers, vampires, and so forth.

I didn't fit into any of those groups either.

The blood tattoo on my spine remained dormant.

Even with the mirror, standing with my back to the room was uncomfortable. Three other Adepts occupied the bar—a lone shifter five stools away and two sorcerers deep in conversation at the far end.

I didn't recognize the bartender polishing the glasses she'd just run through the small dishwasher under the bar. A petite, dark-blond witch, she wore over a dozen different charms on a double-stranded necklace. Most of them looked like potions. Or poisons. Maybe the bouncer occasionally needed help to subdue someone? Or maybe certain clients occasionally asked for their drinks to be dosed knowingly.

The witch bartender shimmied over to me, opening her mouth.

I interrupted. "You aren't Bette."

She pursed her lips, gave me the once-over, then nodded toward the end of the bar. "She just took her break. You might be able to catch her."

Following the direction of her nod, it took me a moment to see the door inset into the dark-painted wall. I stepped through, ignoring the 'Staff Only' sign. I'd been fairly drunk the previous night, but I suddenly remembered Fish heading farther into the club, not out the entrance. Perhaps to the bathroom? Or a back door?

I would check that out after a quick chat with Bette.

Following the scent of roses—perfume, not magic—I traversed a short hall and found a tiny kitchen. Empty. But a sound drew me to the right and through into a change area with lockers.

A dark-haired witch who I recognized from the previous night was freshening her makeup over a freestanding sink. Clad in a belly-button-revealing, high-necked, long-sleeved top and a miniskirt, she flinched when she caught sight of me. A magically sensitive Adept would have known I was approaching.

She swore—in Russian, at best guess. Though I had a hazy recollection that she'd spoken English while pouring my scotch the evening before. Drinks that Fish had subsequently spiked.

"I'm looking for the guy I was here with last night," I said without preamble, leaning back against the wall to the side of the door and keeping my hands in sight. Nonthreatening, but she also couldn't leave the room without coming within reach.

Not that I needed hands to wreak havoc. But she wouldn't know that.

She raked her gaze over me in the mirror, then went back to applying eyeliner. "Don't know you, don't know him," she said in heavily accented English.

I sighed, deliberately affected. Then I tugged a wad of US cash out of my breast pocket. I'd used my credit card at the hotel cafe, but figured I might need something a little less traceable while hunting Fish down.

Her eyes widened, almost imperceptibly.

"How much?" I asked casually.

"How much for what?"

"For you to tell me who the witch was…the one my brother left with last night." I hit 'brother' hard. "I don't have time to be bothered with haggling."

She sniffed, finally turning away from the mirror and leaning back against the sink. Hands on either side of her, fingers curled over the edges.

Nonthreatening.

Like me.

I offered her a grin.

She pursed her lips, glancing slightly away. "How much do you have on you?"

I shrugged, tapping the wad of cash against my thigh. "I have no idea."

"You shouldn't flash that kind of money around so casually."

"There's nothing casual about me."

She sniffed again. "And if I have nothing to tell?"

"Then it's a bad investment. Not my first."

"Three hundred."

"So you do remember us?"

"You do stand out. Half the regulars wanted to fuck you."

"And the other half?"

"Left early." She grinned broadly. "Maybe they knew they didn't have a chance with you."

I laughed—a genuine response that surprised me.

She frowned playfully. "You get that a lot, I suppose."

"Yeah."

"But it was your…brother…who left with the pretty witch, not you." She sneered 'brother' like she didn't believe me in the slightest.

"There are all sorts of familial bonds," I said, my mood souring almost instantly, and my tone abruptly low and dangerous.

She held up her hands placatingly. But the whites of her eyes widened, and some sort of magic flickered around her.

I might not have been as scary as Socks. But then, I didn't try as hard. Though if I was being honest with myself, I didn't think the amplifier who was the beating heart of the Five needed to try at all. She terrified with a single look. And not even Bee had Emma's body count.

Maybe it was just something built into Emma's DNA that triggered the hindbrain of everyone around her. Except for that idiot sorcerer who absolutely doted on her. And the baby dream walker. But Opal had all of us completely beguiled.

I peeled three hundred-dollar bills from my wad, then floated them over to the witch. No muttered spell, no pulling magic to me to do so. An effortless display of power.

She paled. Then she swallowed, squared her shoulders, and plucked the money out of the air. She looked at it, then folded it and tucked it in under her bra strap.

Brave. But without a doubt, all sorts of Adepts came through the club, and not everyone was as sweet a drunk as I was.

"I don't know the witch," she said, her tone stiff now. "But I've seen your brother before. He's rented a room a few times. By the hour."

For meetings, no doubt. "Upstairs?"

She nodded. Once. "They're heavily warded. By the local coven. You need a passkey."

"I rarely need a passkey."

She huffed. "I meant, neither your brother nor the witch purchased one last night."

"Was Daniel meeting someone?" I asked. "Those other times?"

"I'm not paid to notice."

I laughed quietly.

She grinned, relaxing slightly. "He's met with a couple of locals, and the owner of the club. Business, I think. I could give you names."

I shook my head. We weren't in town for Daniel's sort of business. We were looking for Bee. Plus, tracking down extra Adepts would take too long.

The blood tattoo would lead me to Daniel eventually, and more quickly than any other approach. I was just trying to narrow down the radius.

"There's a back exit?" I asked.

She nodded in the direction of the hall behind me. "Keep going."

I dropped two more hundred-dollar bills on the corner of the low bench next to the row of lockers, by hand not magic. I didn't want to scare her any more than I already had. "Thank you."

She eyed the money. "I didn't tell you anything worth that."

"Consider it a future investment, Bette."

She nodded but didn't move to pick up the cash. Smart.

"I'm Samantha."

"Telekinetic." She grimaced. "You stand out."

"Well, blending in would make it too easy, wouldn't it?"

"Make what too easy?"

I just grinned at her, pushed off the wall, and stepped back into the hall.

"What if someone comes asking about you?" she called after me.

"They already know where I'm staying," I said over my shoulder, not at all surprised by the question—or the idea that Fish and I might have been tailed to the club as early as last night. "Anything you tell them will only add to my mystique."

She laughed, seemingly involuntarily.

The exit was only a half-dozen meters down the hall, beyond some more empty offices and a magically locked steel door, which I assumed led to liquor storage and probably a safe. My tattoo didn't flare as I passed, and I would have picked up Fish's presence even through wards.

I flipped the locks on the back door without touching them just in case they too were magically fortified. Even though I could have taken the hit, I never did like getting nasty surprises. Then I stepped through and found myself on the other side of the warehouse. The overhang above the door and an ashtray informed me that I'd uncovered the spot where the staff took their breaks.

Not the great mystery I'd been hoping to solve.

Though apparently I'd also found the club parking lot. The paved area stretching out between warehouses was currently half-full. Over half the cars were luxury models, incongruent to the economic sense I'd gotten of the overall area. But most Adepts were rather lucky when it came to money, with their long lives and even longer family histories. And magic, of course.

The door shut behind me.

I waited, scanning the quiet night, then looking up into the dark, cloudy sky. The warehouse district had already been quiet, shut down for the night, as I'd walked from the hotel to the club. I didn't pick up any traffic sounds or people nearby now either.

The tattoo remained silent.

"Damn you, Fish," I muttered. He was going to force me into action.

I loved action, of course.

I had just recently found there were things I liked a lot more. Like stability. And…family.

I pulled out my phone, ready to actually admit I needed help. The Collective's therapist would have died in shock.

Fish is missing, I texted Knox. *The tattoo is misfiring. I need Paisley.*

The demon dog had spent some time with Fish in the last year or so. Only a few days, but that might have been enough to help her home in on him. And she could teleport—or, rather, walk through dimensions—to get to me.

While I waited for the clairvoyant to answer my text, I started walking in the direction of the hotel, setting up as close to a spiraling pattern as the streets would allow while doing so. Eventually, warehouses and other industrial-type businesses gave way to blocks upon blocks of apartment complexes, none more than a few floors tall. The narrow streets were quiet, with only the occasional car passing as I walked.

Why hadn't we ever tested the radius of the connection between our tattoos? And by that, I meant why hadn't I ever tested my own range? My connections to the others had always been weaker, not that I'd realized that during the time we were all in constant forced proximity. But later, in conversation with Fish, then Knox, I'd come to understand that they felt their tie to Emma more acutely than I did.

I'd done nothing with that information.

And now I was in the middle of fucking Russia with no contacts and no Daniel.

Emma was going to have my head. Though first, she'd get all furious about how it wasn't her job to keep us all in line anymore.

The feel of the residential area was changing a bit, with tiny gardens backing a number of the housing complexes now. The number of lampposts and sporadic pedestrians had doubled. I was preparing to do another outward sweep when my phone finally vibrated to announce a reply from Knox.

>*I'm not in contact with Paisley right now.*

What the fuck does that mean? You've lost track of the demon dog?

>*Ask Socks.*

I swore viciously under my breath, shoving the phone back in my pocket—the clock on which had mockingly informed me that it was now close to two in the morning local time. I had wasted hours of my life fruitlessly waiting on, then looking for, Fish.

I paused, just staring up at the dark sky as I reassessed. The sounds of the sleepy neighborhood filtered in. The murmur of a nearby TV through a partially open window. Laughter from a trio fumbling with keys at the front door of an apartment across and up the street. Back-alley cats or raccoons having a hissing contest, and a car rolling to a stop for the briefest of moments before pulling through a four-way intersection.

Static tickled my nose…from up ahead.

An Adept was near.

I stepped back into a shadowed alcove. Quiet instrumental music filtered out from the apartment directly above me.

More static tickling…from behind.

And…across.

I was being stalked. Maybe even herded. And they were near enough for me to pick up their magical signatures.

A broad grin swamped my face.

The pending, sure-to-be frustrating text conversation with Emma regarding Paisley—assuming she even bothered to answer me after I contacted her—was quickly shoved aside in favor of the confrontation brewing. I might have been willing to forgo such a kerfuffle early on, but now—

The blood tattoo on my T4 vertebra flickered…then quieted. Then it began to simmer. A faint but perceptible connection.

Fish.

Finally.

But he wasn't close. He wasn't one of the three closing in on me. Though the magic tickling my senses, my nose specifically, was starting to feel oddly familiar.

I shoved my hand into my jacket pocket and came out with three medium-sized ball bearings. Then I stepped back out onto the street, walking directly down the center as I headed in the direction the blood tattoo was guiding me.

MY STALKERS TOOK LONG ENOUGH ATTEMPTING TO corral me that I slowed my pace just enough to have a one-handed, ridiculously frustrating text exchange with Emma. Apparently, Paisley had gone AWOL.

And predictably, Socks was pissed that I'd lost Daniel. But as she had to remind me, she had her own stuff to deal with. Finalizing Opal's adoption. It didn't improve my mood, but it put things in perspective.

I made it three more meters before the Adept ahead of me finally tried to get close enough to lay hands on me. By the light of the buildings on either side of us, it took me a moment to recognize the trench coat dude who'd been watching me at lunch.

A step closer, and I could pick up the stench of stale cigarettes wafting off him.

Seriously? Who had trained these guys?

I didn't bother wasting a ball bearing on his unstealthy ass. The open collar of his black trench coat was a perfectly acceptable target.

So while he was stepping into my path—and, judging by his expression, suddenly realizing we were the same height and it was going to be hard to intimidate me physically—I wrapped my magic around his collar and cinched it.

Tightly.

He went down on one knee, clawing at his throat.

I kept walking.

Some sort of spell latched onto my wrist, like an invisible lasso. Again, the tenor of the currently choking Adept's power was oddly familiar. I snapped the spell with a twist of my wrist. Then I squeezed his collar tighter.

He gargled something unintelligible, falling forward to brace himself on one hand.

I could feel more of his magic pouring out of him now as he tried to counter my telekinetic hold with his own power. I had assumed he was a sorcerer, hence not allowing him to speak. But now…

A blast of magic hit a group of garbage cans on my right, emanating from an alley between two apartment buildings and driving the cans toward me. Not even bothering to identify my second attacker, I flicked my fingers, sending them back the way they came. The first can hit what felt like a shield of some sort. So I added an extra push to the next two, breaking through that shield and hitting someone—judging by the grunt that emanated from the darkened area between the buildings.

A witch? Or…another telekinetic?

I continued walking away.

A third Adept darted out onto the street behind me, checking on the dude I was still strangling. Slighter of build and dressed in all-black tactical gear, he seemed rather distressed as he tried to help the trench coat guy, though I was far enough away that I couldn't hear whatever he was saying.

Seriously? So ridiculously unprepared.

Apparently, they had no idea who they were dealing with. If this was the same team that had taken down Fish, they must have blindsided him.

He was vulnerable when wooed by sex.

We all had our indulgences.

And I knew Daniel was pissed that Emma had fallen hard for her dark sorcerer—hard enough that they'd just gotten officially engaged.

Ah…maybe I shouldn't have mentioned that little tidbit to Fish the previous night—

The tattoo on my spine flared, sharpening just a little.

I picked up my pace. My sense of the magic, of the Adepts, I'd just so easily countered still felt oddly familiar. I recalled the kiss of the invisible lasso the sorcerer had wrapped around my wrist…

It felt a hell of a lot like nullifying magic.

FISH WAS SPRAWLED OUT ON THE SIDE OF THE STREET, tucked in beside the scraggly hedges in which I'd hidden the ladder.

An unlikely coincidence.

And yeah, I knew a trap when I saw one, but that didn't stop me from crouching down and pressing my fingers to Fish's neck. The tattoo on my spine flared again, sharper still.

Fish grabbed my hand, squeezing far too tightly.

"Get off me, you idiot," I snapped.

He blinked his light-brown eyes, then closed them, groaning. "Zans. What the hell?" He loosened his grip.

"What the hell? How about what the hell are you doing?"

He blinked again, this time up at the dark sky. "Did I...pass out?"

"Apparently." I wrapped my hand around his wrist. His pulse was strong. His magic, however, wasn't.

It took a lot to drain one of the Five.

"And you just let me drop? What the hell did I do to piss you off?"

Laughing under my breath, I glanced around. The streets were still fairly quiet, and I'd left my inept attackers behind me. But I hadn't knocked them out of the hunt.

"Wait..." Fish groaned, trying to sit up.

"Coming back to you, is it?"

He scrubbed a hand over his face. "I was...dosed?"

"Apparently."

"Stop saying that!" he snapped.

His dark hair fell over his broad brow, highlighting the Asian cast to Fish's features. I'd spent years digging through the data we'd stolen from the Collective, right before Emma implemented the Amplifier Protocol and shredded everything in a five-kilometer radius around their compound. Everything except us. That delightfully destructive act had corrupted most of what I'd managed to retrieve from the servers, so there were gaps in the data. But I had some brilliant tech witches and sorcerers working on sections I hadn't been able to access. Yet. Including our genealogy.

"Just say it," Fish snarled.

"Say what?" I snarled back. "That you got me drunk, abandoned me in the middle of nowhere, then apparently got yourself kidnapped, drained, and now dumped as bait?"

He raised his hand, staring at it. "Drained…"

Of course that was all he'd heard. I grabbed his hand and hauled him to his feet. He was heavy. All of the Five were a bit juiced up, stronger, faster than our magical counterparts among the Adept. We healed quickly and were fairly resistant to magic. Not to the level that Emma was, with all her stolen juice. But yeah, we were magic-wielding, genetically constructed super soldiers. Fifth-generation super soldiers.

So Fish was heavier than he looked—and even though ever-so-slightly shorter than me, he had the physique of a linebacker. In padding.

He swayed. I slung his arm across my shoulders and started pulling him in the direction of the hotel. Five blocks.

"Why are you wearing my jacket?" he asked.

"My jacket," I said. "You abandoned it at the same time as you abandoned me."

He scrubbed his free hand over his face again, opened his mouth, then closed it.

Yeah, he really didn't have much of an argument. Or any way to justify his behavior.

"Text Knox," I snarled, pissed that Fish was already giving me too much of his weight. "Then tell me what you remember."

Those five blocks were going to be hard won. I could lift him with my power, but that had a tendency to screw with internal organs, and I had no idea if he was already injured. Plus, a wanton display of magic was usually a last resort when surrounded by mundanes, and even a subtle touch of telekinesis would make me easier to track by anyone sensitive to magic.

Daniel fished around in his pockets, coming up empty.

I wouldn't have let him have his phone either, if I'd kidnapped him. If I hadn't found him by the time I made it back to the hotel, my next call would have been to a tech contact, to trace his phone. I didn't start with that because it was a bitch to set up new phones every time one got burned.

Fish sighed heavily, taking some more of his own weight, enough so that we hopefully just looked like a slightly intoxicated couple out for a stroll to the few pedestrians and cars currently traversing the streets. I'd been slightly concerned about drawing too much attention, about standing out in a less-populated area, but most of the people we passed kept their gazes firmly ahead. Not scared of us. Just caught up in their own lives.

Fish tugged my phone out of my pocket. He opened it with the password—no face recognition for us while on mission—and scanned my most recent text thread. With Emma.

I waited for the explosion. But amazingly, Daniel just frowned and said, "Paisley's missing?"

I didn't answer, keeping my attention on the street and the apartment buildings to either side.

Fish flipped to my ongoing thread with Christopher and sent one of our all-clear codes. Not terribly explicit, but enough to let Knox know that we were both okay.

Daniel tucked the phone back in my pocket, then took the rest of his weight off me, walking alongside close enough for our shoulders to brush. Close enough to shield us, if he had any magic to call forth.

Three blocks from the hotel—I could see the upper corner of the building—and that static energy of incoming magic tickled my senses.

Fish glanced behind us. "How long have you had a tail?"

"You tell me," I said. "Apparently they're with you."

He swore under his breath. Viciously. "Having a conversation with you is like—"

"A conversation implies the exchange of information—"

"If you would give me one fucking second to get my head—"

"You shouldn't need a second," I snapped. "We were on mission, and you took off with the first little piece that twitched her tail."

He went silent, confused. "She had a tail?"

I snarled at the idiot. "She tried to get both of us in one sweep," I said. "And now I've been under surveillance all day."

Fish shook his head, thinking.

We ate up another block, walking steadily but not running.

"They didn't just grab you…" he murmured. "Because they thought you'd lead them somewhere?"

"Or that I'd draw someone to me."

"Who?"

"Your contact? The one who has info on Bee?"

He shook his head again. "He deals in information. He isn't hard to find."

"For you, maybe."

The front of the hotel came into view. Fish touched my back lightly. "Turn right," he murmured.

"I want my stuff."

"We're not leaving."

"We're not making a mess," I snarled back. But I took the next right anyway, cutting down a darker side street.

"We've been set up," Fish said, picking up his pace.

"That's just become apparent to you?"

"But they don't just want us…" He veered right again at the next street.

The restaurants, stores, and other businesses in the area were firmly confined to the street the hotel occupied. A residential neighborhood with small houses and row houses interspersed among apartment buildings sprang up within a block in either direction. At well past two in the morning now, most of those homes had darkened, curtained windows.

Fish's magic was still so dim that I couldn't feel it unless I was touching him, but we Five healed quickly. Whatever had knocked him out, had drained him, was wearing off.

"We went back to her apartment…" he said, slowly piecing together his memory of the evening and the day that we'd been separated. "Or…a hotel room. There wasn't much furniture…" He stopped abruptly, then tugged up the sleeve of his black sweater. Angling his arm to catch the light from a nearby streetlamp, he exposed three fading bruises. Injection marks.

"A magical suppressant?" I asked.

He swore again, louder this time.

My phone buzzed. Knox's reply to Daniel's text flashed up on the screen.

Fish grabbed my hand, forcing me to meet his gaze. "We solve this ourselves. Emma doesn't need any more ammunition."

It was possible that Fish was actually in love with Emma. Or at least as in love as any of us Five could be, having been bred and trained to be sociopaths. At least Emma had her stolen empathy to help compensate.

"Knox can curate information to Socks. He's been acting as a buffer for over eight years. It's stupid not to keep in touch."

Fish released my hand, shrugged, and started to walk again. We had looped back toward the main street, just two blocks down. "You've kept him informed. I need a taxi." He glanced over his shoulder, his expression lost to me in the deep of the night. "I remember the address she gave."

"You want to hunt down the witch."

He smiled, a flash of white teeth in the shadows. Then he took off.

I followed—and completely against my better judgement, I didn't text Knox. How I, the most destructively powerful of the Five, had become backup just like that, I had no idea. But here I was following in Fish's wake like a dutiful soldier, again and again.

He hadn't even fucking apologized.

THE WITCH'S APARTMENT WAS A BUST. EMPTY. EVEN scoured of magical residual, according to Fish. The single room boasted a bed—sheets still rumpled—and a tiny bathroom.

I pointed to the bed and raised an eyebrow at Fish. "So you got laid at least."

He frowned, checking the single window. "More like passed out."

"And then she…left you? And you made it almost all the way back to our hotel without realizing it?"

"Nope. There was at least one car ride in between those two points."

Using drugs on any of the Five was unreliable. The rest of us didn't have Emma's metabolism, but someone pretty much had to overdose us to keep us down or wipe our memories.

Fish was tapping the walls now, looking for hidden niches.

"It's a safe house," I said, hands on my hips and already itching to move on.

He grunted, not disagreeing as he tugged up a corner of the carpet, then opened a trapdoor set in the underfloor. It revealed a storage space just large enough to hold a few items. "Empty."

"So...they aren't as stupid as they seem."

He sat back on his heels, thinking. "Why attack you so pathetically?"

I shrugged a shoulder.

Fish stood, crossing past me and into the bathroom. He flicked on the light.

"I checked in there," I said pissily.

He ignored me. Like always.

I considered pulling out my phone and checking Knox's text. Or maybe playing a game.

Fish stepped out from the bathroom, glowering. "Clean."

"We grab our stuff from the hotel and leave," I said.

"We reach out to my contact." His tone was dark. "And when we confirm he sold us out, we hunt him down."

I sighed, heavily.

"Got something better to do?" Fish asked caustically.

I smirked. "Well, Emma might want some help with the wedding."

He stomped away.

THE SECOND ATTACK—MUCH, MUCH MORE COORDI-nated this time, as if a new party was now calling the shots—hit us when we were three blocks from the hotel. We'd had a taxi drop us a few streets away, in the residential area, so we could determine if the hotel was under surveillance as we approached before moving forward with our plan to grab our things, then retreat for long enough to regroup and reassess.

The volley of magic hit us both from three different sides, driving us into a boarded-up apartment building undergoing renovations.

Unfortunately for our attackers.

Honestly, it was like they had no idea who they were dealing with.

Fish threw up a nullifying shield with what felt like the last dregs of his power, and we ran into the cover of the building—luring them rather than actually retreating. But apparently, they didn't know that, because they came right at us. The same three unknown yet weirdly familiar Adepts.

I unlocked the front door with a negligible use of my telekinesis, and Fish and I slipped within the darkened entrance on silent feet. Even under attack, we were careful, doing nothing that might draw attention from the sleeping residents of the surrounding buildings. The Five had long been accustomed to fighting as invisibly as possible while in populated areas, at least when factoring in nonmagical senses.

Not even needing to speak because coordinating ourselves was ingrained in our DNA and reinforced by over twenty years of training together, Fish and I spun away from each other into the first openings off the front hall. Me to the right and him to the left, stepping just out of sight, then facing back into the hall. The tattoo tying me to Daniel was steadily humming now, though it wasn't as vibrant as usual.

Had someone asked me earlier in the day, I would have said that connection couldn't have been chemically blocked. But evidently, I was wrong.

I loathed admitting it.

The only time the tattoos had gone truly dormant was after Emma had drained us down so far that I thought my magic might never come back. And I'd hated her for that. Among other things, of course.

Fish gestured toward me, indicating the front door.

The trio breached that doorway in an arrow configuration, with trench coat dude in the lead. The Adept I was beginning to suspect was more than a sorcerer—a feeling reinforced now by the shield he held, which I could feel but not see, buzzing around them.

That was just fine.

I didn't have to penetrate a shield to hurt them.

And again, they really should have known that before picking a fight.

I picked up the stack of lumber neatly piled at the center of the room behind me with a rope of my magic. The contractor had already removed most of the walls around us, and was in the process of reconfiguring the entire first floor. The wood—two-by-fours or the Russian equivalent—was presumably framing material, with a few heavy posts thrown into the mix.

Stepping back so it fit through the opening into the main hall, I slammed the entire pile into the trio just as they paused to make sure the room across the way was empty. It wasn't. But Fish had positioned himself out of my way.

The pile of wood crashed into the shield encasing the trio, and despite its dubious protection, I tossed them all against the far wall in a tangle of limbs, buried under two-by-fours and posts.

Fish was waiting for them with what appeared to be a hammer purloined from one of the tool chests. Fortified with Daniel's nullifying power, that hammer easily cracked the invisible bubble of the shield, slamming into the unprotected forehead of trench coat dude.

Then Fish was suddenly flying backward, deeper into the building and crashing through walls and other things I couldn't see.

Yep. The Adept who I hadn't made visual contact with before—the one who had lobbed the trash cans at me from the alley—was a telekinetic. Not a witch. Clad in black tactical gear as they all were, mixed race like me, maybe in his forties. But his skin tone was shades lighter, and his brown hair was shaved indecently short.

Well, this was going to be fun.

I charged.

Unleashed, my power boiled around me, picking up anything and everything within reach—tools, toolboxes, offcuts of wood, thick metal wiring, some sort of piping.

Trench coat dude, the maybe-nullifier, hadn't moved after taking Fish's blow. But the telekinetic and his other teammate—the one who had come to trench coat dude's rescue on the street—spun toward me, trying to rise to meet me. The third Adept had ten years on Fish and me, with light-brown hair and crystal-blue eyes.

Neither of them made it off their knees.

I slammed all the building detritus I'd swept up around me into the two of them. The telekinetic managed to erect a shield at the last moment, throwing himself in front of the blue-eyed Adept, which was oddly sacrificial of him.

I pummeled them with hammers and nails, a circular saw, and more wood, driving them back until they were pinned against the far wall. Then I kept them trapped there. I could feel their magic welling, trying to counter my effortless deluge.

At peak strength, I could expend magic for over an hour without faltering. Probably even longer now, since I'd been living with Emma for the last few months. Not only did her amplification magic leak, her recent run-in with the entity released by Cerise Myers had unlocked a new aspect of her power. Or rather, it had lengthened her reach, forcing her to train intensely to get it under control.

And since I could handle almost everything Emma could throw at me, I bore the brunt—and the benefits—of that training regimen.

Keeping the other two pinned to the wall, I crouched down by the dark-haired trench coat dude, pressing my fingers to his throat and confirming two things. He was still alive—and he was indeed a nullifier.

To my very far right, Fish threw a pile of plaster and wood off himself with a groan, then slowly made it to his feet—

A sudden, intense pain knifed through my skull.

Falling to the side, I barely managed to support myself on one arm. I lost hold of the tiny tsunami I was pummeling the other Adepts with.

A psychic blow.

The third Adept—the slighter-built male with the crystal-blue eyes who the other telekinetic had been protecting—lunged forward. He managed to get his hand wrapped around my bare wrist, hitting me with another wicked lash of mental power.

He was a telepath. And apparently more effective when holding skin-to-skin contact.

My vision went black around the edges.

Also released from my magic, the telekinetic stumbled forward. Raising his hands, he attempted to choke me with the collar of my leather jacket, duplicating my move against the nullifier earlier.

With a snarl, I punched the telepath in the face, smashing my fist and a wallop of power into his nose. He went down and didn't get up.

That left me facing off with the telekinetic.

I rose to my feet, shaking off his chokehold with a single powerful pulse of my magic. He stumbled back but instantly raised his hands to hit me again.

"Now I'm angry, asshole."

I slammed him through the wall I'd just been pinning him against with a blast of power. He flew back through the neighboring room, bringing more plaster, wood, and insulation crashing down around him. He hit the outer wall, which was of heavier construction, denting it and falling to the ground.

Fish made it to my side. His magic was seriously dim, but I held out hope that he'd have enough juice to question our attackers. That was one of his specialties. So I proceeded accordingly.

With quick flicks of my hands, I grabbed up three rolls of some sort of thick tape. It appeared to be used for sealing the plastic sheathing over the newer areas of construction—most of it half-destroyed now. With the tape, I trussed all three of the unconscious Adepts back to back. Or, more specifically, shoulder to shoulder.

Dragging them farther into the building, I found a room stripped to the framing that we hadn't trashed yet, then dropped them in the center.

Fish found a portable light, plugged it in to a heavy extension cord, and turned it on.

With their backs resting against each other and their legs splayed out on the plywood floor, I wound more tape around the still-unconscious trio, binding them together around their shoulders and torsos, further restricting their movements.

Then Fish and I stared down at them.

The telepath—a slight male with light-brown hair and naturally tanned skin.

The telekinetic—a tall male, more mixed race than me.

And the nullifier—a dark-haired male with pale skin.

"Do they look familiar?" I asked.

Fish shook his head, a little unsteady.

"What about their magic?" I asked.

He frowned at me, shaking his head again as he held out his hand.

I kept my thoughts and observations to myself as I fished three small metal disks out of the pocket on my right thigh. I dropped the disks into Fish's palm. He wrapped his fingers around them, filling each with nullifying magic as he paced around the unconscious trio.

He circled our trussed attackers three times, getting a read on their magic. Then he stopped in front of the telepath—the most dangerous of the three, even while bound—and pressed one of the spelled disks against his forehead.

Fish's frown deepened as he concentrated, entwining the telepath's magic with the nullifying power he'd already infused into the disk.

I couldn't feel any of it, of course, but Fish and I had worked together for years now. I knew the process, and the end goal.

Unfortunately, his magic was still dim. As was the blood tattoo on my spine, even while in the same room as him.

"You still have too much of whatever shit they dosed you with in your system," I said mildly.

Fish flashed me a look. Then, seemingly satisfied, he tucked the spelled nullifying disk into the telepath's jacket pocket and moved on to the telekinetic.

The other nullifier groaned, lifting his head. The wound on his forehead—courtesy of the hammer wielded by Fish—was mostly hidden by his dark hair, but blood had run down his face and neck to soak into his trench coat and tactical gear.

That should have been a killing blow.

The oddest idea had lodged itself in my head, and I couldn't shake it.

I crouched before trench coat dude. He blinked at me as I stared at him, trying to figure out what was disturbing me about the entire situation. I didn't get disturbed. I got even. Or, more accurately, I won.

Every fight, every mission…but there was something seriously off about all of this.

The attack had been sloppy, ill prepared—as if they'd seized a moment rather than luring us into a trap. Yet they'd still effectively taken down Fish. An incredibly difficult feat, in direct contrast with their haphazard frontal assaults and shitty stakeout work.

"Do you speak English?" I asked.

Trench coat narrowed his eyes at me. Instead of answering, he attempted to assess the situation—who he was bound to, the dimensions of the room—without turning his head.

"Whoever sent you after us must not like you very much." I laughed. "But see how nice we've been so far?"

He shook his head, then winced, squeezing his eyes shut against the pain that had to be radiating from his wound.

Fish dropped the second nullifying disk, charged with his power now, in the pocket of the telekinetic, stepping around to stand behind me. Now that the nullifier was awake and aware, Fish didn't bother adding his magic to the third metal disk. He wouldn't want to give away the fact that he'd hidden disks charged with his nullification on the other two, because part of the trick with the disks was that the Adepts Fish used them against had to empty their pockets or change clothing in order to figure out what was dampening their power. The disk mimicked their own magic, making it hard to track.

Not to mention, I wasn't even certain that one nullifier could even nullify another nullifier.

A question for later.

"We can continue with our sweet-and-nice routine," I said, tilting my head and not taking my eyes off the trussed nullifier. "Or..." I lifted my hand, making a show of settling a lick of my magic on his shoulder. "We can see how oxygen deprivation pairs with a nasty head wound—"

Staticky energy shifted behind me.

But the attacker went for Fish, not me. Still nearly drained, he hadn't felt it coming.

He twisted away from the blow too late, but took the hit from a crowbar across his shoulders and neck instead of straight to the head.

I was on my feet, lunging for the attacker before Fish hit the floor.

White flared over her light-blue eyes as she stepped—no, slipped—away from me.

As if she'd seen me coming.

Before I even moved.

Lifting the crowbar like a baseball bat, the petite blond was in black tactical gear identical to the others, similar to my own. She stepped back into the far corner of the room.

Fish wasn't getting up.

Beside me, trench coat dude was wiggling like mad, trying to break through the tape that bound him to the other two still-unconscious Adepts.

I eyed the newcomer. In her early to midforties like the other three, she was the pretty witch who'd propositioned me in the club bathroom, then had taken Fish home.

Except she wasn't a witch.

She was a clairvoyant.

And the plan had been to subdue us, not fuck us.

I pouted at her playfully, stepping over Fish as I kept my gaze fixed to her. "How disappointing," I said. "My ego feels rather bruised."

"That's not all that's going to feel bruised by the time I'm done with you," she said almost tonelessly.

And I realized then that the other three attackers were all a little toneless, a little blank in that same way.

Weird. But interesting.

I lunged forward playfully, then danced a couple of steps to the side and back again. Completely randomly.

The magic flaring in the clairvoyant's eyes increased in wattage, practically whiting out the top half of her face.

"Yeah," I said, as if commiserating. "I'm a little difficult to get a read on, aren't I? That's why you went for Daniel first."

She blinked rapidly, firming her grip on the crowbar. "Untie the others."

"Adorable," I said, tugging a handful of tiny ball bearings out of my pocket. "Do you actually see that happening?" I threw the metal balls in the air, grabbing them with a long lick of my magic as they fell, then sending them into an almost lazy spiral around me.

The first hints of concern flittered over the clairvoyant's face.

"I grew up with a clairvoyant," I said mildly. I added random licks of power into the magic I was wielding, knocking the ball bearings in and out of a set pattern of rotation. Being far more haphazard than I usually would. "And he is far, far more powerful than you, sweet."

I reached up and flicked the nearest ball bearing toward the clairvoyant.

She stepped to the side as it embedded into the wall just a few centimeters from her forehead.

I flicked a second at her, then a third. All randomly timed and not at all precisely aimed.

She stumbled while avoiding the third.

Behind me, Fish groaned, then sat up, rubbing his neck. "What the fuck?" He blinked at the clairvoyant, then looked at the other three—finally putting it all together. "They...they sent a team of...us. Us against us."

"Yeah, but these guys aren't half as good." Keeping my attention on the clairvoyant, I said, "See? My magic already makes me difficult to get a read on, yes? It's rather chaotic. Or so I've been told. And you can't see your own future. You can only see me. See the others in the room."

I focused all my intent, all my will, on visualizing turning the ball bearings on the other three

Adepts—all of whom were now awake and trying to get out of their bindings.

The clairvoyant cried out, darting for me, anticipating that move.

Except I didn't make it.

Instead, I dropped all my magic. I tightened all my power around me. And I stepped forward and punched her in the throat, wrenching the crowbar out of her hands as she fell to her knees gasping, choking.

"Damn, Zans," Fish muttered, finally gaining his feet.

Ignoring him, I reached my power for the loose ball bearings, not wanting to lose any—

The blood tattoo that tied me to Fish sputtered.

I glanced over at him.

He met my gaze and nodded stiffly, warily.

Then without any additional warning, his eyes rolled up in the back of his head, and he fell.

I lunged for him, barely managing to grab his head and shoulders and soften his fall.

The magic embedded in the tattoo on my spine faded completely away. Again. Even though I was crouched over Fish, physically laying hands on him.

I looked toward the open doorway. It was empty.

The clairvoyant had crawled toward the other three and was attempting to release them. As if I couldn't see her.

I could feel something else approaching, crossing into the apartment building and coming toward us.

But it was a dark, black hole...

The absence of power.

I shifted Fish onto his back, getting my hand under his shoulders and dragging him into the far corner of the open room. I propped him up, pressing the crowbar into his hand. When he woke, he'd have a weapon handy.

Straightening, I kept him behind me.

More magic started flickering across my upper spine.

And for the briefest of moments, I thought I was feeling Emma.

As though Socks were the one in the hall, approaching the open doorway now. Except Emma's power had never felt like...nothing.

I reached out, wrapping long tendrils of my power around the four—the other nullifier, the other telekinetic, the clairvoyant, and the telepath. Then I thickened that rope, grabbing their clothing.

Someone stepped into the doorway.

Except no one was actually there. All my senses screamed with that knowing, that understanding. But not my sight.

Honestly, I'd been bumbling around, trying not to kill anyone, for far too long. I was tired of playing games.

Tired of not just being me.

With a burst of power, I shoved the four toward the doorway. They cried out—and most definitely slammed into a fifth person. I saw an odd flash of pink as I shoved them—propelling them back and back with a massive wave of my magic, through the wall behind them, then the next.

Plaster, wood, and insulation collapsed.

The building trembled.

I was just getting started.

I reached up with both hands, flooding the room, and then the entire floor, and then all the other floors above us with my telekinetic energy.

The building began to shake in earnest.

Every single loose object in the immediate vicinity lifted in the air and began to circle around me and Fish. The walls began to buckle, then shred—including the wall behind me.

"The building!" the clairvoyant screamed from somewhere on the other side of the cyclone of debris. "She's bringing down the building!"

I could feel familiar magic flickering. The other nullifier was trying to raise a shield. But even if he was successful, I could still bury him.

Screw keeping a low profile.

I tore the entire building apart.

Then I dropped it on their heads.

Debris and dust settled around me and Fish—he'd regained consciousness enough at some point to curl himself around my feet—in a perfect circle the diameter of my arm span.

An eerie silence came with that sudden stillness. Though soon enough, there'd be sirens and such as the mundanes realized that a random building appeared to have just had its structural integrity compromised by an ongoing renovation. Though that wouldn't explain destruction on the level that I wrought. Maybe they'd call it a rogue tornado or some such?

Fish groaned, rolled onto his back, and blinked up at me. "Really? That's keeping a low profile?"

"Don't be an ass," I said, grinning like a madwoman from the rush of using my full power, even if only for a moment. "You're the one who got kidnapped. You're the bait they used to try to get their hands on me."

Fish ran his hand over the back of his head. "I thought I'd nullified the damn telepath."

What? "You did."

He glowered at me. "I didn't just drop in a faint."

"You totally just fainted."

"Zans," he snapped, "I know what being shut down by a telepath feels like. We all do."

I blinked, casting my gaze toward the large pile of debris where I'd buried the four who had come after us, along with what I assumed was a fifth member of their crew. "They were missing their amplifier."

"What?" Fish shifted up onto his knees.

Lights were flickering on in the apartment buildings all around us, bright against the cloud-filled night sky.

We needed to go.

"Telepath, telekinetic, nullifier, and clairvoyant," I said, reaching down for him. "They're missing their amplifier."

He batted my hand away but didn't attempt to gain his feet yet. "Someone who thinks they're damn clever put a team together, that's all."

The pile of debris across from us shifted...chunks of wood and a tangle of wiring rolled away. I couldn't feel any magic, but...

"They survived."

"One of them got a shield up," Fish said. He pressed his palms to the floor, standing.

Magic rolled across the tattoo on my spine.

Again.

Fish's head snapped to our left, toward the road.

"That's getting old," I groused. Though I was happier to have Fish's tattoo flickering in and out than completely dormant.

"That's not me," Fish murmured.

"What?"

He met my gaze, then laid his hand across my shoulder, fingers dipping into the collar of my jacket. "T1. Amp5—"

"Emma," I interjected.

He huffed. "That's Amp5's blood under your skin, Tek5."

I nodded stiffly, ceding the point to him—though I'd find it highly amusing to see Emma kick his ass for referring to her by her former designation.

He shifted his fingers. The tattoo he was touching on my T4 vertebra flared—his tattoo. "That's me," he whispered.

My heart started pounding in my chest.

I mean, I wasn't exactly slow, but we all had our strengths. And though I was also good with tech, I had always been the second-to-last resort when we worked as a team. I wasn't the strategist in the group.

The tattoo one vertebra higher than where Fish was currently touching was simmering. Bee's tattoo. And it was the one that had flared before...right before...

Fish shuddered, then stumbled back. I grabbed his arm, but he went down so fast this time that he pulled me with him.

I ended up on my knees, looking everywhere at once.

The image of the basil oracle card Knox had texted me flitted through my mind...

Basil...prosperity, protection, and happiness...

Strength...perseverance, courage, patience, compassion...

Why was I thinking of that now?

Why was I thinking of texting Knox...holding my phone, looking at the screen, looking for his phone number...

I pushed back, flaring my power around me.

My head snapped up.

I hadn't realized I'd dropped it.

I hadn't realized that I was just sitting by Fish's prone body like an idiot, ignoring the approaching sirens, the gathering of mundanes on the sidewalks...

The mundanes...

People were frozen on the sidewalks. And not by the chilly weather. They were staring but not seeing.

It wasn't me thinking about the oracle card, or about texting Christopher...

Two tattoos were simmering on my spine.

And Emma and Christopher were on the opposite side of the world.

Even if they had access to a private jet, even if they'd left the moment after I asked for Paisley's help, they still wouldn't be anywhere near enough to be triggering their blood under my skin.

The massive pile of debris I'd dropped on the others trembled again. The other four were—

Pain sliced through my head.

Blackness encroached the edge of my vision.

Fighting back against it, I reached out to the sides, splaying my fingers. Everything that could be touched by my telekinesis—wood riddled with nails, wiring, piping, and more—rose at my bidding.

I should run, I thought.

I'm too exposed.

Too vulnerable.

I should leave Fish and—

"No!" I snarled, shaking with the effort of staying conscious. Even with all my magic churning around me, I couldn't block the person attempting to infiltrate my mind, attempting to manipulate me.

The debris pile split down the middle.

Someone stumbled through the opening. I didn't bother to figure out who it was, or if they were the person trying to shred my mind.

I threw everything I was holding at them, at them and the three others trying to step clear of the building I'd dropped on their heads.

Someone screamed.

But it wasn't any of the other four.

Those four fell under my assault, skewered with steel and wood. Too drained to defend themselves.

An armored figure, oddly cloaked in pink, appeared. Her face and head were completely obscured by a mask and helmet. I had never seen that getup before, yet the DNA embedded in the blood tattoo under my skin screamed a knowledge that my other senses refused to accept.

She'd been standing there for a while, I thought, as I tried to not sway on my knees. She had figured out how to veil herself from my mind. To render me unable to see her...

I reached up and wiped my cheek, thinking I was crying.

Not tears.

Blood.

The cloaked figure spun on me in a wash of pink.

Nothing made any sense.

But I could feel her anger. It poured off her. It struck out at me, knives of rage-filled psychic energy.

I crumpled under the assault. I fell over Fish, losing my sense of sight and sound for a moment.

Then the masked and helmeted figure was crouching over me, pulling off her glove to touch me.

And I knew…in my heart, I knew…

She could kill me with that touch.

Except in doing so, she might just kill herself at the same time.

I focused as much power as I could muster in my right hand, gathering nails and whatever else littered the floor around my fist.

"Tag. You're it," I said. Though we'd never played that game as children. Actually, I wasn't certain I even managed to vocalize the words.

Then I smashed my fist and the last wallop of my power into the side of her helmeted head. It crumpled under my assault, and she fell sideways, half landing on top of me.

Me sprawled over Fish, and she…Bee…slumped over me.

Because none of the Five could actually block another of the Five. We couldn't kill each other either. The blood tattoos bound us in life, and the death of one of us likely meant the death of all.

Except for maybe Emma.

Emma might survive, though she would never risk losing Knox.

A tiny voice in the back of my mind informed me that Emma would never risk losing me either. Or Daniel. But that was a silly, childish wish.

Everything went black.

I spiraled through the pain, falling deeper and deeper into it, until...

... nothing.

I WOKE WITH A START. I WAS COLD, BUT THE FLOOR under me was even colder. I could feel someone beside me, so I instinctively rolled toward them. They were cold as well, but they wrapped their arms around me and tucked me against their wide, well-muscled chest. A hand no warmer than I was settled on the back of my neck, fingers slipping down to cover the blood tattoos inked into my flesh.

The completely dormant tattoos.

I couldn't touch my power, though I could feel it simmering just out of reach.

I had my eyes open, but I couldn't see anything.

The room smelled sweet.

I could hear the faint hiss of air being pumped into the space around me.

I reached up, running my hands over the face of the individual who held me, confirming I was with Fish.

He nodded under my touch, running his hands down my arms, then over my back. Assessing me for wounds while maintaining silence, as per protocol.

If the room was so dark that we couldn't see anything, then whoever was holding us presumably couldn't see us. But they might have the room wired for sound.

I did the same for Fish, running my hands over him. He was clad only in boxers—and apparently, I was wearing only what felt like a cheap cotton tank top and underwear. Not my own. The kind that would shred after a few washings.

I had no doubt that the rest of the room had been stripped of anything that might be used as a weapon.

Both of us were near naked, cold, and—given the sweet scent in the air and my inability to reach my magic—chemically restrained.

Alive.

But well contained.

Selfishly, I sprawled across Fish, leaving him the cold tile floor while I greedily absorbed all the heat he had to give me. I pressed my lips to his ear, whispering so quietly that I couldn't actually hear the words myself. "Did you see who took me down?"

He shook his head—no.

Maybe I'd imagined it all.

I hadn't actually seen the fifth attacker either. But I would have sworn—

The overhead lights flared, wrenching an involuntary gasp from me. Fish rolled me to the side, dragging me up on my feet with him. He had me practically pressed into a far corner behind him before my vision even had time to adjust. Stupid of me for having my eyes open in the first place. Fish's easier adjustment and instinctive protective move made it clear he hadn't been caught as off guard.

I blinked a few more times. My being slightly taller than Fish meant that no matter how broad his shoulders were, I could see over them. A metal door standing directly opposite us and four air vents at baseboard height were the only things that broke the stretch of plain, white-painted walls. I could see the texture of the drywall, so the paint wasn't a thick coat. The room had just been thrown together, perhaps? Another hastily prepared attempt to contain us?

I pressed my lips to Fish's ear. "There's no way those are regular walls."

He nodded stiffly, not taking his eyes off the door.

I knew the drywall had to be hiding more steel. Otherwise, Adepts like us could ignore whatever locks they might have layered on the door and go right through the walls.

Of course, the attack had been so sloppy up to this point. Maybe they were just that stupid.

There was noise at the door—numerous locks being unlatched.

I stretched out my leg, reaching my bare toes toward the nearest vent and feeling a draft. Yep, they were pumping something into the room. Something to keep us, our magic, docile.

If there was a camera on us, I couldn't see it.

Fish glanced down at my extended foot, then nodded to indicate he agreed with my assessment. I settled back on two feet, laying my hand over the dormant blood tattoos on Fish's upper spine. The tattoos were slightly different on all of the Five, but Fish's were the only ones I'd ever had time to fully examine. Being sex partners for most of our teens and into our early twenties meant that I'd lain with him, naked but wakeful, many times.

I presumed that Fish knew what all of our tattoos looked like, intimately, for the exact same reason. Though I didn't get the impression that Emma was the snuggly type, or the type to turn her back on Fish even while having sex.

I almost made a joke about that. But I swallowed the impulse. Fish would have laughed. It would have defused some of the tension tightening his shoulders. But…as I'd slowly come to realize, it wasn't exactly fair. The way the four of us had used Fish, had pretty much taken those intimate moments from him…in doing so, we had actually pushed him away from the group.

Not that it mattered in the end, since Emma had thrown all of us away the first chance she got. Except for Knox.

"Rush the door?" I murmured in Fish's ear.

He shook his head, no doubt wanting to assess the situation. "Don't let them separate us," he said, loudly enough for anyone who was listening in to hear.

"If they try to take you from me," I said just as loudly, my voice flat, "I'll slaughter them all."

Fish nodded firmly. "Same."

The door opened. Five heavily armed mercenaries wearing light armor and gas masks came through. They lined themselves up against the far wall with military precision.

No weapons in sight. Whoever had taken us obviously thought their mercs were good enough to quell us hand-to-hand, fist-to-fist, if necessary.

I was looking forward to changing our unknown kidnappers' minds.

"Adepts?" I asked Fish. Not only the more sensitive of the two of us, he was actually the most magically sensitive of the Five.

"If they are," he said, "I can't feel it. Yet."

'Yet' because they'd left the door open. So far. So if what they were pumping into the room was a similar cocktail that they'd used on Fish—just gas, not an injectable—our magic might reassert itself fairly quickly as the air cleared.

A slighter person in a lab coat stepped into the room, carrying a small but chunky camera on a tripod. They were also wearing a gas mask, but it was sleeker in design...

In fact, it looked a lot like the respirators used back at the Collective's compound. The very ones we Five had worn when we escaped.

I pressed my fingers more firmly into Fish's back, still holding my hand over the inert blood tattoos on his spine.

"I see," he said.

The lab tech set out the tripod, securing the legs and keeping as close to the mercenaries as possible while doing so. The camera was cased in a thicker housing, as if it was fortified, maybe water resistant. Or, more likely, resistant to magic.

With the camera set up, the tech scrambled out of the room.

The door was still wide open.

And it was metal.

I could tear it to shreds, slitting every single throat in the room without effort. No need to get through any armor. No need to even take a step forward.

I reached for the sleepy simmer of my power. Still not quite able to touch it.

A tall, striking woman strode into the room. In her late forties by her look, though that rarely meant much when it came to Adepts. Most had access to anti-aging potions and charms, or aged slowly due to their inherent magic. Her skin was as dark as my own, her bobbed hair straightened to frame her face. Hands clasped behind her back, she gazed at us with large dark-brown eyes and a slight curl of a smile on her lips. She was dressed simply in a light-brown V-neck sweater, black slacks, and sensible shoes. Reading glasses hung from a gold chain around her neck.

I didn't suspect for one moment that she used those glasses for regular reading. No Adept of her obvious position—what with the kidnapping and a dozen mercenaries at her command—had bad eyesight when fairly basic witch spells could heal any such imperfections.

I also got the distinct impression she'd left her lab coat in the other room.

She wasn't wearing a gas mask. Which meant she was immune to whatever was being pumped into the room.

She paused beside the camera, then adjusted its angle. She looked at us again, that same faint smile on her face.

Like she owned us.

I could feel an answering sneer already spreading across my own face.

"My name is Lindiwe Fourie." She paused for effect, tilting her head as if she expected us to fall at her feet. "You may call me Lindi."

I couldn't place her accent. Soft, lyrical—and slightly reminiscent of New Zealand to my very untrained ear.

She laughed almost giddily, clasping her hands in front of her. "I'm the mother of you all." She flicked her gaze at me, her stupid smile widening even more. "Some of you more than the others."

I started laughing.

Fish joined me.

And there was nothing joyous about the sound.

"We've heard that before," I said, actually needing to wipe a tear from my cheek.

"More than a few times," Fish added.

Lindi lost the smile.

"And we all react exactly the same way," I said.

Power sparked underneath the palm I still had pressed against Fish's back, coming from my own blood, from my own magic embedded within his skin.

He lunged forward.

I was on his heels.

Lindi squeaked—and didn't quite manage to dodge Fish. He tossed her into the wall hard, already raising his hands to meet the two mercenaries who had jumped forward.

They were more than human, I noted as I kicked the merc trying to lay hands on me. They moved too quickly. Quicker than I did with unknown drugs still very much in my system.

I tore the gas mask off the second merc while avoiding a retaliatory blow from the first. Out of the corner of my eye, I caught Lindi gaining her feet. But then she kept to the wall, sliding along it.

Toward the door.

She'd realized her mistake. She thought her gas more potent than it was. Or she had no understanding at all of how powerful we Five had become after Socks had drained us down to nothing.

Pulling on the dregs of my power, I slammed the palm of my hand to the chest of the nearest merc, throwing him back into Lindi. They both went down.

Fish had knocked out two other mercs, but the rest were rallying.

I dove for the door—only to find it filled with three of the five Adepts who'd attacked us.

The three males—the nullifier, the telepath, and the telekinetic—squared off with me. Fish, who'd been right behind me, stepped back to finish whichever of the mercs were still conscious, removing their masks at the same time.

"Well, you boys look a little worse for wear," I said, grinning broadly at the trio blocking the door.

"You dropped a building on us," the dark-haired nullifier snarled. His barely healed split lip cracked open and started bleeding. He'd lost the trench coat. He probably had me to thank for that.

He lunged.

I danced back, barely avoiding tripping over one of the downed mercs. The room wasn't big enough to engage hand-to-hand with three more opponents.

The other nullifier got his hand around my throat, his power pouring out of him unchecked.

"Want to know where you went wrong?" I choked out, struggling against the familiar chill as the dude tried to snuff out the glowing embers of my power.

He bared his teeth at me. "You killed our sister."

That made me pause, briefly.

The clairvoyant hadn't survived.

That…that hurt.

That death at my hands lodged itself into the already seething black hole that permanently resided in my chest. Expanding it just a little more.

I shrugged it off, though. "You play with the big kids, and you're going to get hurt." To prove my point, I stopped fighting his chokehold, reached up, and dug my thumbs into his eyes.

He screamed, loosening his hold.

I slammed my forehead into his nose. Hard.

He went down, not even trying to break his fall.

"Stop," Lindi shouted.

I whirled, blinking against the pain shooting through my own skull. Using my head as a weapon really was a last resort, but I was seriously pissed off.

Lindi was pointing some sort of hypodermic injector toward Fish. He was standing, arms loose at his sides. Just watching her as if curious as to what she thought she was going to do.

The other two—the seriously banged-up telepath and telekinetic—hovered at the door indecisively.

I kept them in my sight. "Seriously, Fish?" I snarled.

He shrugged. "She claims to have created us. She's seen us in action. She must know I can snap her neck in the time it would take her to—"

The telepath and the telekinetic both jerked their heads. They turned toward each other in one motion, then stepped away to clear the doorway.

As if being controlled.

And that was what had been bugging me.

Their occasionally delayed responses. The way they seemed almost tethered, and therefore slower than they should have been. Not just in how they moved, but also in accessing their magic.

As if someone had them on a tight leash.

"You're Gen 4," I said, finally snapping the last couple of pieces of the puzzle together.

I had cobbled together enough of the database I'd stolen from the Collective to understand that generations one through three of the project that had created the Five all failed. They self-destructed before they'd even reached their second decade, assuming they'd even been fully functional in the first place. According to that same research, Gen 4 had been decommissioned. At the time, I'd assumed that meant they were all dead.

Apparently not.

"What they are doesn't matter," Lindi purred. She had that stupid smile on her face again, still holding the injector on Fish. "It's not even you who truly matter. Though as individuals, you are magnificent. It took me far too long to figure it out. The key."

"Figure what out?" Fish took a step toward me, uncharacteristically ceding ground. Like he had figured out something himself...or sensed something...

I flicked my attention toward the open doorway, but I still couldn't pick up any magic, not from anyone nearby or beyond.

"Amp5." Lindi grinned. "She's the linchpin. Without her, you'd be mindless killers." She cast a derisive look at the remaining members of Gen 4. "Needing to be controlled every minute of every day. And even then…" She trailed off with a heavy sigh.

The other nullifier lay still at my feet, almost as inert as the tattoos on my spine. The expressions of the other two Gen 4s were blank, their postures stiff.

If Lindi was the manipulator, the uber-powerful telepath who'd taken me out earlier, I felt nothing of her power now. And her obvious disregard for the gas didn't line up either. Everyone else had been masked before stepping into the room. She'd acted like she was immune.

Fish took another measured step toward me, glancing over at the door, then back at me. Reaching for me now…fingers stretching toward my forearm.

Did he want to make a run for it?

No…

The blood tattoo that tied me to him and him to me flickered on my spine, settling into a muted hum…

He was picking up something I wasn't…

I followed his gaze toward the door.

Apparently, Lindi wasn't the Adept who should have been concerning me.

But I knew that already. Didn't I?

I had just refused to believe it. Refused to even acknowledge it as a possibility. So I dove back into the conversation with Lindi. "Emma isn't interested in being your linchpin to anything."

"Oh, I think she'll reconsider." Lindi reached down and grabbed the tripod, which had been knocked over during the earlier brawl but had survived. The sturdy-looking camera was apparently also intact. Lindi turned it on and pointed it toward us.

I snarled obligingly. "Emma is so going to kick your ass!"

Fish snagged my wrist, trying to tug me behind him. Again. I wrenched my arm away from him, but he practically yelled in my face. "Hold on to me!"

Despite feeling pissed about being treated like I was some damsel in distress, I followed orders like the good little soldier I was, plastering myself against his back, arms up around his shoulders, keeping his own arms free.

He was going to try to shield us, even as drained as he was. Whatever was coming through that door had spooked him—

Two of the tattoos on his spine were shimmering. His T4 vertebra was alight with my power. And his T2…was Fish's T2 tied to Knox or…?

A petite figure dressed head to toe in pink armor, helmet and all, stepped into the doorway, drawing the attention of…well, everyone.

"Took you long enough." Lindi sniffed dismissively. Despite her tone, she quickly turned off the camera, as if she didn't want to chance capturing an image of the newcomer. Though I noted that its lights had gone dead. Already burned out by Fish's attempt to shield us, maybe?

Lindi was still holding that injector tightly. She'd angled her body as if expecting a possible assault as well. A subtle move toward the door, but obvious to me.

"What was in that gas, Lenny?" I laughed, annoyed that it sounded forced. "I mean, I'm not the only one who can see the tiny pink Darth Vader, right?" I giggled, trying to be deliberately aggravating. Christopher, Paisley, and I had buddy-watched the original three *Star Wars* films with Opal and her friends only a couple of weeks ago, her at the Academy and me at the farm. So the image was fresh in my mind.

"It's Lindi," the older woman corrected.

I ignored her. "Is that a pretty bow on your helmet, sweetie? And, oh, I dented it, didn't I? That must have hurt. Did you just wake up?"

Pink Vader didn't respond.

"Bee," Fish said. His tone was all sorts of gentle that I'd never heard from him, not even when tangled in his sheets. "Amanda. Are you in trouble?"

My heart, catching up with what my brain had already processed, began thumping wildly in my chest.

Pink Vader reached up and removed the masked section of her stupid helmet, revealing long yellow hair, light-brown eyes, and golden skin.

A tattoo on my back flared, pulsing with power not remotely dampened by the gas I'd inhaled.

Tel5. Aka Bee. Aka Amanda Smith.

Apparently, the stupid armored getup helped her dampen her magical signature, including the blood tattoos. And Bee would never have picked a neutral shade like gray or black if she had a choice.

She had wanted to get away from the rest of the Five, from me, so badly that she wandered around now breathing recycled air, dampening her power. Also, presumably sweating profusely.

That was also her choice.

And that hurt.

I tamped down on a disconcerted moan. I mean, it was one thing to think I was being betrayed, and a completely different thing to face off against that betrayal while it was ongoing.

Fish spread his hands to the sides. "Why not just ask for help?"

My anger flared at his gentle tone, at my own stupidity. Thinking Bee needed me. I interrupted before she could speak.

"You stupid bitch, Emma is going to kick your ass."

"I don't think so." Bee blinked affectedly, her expression placid. "She'd have to lay hands on me first."

I laughed harshly. "She doesn't have to touch you anymore to kill you, Bee."

Bee jerked, a subtle tell. "She can't kill me. Killing me means her own death."

"Not anymore," Fish whispered.

A hint of uncertainty flickered over Bee's pretty face, then was quickly smoothed over. Her nostrils flared as she glanced at Lindi. "They woke up sooner than expected."

"Yes." Lindi clasped her hands, gleeful again. "Promising!"

I was around Fish and up in Bee's face before she could take a step back. Her power knifed into my mind. I had no way to block her even if I weren't drained.

Fish moaned, pained and concerned. "Please, Bee."

I pressed into Bee's power—agony streaking through my mind, my brain—locking my gaze to hers. "You made me kill one of them."

"No," she said, swallowing. "You made that choice."

"I choose Fish," I said. "I choose myself and Fish."

"Exactly."

"You forced that choice."

She shrugged as if she didn't give a shit.

I leaned in even closer, exchanging breath with one of my siblings, one of my heart mates, and vowing, "I will never, ever forgive you."

Bee flinched.

I kept hitting back the only way I could as she effortlessly held me immobile. "When Emma comes to clean up the mess you've made," I whispered, "she will never, ever forgive you."

"Emma doesn't care. Not about you," Bee snarled. "About Fish. Or me."

"If that's true, then we don't make great bait, do we?"

"Not my plan." She flicked her gaze to my throat. Deliberately, it seemed.

Then she did it again. And again.

I narrowed my eyes.

"Enough, Amanda," Lindi said. "We have a schedule to keep, and Nul4 appears to need medical attention. Again."

I couldn't turn my head, but I caught a glimpse of Lindi crossing toward Fish. Then I heard a hiss and the sound of a big body hitting the floor.

Whatever was in that injector could, in fact, take out a nullifier of Fish's power. At least with Bee holding him in place telepathically.

That was why the others had stopped attacking. The Gen 4 crew. Bee couldn't pilot them and attack us at the same time. Though she really should have been able to...so maybe the suit restricted her. Kept her on a tight leash herself.

She deliberately looked at my neck again.

I glanced down at her own neck.

A tiny, barely discernible circle, a woven patch the exact shade of her skin, was attached to her neck. It could have been anything. A comms device...?

Bee stepped to the side, still holding me completely motionless.

Lindi stepped into the spot the telepath had exited, lifting her chin to meet my eyes. "Just magnificent, my daughter," she purred. "Think of all the lovely creatures we are going to make. Together."

I curled my lip, letting all my jealousy, my sibling hatred, infuse my expression and pour into my words. "It's always about Emma."

"That doesn't make you any less special."

I laughed. "It really, really does. I can't wait for you to meet her…Chemist."

One of the two last members of the Collective we had yet to hunt down. An easy guess now.

Lindi sniffed dismissively. Then she injected me in the neck with her knockout potion. It numbed every part of my brain that Bee wasn't already holding in check.

I dropped.

But not before I'd figured out the full scope of what we were facing. The Chemist. The member of the Collective responsible for the actual mix of magic and DNA that had gone into creating the Five. And Lindiwe Fourie wanted Emma for some reason. Because the amplifier's power, embedded under our skin, adhered to flesh and bone and nerves, was what had stabilized the fifth generation?

The Chemist already had Bee on her side.

She had Fish and me incapacitated.

For now.

I WOKE WITH A JOLT, FINDING FISH WATCHING ME INtently as if willing me to wake.

We were moving. Confined in the belly of an armored vehicle, likely a heavily modified Hummer based on the sharp right angles of the stripped interior. No windows. Only one sealed door. A narrow bench was set over the interior wheel wells, running side to side. I was immobilized magically—and based on what I could see of Fish, we were both in metal cages welded to the sides of the vehicle.

"They're getting smarter," I muttered, systematically engaging every muscle, starting with my hands. I could wiggle my toes but not my ankles.

Fish grimaced.

The vehicle went over a bump or rut in the road. Then another.

"How long have you been awake?"

"Since we turned off."

On to the rougher road, he meant. We weren't in a city, if we ever had been.

"Do you remember anything else?"

"A plane."

Fuck. They'd flown us somewhere, and I'd been completely vulnerable for the entire trip. "You have a higher tolerance for whatever the Chemist is dosing us with."

"They've used it on me more," he said dismissively.

I flicked my gaze around the interior of the vehicle. Not spotting any electronics, or anywhere any cameras or microphones could be hiding. "Are we alone?"

"Except for Bee," Fish said noncommittally.

Bee, of course, could listen in on our conversations... hell, she could tap straight into our thoughts, and not only because of her telepathic power. The blood tattoos gave her unfettered access to us.

Unbidden, the image of the basil oracle card rose in my mind. "Protection..." I murmured. "Strength..." I met Daniel's gaze. "Patience..."

"Knox?" he asked, voice cast low.

"He sent me an oracle card."

"And a reading?"

A wide grin swamped my face. I was weary. Being without magic always seemed to sap my physical strength as well. "He hadn't seen it clearly yet."

As if called forth through sheer focused will, the magic of another tattoo flickered on my back.

Daniel stiffened. Then a grin slowly spread across his face, matching my own.

"Christopher sees us," I said, not bothering to whisper.

"No," he said. "Fox in Socks."

As if that flicker had been intensified just by Daniel identifying it, power bloomed across all the blood tattoos on my spine, then settled into a brief, painful flare on my T1 vertebra. Power flooded into me...

Amplification.

Emma was either near—or she could somehow reach for us across an ocean and a continent through the blood bonds.

That was new.

"They're setting a trap," Daniel snarled, though he was still grinning.

"Well…we know what happens when someone tries to get Socks to do anything she doesn't want to do."

"So does Bee."

I shook my head, laughing quietly. "Not even Bee is a match for the amplifier."

"True." Daniel laughed warmly, settling his head back and closing his eyes.

Yes, it was always smart to sleep when the chance was provided. When Emma blazed in with Knox at her side, we were going to need all our strength.

The last time she'd gotten truly pissed—the last time the Collective had tried to kill us all—Emma had destroyed everything in a ten-kilometer swath.

And she'd only been Amp5 then.

Eight years later, Emma Johnson was far more terrifying than the weapon created by the Collective had ever been.

Fully realized and seriously pissy about people fucking with anyone she deemed under her protection, Emma unleashed was going to be a joy to witness.

Granted, I might not survive being rescued by her.

But I'd rather go out like that than face any more days alone.

Acknowledgements

With thanks to:

MY STORY & LINE EDITOR
Scott Fitzgerald Gray

MY SENSITIVITY READER
Natasha Lane

MY PROOFREADER
Pauline Nolet

MY BETA READERS
Anteia Consorto, Terry Daigle,
Angela Flannery, and Megan Gayeski Pirajno.

**FOR THEIR CONTINUAL ENCOURAGEMENT,
FEEDBACK, & GENERAL ADVICE**
SFWA (esp. the Slack/Discord Crew)
Hailey Edwards
Carrie Ann Ryan

About the Author

MEGHAN CIANA DOIDGE IS AN AWARD-WINNING WRITER based out of Salt Spring Island, British Columbia, Canada. She has a penchant for bloody love stories, superheroes, and the supernatural. She also has a thing for chocolate, potatoes, and cashmere.

For recipes, giveaways, news, and glimpses of upcoming stories, please connect with Meghan on her:

New release mailing list, http://eepurl.com/AfFzz
Personal blog, www.madebymeghan.ca
Twitter, @mcdoidge
Facebook, Meghan Ciana Doidge
Email, info@madebymeghan.ca

Please also consider leaving an honest review at your point of sale outlet.

ALSO BY MEGHAN CIANA DOIDGE

NOVELS
After the Virus
Spirit Binder
Time Walker
Cupcakes, Trinkets, and Other Deadly Magic (Dowser 1)
Trinkets, Treasures, and Other Bloody Magic (Dowser 2)
Treasures, Demons, and Other Black Magic (Dowser 3)
I See Me (Oracle 1)
Shadows, Maps, and Other Ancient Magic (Dowser 4)
Maps, Artifacts, and Other Arcane Magic (Dowser 5)
I See You (Oracle 2)
Artifacts, Dragons, and Other Lethal Magic (Dowser 6)
I See Us (Oracle 3)
Catching Echoes (Reconstructionist 1)
Tangled Echoes (Reconstructionist 2)
Unleashing Echoes (Reconstructionist 3)
Champagne, Misfits, and Other Shady Magic (Dowser 7)
Misfits, Gemstones, and Other Shattered Magic (Dowser 8)
Gemstones, Elves, and Other Insidious Magic (Dowser 9)
Demons and DNA (Amplifier 1)
Bonds and Broken Dreams (Amplifier 2)
Mystics and Mental Blocks (Amplifier 3)
Idols and Enemies (Amplifier 4)
Instincts and Impostors (Amplifier 5)
Misplaced Souls (Misfits 1)
Awakening Infinity (Archivist 0)
Invoking Infinity (Archivist 1)
Compelling Infinity (Archivist 2)

NOVELLAS/SHORTS
Love Lies Bleeding
The Graveyard Kiss (Reconstructionist 0.5)
Dawn Bytes (Reconstructionist 1.5)
An Uncut Key (Reconstructionist 2.5)
Graveyards, Visions, and Other Things that Byte (Dowser 8.5)
The Amplifier Protocol (Amplifier 0)
Close to Home (Amplifier 0.5)
The Music Box (Amplifier 4.5)
Moments of the Adept Universe 1
Recon Mission: Bee (Amplifier 5.5)

Please also consider leaving an honest
review at your point of sale outlet.

DOWSER SERIES ★ BOOK 1

CUPCAKES, TRINKETS, and other DEADLY MAGIC

MEGHAN CIANA DOIDGE

DOWSER SERIES ★ BOOK 2

TRINKETS, TREASURES, and other BLOODY MAGIC

MEGHAN CIANA DOIDGE

DOWSER SERIES ★ BOOK 3

TREASURES, DEMONS, and other BLACK MAGIC

MEGHAN CIANA DOIDGE

ORACLE SERIES ★ BOOK 1

I SEE ME

MEGHAN CIANA DOIDGE

ORACLE SERIES ★ BOOK 2

I SEE YOU

MEGHAN CIANA DOIDGE

ORACLE SERIES ★ BOOK 3

I SEE US

MEGHAN CIANA DOIDGE

RECONSTRUCTIONIST SERIES ★ BOOK 1

Catching Echoes

MEGHAN CIANA DOIDGE

RECONSTRUCTIONIST SERIES ★ BOOK 2

Tangled Echoes

MEGHAN CIANA DOIDGE

RECONSTRUCTIONIST SERIES ★ BOOK 3

Unleashing Echoes

MEGHAN CIANA DOIDGE

THE AMPLIFIER SERIES: BOOK 0

THE AMPLIFIER PROTOCOL

MEGHAN CIANA DOIDGE

THE AMPLIFIER SERIES: BOOK 1

DEMONS & DNA

MEGHAN CIANA DOIDGE

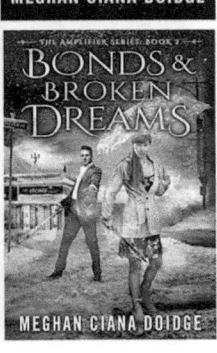

THE AMPLIFIER SERIES: BOOK 2

BONDS & BROKEN DREAMS

MEGHAN CIANA DOIDGE